A CROWN SO CURSED

A CROWN SO CURSED

L.L. McKINNEY

FEIWEL & FRIENDS • NEW YORK

A Feiwel and Friends Book
An imprint of Macmillan Publishing Group, LLC
120 Broadway, New York, NY 10271 • fiercereads.com

Our books may be purchased in bulk for promotional, educational, or business use. Please
contact your local bookseller or the Macmillan Corporate and Premium Sales Department
at (800) 221-7945 ext. 5442 or by email at MacmillanSpecialMarkets@macmillan.com.

Library of Congress Cataloging-in-Publication Data is available.

First edition, 2023
Book design by Veronica Mang
Feiwel and Friends logo designed by Filomena Tuosto
Printed in the United States of America

ISBN 978-1-250-75454-7
1 3 5 7 9 10 8 6 4 2

For My Papa,
Who Knew What I Was
Capable of Even When I
Didn't See It in Myself

One of the deep secrets of life is that all that is really worth the doing is what we do for others.

—LEWIS CARROLL

A CROWN SO CURSED

Prologue
CALLOOH

Through the cracked and crumbling stone of what was once a grand, high ceiling, she could see the lightning dance. Watch it arc and stretch in a webwork of red veins against the stormy flesh of ever-present clouds. Daylight couldn't penetrate them, hadn't been able to in years, which made it impossible to tell how much time had passed. How long had she lain here, clutching at the fractured remains of what was once a throne?

Her throne?

She wasn't certain. Not anymore. Not after . . .

Another bolt bruised the sky and briefly splashed the room with bloodied light. This place, like her, had been vibrant once. It had been bright and shining, full of life and every glorious possibility therein. Now darkness dwelled in its former splendor, and shadows clung to every wall and surface. It stood empty. Abandoned. Forgotten.

Also like her.

Something cold and oily nudged her arm, sending chills skittering across her naked skin. The sensation hurt. Everything hurt. Pain radiated through her body, centered somewhere near her chest. Near where she was broken.

The cold touched her again, harder this time, insistent. The effort to turn her head left her dizzy and aching.

A creature sat hunched at her side, its limbs tucked beneath a bulbous body. Its many eyes fixed on her, sallow and lidless. Inky skin flowed over the length of it, so the beast appeared to move though it remained still.

"You have need of us." A raspy voice touched her mind, words registering though the room remained silent. This thing was speaking, she realized.

"Need of us."

"We are yours."

"Use us."

"Us . . ."

"Ours . . ."

A chorus of silent whispers swelled. More of the creatures prowled into the dim light, undulating in heaps of pitch. They came to her. They called to her, as they had done before. As they had done then.

That night.

The night she first awoke. Had it even been night? She couldn't remember now, and she had known *nothing* then, save pain. Pain and the compulsion to rise, but she had been trapped. Light had flickered somewhere above her, muted and distant. Distorted by the press of crystal enclosing her on all sides. The need to get out had overwhelmed her, and when she tried to take a breath, her mouth filled with fluid. She choked.

She screamed.

The sound had ripped free of her, brutal in its escape. It battered against her shining prison until cracks filled her vision. With a rising roar, everything she knew of the world shattered.

Then she could breathe.

Hacking and sputtering, she had hauled herself free of a vat of watery dark where she collapsed against the aged stone steps and heaved. The muscles in her stomach and throat convulsed wildly. Her body emptied itself onto the floor. The pain had been monstrous.

But there were worse things than lying aching in the dark. The loss of a child. Betrayal by family. A ruining at the hands of a hated enemy. These things had happened, were happening.

"Ours," the whispers asserted. "She is ours, we will take her."

No, she wanted to growl, felt the anger of it hot in her chest. *No, you cannot have her! Have . . . me?*

"Ours. Let us take her. Claim her. You swore."

I swore.

"You failed."

I failed . . .

No, she didn't fail. She was thwarted.

Memories speared her mind like shards of glass. The Eye in her clutches. Her enemies fallen around her. Her victory, her vengeance, finally assured and then . . . The blade so black driven into flesh, breaking open bone, undoing her from the inside, no! No, she couldn't, *wouldn't*, go back to the shadow. It *hungered*. And if she couldn't hold up her end of the bargain, it would take everything from her. She can't lose her daughter again, she can't—!

"*Compose yourself!*" A new voice slammed her with the force of a hurricane.

She doubled over, pinned under the weight of a rage that

threatened to overtake her. A rage that was not hers, yet she knew it intimately.

"They must pay. They must!" she ground out through clenched teeth, though she couldn't remember wanting to speak. Her mouth simply opened, and words fell out. "Every last one of them. For what was taken from me!"

"*So you say*," the voice hissed, the sound low and grating, wide in some places and thin in others. "*But I'm curious, why should I reward your previous failure with opportunity?*"

She went stone still, and somehow managed to stay that way even as panic writhed inside her. "I—I have not failed. I will not fail! I just need more power, please!" Her voice was thick and slippery with desperation. "Please. Do not abandon me now."

Gasping, she clutched at her heart, and her fingers curled around *the* Heart. The flesh of her hand split against the jagged crimson shards still embedded in her chest. Blood and ichor welled between her trembling fingers.

"*Abandon you? As everyone else has? I would never.*" The voice was softer, but no less firm. There were no gentle words to be found here. "*We must tend the wound. Carefully. Or the body will break.*"

The wound?

Her eyes were drawn to where her ribboned hand held fast. This was where the usurper struck her. It should have been a killing blow, *would* have been, if not for her creations. They had carried her away from the Red Palace, brought her here. To where she began.

"*MY creations*," the voice corrected. "*And they are healing what they can as quickly as they can, but your outbursts threaten to tear this body into pieces. Be mindful, I may not be able to restore the bond if it is severed again.*"

She took another ragged breath. Then another. The pain was unbearable. Why did it all hurt so much, what was she doing here on the floor? A fog of confusion settled over her thoughts. "Wh-who's there?" she called to the darkness, her words as tremulous as the rest of her. "Who speaks?" Fear, cold and foreign, coiled in her gut.

"*Hush, child, sweet child,*" the voice cooed, and a thickness filled her senses, clouding them. She was being pulled under.

She wanted to cry out, to batter her way free from the weight settling into her. But she had no strength left, nothing more to be managed than a thread-thin thought.

M-mother . . .

"*There,*" the voice said, quieter now. "*She is ready. Take her.*"

Her body tightened with the return of that rage. It filled her, replacing the damp chill of fear with roaring flame. *Get up.* Her limbs would not listen. She gritted her teeth, and pushed. *Get UP!*

More pain. Merciless. Devouring. Her every nerve went white-hot. She flopped on her side, her efforts melting away. It hurt!

"*Of course it hurts, but you need to get her on her feet!*"

The creatures gathered around her, gripped at her arms with slick and sticky fingers. Their touch was no longer cold and tingling but searing as they hauled her upward.

Another scream threatened to tear its way out of her. She buckled under a feeling like glass flowing through her veins. Her center of gravity shifted, yet somehow her trembling legs held.

"*Well done, Your Majesty. Now, speak the Verse anew,*" the voice coaxed, an eager edge sharpening its tone.

Her lips parted, but someone else's words left her tongue. "Still it haunts me, phantomwise. Moving under screaming skies. In the

5

deepest dark it lies. Never seen by waking eyes." The words were soft, hoarse, but power shivered in the air at her lips.

A burst of jagged black crystal erupted from the floor several feet in front of her, behind the broken throne. The ragged edges snagged on the air, cutting into it, wounding it. Dozens of serrated points aimed outward in the promise of a quick but agonizing end if one strayed too close.

She stretched her hand toward the deadly spikes. Her finger-tips pricked against a few, the sting dulling into the hurt already racking her.

For a moment, nothing happened. Nothing moved. Nothing made a sound save for her labored breaths. Until a few of the spears began to shrink. They drew inward, melting into the body of the crystal. She all but collapsed upon the newly smooth surface.

Bnng-thmmp. Bnng-thmmp. Bnng-thmmp.

At first, she thought it was her heart beating. The steady rhythm seemed to originate somewhere in her chest before rippling out through the rest of her. But as she lay slumped against the cool crystal, the pulse spreading through her body, she slowly realized it wasn't her heart. It was this . . . thing, this . . . coffin of glass and shadow.

"*Speak the Verse anew,*" the voice demanded.

She took a slow, steadying breath, and again another's words left her lips.

"Fury bade me bound to law, and I make no denial. To prosecute in persecution, to test my all by trial. And see me whole with eyes of flame, the witness be my breath. First darkness drawing as it came, I'm thus condemned by death."

Bnng-thmmp. Bnng-thmmp. Bnng-thmmp.

"Bound in blood this given host, gives in turn what I covet most. Callooh . . ."

Bnng-thmmp. Bnnng-thmmmp. Bnnnng-thmmmmp.

"Callay . . ."

The pulsing slowed, receding into the depths of the crystal. As it did, a spark of onyx flame took its place. It burned away the dark, curling it back to reveal something trapped, suspended beneath the surface. A body resting within. Arms, shoulders, torso, legs, everything bled into view. But not the face. The face remained obscured.

Bnng-thmmp. Bnng-thmmp. Bnng-thmmp. Beats in black flame.

The jagged sections of the Heart lodged in her chest pulsed red in answer. Instead of fire, she felt ice dig into her, burrow into her bones. A molten cold excavated and filled the deepest parts of her. The hurt was finally gone, and in its place, she felt the subtle *bnng-thmmp bnng-thmmp bnng-thmmp* resonating through her core. She closed her eyes.

"Thank you," something inside her sighed. "Master."

Mother . . .

One

CONNED

Alice couldn't just sit there. She couldn't escape. All she could do was endure. And it was her own fault, really, wearing a fur-lined cloak while it was ninety-five outside. It was fake fur, but that didn't save her from slowly baking in her extremely intricate, incredibly detailed Trevor Belmont cosplay. Why was it so hot this close to Halloween, anyway?

"Jesus take me before global warming," Nana K had said that morning, her voice carrying over Mom's phone. The two of them spent most of breakfast commiserating over the unusually high temperature. "Hot as the devil's ass crack out there. You be careful at your computer coms, Alice baby."

"Comic con, Nana K," Alice had snickered around a spoonful of grits.

"Right. What I say?"

Both Mom and Nana K then repeatedly reminded Alice to stay hydrated. Mom had even offered her fancy water bottle, the expensive-ish one that claimed to keep your drink cold for twelve hours. Lies. Three lukewarm refills later, Alice debated dumping it over her head instead of drinking it. The only reason she didn't was it meant walking around in soggy clothes. No thanks.

"Uuuuuuuuuuuugh." She scratched at the edge of her wig while her eyes trailed the ridiculously long line of equally miserable con-goers. A river of bodies stretched down the street and curled around the convention center. Most of them wore costumes that would've been perfect on a regular October Saturday. Instead, here they all stood in torment.

Courtney lifted her phone higher, the small fan plugged into the port working overtime to blow hot air against the back of her neck. She'd long since stripped off her red, close-cropped wig and shoved it into the handbag tucked under her arm. She mirrored Alice's miserable moan. "When I'm a puddle on the sidewalk, remember me fondly."

"How are you hot?" Alice asked. "You're wearing a cotton tent."

Without lowering the fan, Courtney glanced down at her Sypha costume. "*Layered* cotton tent." She swiped a hand across her forehead, checking it for foundation afterward. Somehow, her makeup managed to stay in place even though she was sweating buckets. "You *could* take off the cloak, you know. I understand suffering for the aesthetic, but not like this."

Alice shook her head. "It's worse trying to carry it around." Plus, she didn't wanna start peeling off pieces so early in the day. That just made it easier to remove more and more and, before you knew it, you were walking around in half a costume no one could even recognize. "I'll be fine once we're inside."

"If we ever get that far." Courtney tilted to the side to survey the line herself, then huffed in displeasure. "I have seen legless spiders move faster than this."

"That's an interesting visual." Hatta shifted where he stood just to the side of the two girls, his hands in his pockets. It was unfair how unbothered he appeared in his Alucard "costume." No sweat, no flush, no nothing, despite wearing what was pretty much a whole-ass trench coat. Just standing there like he'd stepped right out the show.

Alice would be lying if she said she didn't feel some kind of way about him using an illusion Verse to achieve the look. Lucky for him he was foine. And she wasn't the only one who thought so. Every now and then people took candids as they walked past. Lots of people. Lots of candids.

Truthfully, she was happy he'd decided to come. Thrilled, even. Made being out in this heat all the more worth it. Chess was *supposed* to complete their trio, but he . . . he wasn't into going out much lately.

Pushing the thought aside, Alice propped her short sword against her shoulder and shifted her weight so the handle of the Morning Star whip didn't dig into her hip. Damn thing was heavy, especially after lugging it around half the day. Prolly because it was made from real metal, an exact replica, even. A gift from Hatta. Technically from Tan, since he forged it, but Hatta had made the special request.

"Have to complete the ensemble," he'd said with a grin after surprising her with it that morning. She didn't know if she was happier for the gift itself or that he'd remembered her costume, but she'd spent the better part of twenty minutes screaming and hugging him.

The line shifted forward about five feet before coming to a stop again. Courtney groaned.

"We should've come when the hall first opened," Alice complained, wiping away more sweat.

Court's face scrunched. "I wasn't the only one who wanted to see the Lolita fashion show."

Hatta blinked when both girls glanced his direction. "The dresses are cute," he offered in his defense. "I thought I might see something to take back to Maddi."

Court tapped a finger against her naked lips. "Some of them *were* fairly gorgeous. Others decidedly not. Does she have a favorite color? Because something toward the end caught my eye."

"I think I know the one you're talking about." Hatta wagged a finger in agreement. Alice smirked while the two of them started going on about one dress in particular that Maddi might like. It had teacups embroidered in silver and gold thread against dark blue skirts.

As Court composed a sonnet about the boning in the corset, something over her shoulder caught Alice's attention.

A white girl stood dressed in all black like it wasn't Sozin's Comet hot out here. Blond hair framed her pale face. Thin arms hung at her sides. Her body remained still, a detail that stuck out all the more as people shuffled around her in their shared malaise. That wasn't the weird part, though.

The girl was staring at the three of them. She was too far away to be one hundred percent sure—maybe she was just looking in their general direction, or searching the line for someone—but something at the base of Alice's skull buzzed in subtle warning. And maybe she was imagining things, or it was the sun and heat playing tricks on her, but she got the distinct feeling blond girl wasn't blinking.

That's not creepy af.

"Something wrong?" Hatta's voice snatched at Alice's attention, and she glanced up to find him gazing down the street as well.

When she looked back that direction, the girl was gone.

Alice rolled her shoulders, trying to shake the jitters dancing along her skin. "No, just . . . someone was staring, but she's gone now."

"People have been staring all day," Courtney offered, tugging at Alice's arm as the line crawled forward. "Specially your beau there."

Hatta arched an eyebrow, though one corner of his mouth ticked upward slightly. If Alice didn't know any better, she'd think he liked all of the attention.

Almost on cue, a group stopped on their way by. A Black girl dressed like Cardcaptor Sakura practically bounced as she asked if she could get a picture of them, though her gaze lingered on Hatta.

Courtney fished out her wig, and Hatta dropped Alice's backpack carefully to the ground just to the side. The three of them struck a pose with weapons lifted, ready to attack or cast spells. At least a dozen more phones and cameras came out as people took advantage of the moment, snapping pictures and calling out how amazing they looked.

"We know!" Court hollered back, throwing both hands in the air.

Laughter erupted around them.

"Perfect Sypha," someone shouted as another wave of people approached.

Twenty minutes, at least a hundred pictures, and one zombie-like shuffle through a few metal detectors later, the three of them stepped into the wide, open space of the exhibitors' hall.

The roar of chatter hung in the air, punctuated periodically by someone shouting after a passing character or calling out what they were selling. People moved alone or in small packs, perusing the booths full of merchandise. Other con-goers tucked themselves into corners or settled on the floors near coveted outlets. Within the first handful of seconds, Alice spotted at least six flavors of Deadpool. A wide smile pulled at her face, the discomfort of standing in the heat now forgotten. She'd missed this.

And with a sudden pull at the center of her chest, she missed her father. The want to have him here struck as sharply as any blade, threatening to leave her open and exposed in front of thousands of people.

Keep it together. She breathed through the ache, slowly, purposefully. He'd want her here. Want her to go back to doing what she loved. What *they'd* loved.

"Hey." Hatta's voice murmured near her ear, his tone quiet concern. His gloved fingers weaved between hers and squeezed. "You all right?"

She nodded, sniffing lightly and taking another deep breath. The burn behind her eyes eased. "Yeah, just . . . remembering stuff," she said before he or Courtney could ask for details. "Let's go."

With Alice in the lead, the trio worked their way from booth to booth along rows and columns spread across the massive space. From art to knickknacks to books, memorabilia, posters, pillows, comics, and more, it was a veritable nerdy smorgasbord. One they feasted on eagerly in their own way.

Courtney spent a small fortune on corsets, jewelry, geeky handbags, and a pair of metallic and glittery fairy wings that she opted to wear. Hatta spent more than a brief moment or two perusing booths that housed all sorts of weapons, including replicas from a bunch of different movies, shows, video games, and more. He didn't buy anything, but he appeared to enjoy looking.

"What's the point of a sword without a cross guard?" he asked while eyeing a Mugen replica he'd plucked from one of the tables.

"It looks cool." Alice examined a pair of intricate daggers marked vaguely as "Elven." Why did people think throwing random vine patterns on stuff automatically made it fantastical? "And Kanda's a badass, he doesn't need one."

"I'll take your word for it." Hatta set the weapon down and lifted a battle-ax, testing the weight.

One of the burly, kilt-wearing white dudes sitting at the booth noticed and approached. "You look like you know your way around that thing."

"It and a few others," Hatta said offhandedly. He didn't look all that interested in conversation.

The dude didn't seem to notice and went into his clearly rehearsed spiel about how the ax was handcrafted, one of a kind, blah blah blah. Alice, meanwhile, made her way to the next booth, which was, to her immediate delight, covered in Sailor Moon swag.

Hatta joined her as she finished picking out a Sailor Jupiter phone case, and she gestured for him to lower her pack so she could tuck it in among her belongings.

"It's not too heavy, is it?" Alice asked as she finally managed to wedge her wallet between a change of clothes and a couple Funkos.

The look that crossed Hatta's face made her feel a little silly for asking. "I used to run around in armor, remember?"

"*Enchanted* armor," Alice corrected. "Xelon told me it's not that heavy."

"Enchanted or not, armor is armor," Hatta muttered as he followed Alice along the aisle.

She led the way to the end of the row, then broke off to head for the food court, which was less actual court and more random tables packed together near a handful of snack stands.

After buying a ridiculously expensive tiara to go with her wings, Courtney had mentioned getting something to eat while everyone else finished browsing. Alice searched the sea of people for a sign of her best friend. It shouldn't be this hard to find a Tinkerbell-Sypha hybrid standing nearly six feet tall.

"There she is." Hatta pointed, and Alice followed his finger to where Courtney stood behind a table, waving both arms like she was directing traffic.

Hatta's hand found Alice's again, squeezing as he took the lead. Nearby, a few bystanders tittered and giggled, gesturing at the two of them. This was nice, doing couple stuff with him.

A veritable snack-food feast stretched across Courtney's table. Besides the slice of pizza she was currently nibbling on, there was a plate of nachos, two soft pretzels—one chili, one cheese—and a funnel cake the size of Alice's head covered in slightly gooey powdered sugar.

"Damn, big hungry." Alice snagged a cheesy chip as she settled into a cheap folding chair.

"It's not all for me," Court protested. "Figured you two might be hungry, and turns out the lines in here are as bad as anywhere else, so I grabbed it while I could. Sorry if it's cold."

"No apologies necessary," Hatta said as he went for one of the pretzels without removing his gloves. Must be nice not having to worry about stains. "Thank you."

Alice finally shrugged out of the cloak and draped it over the back of her chair, then helped herself to more nachos.

"So," Court said as she dabbed a bit of grease from her pizza. Two soaked napkins already sat to the side. "How're you enjoying your first con?" Her eyes rolled over Hatta, then pointedly to a nearby table where what looked like a group of steampunk Princesses of Power were sneaking glances and photos.

Hatta rolled his shoulders. "It's . . . interesting, to be sure, but not unpleasant." He licked a bit of cheese from his lower lip. "And it's nice to be able to travel such a distance from the pub for this long without feeling like my heart is going to burst from my chest." He meant it in jest, but the twist of anxiety in Alice's middle didn't take it that way.

Odabeth's pardon had saved Hatta's life after he risked it by going deep into Wonderland to rescue Alice. He'd been willing to die for her, painful and slow. Nearly had. Of course, he claimed he'd do it again, which was sweet but didn't help with the sour feeling in her stomach when she thought about him or anyone else she loved dying. So, she'd been doing everything she could to not.

"I'm glad you decided to come," she said, changing the subject and reaching to snag a bit of his pretzel.

He caught her fingers before she could, then squeezed her hand and pressed a kiss to the back of it. "I'm glad you asked me."

It had been last minute, after Chess told them he wasn't up to dealing with crowds. Alice couldn't help feeling disappointed when he canceled on them, *again*, but she understood. At least, she told herself she did. She was trying to.

"You don't just bounce back from something like that," Hatta had attempted to explain. They were all at the pub one night. Just talking through what was going on, everyone updating one another on Nightmare activity or the surprising lack thereof. Nothing stressful, or so she thought.

Half an hour into it, Chess had gone out to get some fresh air.

Ten or fifteen minutes later, she and Court got a text saying he was going to take the train home, he'd see them later. Sensing both girls' disappointment, Hatta asked if he could offer a bit of insight into a subject he was fairly familiar with.

"Having someone else in your mind?" he'd said. "Not knowing where your thoughts, your *will*, ends and theirs begins? It takes a toll. Trust me. He's going to need time. And for you, his friends, to be patient with him."

Alice was glad to give Chess all the time he needed, she just wished there was something more she could do to help. She'd never been the wait-and-see-what-happens type.

"What else is on the agenda?" Hatta asked as he decimated a hunk of pretzel smothered in chili and *still* didn't get anything on those gloves.

Court ticked events off on her fingers. "There's the costume contest, the Wonder Woman panel, the burlesque show, but that's not until tonight."

Hatta's eyebrows nearly vanished into his newly blond hairline. He tilted his head and pale gold curls fell to his shoulders, looking far more real than any anime wig ever could. "Burlesque show?"

Alice snickered and patted the hand that held hers. "Don't look so worried. It's not *that* risqué. Are you good on time? Don't have to get back to the pub?"

He shook his head while stealing one of her chips. "We're still closed to the public. Maddi and Humphrey can handle things."

The shard of anger that stabbed through Alice took her by surprise. She felt it tighten her expression, and tried to fix her face before Hatta noticed. The way his smile waned just so meant she hadn't quite succeeded.

"Sorry." She wasn't, but she said it anyway. Not for what she felt and who she felt it for, more for . . . She wasn't exactly sure. She pulled a bit of funnel cake free and shoved it into her mouth in lieu of saying more.

"You have nothing to apologize for," Hatta murmured, settling further into his chair. "I shouldn't have brought him up."

No, you shouldn't have, Alice wanted to say, but she bit down on the words harder than she did her food.

Courtney's wide green eyes bounced back and forth between the two of them while she sipped loudly at the ice in her obviously empty cup. "Mm!" she said, brightening and lowering her drink. "Looks like you've got more fans wanting pictures."

Alice glanced over her shoulder, glad for the distraction, though that slight spark of joy quickly flickered out.

The fans Courtney had been talking about stood a few feet behind her; a white boy and, to Alice's surprise, the same white girl from outside. The one that had been staring at him. At least, Alice was pretty sure it was her.

She still stared, her pale face blank, her eyes so dark the color hid her pupils. Eyes that were fixed on Alice, causing the buzz of warning from before to return. The boy stared as well, wearing the same clothes and expression.

Hatta rose from his chair and shifted to put himself between the two "fans" and the table. "Can we help you?" His tone was friendly, but his posture wasn't, if you knew what to look for. He rested one hand on the hilt of his Alucard sword, the other hanging at his side, loose and ready to react.

Neither "fan" said anything. They didn't even glance in Hatta's direction. No, they kept their focus on Alice, unblinking, unwavering. The buzz in her head grew into something more urgent and forceful. A panicked hive. *Leave,* it screamed. *Now.*

Alice pushed up from the table, gesturing for Courtney to do the same. "Sorry, but we're done taking pictures for the day."

Court's chair scraped against the floor as she rose, gathering trash from the sound of it. Alice didn't dare take her eyes off the two until Hatta wrapped his arm around her and guided her away.

"The hell was that about?" Courtney hissed as she fell into step beside them.

Alice shrugged. "I don't know, bu—"

"Strewth!"

Strong hands gripped Alice's shoulders and shoved her forward so hard and fast her feet left the ground. Her stomach dropped as she collided with an equally shocked Courtney.

Alice's body reacted before her mind could make sense of what was happening. She latched onto her friend and twisted, angling her body to take the brunt of the fall. The two of them tumbled across the concrete floor in a tangle of limbs and wire wings. Her elbow slammed into the floor, the impact shooting pain through Alice's left arm. She gritted her teeth and rolled, coming out of it into a defensive crouch. Courtney groaned behind her, but Alice focused on the chaos unfolding in front of her.

The white boy brandished some sort of long, black weapon that swallowed the light. Hatta, wielding Alice's backpack as a makeshift shield, deflected a swipe that should've disemboweled him. Then he lashed out with a kick that sent the boy sprawling. The girl leaped over her fallen partner to get at Hatta. He twisted around her swing and drove his elbow into the side of her head with a crack.

"Dude! Not cool!" someone hollered.

Hatta ignored them, tossing Alice's pack aside and yanking the Alucard sword from its sheath in a single motion. The girl, already recovered, lifted a weapon identical to the boy's. That was when Alice realized it wasn't a weapon at all but the girl's hand, long and blackened, with nails thin and sharp.

Behind her, the boy lifted his similarly transformed arms. The two of them, their lips pulling back to reveal sharpened teeth, loosed low, rattling snarls. Alice's shock sharpened. Only one thing in the world made that sound.

Nightmares.

Two
FRIENDS . . .
SORT OF

Humphrey didn't know what he was doing here, or why. He'd asked himself a dozen times after he left the Looking Glass pub nearly an hour past. Then a dozen more as he boarded the train that carried him across this very strange, very human city. And still a dozen more as he walked the final mile or two to his intended destination.

Now, as he sat in a charming little café, waving off another offer from the server to refill his nearly empty water glass, he asked yet again.

What am I doing here?

Because he requested you come.

That was the simplest answer, but it only resulted in more questions.

You don't owe him anything, so why bother?

The same reason he'd bothered to make this journey the last time. And the time before that. And the time before that . . .

Because you pity him?

Not really. Pity was useless in situations like this. It didn't help anyone and only served as a distraction.

Because what happened to him is your fault?

True, but there wasn't anything he could do to change that. Certainly not these little meetings. Though he'd offered, no other means of recompense had come up.

Because the two of you are the same now, like it or not.

And he did not like it. But that wasn't the real answer.

No. The real answer went much deeper. Touched a part of him he didn't recognize. A part of him from before all this. He was shocked to find such a distant echo still existed.

*Because you **want** to.*

Humphrey couldn't remember the last time he wanted to do something purely of his own volition. While he had sought to harm those who betrayed his la—who betrayed the Bloody Lady, it was clear now that his underlying emotions and desires had been manipulated. He was learning that his actions as the Black Knight might have been seeded in genuine anger and pain, but false conviction was what grew, uprooting any trace of his true motivations.

But this? Coming here. Meeting *him*. Something about the entire venture—about the boy himself—unnerved Humphrey. Still, he *wanted* to do this. He was certain of it. More certain than anything else, right now.

And so, here he was.

Again.

By the Nox, how could a life he'd only started living a few short weeks ago already be so damned complicated?

Motion caught in the periphery of his vision, and he glanced up to find Chester Dumpsky approaching the table.

"Hey." Chess dropped into the seat opposite him, his shoulders still hunched as if to ward off some slight chill only he felt. The rest of the world seemed near to boiling.

"Hey," Humphrey returned, lifting a hand to flag down the overeager server.

She bustled toward them quickly enough, her bright orange pigtails bouncing against tawny cheeks.

Humphrey let her refill his glass this time as she asked Chess if he wanted anything. He stammered out an order for something that sounded ludicrously decadent.

"Got it." The girl set aside her pitcher, then pulled a tablet from the pocket of her apron. She tapped in the order, then aimed a look at Humphrey. "And for you?"

"Water is fine." He waited until the girl retreated before reaching into his jacket to withdraw a vial. The sky-blue liquid inside shimmered faintly. "Madeline requested I deliver this."

Chess frowned, those oddly colored eyes of his dancing between Humphrey and the offered concoction. "I've still got a week's worth."

"This isn't your tonic. She insisted you keep it on you at all times and take it should your tincture prove ineffective."

It was hard to miss the alarm that crossed Chess's face. He froze, having started to reach for the potion. "She thinks it'll stop working?" His voice pitched higher with a note of panic.

"She doesn't *think* anything, she's simply hoping to be prepared." Humphrey shrugged in an act of nonchalance, hoping to assuage Chester's fears. "It's merely a precaution. It doesn't change anything, if you think about it." He wiggled the vial, relinquishing it when Chess took hold. "The tonic has stabilized the Slithe in your system. As long as you take regular doses, you could live a long, natural life."

"Or I could drop dead this afternoon after turning into a magically powered mass murderer," Chess said, his voice quiet as he stared at the ampule of faintly illuminated liquid resting against his palm. He pressed his free hand to his torso, over the wound Humphrey had inflicted the night he'd blackmailed Alice into giving him the Eye.

A swell of guilt attempted to rise, but Humphrey forced it back down. He wasn't here to get wrapped up in his own head. "That's true for any of us, Slithe or no. Perhaps not the mass murderer part." He reached across the table to press his hand over Chess's, curling the boy's fingers in over the vial. "But we're working through that, yes? Accepting that it wasn't you who did those things, even if it was your body. As I said, this doesn't change anything."

Chess held Humphrey's gaze for a moment before heaving a resigned sigh. Then he withdrew his hand, slipping it into his pocket with murmured thanks. His entire being seemed to wilt slightly.

"Of course," Humphrey said. He let his gaze trail off for a moment, giving both of them a chance to take a beat. In truth he felt sorry for the other boy. While Chester's time under the Bloody Lady's influence had been drastically shorter than Humphrey's, it meant that he still remembered who he was before all this. Thus he knew just how far outside of himself she had taken him. Humphrey couldn't remember anything from before. Perhaps that was a blessing. He'd managed to escape the moral trauma. At least, that's what he told himself.

Sunlight poured through the large windows that lined the nearby wall. The day looked bright, cheerful even. Not the sort of day that should accompany hard conversations and potential bad news, even if it couldn't be helped.

"I take it you still haven't told Alice and Courtney about all this?" Humphrey asked, eager to chase his melancholy thoughts away with conversation. "Your condition, the treatment?"

Chess closed his eyes, his expression briefly agonized. "I can't."

"You could."

"I *can't*. At least not yet. I don't want them to worry."

"I'm told worrying is a thing friends do."

Chess made a derisive noise at the back of his throat. "And you'd be the resident expert on that? Having friends?"

At the mention, Humphrey's thoughts turned to Madeline, Anastasia, and . . . Hatta. The three of them insisting he return with them to the pub, that he should be with people who knew him and cared about him while he tried to recover. While they tried to figure out what had happened to him, how he'd gone from Humphrey to . . . well.

"Sorry," Chess said, pulling Humphrey back into the present.

"Don't be." He took a steadying breath to focus on the now. He owed Chester that much. "For one, you're right. I don't know what it is to have such connections."

"The others at the pub don't count?"

"*No*. I mean I don't see myself as friend material."

Chess lifted his shoulders. "Maybe you should. What you're doing here? Helping me? Is pretty friendly." A grin pulled faintly at the edges of his face. "Besides, it's nice to have friends."

Humphrey fought to keep a straight face. "So I, too, can *not* tell them about potential dangers to my health? No. And what I'm doing is paying a debt."

"Here we go!" The server appeared, tray in hand. She smiled brightly as she set a cup topped in whipped cream and drizzled in caramel ribbons in front of Chess. "One caramel crème brûlée latte, double shot, extra whip! Sorry for the wait."

"No problem," Chess said as he drew the steaming mug toward himself. "Thanks."

"You're welcome! Can I get you anything else?" she asked, her gaze shifting back and forth between the two of them, though it lingered briefly on Chester. Not that he seemed to notice.

"We're fine for now, thank you." Humphrey offered what he hoped was a believable smile.

The server, Diwa, according to her tag, dipped her head in a faint nod as she bit into her lower lip. Then she turned to shuffle toward the main counter and her lingering coworkers. Doubtless he and Chess had been a shared topic of discussion.

Humphrey pushed the small dish of sugar packets toward the other boy just as he lifted a hand to reach for them. They shared a brief smile before Chess went about emptying a few into the still steaming cup.

Silence hung between them once more, but not the uncomfortable awkward kind that seemed to follow Humphrey around and linger whenever he was in anyone else's company. This was a companionable and patient quiet.

Perhaps it had been awkward at first, the two of them hardly speaking to one another despite that being the express purpose of their meeting. In fact, Humphrey had been surprised, and more than a little confused, when Chester first approached him outside the pub perhaps a fortnight ago, asking if they could talk.

"Talk?" Humphrey had parroted, not sure he'd heard correctly.

"Yeah." Chess had clutched at his chest, as if he were in pain. "Just talk."

Humphrey eyed him up and down, gaze lingering on where Chess's hand hovered. An unpleasant feeling threaded through him. He struggled to ignore it. "Is it your wound? Should I get Madeline?"

"No." Chess shook his head. "No, I'm—that's fine. It's . . . I'm having these dreams. A voice in the dark telling me to do something awful, and I don't know if . . . I'm worried it might be . . ."

"Her," Humphrey had finished for him.

Chess swallowed thickly and nodded.

Humphrey took a second to look the boy over, examine him closely. He was pale, his features sharper. Circles ringed his eyes, likely from a lack of sleep. Or from the essence of evil holding his body together. Though, unlike the constructs and Fiends that often lingered near when Humphrey served as the Black Knight, he could sense no faint hum of power from the boy. There was . . . something, but it was different. And yet familiar. Just not in that way. Perhaps, he thought, he should use this opportunity to find out what. At least, that was how these little meetings had started.

"It's not her," Humphrey had tried to assure Chess. "Or I don't believe it is."

Then he'd debated whether or not he should reveal this next bit. It was disconcerting, to say the least. Plus, Humphrey didn't make a habit of voicing his thoughts. In the end, though he wasn't completely certain why, he decided to trust Chester.

"I've had similar dreams. Which should be problem enough, my people do not dream. But in mine, this presence? it doesn't *feel* like her, at any rate." He'd briefly considered sharing this development with Hatta and the others but decided against it. He hadn't been in the mood for more questions and awkward glances between them all.

"Two nights in a row," Humphrey had continued, straightening from where he'd tilted against the side of the building. "I don't think it's her influence. I don't feel the pull I used to when she gave an order. Looking back, that should've been my first clue something was wrong." He lapsed into silence, releasing a long, laborious breath. He was tired, he realized. And this conversation might be easier with a bit of lubricant. "Let's go inside. I could use a drink."

"No!" Chess had thrown out a hand to clasp Humphrey's arm,

though he quickly let go afterward. "Sorry. Not here. I don't want anyone else to know. Not yet."

Humphrey cocked his head to the side and narrowed his eyes. It hadn't escaped his attention that Alice and Courtney happened to be inside. "It's not healthy to keep secrets."

Chess's expression twisted. "They wouldn't understand. They don't know what it was like, what *she* was like."

"And I do," Humphrey murmured, putting the pieces together.

Chess had fallen silent then, his gaze roaming the ground in search of . . . who knew.

After a few moments Humphrey heaved another sigh. "Fine. We'll talk somewhere else, just stop looking like someone curdled your whompuss."

Chess blinked rapidly. "My what?"

Humphrey waved off the question. "Don't worry about it. Where would you like Not Here to be? Keep in mind, I'm not familiar with your world and travel might prove difficult."

"You were able to find our school, and Alice's house."

"I used Fiends to track her."

Chester looked decidedly uncomfortable. "Oh . . . well . . ."

Humphrey flapped one hand and used the other to spin Chess toward the road. "Just show me the way, I can find it on my own after."

That had been nearly two weeks and a half dozen meetings ago. They hadn't talked much at first, but slowly began opening up to one another, first about what it had been like to serve his la—the Bloody Lady. Then they discussed the strange dream they apparently shared.

In the dream, they are ordered to complete a truly terrible task. They refuse at first, but by the end agree to do as commanded. They never remember exactly what the task is after waking, but a shared revulsion painted a clear enough picture. Except they had no idea what the dream meant or why it came to them. Humphrey had a theory, but it was circumstantial at best. He'd hoped some clue to the truth would eventually reveal itself with these conversations, but the only new development was Chester's growing addiction to caffeine.

Humphrey wrinkled his nose as Chess took a loud, slurpy sip of his now properly doctored beverage. "Care to get down to business? Now that you have your lah-tay."

"You can just say latte," Chess corrected. "And I had the dream again."

"Night before last, I know." Humphrey traced the rim of his glass with a finger, almost bored. "You're told to do the horrible thing and afterward feel like an ass about it."

Chess nodded, though the movement was sluggish with apprehension. "But it was different, this time."

Humphrey went still. "Different in what way?"

Chess hesitated, taking another sip from his mug. Then he averted his gaze pointedly. "When the voice tells me to do the thing? I still refuse. But this time, instead of giving in, everything goes dark. These hands—I think they're hands—grab me. Pull me. Someone's screaming at me to do as I'm told. I dig my heels in. I fight it! And I'm winning! My heart starts pounding." Chess pressed a hand to his chest and twisted his fingers into his shirt. "Feels like it's gonna pop right outta my chest. And it *hurts*, like I'm being cut open from the inside. I can't breathe, I—I . . . I can't move. My whole body starts burning. Then I wake up, and—Humphrey?"

Humphrey drew his gaze away from . . . he wasn't sure, but he focused on Chester. "What?" His voice sounded distant, thick in his own ears.

"You okay?" Chess asked, his eyes wandering from Humphrey's face to his torso.

"Yes, wh—" He glanced down as well and was genuinely surprised to find he was clutching at his chest as well, only he didn't remember moving. His thoughts stuttered briefly, his mind trying to process this latest development. It took concentrated effort to uncurl his fingers and lower his hand.

Across the table, Chess did the same, mirroring his movement exactly. From the look on his face, it was clear the miming had not been intentional. The two stared at each other for a moment before Humphrey cleared his throat. "I had the dream, too, only it stayed the same. I do as I'm told."

Incredulity crossed Chester's face, followed by a flicker of shock and then confusion. "Why would it change for me? And why would it hurt? Dreams don't hurt."

Humphrey shrugged, trying and failing to shake the unease that had settled over him. "My assumption remains the same. The dreams could be a residual link from her messing with our heads. We were both under her control. Some . . . lingering connection between the two of us without her here to anchor it. It could be any number of things. Or it could be nothing. Stress from shared trauma."

Disappointment poured off of Chess in waves. "That's not exactly nothing," he muttered.

Humphrey sighed. "I'm sorry I don't have any answers, truly. Though I told you I wouldn't."

"I know." Chess pinched at the bridge of his nose. "I know . . ."

"She's gone, and we're left to pick up the pieces of whatever it is she did to u—" Pain exploded over Humphrey, stealing his breath and choking off his words. It felt like someone had reached into him and started scraping out his insides with a rusted blade.

Black stained his vision.

Pressure built under his skin, pushing outward. He was going to shatter.

"*Find . . . her . . .*" A voice dragged over his thoughts like nails scraping at flesh. "*Find . . . her. Bring . . . her. End all who stand in your way.*" Each word drove into his skull with the weight of a boulder being dropped on his head. Then, as suddenly as it had fallen on him, the pain fell away, leaving him empty and reeling.

For a moment, he couldn't move. He couldn't speak. He could barely breathe as his body trembled so hard it rattled his chair.

"Hey," someone called. "Hey!" The voice was heavy with the sway of familiarity, but still unknown.

Hands pressed to his shoulders, shaking him.

He blinked his eyes open, but his vision remained blurred, clouded.

Then he felt himself lifted from where he'd doubled over.

"Hey!"

More blinking. Gradually the café came into focus and with it Diwa. She had hold of him, her face full of worry.

"Oh thank god," she breathed. "Are you okay?"

Humphrey straightened as quickly as he dared, his body aching as his muscles gradually relaxed.

Across the table, Chess looked to be recovering similarly with the help of an elderly man Humphrey didn't recognize.

"Take it easy," the gentleman said. "I called an ambulance. It should be here soon."

Chess gaped at the man for a brief moment before his wide eyes found Humphrey's. "Did you?"

Humphrey nodded as dread crawled through him. Despite his spinning senses, he rocketed to his feet. "We need to go."

Three

BE A FENCE.

Alice swooped in around Hatta, raising her sword to parry the Nightmare boy's attack. She felt the blade catch, felt the give of flesh and bone, and pulled. Something snapped. The boy's hand dropped to the ground as she pivoted into a side kick that flung him into his partner. The two toppled over while an unwitting audience cheered.

"These stunts get bigger every year," someone said.

"The effects are great!"

"Can still tell it's fake, though."

"We need to draw them away from the crowd," Hatta bit through clenched teeth as Alice came to the same conclusion.

There was a flash of light, followed by the rapid click of a shutter. The rising Nightmare girl whirled toward the sound. A dude dressed like Hellboy lowered his camera, his jaw slack as the girl's face contorted with a low growl, her lips curling back from pointed teeth.

Alice snatched the Morning Star loose. She gave the impossibly light chain a hard snap that sent the flail sailing through the air. It slammed into the Nightmare girl's shoulder with a squelch. She howled in pain. People gasped and pointed.

With a curse, Alice flicked her wrist. The flail tore free in a spray of tissue and inky blood, rendering Nightmare girl's entire arm useless.

"Sick!" someone in the crowd shouted.

Nightmare girl shrieked, a high, inhuman sound. Beside her, the boy picked himself up, holding his severed hand. He pressed the torn skin and jagged bone to his equally mangled wrist. His entire arm blackened, sinewy tendrils molding over the joint to bind it.

Similarly, the hole in the girl's shoulder knitted itself together, tethers of tissue slithering across torn flesh and pulling it closed. The Nightmares snarled, their mouths splitting further at the corners. A few bystanders stepped back, uncertainty on their faces.

A hand at Alice's elbow drew her around and pulled her into a stumbling run.

"Go," Hatta urged, reaching to snag Courtney similarly as they passed.

With Hatta in the lead, the three of them darted across the crowded food court, weaving through con-goers, strollers, and tables. Hatta, without so much as a sideways glance, shoved a few folks out of the way when they didn't move fast enough.

"Sorry!" Alice called to someone dressed as Goku sprawled on the ground. A startled Nubia bent to help him up.

There were so many freaking people. Of course this had to go down on a Saturday. *Shit.*

But why was it going down at all? Nightmares didn't come out during the day! What the hell?

"Damn!" Hatta slid to a stop, and Alice barely had time to catch herself before slamming into him from behind. Courtney wasn't so lucky, or quick, and she would have gone tumbling by if Hatta hadn't snagged her around the waist.

Up ahead, three more Nightmare people blocked the exit, their hands and fingers lengthened into talons, their faces distorted.

Alice yanked on Hatta's arm. "This way!" She bolted down the nearest aisle, trusting that he was behind her, Courtney in tow.

If she remembered correctly, there was a curtained-off area nearby that served as an arena for con-hosted Pokémon battles. If they could reach it without being seen, it'd hopefully provide some cover for them to come up with a plan.

The top of the "tent" came into view over the heads of surprised vendors. Alice pivoted toward it, running full tilt when the crowd thinned out. Hatta was on her heels, from the sound of it.

Without slowing, she dropped into a slide, skirting beneath a divider and through the heavy curtain. It was dark inside, and thankfully empty. As she stood, Hatta swept in beside her, clutching Courtney tight in a bridal carry.

Alice had to hand it to her bestie, Court looked close to screaming but had managed to lock it down. Her eyes were wide and her face flushed, though slightly green at the edges.

"Sorry for the bumpy ride," Hatta murmured.

Courtney made an acknowledging noise that sounded like she'd swallowed a golf ball.

Hatta drew his sword and moved toward the still swaying curtains. He hooked one edge of fabric with his fingers and parted it just enough to peer through. Alice waited, her hands on her own weapons, her body tense and ready for a fight.

"I don't see them," Hatta murmured, the tightness in his shoulders easing. "Take a moment to catch your breath," he encouraged. "We'll have to move again, soon."

Alice reached to squeeze Court's shoulder. Girl looked like she was about to pass out. "You okay?"

Courtney nodded, though it took a few seconds before she could manage words. "If by okay you mean in one piece physically," she said around gulps of air. "Mentally is a whole other matter." Humor was Court's default de-stresser. If she was cracking jokes, she was managing. "Were those people, those *things*, Nightmares?"

Alice chewed at her lower lip. She was still trying to work that part out herself. The last time she'd seen anything even close to whatever those were had been outside her school a few weeks ago, when a creature pretending to be Chess dragged her through the Veil. That hadn't been a Nightmare, though, had it?

"I think so," she answered, then glanced at Hatta, hoping for a bit of input, but he remained fixated, keeping watch. "But what're they doing out during the *day*?"

A soft *patpatpat* filled the tent as Hatta tapped a gloved finger against his sword's hilt. The rest of him remained perfectly still, but that bit of movement was enough to give away how anxious he was.

Addison Hatta didn't do anxious as far as Alice knew. At least, not when it came to facing the enemy, even one with unknown strengths and abilities. She'd never seen him agitated by the prospect of a fight. No, this was something else.

She quietly promised Courtney it would be all right, then crossed the dim space to join Hatta near the curtain. He spared her a brief, questioning glance.

"What aren't you telling me?" she asked.

He aimed another look at her, this one lingering. Finally, he murmured, "Nothing."

Her hand fell over the one gripping his sword. The tapping stopped. "*This* doesn't seem like nothing."

He grimaced, pretty much caught. "Speculation. Nothing more."

She pressed her lips together with a disbelieving *mmhm*, which made him sigh. But there was a faint quirk to the corners of his mouth.

He finally admitted, "Nothing we have time to get into, especially while we're being hunted."

"*Hunted?*" Courtney squeaked. Of course she was listening.

Hatta's gaze slid past Alice to Courtney. "I recognize the young man from the crowd outside the fashion show. They've been following us for that long, at least."

"And I saw that girl while we were lined up to come in here," Alice offered while staring up at Hatta. She waited until his eyes found hers again before mouthing, "We're *going* to talk about this later."

Satisfied with his resigned nod in answer, she made her way back over to Courtney. "We need to get out of here, without starting another fight, if we can."

"They seem eager to force the matter." Hatta went back to survey the passing crowds.

Court finally managed to climb to her feet. Her wire wings were askew, and her crown was missing, but she looked otherwise fine, thank goodness. "Can't you just superhero it up and kick their asses?"

"I don't have my Figment Blades." Alice splayed her hands, a tide of guilt rising in her chest. There was no reason to feel a way. She couldn't have guessed she'd need her weapons at a fucking con in the middle of the fucking day! But here they were, reason be damned.

"And we need to get away before someone gets hurt," she continued. "You saw how people acted, they think we're putting on a show."

"Why the hell would they think that?" Court blurted.

"Damn near everyone is running around in a costume," Alice said, gesturing at herself and then at the three of them together. "And we're dressed like monster hunters. Makes sense we'd be fighting monsters!"

Hatta said, "Plus, most humans don't recognize Nightmares by sight, unless they are aware Nightmares exist. Otherwise, the creatures appear as large dogs, wolves, or bears. No idea what these things might look like." He finally stepped away from his post. The curtain swept shut behind him, plunging them further into shadow. "The glamour Verse I'm wearing doesn't help. Everyone within twenty feet is affected. Such things are usually harmless, though it *is* an illusion. Tends to warp reality a bit for anyone nearby."

Alice scrubbed at her face. Couldn't just have a normal weekend. "Then our best bet is to sneak off. Hope those things follow." To where? They'd figure that part out as they went. Honestly, anywhere was better than here.

Court gave a low whine as she pressed circles into her temples. "Jesus be a fence."

"Fences won't help," Hatta said. It was hard to tell if he was joking, but Court sniffed a laugh at least.

Alice sympathized with the trepidation coating her friend's

voice. Hell, she empathized with it, felt her own panic rear its unhelpful head. But she needed to focus. She turned to search their hiding place.

There wasn't much to it, just a hastily built stage elevated a couple of feet off the ground. White tape along its surface marked the outline of the "arena." Toward the rear, where the curtains didn't fully reach the walls, she noticed another stretch of blue tape. And then a light bulb went off.

"Over here!" Alice pointed to the lines. "This marks a no-sitting zone for a clear path to the elevators. We should be able to follow this to an exit."

Without warning, the entrance curtains flew open and flooded their little hideaway with light and sound. About five people wearing STAFF shirts froze in the "doorway."

One of them, a brown woman clutching a clipboard to her chest, brandished a walkie-talkie like a weapon. "You cannot be in here!" she declared in a thick Indian accent.

An apology hovered on Alice's lips, but she swallowed it when she spotted three Nightmare people over the woman's shoulder. She tensed as all three heads swiveled toward them simultaneously.

"We need to go," Hatta insisted. "*Now.*"

"Get Courtney." Alice turned on her heel and bolted out the back side of the tent.

Hatta followed. Court squawked in surprise as he swept her into a fireman's carry.

"H-hey!" the Indian woman hollered.

Alice ignored her, racing out into the open.

As she ran, she tried to search the wall for sign of elevators, escalators, anything. Hell, she'd even take the freight—there!

Extended high on the far wall, an illuminated sign marked an elevator, and where there was an elevator, there was likely a staircase. If they made it to the ground floor on this side of the building, it was a straight shot past the loading dock and out a service entrance she knew about after Dad snuck them in a few years ago thanks to knowing a guy who knew a guy. Practically home free.

Just as Alice reached the end of the row, intending to adjust course, something slammed into her. Pain radiated through her body. The world tilted and spun wildly. Somewhere overhead, or behind her, then in front of her, Hatta shouted her name as Courtney screamed.

Four
DUTY

Addison tried to call a warning, but before he could open his mouth a brute of a man collided with Alice.

"No!" The panicked shout escaped him as one of the other Nightmares took to the air in an impossible leap. It was the girl, half-transformed, fingers and teeth long and deadly. She landed between him and Alice, fangs bared.

"Traitor!" Her voice was high-pitched and grating.

Addison let Courtney down, then hastily swept her behind him with one hand while the other went for his sword. "Run!" he ordered, and when she didn't move, "GO!"

His shout shook her from her terror. She whirled to disappear into the crowd just as the Nightmare girl struck. "Traitor!" the Nightmare girl howled again as she tore at him with nails as long and sharp as daggers. Her fevered swings glanced off the flat of his sword.

Courtney would be all right, he told himself when he lost sight of her. These things weren't after her, so the further she went, the safer she'd be.

Around him, the human onlookers had withdrawn, many of them pointing and shouting, some in fear and some in excitement. There were other cries as well, calls from security guards demanding to be let through.

Addison shifted his stance and, instead of dodging the Nightmare girl's next attack, he stepped into it. Those knifelike claws caught him across one side but allowed him to latch onto her wrist and pull. At the same time, he thrust the tip of his blade up into her chin.

She went still, her dark eyes glossy, her mouth slack with blackened lips pulled back from sharpened teeth. The end of the sword was visible where it protruded from the back of her head, stained with yellowed blood.

A wave of shock rippled through the crowd. "Oh my god," someone gasped.

Addison drew the sword free. The body crumpled to the ground with a wet thump.

"Come on," he whispered, trying to ignore the cloudy, deadened gaze that stared at nothing over his shoulder.

"Hold it!" The human authorities were close now.

From the corner of his eye, he could see them hurrying up the aisle, but his focus remained on the girl. No, the Nightmare. "Come on!"

Finally, the skin began to shift. It slackened as if melting, the bones of her face deflating beneath it.

Relief nearly pulled him to his knees. He hadn't just killed some poor soul suffering from heavens only knew. What these creatures were and how they came to be were questions to be answered later. He had to help Alice.

Just as the authorities reached the edge of the crowd, shouting for him to get on the ground and put his hands on his head, Addison released a breath and let go of the idea of himself.

I was never here. He didn't move, but he heard surprise wash over the crowd as he faded from sight, the invisibility Verse taking hold. He waited just long enough for those gathered to start questioning themselves and each other. What was happening? Who was that guy? What guy? There was a guy?

Then he was on the move, his stride long, his pace quick.

He ducked between people, brushing against a few who floundered in his wake when they turned to see what they'd bumped into, only to find nothing.

At first, there was no sign of Alice or the creature that had attacked her. This was good, Addison told himself. It meant she was on her feet. Or had been long enough to get away. And he wanted to follow, to track her down and make sure she was all right, but there were more of those things up here somewhere. On his own, he could find and dispatch them quickly and quietly. This was his duty.

Alice can take care of herself. He knew the truth of this, had sent her into danger numerous times, and often alone. But that did little to assuage his still mounting worry.

Around him the energy of the convention had changed. Before, there was an excitement and intensity, similar to what he remembered of the days when he would visit the Wonderland markets. But now things were more frantic, people drawing tarps and covers over their booths, others dressed in security vests and T-shirts giving orders to close down.

Vendors argued with some hapless staffers who didn't know

what was going on. A particular section of the floor was being shut down due to . . . a fight? They weren't sure.

As Addison moved, he fished through the many pockets on his costume for his phone. It was a long shot, by far, but if he could reach her, at least—

"Hatta! Oh thank god," Alice's voice exploded from the speaker. She sounded winded, distracted, but not pained.

"Are you all right, luv?" The words left his lips in a rush.

"Yeah, yeah, I just—oh shit."

The line went dead.

He swallowed the dread rising in his throat and called her back.

"Hey, this is Alice!" her voice mail started. He hung up before it could finish and dialed again.

Each unanswered ring felt like a railroad spike being driven into his chest. Something was wrong.

Five

CORNERED

The force of the impact launched Alice into the air, or would have if a pair of meaty arms hadn't closed around her. The two of them slammed into an occupied booth.

More screaming. More pain.

Bodies fell on top of her and her assailant. Hands pushed and slipped as people tried and failed to get up. Her trapped arms left her face unprotected, and she caught a knee to the chin. Her vision blinked out. She tasted blood.

Hatta shouted. He sounded so far away.

Alice twisted hard as she could, bringing her knees up and wedging them against whatever had hold of her. Then she shoved with everything she had, driving the toes of her boots into something soft and fleshy.

The grip on her slackened the barest bit, but it was enough. She managed to get her arms up and bring her elbows down. Bone gave with a familiar snap. Her attacker yowled, the sound painfully loud in her ears, foul-smelling breath hot in her face. She struck again and again until the hold came loose entirely.

Free, Alice rolled away and struggled to her feet just in time to face off with a middle-aged white man dressed in black.

Her eyes went to his hands, to his fingers, stained and lengthened like talons. One of his arms hung useless at his side, but it was already correcting itself with a series of sickening pops. He snarled, baring a mouthful of fangs.

With a hiss he came at her, his strikes impossibly fast but wild, undisciplined. These Nightmares were powerful, but they weren't fighters, and they didn't have the raw, animalistic ferocity normal Nightmares possessed. Their human forms got in the way. That was the only thing that saved her from being shredded.

Alice dodged another blow, then twisted into a spin that delivered a solid heel kick to his stomach. It sent him tumbling over into the already partially demolished booth.

Someone shouted about paying for damages. She ignored them, searching the throng of faces for signs of Hatta and Courtney, but she didn't see them. She *did* see the Nightmare boy from earlier racing toward her.

"Shit!" Turning, she leaped the remains of the stall and darted for the elevator she'd spotted earlier. There were fewer people on this end of the floor, most of them making themselves scarce now that booths were collapsing, in turn making it easy for Alice to cross the space at a dead run.

Ahead, a couple of hooded Jedi with a BB-8 stroller waited in front of the elevator, and beyond them stood a door marked STAIRS.

One of the Jedi noticed her speedy approach and shouted for her to stop, but she didn't, *couldn't*. Instead, she jumped, letting her momentum and strength propel her up and along the wall at a run, over the heads of the ducking masters and their youngling. Landing on the other side of the little family, she exploded forward, slamming into the door with a resounding clang. It flew open. She ignored the pain in her shoulder and kept moving.

At the bottom of the stairs, she spun, drawing the Morning Star free once more and holding it at the ready. In here, with no one around, she could take one, maybe two of those things. But as she stood there, adrenaline surfing her limbs, the stairwell remained empty, silent save for the echoing of her own panted breaths. At least until they were joined by the violent buzzing of her phone. She dug it from her pocket, her eyes playing over the name on the screen.

"Hatta!" she shouted before the phone even reached her ear. "Oh thank god." Her eyes fell shut under the weight of her relief.

"Are you all right, luv?"

"Yeah, yeah, I just—"

Bang! The nearest stairwell door flew open and smacked against the concrete wall. A hulk of a man, or what used to be one, bent to duck through the opening.

It was the same dude that had tackled her upstairs, only now he was *huge*. Thick-necked, barrel-chested, each arm as large as her entire body. The black of his talon-tipped hands coated his entire torso, flowing along his grayed skin and ending in thick tendrils that wrapped around his neck, bulging and pulsing like veins. His lips peeled away from pointed teeth, pitch oozing between them and dripping from his mouth in rivulets. His eyes had gone completely black, and they locked with hers, unblinking.

"Oh shit . . ." Alice tucked her phone away and slid into a defensive stance, lifting the Morning Star in one fluid motion. He smiled, slow. Then lunged.

Alice threw herself backward, barely avoiding those talons.

Their tips snagged her shirt. She felt wind from the swipe fan her face. Damn that was close.

The man-beast turned to come after her again. She flung the whip out, twirling the handle so the chain coiled itself around the guy's neck. Then she jumped at the same time she pulled, hard, yanking his head down to crack his skull against her knee.

At least that had been her plan.

Lightning quick, a massive hand shot up to catch the chain and tug. Alice didn't let go fast enough and he hauled her forward. She stumbled, then dug her heels in, but it was too late.

The claws of his free hand, splayed and lethal, came at her unprotected stomach. Strong as she was, she couldn't fight gravity as it delivered her to the monster.

She braced herself.

Six

THE BEST LAID PLANS

Addison pushed through the crowd, fighting the panic grating against the sorest parts of him, those echoes of the past. He'd been too slow, again, and now Alice . . .

He didn't want to assume the worst. Alice was a Dreamwalker. A powerful one at that, more powerful than she realized. She would be fine.

But what if she isn't, a small part of him whispered. *You've been through this before. You thought* she *was fine.*

"No," he spoke softly as he rounded a corner, his gaze darting about. He couldn't lose himself to the past, not now.

It rose up to swallow him, anyway.

"Odette? She's probably playing near the river," Portentia had said that fateful day. "During breakfast, she mentioned wanting to pick some of the roses that grow there." The Queen had been so certain of this, and the easy smile that took her features had assured Addison as well.

"Roses?" he had asked. The royal gardens were full of them. Plus, the ones that grew near the water were always soggy. "That . . . doesn't sound like her."

"True," admitted the Queen while drifting back into the overly large chair on which she perched. The casual way she carried herself helped sell her lack of concern. "Which is why I think it was an excuse. You know how she likes to sneak down there to feed the frost fish." Something the youngest princess had been warned against on more than one occasion. Get a frost fish too used to being fed, and it would follow you home. Then eat you out of said home.

"Well, *that* sounds like her," Addison had murmured in reluctant agreement.

Portentia had chuckled. It was one of the last times he'd ever heard her laughter. Her face lit up with it, her bronze skin glowing in the daylight as it danced through the crystal finishes of the throne room. "Doesn't it just. Fortunately, most frost fish are out to sea until the end of the season, so no danger there. We have a bit of time yet before dinner, let her have her fun."

Addison had sighed, the want to lay eyes on the youngest princess simply to be sure threading through him, but he eventually relented. Just as he had the few times he'd brought up the need to assign the youngest princess her own knight now that she had taken to venturing off so often. "Very well, Your Highness. By your leave."

Portentia waved a hand as a teasing smile played over her lips. "You have it."

He bowed and departed, exiting the throne room, though pausing when he spotted a familiar figure standing nearby in red armor.

"Still no sign of her?" Addison asked.

Humphrey shook his head as the two fell into step. The black of his cape swirled in his wake. "You want to go out again."

Addison tilted his head to the side just so. "What makes you think that?"

"I know you." A smirk pulled at Humphrey's lips, drawing Addison's attention to them. Humphrey briefly passed his tongue over the lower one. "If the Queen isn't concerned, why are you?"

"Because it's my job." Addison faced forward again, lest he give in to the urge to pin Humphrey by his shoulders to the nearest wall and kiss him until both of them were dizzy from lack of oxygen. But they were on duty. For now. "And because . . . something doesn't feel right." He couldn't explain it beyond that, the odd twisting in his stomach, the weight of unknown wrongness he couldn't adequately put words to.

"I can send out another patrol," Humphrey offered. "Anastasia even volunteered to lead them."

That earned an arched eyebrow from Addison. "Lead a hypothetical patrol that hasn't even been dispatched yet?"

The two of them rounded a corner, the guards stationed at this juncture of corridors standing at attention as they passed. Addison nodded in greeting, putting the soldiers at ease.

Doing his best to ignore the fact that he was being scrutinized, Humphrey scratched at a cheek with one finger. "I maybe knew you'd say yes and got things in place already. Just to save time."

Addison chuckled, shaking his head. "Am I so predictable?"

"About this? Absolutely."

"I suppose there are worse character traits." He sighed, feeling the weight of the day press on him. "All right, send out the patrol. And let's see about finally assigning the young princess her own knight."

Humphrey paused in order to place a fist over his heart, bowing partially at the waist. "Of course, Captain."

Addison had started to return the salute when Humphrey stepped into his space. "What—" The question fizzled out when Humphrey's lips found his.

In the next instant, the Red Knight curled fingers around the back of Addison's neck and held him fast. His faint noise of surprise was lost to the kiss, bleeding into the slightest groan, just as Humphrey drew back. While the kiss didn't leave Addison light-headed, a pleasant, gentle rush swept through him.

"I'll see you later." Humphrey, with a telltale twinkle in his eye, turned to depart, leaving Addison staring after him. "Xelon already agreed to supervise tonight's watch, so you'd have some extra time. Yeah, I predicted that, too." He flashed a grin over his shoulder and was gone.

For a moment, Addison hadn't been able to do much more than blink rapidly, his mind still stuck on the feeling of lips pressed to his. The two knights had been together for some time now, but every so often, Humphrey managed to make it all feel so fresh and new. That damned spontaneity, both a blessing and a curse.

Mouth still tingling slightly, and face flushed the barest bit, Addison smiled to himself as he turned to head toward his study. He would focus on putting together a list of potential candidates for guarding the youngest princess. Then he would meet Humphrey for what promised to be a pleasant evening.

He'd had no idea that it would be one of the worst nights of his life, and the beginning of the end of . . . well, almost everything.

He should have listened to his gut back then. If he had, perhaps he could have prevented so much of what went wrong. But he'd ignored his finely tuned instincts. A mistake.

One he was determined not to make again.

His phone buzzed, snatching him back into the present. He

tugged it free. Then his racing heart sank when the name that popped onto the screen wasn't Alice's.

"Courtney," he said into the receiver. "Are you all right?"

"Y-yeah, I'm okay." She sounded as frazzled as he felt. "Where's Alice? She's not answering!"

The weight of those words pressed down on him. "She'll be fine." He tried to sound confident. "This is what she does, remember? But you need to get out of here."

Courtney made an incredulous sound. "I can't just *leave* y'all!"

Addison dodged around a family with two small children dressed as what looked like tiny ghosts and kept moving. "Courtney, this is my job. It's Alice's job. We can handle this, but if anything happens to *you*, Alice will never forgive me."

Laughter trickled over the call, light and slightly unhinged. Addison felt a pang of empathy. What was the saying? Laugh so you don't cry? Or something like that.

"Courtney?" he asked. His gaze swept the floor, searching. "You have to start moving. Find the nearest exit."

"I—I . . ." Her voice was small, frightened. "What if I run into one of those things?"

"They're not after y—"

"N-no, I can't, I-I'll just—I'll wait."

He bit back the curse that rolled along his tongue and collided with his teeth. He didn't have time for this. "I'll come escort you to the exit, but then you must go. No waiting, no hesitating, you run. Understood?"

"Y-yes."

"Where are you?"

"Near aisle eighteen hundred," she said. "There's, um . . . bathrooms."

His eyes trailed along the walls and ceiling until he spotted the sign and started that direction. "Be there in a moment." He would find Courtney, get her to safety, then come back for Alice.

Another plan. Just like before.

Hopefully, this time, fate would prove kinder.

Seven

ENEMIES. DEFINITELY.

Alice closed her eyes and braced for the pain of claws digging into her. Instead, arms enveloped her and pulled with a jerk. A sound like paper tearing filled her ears, followed by a grunt of pain that didn't come from her.

Alice's eyes flew open. Standing between her and the Nightmare, Humphrey had pulled her out of the way of the blow, but it looked like he'd caught part of it along his side.

"W-what?" she gasped, her brain trying to catch up with what she was seeing.

He smirked through a grimace, his bright red hair falling around his face. "Hold tight, kitten."

Before she could do or say anything, the sickening, familiar rush of cold and wind snatched at her. Everything tilted, a feeling like air in her veins swelling to bursting.

Darkness pushed at the edges of her vision. Her stomach threatened to turn itself inside out. And just when she felt she might give in to the black, it faded. Air and warmth returned to her body. She gasped, her lungs struggling as if she'd broken the surface of water, leaving her dizzy, though not so much so she couldn't tell she was outside. She could smell dirt, exhaust, and a hint of something nasty that she didn't have the capacity or desire to identify.

Humphrey drew back, wincing as he did, though he didn't get far before Courtney pushed in around him to get at her.

"Alice!" Court squeezed so tight Alice's sides ached. "Thank god, you're okay! You're okay, right?"

"I—I . . ." Alice blinked at Courtney, then past her to where Humphrey stood for a second before vanishing from sight.

With his departure, Alice's thoughts could move again. Slowly, at first, as if his presence had trapped them in her brain. She focused on her friend. "I'm okay. What about you?"

Courtney looked a mess. Her costume was torn in a few places, her makeup smeared, but she'd somehow kept her wig in place, which was more than Alice had managed.

"And where's Hatta?" she asked, looking around.

Court made a noise that was half laugh, half sob. "I'm okay, and he is too."

"But where is he?"

Court fidgeted with the sash wrapped around her waist, her fingers twisting and wringing the fabric. "He stayed inside to find you while Humphrey got me out. Don't worry!" She tightened her grip when Alice started to pull away. "Humphrey'll find him."

"Y-yeah." Alice frowned, her mind finally catching up to the fact that *Humphrey* of all people had rescued her. At the risk of sounding ungrateful, she wanted to know, "Why is *he* here?"

"I brought him," said an achingly familiar voice from nearby.

Alice spun that direction, her heart in her throat.

Chess stood off to the side, tilted against a tree like this was some dramatic reveal in an anime. There were bags under his eyes, and faint lines pinched his face with exhaustion. But those same violet eyes still managed to twinkle a bit when he grinned faintly, and that was all it took before she hurried forward, her arms going around him.

"What are *you* doing here?" Joy pitched her voice up an octave or two, along with the threat of tears now pressing at the backs of her eyes. She breathed through it. "And where *is* here, exactly?"

He returned the hug, stiffly, then hastily withdrew. "Behind the convention center. Out of the way."

The rejection stung and left her reeling. Unsure of how to respond, she turned to take in their surroundings. Sure enough, their new hiding spot—better than the tent—was nestled behind a row of hedges, shaded by a few trees that protected the space from the worst of the heat. Through the neatly trimmed twigs and leaves, Alice could see a small stretch of green littered with con-goers having picnics and taking pictures. A couple of guys dressed like One Punch Man and All Might tossed a Frisbee back and forth.

"No one can see us, if that's what you're worried about," Chess assured them.

"I'm not." Alice pulled her gaze away from the smattering of people and fixed her attention on him. "You didn't answer my question—what're you doing here?" Then she remembered he hadn't come alone, and her brow furrowed with irritation. "And since when do you hang out with Humphrey?"

Chess's smile, small as it was, faded under the force of her questions. "I . . ."

He was saved from having to answer when Humphrey popped into view holding on to a somewhat startled-looking Hatta, still very much dressed like Alucard, who blinked his wide gold eyes rapidly. "Still not used to that," he murmured.

Humphrey jerked away as if being so near to Hatta hurt him physically. Which was just fine with Alice, who practically tackled Hatta, similar to how Courtney had first latched onto her. "You're okay," she breathed, the tension that had been winding up inside her fading.

Hatta's arms fell around her, and she felt the rumble of his chuckle as much as she heard it. "I'm all right, milady. I trust you and Courtney are similarly unharmed?"

"I'm fine," Alice said, though she didn't let go just yet.

"Me too," Courtney chimed from somewhere behind her. "Besides the psychological scarring, that is."

"Good," Hatta said, then paused and shook his head. "About the being fine, not about the scars."

"This is cute and all," Humphrey grunted, an edge of pain to his words. "But we really should focus on getting very far away from your new friends."

Alice shifted around to face the former knight. He'd moved to tilt against the same tree Chess occupied.

"You all right?" Chess asked, concern clear in his voice and gaze as he eyed Humphrey, who was obviously injured.

"I'll live," Humphrey shot back, one hand pressed to his side.

Alice couldn't see any blood, but she knew he was wounded. He'd taken that hit for her.

You should thank him. Instead, she muttered, "What were those . . . things?"

Humphrey blinked, looking more than slightly surprised she was talking to him. He even glanced around as if to double-check and then pointed at himself, a single brow arched in question.

57

She rolled her eyes in answer and continued, "Why are they here? During the day! They're *Night*mares, it's in the name!" Then she hesitated, uncertainty creeping in. "They *are* Nightmares, aren't they?"

Humphrey pushed away from the tree, his hand going to his side. "All very good questions to which I do not have definitive answers."

Then what use are you? Alice wanted to snap, but she managed to lock it down. Barely. Hatta made a thoughtful sound at the back of his throat.

"And while I'm happy to speculate," Humphrey continued, "I suggest we do so elsewhere."

Alice felt her face fall into a frown. "So, what, we just walk away? What if they attack someone?"

"I don't think it'll be a problem," Chess said. He glanced around at all of them then at the ground. "They're only part Nightmare."

"They looked fully Nightmarish to me," Courtney muttered as she folded her arms around herself for comfort.

"What he means is they're not *completely* Nightmares. They're more like Fiends," Humphrey said, which presented a number of implications Alice didn't want to think about. And what happened to him not having any definitive answers?

"They were created," Hatta said, his voice low and calculating. "Is that what you mean?" There was a severity to his words, one Alice couldn't place, but she felt the weight of it all the same.

Humphrey's gaze snapped to Hatta. His shoulders lifted slightly, defensive almost. "What I mean, specifically, is they follow the orders they're given. They don't act on the instinct to go after humans. Which is great, for the humans, but *we* should go."

Hatta squeezed Alice before breaking away, approaching the

former knight. Other former knight? "If these things have been ordered to attack us, simply relocating will not deter them."

"Maybe not," Humphrey started. "But it buys us time. I mean, look at you lot," he said, his words a half laugh. "Done up in those outfits, no real weapons, you're not ready for a fight."

He had a point, though Alice hated to admit it. She also hated the idea of just leaving this mess behind. She *also* also hated that slightly condescending look on his face, but the first thing was more important.

"We were able to hold them off," Alice said, perhaps a tiny bit petulant. His comment stung a lil, no lie.

"Barely." Humphrey adjusted his hold on his side, wincing in the process. "Say we do stay. Fight. A full-on four-way brawl, illusion Verse or not, will cause a panic. People are already confused and concerned. We introduce fear into the mix, it'll just make those things stronger."

Shit. He's definitely right about that. One thing *all* Nightmares had in common: they fed on negative emotions. Fear had the greatest and gravest effect. "Fine," she conceded, flinging her hands up. "Fine. We'll split the difference. Humphrey and Hatta can go invisible or whatever, stay behind and kill those things so they don't hurt anyone—I know what you said," she aimed a scowl at Humphrey when he looked ready to argue. "But I'm not good with leaving monsters here unchecked. And if people can't see you, they won't freak out. The rest of us will go." It wasn't a bad plan, in her opinion. Certainly better than just letting those things run wild.

"They do fade when slain," Hatta offered. "At least, the one I killed did. I don't know how long it will take them to re-form—I don't know anything about them, to be honest." There was some accusation in his tone, a little attitude.

Both Humphrey and Chess shifted their weight but said nothing, which wasn't suspicious at all. Alice narrowed her eyes while Hatta kept talking, his point made.

"It stands to reason putting them down, even if only briefly, is our best option. My only concern is your injuries." Hatta looked to Humphrey. "Can you fight like that?"

The Red Knight met Hatta's gaze. His face was blank, but a muscle worked at the back of his jaw. After a handful of seconds he finally looked away, glaring off to the side and grumbling, "I'll manage."

Hatta's face fell. "I didn't mean—"

"Don't," Humphrey snapped, then repeated, softer, "Don't. If you know me, you know I've had worse." He let his hand drop from his side. His palm came away stained red.

Hatta looked more than ready to argue the point, but instead he cleared his throat loudly and simply nodded.

Appearing satisfied, Humphrey aimed a finger Alice's way. "Might I borrow your sword, in that case?"

Her hold on it tightened. She didn't want to give it up any more than she wanted Hatta and Humphrey going at this without her. Sure, the whole thing was her idea, and those creatures definitely had to be handled, but this little exchange made her wish she'd kept her mouth shut. She undid the belt before tossing the entire thing toward him. "It's blunt."

He caught the sword and drew it in one motion. "Not for long."

"Just don't break it," Alice warned before her attention returned to Hatta. The anger that had started to simmer cooled. "Be careful, yeah?"

"Of course, milady. And before I forget." He took her hand, bowing at the waist, then placed the strap of her bag into it.

Her eyes and smile widened. "How did you manage to hold on to this?"

"Magic." Hatta winked, then made his way over to a waiting Humphrey's side.

Said former knight looked like he'd rather be anywhere, doing anything, but here and this. "Hold on to me," he said.

Addison seemed to hesitate, unsure of just how to do so, before deciding to curl one arm around Humphrey's shoulders.

Then, with a slow inhale from Humphrey, the two of them shifted out of sight.

Alice stood there with her friends staring at the now empty spot near the tree, then at the building. She wasn't sure what she was waiting for, maybe a sign that everything was okay, or that the two were getting the job done; she just knew she wasn't ready to walk away just yet. But that wasn't the plan, was it?

Courtney took Alice's hand at the same time Chess cleared his throat. He asked, "So you two drive, or . . ."

"We parked over by the school," Alice said, her eyes returning to the empty space where the pair of knights had stood just a moment before. "Took the train."

"If I remember correctly, the nearest station is this way." Courtney pointed, squeezed Alice's hand once more, then started off. She curled her arm around Chess in passing, drawing him along with her. Alice followed behind them.

As they moved into the open, she kept her head on a swivel, checking and double-checking groups they passed for anyone that might be one of those things. She wasn't the only one. Chess seemed to be taking careful note of their surroundings despite Courtney chatting his ear off about nothing important from the sound of it. Breakups and makeups at school, one of the teachers apparently cheated on his wife with the volleyball coach, etc.

Alice couldn't blame her. She missed Chess, too. They hadn't seen him for nearly a week! Giving him space and whatnot. The band was technically back together, but did this really count? He was only here because those things had attacked.

He's still here. *That should be enough.*

Then why wasn't it?

Eight

GOOD. MAYBE.

Alice's unease had settled by the time they reached the station. Sort of. It helped that Courtney had kept up chatter about this or that she'd seen at the con, or lamenting what she would miss now that they were heading home early.

Thankfully, there hadn't been any Nightmare sightings since leaving the convention center. With any luck that meant Hatta and Humphrey were able to deal with them without much trouble. But if that was the case, why hadn't Hatta called with the all clear?

"They're fine."

"What?" Alice glanced up to find Chess watching her.

"Those other two? They're okay. You don't have to keep checking your phone." He dropped his gaze to her hands.

She quickly tucked both behind her back. "O-oh, I wasn't . . ." Clearing her throat, Alice slid her phone into a pocket, trying not to think about how she was acting like a toddler hiding a toy. "I'm not *worried,* worried. Just wanna make sure they don't need backup or something."

Chess lifted an eyebrow but didn't say anything else, which was somehow worse. Then he quickened his stride just enough to pull ahead a little.

Court chewed at her lower lip, shooting Alice a look. She'd been unsuccessful in getting him to join her one-sided conversation. Alice shrugged, equally helpless. There wasn't much they could do if he was still shutting them out.

"You sound so sure," she called after him.

He didn't stop but did look back. His expression was guarded, almost wary. After another few seconds of silence, he finally said, "I *am* sure. Just like I'm sure you're not gonna like how I know. I don't want you angry with me."

That pulled at something in her chest. "Why would I be angry with you?"

He lifted his shoulders. "Because you don't like Humphrey."

Her mouth worked a moment. "I— That's not . . ."

Chess pursed his lips and twisted his mouth to the side in a look that reminded her waaaaaaay to much of her mom.

"Okay, yeah, so, I don't like him." She folded her arms over her chest. "For damned good reasons if you ask me."

"Not disputing that," he said.

"But," she stressed. "He's not you. *You're* my friend. I won't get mad."

He was clearly reluctant to say more, but eventually his shoulders sagged with the decision. "We're connected. Him, me. Because of whatever was done to us. We can sense each other, same way we can sense the Nightmares."

Alice frowned, and it deepened with each word he spoke until, finally, the reality of what he was saying settled over her. "What do you mean you can sense Nightmares? Like, detect them?"

"Sort of. It's more complicated than that, but that's the easiest way to describe it." His gaze bounced from Alice to Courtney then back ahead again. "Anyway, he's fine. I'd know if he wasn't. And if he's fine then Hatta's likely fine, so you can stop worrying."

That was easier said than done. Much easier. Especially after that particular bomb was dropped. Sense Nightmares. Connected to Humphrey. Alice had so many questions, but they were going to have to wait. Down on the platform, a couple dozen people who'd obviously been at the con milled around. Some were in various stages of costume removal, others carrying merch from artist alley or the vendor floor. While the dull roar of voices echoed against the concrete, the three of them lapsed into silence. Awkward, loud as hell silence. Courtney kept pitching looks between Chess and Alice while they waited.

After a few minutes of whatever this was, Alice cleared her throat. "Sooooo, what happened to the thing you had to do?"

Chess looked up from where he'd pulled out his phone. "What?"

The way Court's eyes widened would've been hilarious any other time. She shook her head adamantly, just outside his line of sight.

Alice ignored her. "You said you couldn't come with us to the con because you were busy?" She checked over her costume while she spoke, tightening the straps and whatnot. Partly to try and act all nonchalant or whatever, but also to genuinely see what needed fixing. Some of it would have to be patched.

As if not certain what she meant, Chess blinked a few times before understanding flattened his expression. "I was. Busy."

"With Humphrey?" she guessed, trying not to sound suspicious or annoyed. Chess definitely looked the latter when she posed the question, so she quickly followed up with, "You said you brought him, I assumed you were together."

Chess muttered something under his breath before putting his phone away. "We were talking. I assumed you'd ask," he said when she opened her mouth to do just that.

Why the hell did *he* have an attitude? He was the one hanging out with otherworldly evil entities instead of his best friends. Instead she asked, "What about?"

"Does it matter?" His brow was furrowed, his words sharp. "It's a good thing I was, or who knows what would've happened."

Alice felt her nostrils flare as she traced the inside of her teeth with her tongue. True, she didn't know what she would've done if Humphrey hadn't come to her rescue, but that didn't fucking matter. So what if he did one nice thing after terrorizing her for days? Poisoning the White Queen and Hatta, stabbing Chess!

Chess, who should be angrier than her about it, but had forgiven Humphrey or some bullshit? Why, she wanted to ask, but that's not the question that escaped.

"You didn't blow us off so you could hang out with him, did you?" Her voice sounded small in her ears, and she hated the way it frayed slightly at the end.

"We're not hanging out," he said while glaring down the tunnel in search of their awaited train. "Not like that. Besides, it looked like you found a replacement, so what's the problem?"

Alice's breath caught faintly. That . . . that hurt. "Hatta isn't your replacement," she snapped. "He's a friend who we asked to go since we had an extra badge and didn't want it to go to waste."

"Just a friend, huh?" A smirk sliced across his face, his tone equally cutting. "Looked like more than friends to me."

Ice filled her body, freezing her in place. Her thoughts, on the other hand, raced, frantic to get away from the moment. Too bad her panicked mind ran straight to the memory of Courtney's party. Chess offering to drive her home. The almost kiss. Then the actual kiss outside Nana K's building, and—Christ. If she closed her eyes, she could feel the press of his lips against hers. The way his arms folded around her, the strength in them, in him, enveloping her.

A faint flush of heat filled her cheeks as a war of emotions raged inside her. She'd tried to say he hadn't been himself, that she shouldn't read too deep into it, but . . .

"Oooooh dear," Courtney murmured, her eyes wide as they ping-ponged between Alice and Chess.

Alice swallowed thickly, her throat tight. She couldn't think of anything to say. Which might be good since the look on Chess's face said he probably didn't want to hear it.

"Um, m-maybe we talk about this another time," Court said hurriedly as she glanced around. The train would be arriving soon, and the platform was starting to fill up. "Somewhere less crowded. Oh, how 'bout we go to Yonnie's tomorrow! My treat."

Alice barely heard the suggestion. Her heart was in her ears like a siren, her attention fixed on Chess.

He held her gaze, the light in those violet eyes flickering. Then they dimmed just before he looked to Courtney. "Yonnie's. *That's* supposed to be less quiet?"

"Relatively." Court hunched her shoulders. She clearly wasn't comfortable with the almost antagonistic energy growing between them. "Plus it's always good to have these conversations after eating. Makes everyone less likely to potentially say something they may regret to their friends."

Alice didn't know if that was for her or Chess. Probably both.

Either way, she appreciated the save. She couldn't have this conversation right now.

"A-all right," she said quietly.

"Fine," Chess agreed.

Court heaved a relieved sigh just as the rumbling of wheels against metal and the whoosh of wind preceded the glow of lights. The train was finally here.

◊ ◊ ◊

Silence hung between the girls as Court's Camaro carried them toward home. It wasn't the awkward, just-the-right-side-of-hostile quiet, but Alice still didn't like it.

And she didn't know how to fix it.

It was sort of her fault the way things went with Chess earlier. After the exchange on the platform, they rode to where Court had parked. When she offered to give him a ride home, he said he needed to take care of something first, but thanks for the offer. Then he was gone, without a real good-bye.

Briefly Alice had wondered if he was running off for another secret meeting with his new buddy, but then she kinda felt bad. Not bad enough to say anything, though. There would be plenty of time for talking tomorrow.

After another quiet mile or two, Alice sighed and slumped further into the passenger seat. "Okay, say it."

"Say what?" Court asked, her eyes on the road.

"Whatever you think I should've done or said differently with Chess."

For a moment, the silence returned. Then Court made a sound

that was part groan, part whimper. "I'm not sure there was anything that could have been done. Differently, I mean."

Alice tilted against the door, pressing her forehead to the window. "So, you're saying I fucked up."

"I'm not saying that." Courtney picked through the words like she was navigating a minefield.

"You're not *not* saying it." Alice waved her hands, mostly because she couldn't think of anything else to do with them. "I'm sorry, I just—Things were fine, at first. At least, I thought so. But then he falls off the face of the earth, avoiding us for weeks, all withdrawn, he looks like hell, something's definitely wrong, he's trying to act like it's not and pushing us out a-and . . ." Feeling the sting of tears, Alice took a slow, tremulous breath. "And then he shows up with Humphrey? He's been hanging out with *Humphrey*?!"

Courtney cleared her throat slightly, stealing a glance at Alice, then looking back to the road. "Your feelings are valid."

Alice snorted, unable to help the faint smile that broke through. "Your feelings are valid?" she repeated. "You been listening to self-care podcasts again?"

Court choked on a giggle. "No. No, I started going to a therapist. You know, after the whole seeing one best friend die then come back to life under the control of a demon witch, then going to Wonderland to save my other best friend after watching her get dragged into another dimension by literal living darkness, so . . . yeah, I needed to talk to someone."

And just like that, Alice felt like an ass. "Oh, I didn't mean—"

"I know," Court said.

"I think it's good. Therapy. And you going to it." Alice smoothed a hand over the side of her face. "I could probably use some myself," she murmured, then paused when something occurred to her. "You didn't talk about what *actually* happened, did you?"

"Of course not, I acted like I was having trouble with my family, which wasn't far from the truth." Court smiled. "And your feelings really are valid. A lot of not-great shit happened, and Humphrey was the cause."

Alice snorted. "That's putting it lightly."

"So, yeah, it makes sense that you're not thrilled about the situation."

"Again, putting it lightly." Alice picked at a loose thread in the seat. If she brought it to Court's attention, it'd likely be fixed in time for school Monday. "I mean, I'm low key salty as fuck. Humphrey tried to kill us!"

"While he was being mind-controlled."

"While he was being mind-controlled." Alice cut a side look at her friend. "But it still happened. And I know it's not entirely his fault or whatever, but I'm still pissed. I have every right to be pissed, and I don't appreciate Chess getting all defensive and acting like I don't!" She folded her arms, her shoulders hunched. It felt childish, probably looked it, but she didn't care. She just. did. not. care.

But as quickly as the anger flooded her body, it evaporated. Damn, she was tired.

Courtney looked like she wanted to say something, but decided against it. Which was great, because Alice was honestly done talking and thinking about all this, at least for now.

By the time they pulled up to her house, Alice had received an update from Hatta. He was fine, like Chess said he would be, and the creatures had been dispatched. Turns out Humphrey did know what they were, the liar. Or rather, he was able to make an educated guess. Something to do with the time Maddi spent as the Bloody Lady's captive. The whole thing sounded vague and cryptic.

"We can discuss details tomorrow at the pub," Hatta had said.

"It'll have to be after brunch. I'm going with Chess and Courtney."

"Mmm. Keep your daggers handy just in case. If Humphrey's hypothesis that these things are acting on that woman's final command to go after you is correct, it might not be the last we see of them. Take care, milady." Then he hung up, leaving Alice with way more questions than answers.

Greaaaaaat.

"Damn," Court said, sounding far too appreciative. "Don't take this the wrong way, but I hope I cause problems for my enemies after I go."

Alice stared at her friend. "Really?"

Court lifted her hands. "I mean in a I-want-her-to-know-it-was-me sort of way. There's only so much I can manage, I'm not a . . . what did you say? Evil entity from another realm?"

"You sure about that?"

"Ahh!" Court yelped in mock offense. "Get out of my car this instant!" She aimed a finger past Alice's nose and toward the porch.

Grinning, and feeling a bit better, Alice climbed out of the car. Then she leaned down to peer in the window.

Court had taken off her wig and tossed it somewhere in the back, along with most of the costume. She was left wearing the sports bra and leggings.

"You still down to take me to the convention center tomorrow?" Alice wasn't sure how she was going to sneak in and purge the Wraiths during the final day of the con, but she'd figure something out. Maybe a potion from Maddi would conceal her as well, or at least confuse anyone nearby so they don't see what they think they saw. Wraiths. A fitting name, and another revelation from Humphrey. Not definitive indeed. Ass.

"Of course." Court blew a kiss. "See you tomorrow. Love you!"

"Love you."

Alice waved from the porch as the Camaro disappeared down the street, then pushed into her house. The smell of meat loaf and the sound of Janet Jackson wafted in from the kitchen.

"I'm home," Alice called as she headed for the stairs.

"Already?" Mom's voice carried over the music. "You're usually at those things all day."

"Yeah, it . . . Costume malfunction. And we saw everything we wanted, so we called it early." There was no need to lie anymore, her mother knew what was up, but damn, it was almost like second nature at this point. She was gonna have to work on that, for real.

"Oh," Mom said. "Well, dinner's not ready yet."

"That's okay. I need to get out of this first, anyway." Alice headed up to her room, pausing to scratch Lewis between the ears where he lay on one of the steps.

First things first: She bent to draw a duffel bag out from under her bed, unzipping it to reveal a set of Figment Blades. Two daggers and a sword. She preferred the former, but knew how to wield the latter in a pinch. It never hurt to have a backup plan.

"Always be prepared, Baby Moon," Dad used to say. "If you stay ready, you never have to get ready."

After being attacked at school and then her own damn house, she finally decided to keep a few weapons at home.

Closing the bag, but not putting it away, she stood and started peeling off parts of the costume. As she went about getting undressed, her mind tumbled over everything that had happened today. From the ambush to the sorta argument with Chess, her brain was on overload.

It *was* good to see him, though, even if he did come with unwanted Black Knight baggage. She'd missed her friend, more than she realized. Missed hanging out with him, hearing him laugh, seeing him smile, and the way his eyes twinkled with it as he leaned in toward her . . .

Smack!

She jumped when Carol landed on her dresser, knocking over a few bottles of perfume. "Hey, girl," Alice murmured, reaching to give the kitty scritches as well. "Hiding from Lewis or the construction?"

The house was still in partial shambles, something else that was Humphrey's fault. Their little battle had busted stuff up, but the repairs were coming along. The house wasn't the only thing broken, though.

After that fight sort of forced Alice to come clean to her mom about the whole Wonderland situation, shit got weird. Like, weird-even-for-her kind of weird.

Mom had handled the news like a champ, all things considered, but now . . . well . . . Every time Alice bumped into something, or the cats knocked stuff over, Mom pulled a kitchen knife or a Taser or one of Dad's golf clubs seemingly out of thin air, ready to knock some heads.

Of all the potential outcomes of revealing your secret life of killing monsters to your parents, the last one Alice expected was her mother to turn their house into a domestic Thunderdome. Mom had makeshift weapons fashioned from various kitchen tools tucked between the couch cushions; it was like Mad Max meets Martha Stewart up in here. Seriously, there was a meat cleaver hidden in the magazine rack.

After a quick shower, Alice started the process of taking down her cornrows. She was nearly finished when Mom hollered that dinner was ready. She entered the kitchen to find her plate already made and waiting for her—meat loaf, mashed potatoes, green beans, and mac and cheese. Her stomach gave an eager gurgle.

"Hey, baby." Mom piled more food on another plate. "Was the comic club fun?"

"Con. Comic *con*, and it was . . . unforgettable." Alice settled onto one of the stools near the island.

Mom paused and turned to pin Alice with a look. "What does that mean?"

She felt her eyes widen slightly and fought like hell not to look away. "Nothing! It don't mean nothing." Man, she had to choose her words more carefully.

"Nothing, huh?"

"No. I mean, I got into a fight with Chess. I think. It's complicated." She turned her focus to her food. It wasn't a complete lie. Mostly.

"Oh." Mom fetched a Pepsi from the fridge, then joined Alice at the island. "Do you wanna talk about it?"

Not really. "Mmm."

"Sometimes a fresh perspective could help uncomplicate things."

"I don't think it will with this." Alice shoved a forkful of meat loaf into her mouth. Daaaamn, but that was good. Tender and juicy, perfectly seasoned. She went after the potatoes next. "How's construction going? I saw the stairs and hallway were done."

"And the rest will be finished over the weekend, thank the Lord." Mom shook her head and swiped her brow. Her hair was pulled back into a fluffy ponytail lined with faint rivers of silver. She'd stopped dyeing it.

When did that happen? Alice wondered.

Mom continued, "It'll be like nothing happened. Or it'll at least *look* like it."

"That's good. It'll be nice when things are back to normal."

"Mmhm. So, besides your complications with Chess, you have a good time with your *other friends?*" Mom lifted her voice slightly, emphasizing those last two words.

Sensing a trap, Alice pretended not to notice. "Yeah. Took some pictures, saw cool costumes."

"Good."

"Always do." Alice shoved more food into her mouth so she could be preoccupied with chewing.

"Mmhm. And when am I going to meet these other friends?"

Alice swallowed a groan. *Here we go.* She kept her focus on her meal. "I still don't think that's a good idea."

Mom sniffed, clearly not agreeing. "It's been a month, Alison."

"Actually, it's been three weeks."

"Don't get hurt."

Her shoulders hunched. "Sorry."

"It's been *nearly* a month, and you haven't introduced me to any of these people you've gotten yourself mixed up with." Mom's voice hardened a bit.

This time Alice's groan escaped, though it was faint. "I know, but I still think it's too dangerous right now. And they agree." Plus, she still wasn't entirely convinced her mother wouldn't try to strangle Hatta. He was the one who introduced her to the notion of being a Dreamwalker, after all.

"They agree? Oh, *they* agree." Mom snorted. "And, what, you expect me to be okay with that? You hanging around these dangerous people I've never met just because they agree?"

"What? No, it—*they're* not dangerous, it's the situation. Which is why regular people don't normally get involved." They end up hurt, or worse. Of course, her mind went immediately to Chess. To the memory of Humphrey as the Black Knight stabbing him with the Vorpal Blade. To the desperation in his eyes when he begged her to help him. Then the cold disregard when, resurrected under the Bloody Lady's control, he turned a sword on her. She shook her head, pushing the memories back. "For good reason."

"Courtney got involved," Mom said, her voice dangerously low.

"Not at first. Plus, she's really just my ride." And she still ended up being dragged into the bullshit.

"But she's met them," Mom pressed.

Alice fought to keep from fidgeting. It'd taken every excuse she could think of to keep her Dreamwalker life and normal life separate after her mom found out the truth. Everyone was busy. They were in Wonderland. They actually lived halfway around the world. Well, a few of them did.

She didn't really know why, but the thought of her mom meeting Hatta and the others? Finding out where the pub was and being able to just pop up whenever she wanted to? The very idea threatened to send Alice into an anxious spiral.

And while Mom had accepted Alice's reasons for postponing the introductions in the beginning, it was clear her patience was running out. After all, one of the contingencies for Alice being able to keep this up was a meet and greet. Mom wanted to know who was sending her baby girl into danger, which was fair. Potentially deadly for Hatta, but fair.

"Okay," Alice caved. "I'll ask. But even if they agreed, the puuuh-lace they operate out of is closed right now. It got hit, kinda like the house, only lots worse. No outsiders, not even Courtney." Which was true, thank god.

Mom twisted her lips to the side, clearly not buying it. "Is there something preventing them from coming here?"

"I mean, they're still busy dealing with all that."

"But they made time to go to this con thing with you."

"That's actually part of the 'all that.' And it's not like I can just invite them over to dinner or something," Alice said, then instantly regretted it when a thoughtful look crossed her mother's face.

"That would work for me."

"What? Wait, no, I didn't mean—"

"Sunday dinner. Extend the invitation." Mom got up, moving to snag a fork from the drying rack. "I know it's short notice for this weekend, so next is fine."

Alice stared, her mouth working uselessly for a second. "I can't just invite them to dinner—they're busy saving the world and . . . stuff!"

"Mm, if I recall correctly, *you're* the one that does the saving while they help out, so if you're not busy, I'm sure they're not busy." The look that crossed Mom's face left zero room for deals, debates, or discussions. "Extend the invitation, Alison."

Nine

DISTANT DREAMS

Addison slipped his phone into his pocket and poured the last few ounces of whiskey over the half-melted ice in his glass. He took a swig, letting the familiar burn crawl its way over his tongue and down his throat. He had to hand it to humans, they made a decent drink. It was not ember weave ale—few things were—but it got the job done.

"There is none, but so see the songs of tomorrow!" Madeline snapped, loud enough for her voice to carry from the back and out over the empty bar, her tone annoyed.

"I'm not squirming," Humphrey returned, his voice just as loud and tight with annoyance. "Maybe if you didn't—ouch!"

"Made you ring the bell," she said matter-of-factly.

Amused, Addison followed the sound of their squabbling down the back hall of the Looking Glass, past a few closed doors, until light spilled from an open one.

The space was fairly basic, a simple bedroom that boasted little more than a bed, wardrobe, and a few chairs for visitors. The window looked out over a majestic stretch of white sand glittering in the sun, the crystal blue waters of the sea beyond. Which sea, he wasn't entirely sure. Maybe the Adriatic? Perhaps he'd visit now that he could explore the human world.

Humphrey sat on the edge of the bed, undressed from the waist up, with one arm lifted in the air. His bright red hair curled against his furrowed brow, his face drawn up in irritation, along with a touch of pain.

Maddi—seated on a small stool beside the bed—tended to a rather nasty-looking set of slices in Humphrey's side.

Worry cut through Addison at the sight of them, swift and sharp. "Just a few scratches indeed."

"That's what I said, isn't it?" Humphrey flinched when Madeline pressed something over the wounds.

A morfasil, Addison realized. As she molded it into place, he was able to take in the state of her patient. Humphrey had always been lithe, but without the deceptive shroud of baggy clothes he'd taken to wearing, Addison could see he was thin. Noted how he seemed a little too pale under the lights.

"Don't look at me like that," Humphrey said.

Addison blinked, caught, but simply swirled his glass. The ice clinked. "Like what?"

"Like I'm some injured puppy."

"But you *are* injured."

"I'm certain you did worse to me in that healer woman's house."

Addison's mouth snapped shut as embarrassment moved through him. He hadn't known the Impostor was actually his—was Humphrey—but that was beside the point. "Fair enough."

Humphrey finally lifted his gaze. It met and held Addison's, then broke away to look him over—twice, in fact. "I meant to ask earlier, what are you wearing?"

The "costume" was still intact, and would be until he released the Verse that held it in place. Truth was, he'd all but forgotten he was "wearing" it, until just this moment. But he wasn't about to let the other knight know that. "It's called cost-play, and it's quite serious, so I'm told."

"You look ridicu—ah! Hey!"

"There is a river that flows west twice," Madeline murmured.

"I *was* holding still," Humphrey objected. "Your hands are cold." He jumped slightly when she patted at the bandage, the color melding to match his skin.

As Madeline busied herself with cleaning up her supplies, Humphrey slowly, stiffly, tested his range of motion. It was easy to tell how hampered it was when he shifted his right arm back and nearly buckled under the pain.

"But the way the moon melts is to the north twice," she said without looking up.

Humphrey choked lightly and blinked at her, eyes wide, his mouth open on a protest that didn't quite reach his tongue.

"She has a point," Addison said after taking a sip of his drink.

For a moment, it appeared the former Red Knight might disagree. Instead he bowed his head and simply said, "Thank you."

Madeline nodded, then hurried for the door without another word.

Addison stepped to the side to let her depart.

Humphrey watched her go before sinking into the half dozen pillows piled against the headboard. Each room in the pub was stocked with two pillows on the bed and one extra tucked away, which meant Humphrey had pilfered three more from somewhere else to make this nest. It brought a small smile to Addison's face. That was more like the Humphrey he remembered.

"I don't think she likes my being here," Humphrey said, gazing after the Poet.

"Probably because you still steal pillows."

"What?"

"Nothing." Addison waved a hand, then finally stepped into the room. He slowly made his way toward the bed, still sipping at his glass, fully aware of Humphrey's wary gaze on him the entire time. "Believe it or not, she's actually quite happy about it. We all are."

"I can think of one person who isn't."

So could Addison. "She'll come around. In her own time."

"I wouldn't be too sure about that." Humphrey propped one knee up, his elbow draped over it.

"What makes you say that?"

"She only knows me as the Black Knight, for one." Humphrey watched as Addison came to stand at the foot of the bed. That seemed like neutral enough territory, still close without being invasive. It was a fairly large bed, after all.

After a brief staring contest, Humphrey glanced to the side.

Addison took the unspoken invitation and lowered himself to sit. "But she knows that's not who you really are. That you were controlled by the Bloody Lady. Heavens, we need to come up with a better name than that."

"Agreed." Humphrey smirked, though it was brief. "I won't be much help in the moniker department. I don't know who she is. Who she could be. She's just . . . my lady. Rather, she was." He pressed a hand over his eyes, fatigue rolling off him. "I can't believe I was so willfully obedient to someone and never knew their name."

For a moment, Addison considered *not* verbalizing the thought that popped into his head. But the longer it tumbled around between his ears, the more difficult it became to hold it in. Little good would come of giving it breath, giving it life. He knew that. Not in its rawest form. So, instead of the initial musing, he settled for saying, "Trust me, you'd feel worse if it was someone you knew. If it was your choice from the start."

Humphrey lowered his hand, and their eyes met. There was a time Addison could stare into those eyes for hours. Lose himself in them. He wasn't sure he'd ever get used to how they regarded him now; as a stranger, just shy of an enemy.

Addison smiled, or at least he made the attempt. "Have you remembered anything else?" he asked, changing the subject. "Any more flashes or visions?"

Humphrey hesitated, his gaze shifting to the side again. His lips thinned and his jaw flexed as he chewed at the inside of his cheek a little.

Addison's smile widened. Even after all this time, Humphrey's little tells remained, the things that gave up the game to anyone who knew him well enough. That meant there was still a part of the other knight in there.

That also meant that he was hiding something, or thinking about lying.

"What happened?" Addison asked before the untruth could be spoken.

Humphrey's jaw tightened. "What makes you think something happened?"

"You may not remember who you are, but I do. And I can read what little bits of you manage to rise to the surface."

Humphrey narrowed his eyes. "Meaning?"

"I can tell you're not being forthcoming," Addison said, amused.

Surprise swept across Humphrey's face. His brows rose, his eyes widened. Then he averted his gaze, and his expression fell flat. "Stop."

The force of the word knocked the smile clean off Addison's face. "What?"

"Reading me. Recognizing me. Whatever you want to call it!"

"I . . . I'm sorry. I didn't mean—"

Humphrey waved a hand, glaring at a spot on the bed. "Just. Stop. Between dealing with the ramifications of what I was made into, and tiptoeing around the idea of who I used to be, I'm having a hard time grasping the notion of who I actually am, so I need you to stop," he growled, his teeth clenched, his body tense. Then he slowly relaxed, letting it all melt away as he begged, quietly, "Please."

That final plea is what did it. What knocked against Addison's heart, resulting in the first crack. It was small, harmless really, a hairline thing. But if asked in the distant future whether he could pinpoint what put him on the path that led to so much coming undone, he'd remember this moment—and how he had no one to blame but himself.

Silence, long and thick, stretched the air so thin that the few feet they sat apart felt more like miles. Nothing so vastly empty had ever passed between them before. They'd had their spats—what lovers didn't quarrel—but there was never such . . . animus. He didn't like this, couldn't stand it, really. But he also knew he couldn't be too eager, couldn't push. Humphrey had to go about this at his own pace, on his own time, no matter how badly Addison wanted his friend back.

"I'm sorry," Addison repeated. Then he prepared to depart.

"I've been having dreams, not visions," Humphrey blurted, still glowering at the comforter.

Addison's spine straightened. "Dreams? But that's—"

"Impossible. I know." Humphrey shrugged. "And yet, it's happening. And I wouldn't say anything except I feel . . . I think it may be tied to what's happening."

At first, Addison didn't have the words. Neither did Humphrey, it seemed. The other knight appeared intent on retreating as far into his pillow nest as possible.

After a couple of slow breaths, Addison carefully, quietly pressed, "What do you dream of?"

At that, Humphrey once again met his gaze.

In those breathtakingly blue eyes, Addison saw an achingly familiar hurt. The need to soothe it, soothe Humphrey himself, nearly overwhelmed him. He bit into his cheek hard enough to taste blood.

"I'm not sure," Humphrey began. "It starts with me sitting with a woman. I don't know her. I can't see her face. But she's familiar, somehow. Very familiar. I love her, I think, though I'm not in love with her." He snorted. "Funny, I can remember what love feels like."

Something inside Addison's chest crumpled, but he remained silent, waiting.

"This woman," Humphrey eventually continued. "She's important. To me, but also she just *is*. She tells me to take care of something. I don't hear her say what, though I somehow know it's equally important. Then she's gone, and I'm alone. Everything is . . . dark. Something's wrong. I lost it, the thing I was supposed to take care of." His expression twisted before he tore his gaze away.

A hollow sensation trapped somewhere between empathy and sympathy but deeper than both lodged itself in Addison's middle. He wanted to reach out to Humphrey, touch him, hold him, tell him it would be all right. Instead, he curled his free hand into a fist and rested it against his knee.

"Continue," he urged softly.

Humphrey's gaze flitted about the room like a restless bird. "After I realize I've lost this . . . important thing . . . I hear a voice. Not her voice, and no, I don't know who it belongs to. It tells me I have a job to do. Something horrible. I never remember what after waking, I just know I feel terrible about whatever it was. Bad enough I want to be sick. I don't want to. In fact, I outright refuse. That's when the pain starts."

Addison frowned. From what he knew of dreaming, pain did not transfer truly. There might be a dull ache akin to knowing something should be felt, the sensation remaining just out of reach, but actual pain? It seemed the number of possible impossibilities was growing.

Humphrey set a hand against his chest. "It starts here. Dull at first, like someone is poking me, hard. Then it starts to dig. It cracks my chest open and pours fire into me. And when I think I can't take any more, the pain vanishes. I'm standing in the dark again. The voice returns. Tells me to do the horrible thing or suffer more. So, I obey. Then I wake up." As Humphrey finished his tale, his eyes now bright with pain and fear locked with Addison's.

And like that, he was stuck.

Everything he'd thought he'd buried, twice now, came rushing to the surface. Every fond feeling, every urgent need, every bitter sweetness of knowing and loving the other knight came pouring out of that hair-thin crack, which widened with *that* look. Vulnerability clear as crystal, the silent ask for help Humphrey likely didn't realize he was making, because he didn't remember this was how he'd make it.

Somehow, Addison found the strength to turn away. He

knocked back the last of his drink, holding it a moment so the burn could purge the ache. When he swallowed, he winced. "How often do you have this dream?"

"One, two times a week," Humphrey said with a shrug, oblivious to the hurricane raging inside Addison.

"The same dream every time?"

"Near as I can tell."

"For how long?" Addison asked, though he could venture a guess.

"Since I came here." Humphrey gestured around them. "To stay, I mean. That first night is when they began."

Which didn't give them much to go on. Perhaps it had something to do with time spent in this world, but it wasn't as if this was Humphrey's first extended visit.

Happy for the distraction of a mini-mystery to solve, Addison tapped his fingers against his now empty glass, his mind working over the information. In all his knowledge of both worlds, considerable yet nonconclusive as it was, he couldn't recall any tale, legend or otherwise, of any Wonderlandian dreaming. Which left him without anyone he could think to reach out to for potential answers.

"There's more," Humphrey said, pulling Addison from his thoughts.

Oh, lovely.

Addison waited for an explanation, but Humphrey seemed hesitant, nigh on loathed, to offer one, even though he'd declared there was one to be offered. This was another of his older quirks. There was nothing for it but to wait it out, and Addison was quite adept at this in particular.

Finally, the former Red Knight drew in a breath and muttered, almost in defeat, "Chester is having the same dream."

Ten

SO . . . THIS IS AWKWARD

Alice tried not to take it personally when Courtney arrived at her house the next morning with news that Chess had declined to ride with them to the restaurant.

"He said he'll meet us there," Court had offered in a hopeful tone as she pulled away from the house.

Then Alice tried not to hold it against him when, damn near forty-five minutes after they got a table, Chess finally showed up.

And she did her absolute best not to feel a way when he sat down and picked up a menu without a word. Not an "okay, so listen," "what had happened was," "fuck y'all"—nothing. Hell, he barely apologized, and it was only after Courtney said something about being glad he remembered where the restaurant was.

So yeah, Alice tried not to let any of that get to her. She tried her very best. But as her eggs grew cold, her temper flared hot. Which sucked—she usually loved eating at this place.

The clamor and commotion of Yonnie's bistro was a welcomed

familiarity. Everything, from the floral wall decal, to the smell of bacon sizzling, to the slight squeak of the server's shoes against the tiles on the floor, pressed in from all directions. Which made this awkward-ass silence hanging over their table that much worse.

Chess poked at his home fries, Court stirred her sweet tea, and Alice was beginning to wonder if this whole meeting wasn't a mistake.

"So," she breathed as she resisted the urge to twirl her knife.

"So," Court repeated, then promptly sipped at her drink to occupy her mouth. Cheater.

"So." Chess sank into his seat like the word threatened to pull him under the table. His expression drooped similarly.

Alice cleared her throat a little. "How are you doing? With everything."

"Fine." His response was automatic, and robotic. He didn't look at either of them.

A muscle twitched in her jaw. "Just fine?"

"Mmhm." He took a bite of his waffle. First one since he got his plate almost ten minutes ago.

"You don't *look* fine," Court pressed gently.

Chess sighed. "And if I'm not? Would you really be surprised?"

Courtney blinked, clearly taken aback. "Well, no."

"Then why'd you ask?" Chess murmured.

Court pressed her lips together, the lower one trembling slightly, before going back to her own neglected plate.

Alice, once again, tried not to take his attitude personally, but he was making it real, *real* hard. "Because that's what friends do. You remember the concept of friendship, don't you?"

This time Chess was the one to shrink slightly.

"Or did you find a new definition, like you found a new friend?" She folded her arms.

"Alice," Court warned in a whisper.

"He's not my friend." Chess frowned and dropped his fork.

"You sure? Since, apparently, you'd rather spend time with him instead of us." All right, fine. She was pissed. Had been all night, and she had tried to push it aside as well. Today was supposed to be a fresh start! They could talk to each other, about Humphrey, about Hatta, about all the relationships therein. But not if he was gonna act like this. That was the dealbreaker.

She didn't care that he needed space—it was understandable. She didn't even care that he was being a bit of an ass—sometimes trauma gave you an attitude for a while. What set Alice off was that all of this was aimed at her and Court while he made nice with the person responsible for everything. So yeah, she was angry. But, most of all, she was hurt.

"You ignored us for weeks," Alice hissed. "*Weeks*. When you stopped answering our calls or responding to the group chat, we figured you needed space. We backed off, hoping it—we were so . . . worried." She couldn't keep the tremble out of her voice. "It's a little upsetting to find out you been hanging out with the asshole who started all this."

Chess ran a hand through his hair while making a frustrated sound at the back of his throat. "We're not *hanging out*." He flexed his fingers in air quotes. "It's . . . You wouldn't understand."

"You think maybe you could let us try?" Court asked. It was more of a croak, really. "To understand, I mean. You're our friend. No matter what's wrong, we wanna be there for you. The way you've been there for us."

Alice felt some of the heat go out of her anger. She reached to squeeze Courtney's hand where it fidgeted with a napkin on the table. Then she looked to Chess.

He released another slow sigh, sinking even further down into his chair if it was possible. He didn't say anything, his gaze aimed at the ceiling. Of course their server chose that moment to drop by, setting out drink refills and asking if there was anything else he could do. Then the poor guy took one look around the table before his sunny expression clouded a little. "Y'all let me know if you need anything," he said before vanishing into the bustle of the bistro.

The seconds stretched on. Chess didn't move. Courtney ate some of her food but didn't seem half as excited about it as before. Alice's appetite abandoned her completely. She'd just take her plate home to Mom. She loved Yonnie's.

Finally, after what felt like forever, Chess shoved his plate away and murmured, "Maybe you should just worry about yourselves."

Alice opened her mouth, immediately ready to clap back, but Courtney squeezed her hand so hard she yelped instead of speaking. Court bucked her eyes, then knifed a look at Chess and back. He was slumped in his chair, jaw tight, glaring at his food. But it wasn't anger Alice saw on his face, it was pain.

Her friend was in pain.

She swallowed the lump forming in her throat. "You have . . . no idea how fucking furious I am at Humphrey for what he's done. How he took one of my best friends from me. Turned him into something I didn't recognize. Into someone who didn't recognize *me*." Her throat tightened and her voice cracked.

Chess glanced up, his violet eyes finding hers.

"And I know, I *know*, he was being controlled. I know, but I'm still angry. I don't know how to not be angry." She sniffed and took a few swigs from her glass of water.

Courtney's hand squeezed again.

"And I don't know when I'm not gonna be pissed about what happened, but I'm not judging him. And I'm not judging you for what you did. I, *we'd*, never judge you, o-or hate you, or anything like that. I hope . . . I hope you know that." That was it, then. Everything she felt, everything she had to say, everything that built up over the past weeks, laid bare. She hoped, she prayed, it was enough. For what, she wasn't sure. But she missed her friend, and she just wanted him to be okay.

Chess straightened in his chair, his expression easing, the tension in his body melting away a little. He gazed at Alice, then looked to Courtney, who smiled and nodded. Tears glistened in the corners of her eyes.

"Gonna get some air," Chess said abruptly as he pushed up from the booth. He made a beeline for the front of the bistro, nearly ran over a server but sidestepped with an apology at the last second, then eventually pushed out the door.

Alice couldn't tell if it was her imagination or not, but it seemed like the restaurant quieted a little. Like everyone knew what just happened and was waiting to see what came next.

Courtney set her hands on the table. "Should we get a to-go box for him?" she asked quietly.

Alice, her heart in her throat, stared at the mostly untouched plate in front of the now empty chair. Biscuits and gravy was his favorite. He never left a crumb. "Y-yeah." Her vision blurred briefly with the threat of tears, her face and throat burning. "Get me one, too. I'll . . . see if he's okay."

Hurrying for the door, Alice pushed through and out into the bright Sunday morning. It was nearly noon, but a chill thickened the air and slid along her arms. Where was this cool weather yesterday when she was covered in leather and fur? Shit, she'd left her jacket in the booth. Rubbing at her bare skin, she glanced around for signs of Chess. He couldn't have just left, could he?

The beginnings of panic blossomed in her chest, but then she caught sight of him near the end of the building, sitting on an overturned bucket. He leaned back against the brick, his long legs extended across the walkway, looking like a lanky snack.

Heat flared in Alice's cheeks, and she quickly bottled that treacherous line of thought. Memories of what had passed between them, the moments shared at Court's party and outside Nana K's, had plagued her last night. Ever since they . . . well.

Let's not, okay, brain?

He glanced up as she approached, his violet eyes taking her in with a quick play from her head to her toes. Was the color dulling again? She couldn't tell without staring.

"Hey," he murmured.

"Hey." She stopped a short ways off and tilted back against the wall. A chill shot through her, the cold of the stone stabbing at her through her shirt.

"I meant it. When I said you could talk to me. To us," she said while stealing glances at him. "You don't have to be alone with what you went through—"

"What I did?" There was a bite to his words colder than the air around them.

"What was done *to* you," she insisted. "But my point still stands. And if you can't talk to us for whatever reason, you should still try and talk to *someone.*"

Another stretch of silence passed between them, and Alice couldn't tell whether he was upset or not. Not knowing bothered her, more than she thought it might. He used to be such an easy read for her, with his gentle smiles and chill vibe. She didn't like not knowing what he might be feeling.

"You don't seem to like my choice in therapist." His voice was so quiet she almost didn't hear him. "Which is fine. You don't have to like the guy. But if he helps, *actually* helps me deal with all this? Isn't it worth it?"

Each word was like a stone in Alice's stomach. He made a fair point. She hated it, but that didn't make it any less true.

"You're right," she admitted with a shrug. "What helps you should be the priority. I'm sorry. Really." If talking to Humphrey somehow helped Chess, then fine. Two things could be true: She could hate Humphrey's guts, and he could be good for her friend. But the second Chess didn't need him anymore? All bets were off.

She reached to lay a hand on his shoulder. "Look at me."

He didn't at first, not until she shook him gently.

"What happened still isn't on you. I know it may not feel like it, but that don't make it no less true." She pressed her lips together. "Say it."

"What?"

"It's not your fault. Say it."

"Alice—"

"Say. It."

He sighed, his shoulder sagging under her touch. "It's not my fault."

"Again."

"It's not my fault."

She nodded, pleased. "Good."

Chess watched her for a moment before a smirk plucked at the corners of his mouth. "If it's any consolation, you being jealous of any potential new 'besties' is pretty nice."

"Ah!" Her mouth dropped open, and she shoved him, earning a chuckle. "I wasn't jealous—I was pissed! Still am! But . . . I love you more than I dislike him." She barely managed to avoid saying "hate." In fact, she was so focused on it, she almost missed what Chess said next.

"I love you, too."

Shock nearly squeezed the air from her lungs. When her gaze cut toward him, he was still grinning. Almost like his old self.

But then his smile faltered. The light in his eyes dimmed and went unfocused. The change was sudden and stark, but brief. One second he was gone, the next he was back, blinking up at her, his brow furrowed.

"What's wrong?" Alice asked, suddenly on alert.

"I don't kn—ahh!" Chess doubled over, clutching at the sides of his head.

Alice reached to catch his shoulders. "Chess! CHESS!" She came around to kneel in front of him, ignoring the looks from the family on their way into the restaurant.

Pain twisted Chess's face. His fingers tugged at his hair as he shook his head, curling in tight on himself.

"No. No, I—I won't!"

"Chess, what's wrong? Talk to me, come o—"

"I won't! You can't . . . No!" He straightened with a jerk.

Alice recoiled.

The violet of his eyes had gone black at the edges. Amber burned in his pupils. The flames swept outward, filling his sockets completely. And then they vanished. Poof, gone. He blinked rapidly, his chest heaving. His now normal gaze danced around, almost uncertain of where he was or what was going on. His eyes found hers for the briefest moment, then lowered to her waist.

Alice looked down as well and realized her hands had gone to her hips as if to reach for daggers that weren't there. Guilt burned through her. "I-I'm sorry, it's reflex, kinda."

He waved off her words, and her offer to help him up, rising on his own. "Get Courtney. We need to go, *now*."

Eleven

WHISPERS

Addison massaged a temple with one hand and stirred honey into a steaming mug of chamomile with the other. This was his fourth cup today, and if the pounding between his ears had its way, it likely wouldn't be the last.

"Did you hear me, Mr. Hatta?" a voice droned from over his shoulder. "About checking the foundation?"

With a deep breath, he set the spoon aside and took a long, slow sip. The heat and earthy flavor were like a balm against his agitated soul. A shot of whiskey would help but, for the first time since opening its doors, the Looking Glass was fresh out. How unfortunate. He should have gotten a fresh bottle when he emptied the final one last night. Just the one would've been fine.

"Mr. Hatta?" the voice pressed.

"I heard you." Addison turned and faced what was left of the bar and the gentleman standing at the center of it. "And I told you before, I've already got someone handling that."

The man, a middle-aged, balding fellow with pale skin, nervous eyes, and fingers that never seemed to stay still for more than a handful of seconds, tightened his hold on a clipboard. "And I've told you it has to be a certified inspector."

"She is," Addison said over the rim of his mug before taking another sip. "One of the best, in fact. Now, could we hurry up? I've got other meetings to take, as I'm sure you can imagine."

Gerald, the unfortunate soul assigned to making sure the repairs to the Looking Glass were up to code, huffed his very apparent displeasure. "Sir, we attempted to contact your establishment several times in order to schedule a meeting, but were never able to reach anyone. It's come down to the wire, and if you want the blessing of the city to reopen, we need to finish this."

Addison barely resisted the urge to roll his eyes, juvenile as it might be. "I promise, I want nothing more than to be *finished* with this entire affair."

"Frankly, I'm surprised a structure this old survived an explosion caused by . . . what was it again?"

"Gas leak," Hatta sighed, taking another sip of his tea.

Gerald plucked his glasses free, folded them together, and slipped them into his breast pocket. "How did someone so young end up the proprietor of such a . . . distinguished establishment?"

Ahh, there we are. "I inherited it," Addison offered without missing a beat.

"Mmm. Well, if you want to keep it operational, I suggest you take these requirements more seriously." Gerald patted the packet of papers on his clipboard.

Addison smirked behind the lip of his cup. Little did Gerald know, this was not his first run-in with human authorities regarding the pub's operations, and he doubted it would be the last. He supposed it was good things were less fraught this time around. The prohibition was many things, but dull was not one of them. Including now, the Looking Glass had needed to be rebuilt thrice—3.5 if he counted that little dustup with the wild Nolsi. He shuddered faintly at the memory. So much . . . goop . . .

Bzzzt. Bzzzt.

His phone buzzed in his pocket. Maneuvering the mug to one hand, he pulled the device free.

"And of course it would behoove you to . . . Am I boring you, Mr. Hatta?" Gerald asked, his tone indignant.

"Go on, I'm listening." Addison didn't glance up from the screen, where a text from Humphrey had appeared.

Felt it again. Chess did, too. He's on the way with Alice.

Pressure rose behind Addison's eyes, sudden and sharp. Seems Humphrey's hypothesis had proved correct.

Gerald cleared his throat faintly and flipped through a couple of his papers. "Now, the foundation isn't the only thing you have to—"

"I do apologize—Gerald, is it?" Hatta responded to the message as he spoke, asking for an ETA. "I appreciate your dedication to making sure the Looking Glass is back to one hundred percent as soon as possible, but a personal matter has come up."

Gerald huffed, his already ruddy face darkening. "Mr. Hatta. This inspection is required for you to operate your business. I'd hoped you'd understand the importance of seeing it through."

"Oh yes, so important." He turned to make his way toward the exit. "But as I said. Personal matter. We can reschedule for a better time that suits the both of us, yes? Thank you for coming." He held the door open and smiled.

Gerald went another shade darker. "If I don't conduct this inspection today, your reopening could be pushed back weeks, months even! And I have to say, I don't appreciate my time being wasted like this. There are a number of other establishments that are serious about their businesses and would have gladly taken this spot, and I—"

Without warning, a headache exploded behind Addison's eyes, and his vision went white. The beating of his pulse rattled inside his skull. Each slam sent fire through the rest of his body, and just beneath the frightening familiar burn, he felt, he heard . . . something.

A voice at the center of the hurt called to him.

I can see you.

It reached for him.

I can feel you.

It wrapped around his heart and pulled.

Take up your sword and come to me.

Then, as suddenly as it had come, the pounding faded. His vision started to clear. First colors, then shapes, a kaleidoscope that solidified with a few blinks.

His chest heaving, his body tight, he was surprised to find himself on his knees. Hot tea soaked into his jeans, the shards of his mug scattered around him.

"M-Mr. Hatta?" Gerald stood over him, his scuffed loafers visible just to the side.

"I'm all right." Addison focused on breathing.

The slap of shoes echoed from the hall, and within seconds Madeline filled the doorway, her wide purple-then-blue eyes homing in on him.

"Flutter? A bird cries two bushes?" she squeaked, her shoulders rising and falling with quick breaths.

He nodded, and she disappeared back down the hall to fetch her tinctures. "I'm all right." Addison glanced up.

Gerald had extended a hand in a gesture of offering help, though the instant his eyes met Addison's, he recoiled.

"W-what in the—" The man stammered as Addison carefully regained his feet.

"Migraines." Addison pinched the bridge of his nose.

"Migraines?" Gerald parroted, his voice pitched high in disbelief.

"Yes." The burn behind Addison's eyes had lessened, though it smoldered dangerously. He chanced a glance at Gerald, and when the man didn't react beyond what appeared to be mild confusion, he loosed a faint sigh of relief. "They sneak up on me every so often."

Gerald's lips worked a few times before he swallowed. "I thought I saw . . ."

"Sorry for the scare." Addison bent to gather up the remains of his mug.

"Your . . . eyes . . ."

"I promise the foundation inspection will be completed and certified within the required time frame." He straightened and forced what he hoped was a polite smile. "In fact, I'll call you day of."

A gesture toward the exit had Gerald shuffling that direction, stealing side-glances at Addison as he escorted him through the brand-new doors.

"V-very well. Good-bye."

"Good-bye." Addison closed the door just as Madeline returned carrying a small chest and hauling one of the chairs from the back. The furniture had been cleared out of the bar proper. All that remained were unsettlingly bare walls and a large scar on the floor where the bar itself once stood.

"Won't wake the sunrise?" Madeline asked as she knelt with the box.

He handed her the key from around his neck. "I'm not sure. It was similar to an episode but . . . different." And at the same time entirely too familiar. This couldn't be happening. *She* couldn't be happening. Sinking into the chair, he dropped his still faintly throbbing head into his hands.

It seemed all sorts of nightmares were coming back to haunt them.

"Down," Madeline said.

She held out a vial of purplish green liquid. He took it with thanks, tore the cork free with his teeth, then swallowed it in one pull. The liquid tasted of copper and slid cool down his throat. A second potion followed. He was about to down a third when the sound of footsteps approaching caught his attention.

Madeline glanced up just as Humphrey came around the corner. He tilted heavily into the archway, his already pale face even more ashen. Circles darkened the area beneath his eyes.

"What in the nine hells just happened?" Humphrey panted faintly.

Addison frowned. "You tell me." He had his suspicions, but those wouldn't be enough. He needed to be sure.

Grunting, Humphrey crossed the room and bent to pluck one of the vials from the open box. He ignored Madeline's warning, uncorking and drinking the contents. "I don't know, I—my head started pounding. I heard someone calling to me, telling me to join them . . . in battle?"

Madeline squeaked but didn't say anything as her wide eyes moved back and forth between them. Her hands pressed over her mouth.

Humphrey straightened as the effects of the potion started to take hold. "It wasn't like the dreams, though. It was different. Sharper."

"I think there may be more going on here than we originally assumed," Addison murmured. His gaze trailed toward the hallway, beyond which lay his office. In that small room, tucked into a cabinet in the corner, locked away from the world, was the anchor for something he hadn't felt actively call to him in an age.

At least, not until today.

Twelve

AWW HELL

Alice once again clung to the oh-shit bar on the passenger side of the Camaro as Court dodged through traffic, whipping them onto a side street she said would be faster than the choked highways.

"Y'know," Court started, jerking the wheel to the left, "I'm starting to sense a pattern."

"What?" Alice kept pitching glances at Chess in the rearview mirror. He sat behind Courtney, staring out the window, the color in his eyes shifting just slightly every few seconds. It was a bit unsettling, but he assured them he was fine. Then he insisted they go to the pub as fast as possible and hadn't said a word since.

Court nodded. "Shit goes down, we deal with it—well, *you* deal with it—things get better for a bit, but then we end up rushing to the pub because, once again, shit has gone down."

Alice smirked faintly, despite the nerves rolling through her. "I mean, that's been life for a while now."

"I know! And it was cool, you doing superhero stuff, but you can't tell me things haven't gotten out of hand lately."

She's not wrong. Alice couldn't help feeling this sudden negative outlook had to do with Court's little vacation in Wonderland. After more than a year of gushing about how dope everything was and how awesome it must be doing what Alice did, she was pretty lukewarm on it all lately. Still supportive, but clearly less enthusiastic about potential threats to their lives.

"Look out!" Chess screamed.

Something slammed into the car. Metal buckled with a deafening *wham*. Glass shattered, sending a hurricane of shards spinning through the air. The Camaro pitched onto two wheels, flinging Alice against the door. Pain erupted from her pinned shoulder and tore down her arm.

The world spun in a blur of sky then ground then sky, over and over as they tumbled. Her heart leaped into her throat. The seat belt dug into her chest, her neck, her stomach. Everything tilted to the side, then came crashing to a stop.

An alert pinged over the radio before a woman's voice filtered through, saying, "You have been in an accident."

No shit! Alice blinked her eyes open. Her vision waxed and waned, fighting to bring the world into focus. White smoke choked the air, making it hard to breathe, even harder to see. "Court? Chess?"

No one answered.

Head throbbing, she craned her neck to look around. The car was on its side, leaving her dangling slightly above an unconscious Courtney. Blood slicked her face, stained her hair, and dripped toward the roof.

Chess hung similarly in the back, but Alice couldn't see whether or not he was hurt.

Panic ate at her, but she pushed it down. "G-guys? Somebody talk to me. Hey!"

Silence, save for the grind of some engine part as it worked uselessly and a steady *ping ping ping* from some alert.

Alice shifted where she half hung from her seat, reaching to undo the buckle. It came loose with a click, and she caught herself against the warped dash, bracing to keep from falling onto her unconscious friend. "Courtney?" she called softly, reaching to gently shake her shoulder.

Court's body shifted with the slight jostle, but she didn't wake. For a second, Alice feared the worst. Then she saw the shallow rise and fall of Court's chest. She was breathing.

Oh, thank you, Jesus. Alice twisted to try and get a look at Chess, but the seats were in the way, and she was upside down. She had to get out, get help.

Ignoring the burn of cuts and bruises along her body, Alice shifted to brace against her seat. Her right leg throbbed. It wasn't broken, that much she could tell, but the pain shooting through her made maneuvering that much more difficult. Still, she managed to angle herself around and lash out at the fractured windshield with her good leg.

Wham! Wham! Wham!

The dense webwork of cracks thickened as tiny shards rained across the destroyed console like sand, more and more until the edge of the windshield finally came loose.

A groan spilled in from the back seat. "Jesus Christ . . ."

"Chess?" Alice's heart kicked against her chin.

"Y-yeah."

"Are you okay?"

There was a pause, punctuated by a hiss of pain. "Mostly. You?"

"I-I'm okay. Courtney's unconscious." Alice pushed at the windshield with her feet.

"What . . . what happened?" Chess croaked.

"Don't know. Can you move?" Another kick and the slab of fractured glass bent outward, leaving a space nearly big enough for her to crawl through.

Chess grunted. She could hear him shifting around back there, no doubt trying to get loose.

"I-I'm pinned," he said.

"I'll get help," Alice promised as she finally managed to fold the windshield in on itself and start to pull herself through. Glass tore at her arms. But she gritted her teeth and kept going. She'd had worse.

With a cry she fell free, hitting the pavement in a roll, chest heaving. She scrambled to push onto her knees, trying to see what was happening, where they were, what hit them. There was nothing. No one. They were alone where the car had tumbled into an empty parking lot. One Alice recognized.

Her stomach dropped. This was the football field where Brionne had died. Where Alice, just weeks ago, had faced off against Humphrey as the Black Knight along with the biggest Nightmare she had ever laid eyes on. The field had been nearly destroyed in the fight. The entries to the tunnels and the stands were still roped off.

Favoring her sore leg, Alice managed to stand, limping around the car to see if she couldn't open a door or break a window to get her friends out. She grabbed a handle and pulled. The metal groaned.

No. That wasn't metal. Alice's insides went cold as an all too familiar howl filled the air. She spun, and the ice in her stomach spread through the rest of her.

A Fiend emerged from the nearest stadium tunnel, sniffing at the ground. It raised its catlike head and loosed another howl that was answered from somewhere behind Alice. She whipped around to find a second monster creeping toward them from across the street.

Every muscle in her body tightened. *Shit shit shit!* She hurried over to the car, bending to push through the space where the windshield had come loose. Her bag, she had to get her bag! She winced where bits of glass caught at her arms, but managed to squeeze far enough inside to look around. There. It had fallen against Courtney's window. Alice snatched at her bag, surprised by how light it was. That was when she noticed her things scattered through the car. *Are you fucking kidding me!*

Another growl, closer this time. The sound was accompanied by a low cackle, the beasts laughing as they cornered their prey.

"Delicious fear," one hissed.

"Split the bones. Drink the blood!" the other growled.

Alice thrust her hand into her bag and fished around until she found the hilt of a dagger. The other was gone, and she didn't have time to look for it. Drawing the Figment Blade, she shimmied back out of the car and landed on her ass just as one of the Fiends pounced.

With a cry, Alice brought the dagger around to catch it in the chest. It howled, clawing at her, talons catching in her shirt and skin. The pain was white-hot against her nerves.

She grit her teeth, curled her legs in, and kicked out, driving the heels of both shoes into the beast's underbelly. The creature went flying with a yelp. Her injured leg threatened to give as she regained her feet.

"Poor child," one Fiend rumbled.

A chill slid down her spine. That voice. Flashes of the night her father died raced across her memory. The creature emerging from the shadows, moving with the lethal certainty of a predator stalking prey.

These Fiends moved similarly, one going to the left, the other to the right. Alice brought up her dagger, her gaze dancing between them, her body tense. If they came at her at the same time, she wouldn't be able to defend herself. The sharp talons of fear gripped her heart.

"So alone," one Fiend growled.

"So afraid," the other hissed.

"Not alone."

Chess slammed into one of the Fiends from the side, feet-first. He landed in a crouch as the creature collided with its partner and the two howled as they went tumbling. Alice's brain stuttered to a stop.

This wasn't the first time she'd seen him fight, but that hadn't been him, at least not *him* him, and this was, wasn't it?

She was saved from trying to puzzle things out further when Chess came running toward her, something glinting in his hand. Her other dagger, she realized.

"Are you okay?" he panted, his face drawn up with worry.

"I'll manage." Her eyes dropped to the weapon in his grip. She hated the idea of her friends in danger, but she was hurt and couldn't face the Fiends alone. If he was half as good with a dagger as he'd been with a sword . . . "Think you can use that?"

He rolled his shoulders, a bit of color filling his face. A bruise had started to purple near one of his temples, and a cut still bled where it split his lower lip. "Don't know, guess we'll find out together." He gestured at the Fiends with the blade.

The beasts had regrouped, coming toward them slowly with fangs bared and heads lowered.

Alice took a breath and centered herself as best she could with her leg. She could feel the muscles tense and relax as her body worked at healing itself. She stole a side-glance at Chess as he took a similar stance, his eyes narrowed. That . . . that was not a look she was used to seeing on him.

Refocusing on the creatures, she tightened her grip on the dagger. "I got the one on the left."

"At your side."

The Fiends came at them.

This wasn't the first time Alice had fought alongside someone else, and it surely wouldn't be the last, but a sense of surety rested in her limbs. A feeling that was more than familiarity—no, this was a comfort born of repetition. Chess seemed to *know* what she was going to do before she did it. The two of them moved in tandem, guarding openings in each other's stance, pressing in attacks where they could, methodically taking the Fiends apart whenever they came within range.

The monsters seemed to notice, their attacks coming slower, more time spent circling the humans to try and sniff out weaknesses in their formation. But there were none. And within minutes, their combined efforts saw Chess parrying a swipe of claws, which gave Alice the perfect opening to draw her blade along a fleshy underbelly.

The Fiend yowled in pain and toppled over, claws scrabbling

at the ground, too wounded to regain its feet. Alice pounced, driving her dagger home with a crack. There was a sound like bottled thunder, and the body started folding in on itself. A glance over her shoulder revealed Chess standing over a similarly dissolving body. Holy shit, that was probably the fastest she'd ever taken down a Nightmare. And not a drop of that putrid shit on her, a personal best.

BEEEEEEEEEP! BEEP BEEP!

Both Alice and Chess whirled toward the car as blasts from the horn filled the air.

"Courtney!" Alice gasped.

"I got it." Chess tossed her the second dagger, which she caught with ease. "You finish up." He started across the lot in a run, coming to stop beside the Camaro and kneeling to crawl partway through the widened space where the windshield came free.

Alice gripped her weapons and turned to the now-darkened patches on the asphalt. She drove the blade into the ground. It gave like sand. The dagger flared, there was a hiss, and soon all that remained was a scorch mark that would eventually fade. She did the same to the second patch of black, then hurried toward her friends as fast as her throbbing leg would carry her.

By the time she hobbled over to the car, Chess had managed to get Court's seat belt undone. Alice reached to get her hand under Court's other arm and, together, they carefully pulled her free.

"God*dammit*!" Court hissed as she curled against the ground.

"Go easy," Chess cautioned.

"My arm!"

Alice flinched in sympathy as she caught sight of bits of glass dug into sluggishly bleeding and torn skin. She had cuts and bruises as well, but hers were already starting to heal. By tomorrow, most of them would be faded.

"Fuck," Court groaned, stretched on her back. A cut on her face still bled as well. She looked to be moving okay, though.

Alice prayed there was no internal damage. "What hurts?" She knelt beside her friend, hands hovering. "Anything feel broken?"

"Everything hurts." Courtney complained as she winced and set a hand over her side.

A flare of worry washed over Alice. "Try not to move too much," she cautioned. "We'll get help."

"It doesn't look like there's any help to get," Chess said, glancing around. The lot was still empty, but so were the neighboring streets. No one jogging or playing or anything. Not even any cars passing by. A park across the way was also void of a single soul. This . . . this was weird.

"Well, we damn sure can't stay here," Alice said, not wanting to stick around and find out just why there weren't any people. "You got your phone on you?" She aimed the question at Chess.

He shook his head.

"Mine is in there somewhere." Court glanced at her totaled car. Her lower lip stuck out slightly.

"I got an idea." Alice made her way over to the car, bending to crawl into it again. She maneuvered her way carefully around warped metal and over broken glass until she could reach out and press the ignition button.

A few of the lights on the dash flickered to life, those that weren't broken, at least. Holding her breath and sending a prayer up to the tech gods, Alice held the call button on the wheel and waited.

. . . . . . *Ping!*

Yes! "Call Hatta!"

There was a brief pause before a robotic female voice responded. "Calling Hatta, mobile."

He picked up on the first ring. "Courtney? Is everything all right?"

"Hatta! It's Alice. We were attacked by Fiends. Courtney's hurt."

Hatta cursed quietly. "Where are you?"

"At the field where we fought the Black—Humphrey that time?" Her throat tightened.

He said something to someone, his voice muffled briefly. She thought she heard Maddi answer, then he was back. "We're on our way."

The call ended, and Alice carefully crawled out of the wreckage and made her way over to her friends. "Hatta's coming. Maybe Maddi." At least she hoped that was the case. All three of them could use a couple potions.

Alice reached to take Court's hand, squeezing her fingers before her gaze shifted to Chess. "Keep an eye on her. I'm gonna have a look around."

"You think that's smart?" he asked. "There could be more monsters out there."

Alice's gaze slid toward the stadium. Most of the stuffed animals and flowers from Brionne's memorial had been replaced with new ones, though some were wilted and discolored from the weather. A few pieces of the yellow caution tape that roped off the tunnels hung in flowing ribbons, torn free when the Nightmare emerged. The place looked quiet enough, but that didn't mean anything. "Those Fiends showing up here can't be a coincidence. I'm gonna go check on the purge site."

"I'll come with you," Chess said, already rising to his feet.

"No. Stay with Courtney. And here." She held out one of the daggers. "Just in case."

He hesitated, eyeing her with a look that said he didn't like this, but took the dagger anyway.

Alice limped toward the tunnel. Her leg was already feeling better. She ducked under the remaining tape and made her way into the shadows. Her body thrummed. Her heart kicked against her ribs. Her free hand fisted at her side. This place . . .

Even as she emerged into the sunlight, a chill slid down her spine. Visions of that night spun through her mind: Humphrey as the Black Knight, flanked by Fiends. Chess, bloodied and bruised. Hatta and Xelon facing off with that thing. She could still hear its roar, feel the heat of its fiery breath, smell the stink of sulfur and Slithe rolling off it.

Breathe. It's okay. This is . . . not fine. But you're here. You got this. Alice ran her gaze over the area. The ground was still carved up from the battle, grooves carved into the turf and dirt. Machinery had been brought out to make repairs, but it looked like they'd only gotten to part of the field. Eyes squinting in the sunlight, she lifted a hand to shield them. Then she froze. Something was moving out there. It was small, dark. Maybe an animal. She tightened her grip on her dagger all the same.

Very much on the alert, Alice made her way toward the purge site. As she drew nearer, she could tell that whatever was out there wasn't an animal. A cold sense of fear skated through her as what she was seeing started to register.

At the center of the damage, black liquid bubbled up out of the ground. Sunlight reflected off the inky surface as the stuff ran up and over, folding into itself but never soaking into the ground or flowing outward. Same as she'd seen in Ahoon. This shouldn't be here. When they got back from Wonderland, she'd purged the site before anything re-formed, Hatta had confirmed. So what the fuck?

It didn't matter, Alice decided. She dropped into a crouch,

lifted the weapon, and murmured, *"Moon Prism Power,"* under her breath, then drove the dagger down.

CRACK! It snapped in half, and Alice's hand slammed unprotected into the ground.

"Shit!" She clutched at her throbbing fingers as the pain from the impact gradually faded. A few inches away, the blade lay against the grass, broken off from the hilt. Chunks of silvered glass were scattered like confetti, catching the light of the sun. Alice sank onto her backside, her eyes ping-ponging back and forth between the bubbling Slithe and the now useless Figment Blade.

". . . Aww hell."

Thirteen

WRONG

Addison turned the hilt of the now broken Figment Blade over in his hands. "Well, this is unfortunate." Especially since he didn't have a readily available replacement.

Alice scoffed. "Among other things."

"I'll reach out to Tan soon as I can." He slipped the hilt into the small velvet bag where he'd placed the gathered fragments of the blade. His gaze played between it and a very anxious-looking Alice as she stood nearby, her arms folded over her chest, one lifted so she could chew at the end of her thumbnail. "What is it, luv?" he asked.

"This isn't 'sposed to happen," she murmured. "The whole point of this Dreamwalker thing was to keep Nightmares from popping up whenever they damn well please on this side of the Veil."

"Indeed." He released a breath. "To say the past twenty-four hours have been out of the ordinary, even for us, would be a bit of an understatement."

"What the hell is going on, Addison?"

"I'm afraid I'm not sure." He eyed the bubbling fountain of Slithe nearby. Revulsion slid through him, like something cold and wet pooling beneath his skin. He rolled his shoulders to shake it off and returned his attention to Alice. "All we have now are guesses and assumptions. I've put out a few calls to see if this rings any bells for anyone. I'm afraid I may be out of my element."

"That makes two of us." Irritation coated her words. He couldn't blame her.

His gaze wandered back to the bubbling pitch. Alice had explained that this was the same occurrence she and the Tweedles had investigated in Ahoon, only that one was smaller and had purged with no problem, while this one was giving Alice an oddly difficult time. He was going to have to reach out to Anastasia about this. "Curiouser."

"And curiouser, yeah yeah, what do we *do*?" There was a sharpness to Alice's tone that pulled at Addison's heart. She'd been through so much these past not even twenty-four hours, and he wanted nothing more than to draw her close and offer her any sort of comfort. But he knew that look in her eye, and while a hug might provide a small bit of respite, answers would help even more. Unfortunately, he had none. Still, he reached to take her hand.

She glanced up at him, surprise flickering through those brown eyes as her expression eased. Her lips pursed before she blew out a breath. He felt her hand shift in his, their fingers wove together, and he squeezed.

"Have you tried the other dagger?" he asked. "For the purge."

Alice shook her head. "Didn't want to risk it in case more nasties showed up."

"Well, we'll be prepared if they do. Go ahead and give it a shot," he offered.

Alice nodded, then used her grip on his hand to tug him toward her. When he was in range, she brushed her lips against his cheek. "Chester has it, be right back," she explained, already headed for the tunnel.

Warmth lingered where her lips had pressed. A similar feeling settled into his chest. Smirking to himself, Addison looked back to the bubbling black. That fast, he felt the smile vanish under a frown.

While he'd known Figment Blades to break during battles, he'd never seen one shatter during a purge. Well, *he* hadn't. And this didn't seem like what Anastasia had described all those years ago, but there was only one way to be sure.

Pulling his phone free, he took several photos from various angles, as well as a brief video, then attached them to a text.

> Take a look at this. It's in the field where we battled Humphrey.
> Alice's blade broke when she attempted a purge. What do you make of it?

He sent the message and settled in to wait for a response. Alice returned first, carrying the dagger and walking with a faint limp. His frown deepened.

"Are you sure you don't want Madeline to take a look at you?" He gestured to her gait.

She shook her head. "Think I pulled a muscle or something. It's already better than it was."

He nodded, though he played his gaze over her carefully. "How's Courtney?" Poor girl had looked like she'd seen the angry end of a trash compactor. Lucky for her, Madeline came prepared.

"She's complaining about her car, so much better." The smile that pulled at Alice's face sent Addison's heart fluttering. "Maddi says she'll make a full recovery in a few days."

"Madeline is gifted. We're fortunate she puts up with us."

Alice moved forward, her dagger in hand. She knelt near the sludge, her fingers tapping at the hilt. She hesitated, no doubt thinking about the failed previous attempt. But then she seemed to shake it off, lifted the dagger, and brought it down.

The tip of the blade sank into the ground an inch or two, but it didn't go further than that.

"Sonuva . . ." Alice leaned forward to put her weight onto the pommel.

For a moment, it appeared as if nothing was happening. Then the dagger started to sink slowly into the ground. As it did, the bubbling Slithe slowly descended into the dirt, until all that remained was the black taint that surrounded the immediate area. Alice sat back, staring at the space.

"Is . . . is it supposed to do that?"

"I—" Addison blinked rapidly and shook his head. "I'm not sure, luv. This is—" He broke off when the ground around the dagger began to darken even more. Alice withdrew with a gasp, scrambling to stand. The shadow crawled outward beneath their feet, spreading like water through cloth.

Addison spun, eyes dancing over their immediate surroundings. What in the world?

"Fuck it," Alice said.

He turned in time to see her grip the dagger and pull. She struggled at first before digging in her heels and using both hands. Finally, it came free, throwing her back in the process. She landed on her backside with an *oomph*.

It was like someone flipped a switch. The gradually widening stain withdrew in a blink, and vanished entirely when the dagger came free.

For a moment, the two of them stared, neither saying a word. Then, tentatively, Addison stepped forward and kicked at the area where the Slithe had bubbled. Nothing but grass and dirt came away with the toe of his boot.

"That do it?" Alice asked as she inspected the weapon.

"Looks to have. But we'll want to keep a close eye on the area, just in case. How's the dagger?" Addison extended his hand.

She took it, and he pulled her gently to her feet. "Still in one piece. Mostly." She held the weapon out for him to get a look.

The blade remained intact, though there were what looked like small strikes of lightning throughout. It likely wouldn't last another fight.

Alice ran her fingers over the silvery surface. She narrowed her eyes, bringing it closer to her face.

"Something wrong?" he asked.

"Thought I saw a . . . hole? Just a trick of the light, or the fractures."

"Light is just as playful as shadow," he said with a faint smile. "We should get back to the others."

As they departed, he chanced one final glance over his shoulder.

First Wraiths, then Fiends rising from a purge site, then a purge refusing to take at all. Something very wrong was happening here, and he feared it might consume the lot of them before he riddled it out.

Fourteen

PARTNERS . . .
ALSO SORT OF

Humphrey watched as Hatta and Alice emerged from the tunnel. They moved with a matching rhythm, attuned to each other in a way they themselves were likely unaware of. When her step faltered slightly as she favored her injured leg, he stepped in so she could catch her balance on his arm. He smiled at her. That smile . . .

Once upon a time, that smile had been reserved for Humphrey. He couldn't recall any specific memory, but some part of him knew this. An ugly feeling he didn't fully recognize, and honestly didn't want to give much thought or space, swelled inside him. He pushed it aside. It promptly resurfaced when, a handful of seconds later, Alice scowled at him. Even at this distance, he felt the heat of it. Just as he had the last time they were all here.

Memories of that night tried to surface. He looked away, not wanting to be taken by them, and instead focused on the group a short way off. Madeline tended to the injured Courtney. Chess sat on the ground nearby. Every so often, the boy would glance up, scanning their surroundings, same as Humphrey himself had been doing since arriving.

There was no sign of any Nightmares, but that could very quickly change.

At the sound of footsteps, Humphrey turned to find Hatta approaching.

Alice had split off to make her way over to her friends.

"All clear?" Humphrey asked, shifting to try and mask his discomfort with being back here.

"Yes . . . and no," Hatta murmured, looking back toward the tunnel. "That morning we faced you here, as the Black Knight, do you recall what method you used to summon that massive Nightmare?"

Humphrey blinked, somewhat taken by surprise at the question. "I . . . used my sword to summon the darkness. Her Majesty wanted . . ."

Pain stabbed at the center of Humphrey's head, so sharp and so deep he felt the aftershock along the rest of his body. Everything went white with the hurt. His ears rang with it. His vision blanked. Eventually the bombardment along his senses lessened and he heard . . . he wasn't sure. The sound was muffled, hushed beneath the thunder of his heart. Then, gradually, he was able to make out a word.

"Humphrey. Humphrey!" Hatta was calling his name.

He fought to come out of the fog. Control returned to his limbs, and he shifted them. It was like trying to move through water.

"Humphrey! Look at me."

He blinked his eyes open. Blobs of color and light danced across his field of vision. They gradually solidified, and slowly the blurred edges of distinct forms began to take shape. That's when he realized he was on the ground, at least partially. Hatta had wedged himself beneath him so that Humphrey rested against his lap, with Hatta bent over him. Madeline knelt to the side, her fingers moving over him. When had she come over?

"What . . . what happened?" Humphrey rasped, his throat feeling like it was on fire.

"Chess! CHESS!" Alice's voice filtered in over his already fuzzy senses.

With some difficulty, he angled his head in the direction of her frantic cries.

Similar to how Hatta leaned in over him, Alice had hold of an unconscious Chester. A newly mended Courtney pressed in close as well.

"The light shines at midnight." Madeline waved fingers in Humphrey's face.

Annoyed, he shoved at her hand with a grunt.

"But for the forests, no way," she said, an edge of relief in her words.

Hatta released a breath. "Looks like it. Go check on Chester."

She nodded and scurried away.

Humphrey groaned as the pounding between his ears lessened but lingered. His senses swam with the pain. "What happened?"

"The two of you appear to have fainted. Simultaneously." Hatta snorted. "It'd be comical if it weren't so concerning."

"I'm sure," he muttered and shifted to sit up.

Hatta helped him, hands on his shoulders. "You were in the middle of telling me how you summoned that Nightmare. Then you both just dropped."

"Oh thank god," Courtney cried.

It seemed Chess was coming around as well.

"Do you know what laid you out like that?" Hatta asked.

Humphrey frowned. The throbbing in his head returned when his line of thought turned toward that previous battle once more.

"When I try to remember that night, I only get flashes. Pain. Then I guess I pass out?"

His thoughts were flooded with fractured memories; receiving orders to secure the Eye and the contingency that involved capturing her friend if things went astray. He couldn't quite recall what he had been told to do, and trying to dig around for answers sent another shard of agony ricocheting between his ears.

It bothered him that he couldn't remember his life before becoming the Black Knight, and now it seemed he was starting to forget even that. If this kept up, he was going to be no one. Nothing.

"Curiouser," Hatta said. "Those symptoms are similar to mine. But that's impossible."

"You keep saying that word."

"Mmm. Perhaps I should find a new one. My point is, you just described what it is to suffer from the Madness. At least in part. Which, as I said, should be impossible. But so should the existence of a second Black Knight, another Vorpal Blade, and most of what's happened the past couple of days." Hatta slowly shook his head, a frown etched into his features. "Something's afoot. Can you stand?" He offered a hand, and Humphrey took it.

A sense of vertigo joined the stubborn aching, but once the former knight was upright, it all faded to a dull scratching at the base of his skull. Symptoms of the Madness. He filed that away to dig into later.

To the side, Chess got to his feet as well, with Alice and Madeline's help. Courtney remained seated.

"I wonder if it's the same for him," Hatta said, eyeing the three of them.

Ping.

Hatta pulled his phone from his pocket and peered at it. Whatever he saw made him stiffen, and the color fled his face.

Something uncomfortably close to concern pulled at Humphrey. "What's wrong?" he asked.

"Nothing," Hatta murmured. "Yet." He put the device away and turned to head over to the others. Humphrey followed, though he hung back.

Alice was the first to notice their approach. Her eyes slid from Addison to Humphrey and narrowed. It was brief, but there. "Any idea what the hell just happened?" The question was posed to Hatta, but Humphrey got the distinct feeling it was meant for him as well. The accusation in her gaze certainly was.

"None," Hatta admitted. "Which seems to be a persistent theme, at present. That being said, we should get back to the pub, make sure everyone's wounds are treated."

Alice nodded her agreement. "I have a Figment Blade at home, a sword. I should grab it first, just in case, since we seem to be running low."

Madeline looked up from where she had knelt to look after Courtney again. "The road to travel is a tempest tossed. All tea."

Alice's gaze flickered back and forth between Madeline and Hatta. "Aaaaaaand that means?"

"She said there's only one vehicle," Hatta explained. "And even if we could fit everyone in it, we still have two destinations and only one mode of transport."

Alice's expression fell. "Crap."

Humphrey shut his eyes as he released a breath. He couldn't believe he was going to say this. In fact, everything in him screamed it was a bad idea, but . . . "I can take her," he offered.

Alice looked at him like he'd offered to behead her instead.

He found and held her gaze. "It will take a handful of stops. That's too far a distance to cross at once, but we pop in, you get your weapon, and we pop back to the pub. It leaves enough room for the others in Madeline's . . ."

"Truck," Maddi finished.

"Truck," Humphrey repeated.

Alice's nose crinkled. "By 'pop,' you mean that teleporting thing you do?"

"No, I mean like a balloon."

She rolled her eyes.

"Are you sure you're up for it?" Hatta asked.

"I'm fine. Fainting spell aside." He brushed off his shoulders. "Besides, with everyone else at the pub, there's no one to warn her if we sense any more Nightmares. This, as luck would unironically have it, is the safest option."

"Fair point," Hatta conceded.

"Ugh, fine," Alice grumped, then tromped over to join Humphrey. "Let's just get this over with."

"Trust me, princess, I'm just as thrilled as you are," he muttered.

"See you two back at the pub as soon as possible," Hatta said, his eyes playing over them. His gaze lingered on Humphrey, and there was a brief moment when he seemed on the verge of saying more.

Humphrey looked away, trying to ignore the slight tremble at his center. He was probably imagining things. A result of fainting. Clearing his throat, he offered a hand to Alice, who took it reluctantly. Then he drew her in, his other arm curling around her.

"Just like old times," he murmured. "Partner."

"I *will* murder you with your own shoes."

"Threaten me with a good time. Hold on tight."

With a breath, he felt the swell of the ether, tightened his hold on her, and allowed the pull to swallow them whole.

Fifteen

OKAY . . . MOSTLY

Alice gasped when the cold fled her body and solid ground pushed up beneath her feet. She shoved out of the arms wrapped around her and doubled over, panting. Her body trembled, her lungs rebelled, and she fought to stay upright.

"Nnnnnng . . ." she groaned.

"Just breathe," a voice cautioned, reminding her she wasn't alone.

She blinked open her eyes and nearly fell over in relief when she realized she was finally, finally, standing on her front porch.

"Hnnnnnnnever want to do that, again, dear Jesus," she sighed.

"I wouldn't go that far," the voice said, "but you're welcome."

Said relief melted away under irritation, and she straightened in order to glare at Humphrey where he stood nearby.

"It's just a joke, ki—Alice," he corrected when her glare sharpened.

"Ha. Ha." She drew in one deep breath, and then another, and another, willing the churning in her stomach to lessen. "There a reason you aimed for the porch and not my window this time?"

Humphrey arched an eyebrow. "Besides how creepy that was?" He shrugged. "Figured you'd want to go through the front door."

"Whatever. Look, just . . . wait here, and stay out of sight. I won't be lo—"

The click of the dead bolt drew Alice's attention. Panic sparked in her chest, and she spun, her eyes widening, as the door swung open, revealing the absolute last person she expected to see. "N-nana K?!"

"Hey, baby!" Nana K swept forward and pulled Alice into a hug. "Mmmmm-*mm!*" Nana squeezed hard, and it sent a feeling through Alice she couldn't quite explain. Her grandma's hugs were like actual magic. Though she was still slightly panicked.

"H-hey! What, uh . . ." Alice pulled back and threw a glance over her shoulder. She didn't know why she was surprised to find the porch empty. "What're you doing here?"

Humphrey must have vanished when they heard the door unlock.

"Just checking in on my girls, and making sure them people are building this house right." Nana K peered at Alice over the tops of her glasses, the front of her silver Afro casting a shadow across her face. "How 'bout you? You doing okay? You look like you been in a fight."

Why did old Black lady intuition have to be so on point? Alice shook her head quickly. "No fight. Just brunch with some friends. Went to a . . . park for a lil bit. Touched some grass, you know." She brushed a bit of dirt from her jeans.

Nana K sniffed a couple times. "You do smell like outside. Been behaving otherwise, then? No more sneaking out or nothing?"

"Nope!" Alice squeaked. "All reformed. On my best behavior."

"Mmhm." Nana K tilted her head back, but didn't adjust her

glasses. She was probably the only person on the planet who could peer *up* her nose at people. "Well, I brought some banana puddin' to help."

"Oh!" Alice clapped her hands together in genuine delight. "I'll be right in. Wanna . . . check the mailbox. Waiting on a package."

Nana K blinked at her flatly before chuckling and shaking her head. "I swear, people can't just go buy nothing anymore, gotta have everything delivered. All right, then, go get your doodad. I'll see you inside." She leaned in to kiss Alice's cheek before slipping back into the house.

Alice watched her go before heading down the steps to the mailbox. She doubted there would be anything in there; her mother was almost obsessive with the way she collected the mail.

Instead, when she reached the box and pulled it open, she glanced around. "Humphrey? Humphrey. Humph—"

"No need to shout." The voice came from her left. He stood not too far off, his hands in his pockets. "Close call."

"You have no idea. Getting in and out might be harder than I thought." Especially now that Nana K was here for a visit. She couldn't just run off so soon after getting home; it would be rude *and* raise questions. The last thing Alice needed was her grandmother asking questions, especially right after she just started telling her mother the truth.

Humphrey made a faint sound at the back of his throat. "Should I wait around?"

"Probably not smart. My mom is still pretty upset you trashed our house."

His shoulders hunched slightly as he glanced away. "Mmm. Sorry," he murmured.

"You already apologized."

He shrugged. "Can't hurt to do it more than once." His gaze found hers again. "What do you want me to do?"

Alice pinched at the bridge of her nose, trying to think. "Okay. Okay, I don't know. If I say I'm going to spend the night with Courtney, I can probably get away after dinner. Come back later tonight?"

"Can do." He saluted, then vanished from sight.

Alice pressed the heels of her hands to her eyes. Could this day get any worse? Closing the mailbox, she hurried back up the stairs.

Nana K's laughter spilled onto the porch when the door swung open. She was in the middle of recounting the grand adventure of her first time using "the Lyft"—and her subsequent hitting-on of the cute driver.

As Alice stepped further into the living room, Nana K paused in her storytelling to eye one of the construction zones. She shook her head and "mm-mm-mm"-ed on her way to the kitchen. "You not paying too much, is you, Missy?"

"No, Momma. The insurance is taking care of it anyway. After nine million calls and a threat to go down there," Mom muttered.

"Sometimes you need to pop up on people to get shit done," Nana K said, sounding like she'd done just that on more than one occasion.

"Momma!" Mom admonished, though any harshness was undercut by her laughter.

"*Well!*" Nana K smiled and winked, her eyes crinkling at the corners.

"What about you?" Mom asked. "You breaking out? Need somewhere to lay low after tormenting your neighbors?"

Nana K sniffed and shifted her shoulders as a I-don't-know-what-you-talkin'-'bout look crossed her face. "I just thought I'd come visit, like I said. Make sure y'all doing all right."

"Uh-huh. Is that what *that's* for?" Mom gestured at the pastel pink bag tucked on the other side of the love seat.

"I plan to be thorough," Nana K said without missing a beat. "And thoroughness takes time."

Alice's eyes widened. "You're spending the night?"

"I sure am. *And* I'm making breakfast, I don't wanna hear nothing about it."

Mom sipped at her mug of tea. "Oh, you won't."

"Good. Now then, are you gonna finally get rid of this carpet? White is just not smart, baby."

Alice nearly pouted. She loved when her grandmother stayed with them, had since she was a little girl. It was always an amazing time, full of love, laughter, and so much good food. The past few years, the sleepovers happened less often. Hell, the last one was nearly a year ago, shortly after Dad passed.

She couldn't miss this. Especially since there was no telling when the next one would happen. If it happened. They didn't talk about it much, but Nana K *was* getting worse. She hated thinking about this shit. Even now, her throat closed off and her face flushed. She blinked rapidly to fight the tears. Naw, she wasn't going to miss this.

"I'll be back," Alice said, heading for the stairs. She'd call Hatta, let him know what was happening. She could go to the pub in the morning.

Mom and Nana K were deep into a not-argument about the pros and cons of wood flooring versus carpeting in general, and didn't seem to notice her departure.

Upstairs, Alice tossed her pack onto the bed, set the fractured dagger gently on her dresser next to her Iron Bull bust, and bent to retrieve a duffel from beneath her bed. The sword she'd borrowed from the twins rested inside, the silvered-glass blade twinkling in the light. *Borrowed* might not be the right word. They'd insisted she keep it, so she'd have something at home, in case of emergencies. Good thing, too, since she was down one dagger, which wasn't looking too hot.

She stuffed some clothes in on top of the weapon, also just in case. Having a spare outfit on standby never hurt. Not long into packing, she was distracted by a knock.

Nana K filled the doorframe. "Hey, baby." She glanced from Alice to the bag and arched an eyebrow. "Hope I'm not interrupting. You going somewhere?"

Alice waved off the concern. Or maybe that was suspicion. "N-no! No. At least, not tonight. I'm staying over at Courtney's tomorrow." Wild how she was finally done lying to her mother only to have to start lying to her grandma. Freaking fantastic.

Nana K nodded, though her brow remained lifted. "Oooh, hope you have fun. Tell Courtney I said hi. Ain't seen her for a while."

"Promise I will."

As they spoke, Nana K's gaze roamed Alice's room. "Missy said you had some damage, too, but I didn't wanna come up here while you weren't home."

"Most of the damage is in Mom's room and the hallway," Alice said. "She used it as an excuse to get a new bathroom, heh."

"I saw that not-so-little addition. Told her I was gonna come over here more often and climb in that tub," Nana said with a smile. Then her brow furrowed just so. "Those hooligans didn't steal nothing of yours, did they?"

"Who?" Alice asked, before she remembered the lie about the house being broken into. "Oh! Oh, no. My stuff ain't worth nothing, so."

"Sure it is. Money isn't everything." Nana K's eyes trailed down to Alice's neck and widened in delight. "Oh, you're wearing the necklace!"

Alice's hand went to her throat and the chain hanging from it. The pendant her grandmother had given to her a few weeks ago dangled at the end, tucked beneath her shirt. "I hardly take it off." Only when she had to fight Nightmares. Well, when she knew she had to fight them ahead of time, not when they were jumping people.

Nana K smiled, her eyes glittering with appreciative tears. "Good. I mean to ask about that earlier, but you know I—I be forgetting things."

Alice fought to keep her smile from dipping. "Not the important ones."

With a knowing and slightly saddened look, Nana K kissed, then patted, Alice's cheek. "Anyway, I really came up to ask if you'd like chicken and dumplings for dinner."

Alice's stomach gave an eager gurgle. "I'm always good for chicken and dumplings."

"I thought you might be." With that, Nana K slipped out of the room, but paused in the hallway and lifted a finger. "Before I forget, your computer was making an awful lot of noise earlier. I thought a bomb was 'bout to go off in here or something."

Alice stole a glance at the laptop at the foot of her bed. "What did it sound like?"

"A whole bunch of beeping."

She had a pretty good idea what the cause was. "It's nothing to worry about," she assured her grandmother, who nearly turned to continue on her way but stopped short one more time.

"Last thing, then I'll leave you be." The slight smirk that crossed Nana K's face should've been a warning. "Was that the not-boyfriend from a while ago I saw out there by the mailbox?" she asked in a low, conspiratorial voice. "Cuz it looked like somebody new. You doublin' up?"

Alice's face felt like it might explode, both from the realization that her grandmother had seen Humphrey and the notion that she thought they were dating! "Nana!"

"You take after your nana more than you realize. I'm out!" She lifted both of her hands and slipped from the room, laughing as she went.

"What you up there cackling about?" Mom called from downstairs.

"Just messing with my baby."

Alice groaned, wishing she could close her door. But there wasn't one. *Thanks, Humphrey.*

Instead she crossed to her bed and reached to prop open her laptop. Just like she'd suspected, a veritable monsoon of notifications from the Discord she shared with Haruka and the twins poured across the screen. The initial goal was to discuss Dreamwalker business, but they talked about other stuff, too. When discussing "work," they made it sound like they were talking about a game, just in case anyone ever got hold of the chat logs. Haruka had suggested Dungeons & Dragons. Alice had to admit, it was kinda brilliant. But Haruka was a genius, so.

Catching up on the conversation, Alice was surprised to find the twins complaining that the Duchess was sending them to Ahoon, again. Her fingers flew over the keyboard.

Alice: Probably because of what we found today.

The twins greeted her in all caps, their excitement palpable through the screen. They'd heard about the attack and were glad she was okay. Haruka wanted to know what they were all talking about. What attack?

Alice proceeded to lay out everything that had happened, from the car accident to the Fiends to the Slithe in the football field and how it had broke one of her daggers clean in half.

Dee: Damn.
Haruka: That's strange.
Dem: Understatement.
Alice: Hope you guys find some answers. Be careful.
Dem: Always.
Dee: 👍

Alice skimmed her other messages, though she paused when a DM popped up.

Haruka: Are you okay? Really?

Her fingers hovered above the keyboard while she did her best to ignore the resurgence of butterflies in her stomach.

Alice: I'm good. It was a lot but everyone is in one piece.
Haruka: You wouldn't say that so I won't worry would you?
Alice: Not when I know it'd only worry you more.
Haruka: ♥ Just making sure.
Alice: I know. Thanks for having my back.
Haruka: Happy to have that and more.

Now Alice's butterflies had butterflies. Seriously, her insides were gonna tie themselves in knots. This wasn't fair, Haruka *knew* she was in an entire relationship. And Alice knew she kinda liked it when the other girl pressed her, anyway.

Alice: You're sweet. Are we still on for tomorrow night?
Haruka: Of course.

The plan was to watch a movie together, or maybe a few episodes of a show. They were going to pick between the new season of *Bridgerton* or this new anime about monster slayers in Chicago. The anime was probably the safer bet.

Alice: See you then.

She closed the laptop altogether. With everything going on, dealing with those feelings was the last thing she needed.

"Alice," Mom called, her voice carrying from the kitchen. "Come give us a hand with dinner."

"Coming!" Alice gladly headed for the door.

Sixteen

MISSING: PART TWO

Addison paced in his office as much as the small space would allow. Every third turn or so, he stole a glance at his phone lying at the center of the desk or at the locked cabinet in the corner where he kept the Vorpal Blade. It was taking entirely too long for Anastasia to get back to him. Ahoon wasn't that far—without incident. The twins should be there and back within a handful of hours, if that. Dammit, if everyone still had their mirrors, he'd be able to contact them directly, but the Eye had been re-formed, leaving them all cut off from one another when crossing the Veil.

"Perfect," he muttered.

"Hey."

Addison turned to find Humphrey standing in the doorway. "Were you able to get Alice home and back safely?"

"Home, yes. Back, not yet," Humphrey said. "She told me to return for her later. Looks to be something to do with her family."

"And the journey didn't tax you?" Addison asked, worried.

Humphrey snorted. "No, Mother. As I said before, I'm *fine*. How are the others?"

"Courtney has been seen to and is resting. Chester seemed to be relatively fine as well, all things considered." Hatta frowned as he realized he hadn't seen much of the young man since their arrival. "Not sure where he's disappeared to. Can't get into too much trouble here, though."

"You'd be surprised," Humphrey said, then waved it off when Addison shot him a quizzical look. The former Red Knight continued, "Now then, about that message you received at the field. You said you would explain."

"So I did." Addison shifted to tilt back against the front of the desk. He gestured for Humphrey to take a seat on the small couch if he wished. "I'm waiting on word from Anastasia. She's looking into something for me on the other side. A hunch concerning recent events. And, perhaps, past ones."

Humphrey eyed the couch, then shook his head in refusal. "And so, you're going to sit here staring at your phone until she checks in?"

"Indeed. I've stopped asking for updates. She informed me that if I inquired one more time in the next quarter hour, she was going to feed me my hands."

"Tasty."

"Through a straw."

"And imaginative—next item, you mentioned impossible symptoms concerning the Madness?"

Addison nodded, weighing his next words carefully. He didn't want to jump to conclusions, especially the wrong ones. But the evidence was piling up.

"Your symptoms," he began slowly, "and Chester's bear a remarkable resemblance to my own. Remarkable in the sense that no one else should be exhibiting them, since the only person able to inflict the condition on others has been in stasis for the better part of two centuries."

It didn't take long for Humphrey to catch on, his lips pursing. "I see."

"I figured you would. The same could have been said for the existence of the Black Knight and the Vorpal Blade, and yet." Addison gestured between the two of them.

"And yet here I stand," Humphrey sighed, massaging one temple. "A walking impossibility, possibly twice over."

"Rather impressive, regardless of the implications."

"Which are?" Humphrey asked, sounding exhausted.

Addison sympathized. "There's a larger picture here we're failing to see. By the time we realize what's going on—"

"If you say 'it may already be too late,' so help me, I will stuff your dramatic arse in one of those desk drawers."

The joke was unexpected, but Addison grinned all the same. That was more of the old Humphrey peeking through.

"Mmm. It's just my own thoughts giving me trouble now."

"Have you recalled anything more about the Wraiths?" Addison asked, careful to keep his tone even. "What their purpose is, why they've been created now?"

"No." Humphrey lowered his hands from where he'd been rubbing at both temples. "Mostly because I didn't ask questions, I just did as I was told." A shadowed look crossed his face. "At least I was an obedient dog, if nothing else."

Addison started to press the issue when—

WHAM!

Both Addison and Humphrey spun toward the hallway at the sound of a door slamming closed somewhere farther into the pub.

Or did it slam open? The commotion was quickly followed by the sound of feet shuffling hurriedly in their direction, accompanied by labored breaths and pained groans.

"Hold on, my friend!" someone urged in English, though the accent was airier, rolled toward the back of the tongue slightly.

Addison knew that voice. "What in the world?" he muttered just before Dem went stumbling past, held up by a tall man with dark brown skin, a silver beard, and no hair. That was Theo. What in all hells was the Southern Gatekeeper doing here?

Frowning, Addison shared a brief look with Humphrey before the two of them hurried after the sudden visitors.

Out in the bar, Theo paused to look around, carefully adjusting his hold on Dem. "I need help here!"

All questions died on Addison's tongue when he got a good look at the elder Tweedlanov.

The boy was covered in black goop, red smeared here and there. He clutched his side, his left leg nearly giving out. His face and arms were littered in bruises and cuts. Gashes dashed one side of his face and split his lips. The rattle in his breath was extra worrying.

"Madeline!" Addison bellowed as he moved to grab one of the folding chairs tilted against the wall. "Put him here," he said to Theo. Together, they got the young man down just as Maddi came scrambling into the room.

Her eyes widened, the colors shifting as she blinked rapidly. "Bubble-gum dreams!" she shouted, then hurried back down the hall to fetch her supplies.

Dem groaned, the sound ending in a hiss. "Got . . . got to go back!" he said in strained Russian.

"Stay still," Addison ordered. He wasn't a talented healer like

Madeline, but he knew enough first aid to start checking vitals. "Is anything broken? Any puncture wounds? What's the worst of it?"

"Stabbed in his side," Theo said as he stepped out of the way.

"Dee," Dem wheezed before coughing. He pushed at Addison's searching hands.

"Hold still," Addison chided as he helped maneuver the Dreamwalker in order to search out the wound.

While he worked, his attention shifted to Theo, whose dark brown face was pinched with concern. "What happened?" Addison asked. "And what are you doing this far north?" He withdrew his hands as Madeline returned, sliding in beside him to take over.

"Patrol," Theo said, watching closely as Madeline shushed a distraught Dem, who stammered repeatedly, almost drunkenly, that he "needed to go back."

Dem struggled to try and rise, but was so weak with blood loss and perhaps pure exertion Madeline was able to hold him in place on her own.

Theo continued, "With the increased activity lately, I figured it was all hands on deck."

While Addison was the only Gatekeeper who had been physically bound to his post, the other three rarely left their stations unless absolutely necessary. And Theo least of all. It had been more than a decade in the human world since Hatta saw him last.

"There was . . . an ambush in Ahoon. I think," Theo explained. "We found him like this."

We? That's when it struck Hatta that Theo was here without his Dreamwalker. "Where's Mpho?"

Theo finally met Addison's gaze. "Gone after this one's brother. The Nightmares carried him off."

Seventeen

NIGHTMARES

Alice hadn't meant to fall asleep after dinner, but eating three bowls of Nana K's chicken and dumplings was like injecting the itis straight into your veins.

Just a cat nap, she'd told herself while making sure everything was packed and ready, yawning the entire time. Twenty minutes and she'd be good.

She should have known better.

The next time she opened her eyes, it was dark outside. It was dark everywhere, actually; she couldn't see a damn thing despite the moonlight pouring through her window. *Shit.* This wasn't supposed to happen. She needed to get up, get moving, her friends were waiti—

Alice froze. Her body went tight, her senses suddenly on alert. Something was wrong. She didn't know *how* she knew, only that she did.

"Trust your instincts," Hatta had told her, more than once. "They'll save your life."

Right now those instincts were telling her to run, get away. Now, go *now*! She blinked rapidly as fear threw off the remaining weight of sleep. The shadows of her room came into sharp focus, and with them a clarity that revealed the horror poised at the foot of her bed.

Three amber eyes blinked at her in the dark, staring from the center of an inky head. Lips peeled back from fangs that glowed a sickly yellow. The Fiend growled, the stink of death and ruin hot on its breath.

Alice felt a tremble of terror in her gut. The sword. It was her only hope, tucked in the bag on the floor. Could she reach it before the Nightmare tore her throat out? *I'm gonna die. Fuck. I'm gonna **die**.*

The monster lunged.

She threw herself over the side of the bed.

The Nightmare should have landed on top of her and torn her to pieces. Instead, it bounced off the air like a rag doll flung against the wall.

No. Not the air. There was a barrier encircling Alice, glowing a faint red. A sort of transparent bubble. *It* had deflected the Nightmare's attack. Had saved her. Just like the one that kept her from falling to her death when she fell out of Chou's basket. But she didn't have the Vorpal Blade, so how?

The answer tapped lightly against the underside of her chin. Floating, though still anchored by the chain around her neck, was Nana K's necklace. It pulsed faintly, glowing the same crimson as the energy that made up the barrier.

"What?" Alice breathed, bewildered, before recoiling with a shout as the Fiend came at her a second time. It rebounded off of the shield again, spilling across the carpet in a flail of limbs and claws, snarling the entire way.

Alice scrambled to get free of her blankets. She dropped to her knees beside the bed, snatching at the zipper on the duffel bag.

The Fiend paced a short distance away, its jowls vibrating as it growled. "You cannot hold us off forever."

Long enough to take your head, Alice thought, her frightened shock now replaced with furious determination. These fucking things were in her house again!

Back on her feet and armed, Alice hefted the sword in both hands. Her palms warmed. She felt pressure begin to build in her skin, the anticipation of the fight to come.

Then it all evaporated when she saw her dresser, more notably the single dagger resting on the surface.

The Figment Blade was coated in Slithe. It poured from the weapon, oozing down the front of the drawers, pooling on the ground in a shifting, writhing mass. A trail of yuck snaked from the puddle to the foot of her bed and up along her blankets.

That's where it came from, she realized with a start, just as another pair of double-jointed limbs burst free of the black. A second Fiend scrabbled to be born, right there on her floor.

Alice stood transfixed until her shock was broken by the sound of Mom's bedroom door banging open.

"What in the hell?" Mom's voice filled the hall.

The Fiend that had been pacing at the edge of her bubble snapped toward the sound. Alice's stomach sank to her feet.

"No!" She swung as it leaped to get past her. The sword caught it across the side, flinging it into the wall. A few pictures and books on floating shelves toppled free.

Alice threw herself out the door, pivoting just in time to avoid being tackled as the Fiend flung itself after her. It slammed into the newly replaced railing. Wood splintered and snapped as both monster and banister tumbled into the dark.

"My rail!" Mom stood outside her bedroom door, her eyes wide, her bonnet lopsided, and a baseball bat clutched in her hands. Her gaze trailed over the bits of broken timber scattered at her feet. "What in Jesus's name?" she breathed, inching toward the edge to try and get a look at whatever just bulldozed through part of her house.

Alice latched onto her mother's wrist and hauled her away from the railing. As she did, the shield flowed down her arm to envelop her mother, enclosing the both of them.

"Go in your room, lock your door!" Alice ordered.

Mom, who was staring at the mess all Pikachu face, looked at Alice like she'd starting speaking Klingon. Then Mom screamed and brandished the bat with one hand, the other tangled in Alice's shirt, trying to pull her close.

The second, now fully formed Fiend ricocheted off the shield and flew back down the hall, nearly down the stairs. Its claws scrabbled at the floor as it tried to right itself.

Alice breathed a brief sigh of relief. "I'm fine," she cautioned. "But you gotta go in your room while I handle this!"

A low thump pulled Alice's attention to the hall again. She readied her weapon for another attack. Instead, the door to the guest bedroom swung open.

"What's all that racket?" Nana K stepped out into the hall.

And right into the path of a charging beast.

Eighteen
. . . WHAT?!

Three things happened at once. A Nightmare leaped for Nana K. Alice's heart leaped into her throat. Then she leaped forward to try and get between the monster and her grandma.

Alice's trapped heart thrashed.

She wasn't going to make it.

Panic hammered a tattoo against the inside of her skull. She wasn't. going. to make it.

Everything slowed. It felt like moving through a world made of pudding: her limbs heavy, her mind shrieking that she needed to go faster but her body simply could not.

The Fiend opened its mouth, teeth slathered in yellowed drool, sharp and hungry for the kill.

No! Alice tried to scream, but the word caught in her throat.

Nana K turned. The Nightmare pounced.

Claws the size of fingers went for her throat.

Suddenly, everything exploded in a rush of energy and soft red light. Alice felt herself lifted off her feet and hurled bodily through the air. She didn't go far, only a yard or so before landing and rolling across the floor. Behind her, Mom shouted her name, asked what was going on.

Alice had no idea. She couldn't see anything, could only hear the sound of her mother's voice and her own flailing heart.

The panic threatened to spike into full-blown hysteria. A monster had attacked her grandmother, would tear her to shreds. There was nothing more Alice could do. She wanted to cry. Drop to her knees and weep. But something wouldn't let her. She blinked against the haze, trying to see, her hand lifting to shield her eyes.

Her hand. The bubble, the force field or whatever, blazed red hot along her skin. But she didn't burn. She didn't feel anything except an odd tingling like her body was falling asleep, and a familiar warmth gathering in her palms.

Alice knew this power. It had filled her during battle on more than one occasion, filled her weapons as well, come to her rescue twice now, but always from within.

She was not the source of this. What the hell was happening?

The crackle of electricity singed the air and left it smelling like rain. The crimson energy surrounding them began to withdraw. It folded in on itself, a curtain drawn open before swirling into a single point like water flowing down a drain. But instead of vanishing into some invisible pipe, the energy condensed into an orb about the size of a basketball.

Alice blinked the world into better focus. She heard the Fiends before she saw them and tensed in preparation for a fight, but the monsters merely paced where they stood at the top of the stairs, hackles raised, spitting curses. They didn't draw nearer. They couldn't. Energy from the orb held them back. The orb now hovering above Nana K's open palm.

Small pulses of red and gold licked along the orb's surface like arcs of radiation dancing across the sun. They poured over Nana K like rivers, dipping in and around the folds of her nightgown. Her silver afro glowed like a wreath of holy fire.

"Traitor!" one Fiend shrieked and scrambled when a crimson tendril lashed near its feet.

"You will die!" the other snarled.

Despite their threats, they didn't move. Sure, they stalked side to side, clawing at the floor, their talons digging grooves in the wood, but they pretty much stayed put.

Nana K looked completely unbothered. She regarded the Fiends coolly but not uncaring. It was a look Alice had seen plenty of times when she got caught doing something she knew full well she shouldn't be doing.

"Begone." Nana K's voice echoed, the dual tones harmonizing with each other. It was . . . beautiful. She flexed her fingers, then splayed them wide. The orb pulsed before bolts of red light shot forth. They hammered the Fiends, who turned to run. One tried to dart into Alice's room, but the light tore into it, leaving a heap of charred monster against the floor. The other went for the stairs, clearing the banister in a single jump, but the bolts tore into it in midair. The body hit the carpet below, melting away.

For a brief moment there was complete stillness, save for the faint rippling of Nana K's gown. Then she closed her hand and the orb was snuffed out, plummeting the hall and the rest of the house into darkness. Curtained moonlight poured in through the windows.

No one moved. No one spoke.

Finally, Nana K turned to look at Alice. Her expression softened, the lines in her face deepened by the night shadows. She looked simultaneously older yet something else entirely. Something eternal.

She held Alice's gaze a moment, then released a breath. Her body sagged with a sudden heaviness, and she braced herself against the nearby doorjamb.

Click.

The cold, lifeless glow of energy-efficient bulbs filled the landing. Everything was suddenly washed out, as if some sort of filter had been placed over the world to block out the fantastical. Gone was the fiery goddess who had vanquished two monsters with a gesture and in her place stood a woman who looked exhausted, far more so than Alice could ever remember her grandmother being.

That's right, Alice's stunned brain finally rebooted. This was her grandmother. Somehow. What the hell just happened?

"Momma?" Mom squeaked where she stood nearby, eyes big as pot lids, one trembling finger still pressed to the switch.

"My, my." Nana K fanned at her face with one thin hand. "Ain't had to pull that one out in a while. Sorry for the mess, Missy."

Alice continued to gape.

Pop! The telltale crack and fizzle of dissolving Nightmares made Alice jump. Mom's gaze roamed over the dissolving bodies. The one in Alice's bedroom doorway was nearly gone, and the stink seemed to hit everyone at the same time, judging by the way they all slapped their hands over their noses.

"What in—" Mom started, disgust coating her words. She gagged. "Oh Jesus. *Jesus!*"

"Whew. Forgot about the smell," Nana K complained.

"Forgot about . . ." Alice sank back against the wall, her attention returning to her grandmother. Her superpowered grandmother.

"Demons in my house," Mom kept going, then retched again. "*Huech.* That's it, I can't. Nope. No more. Fuck it. We're moving."

While Mom ranted about refusing to live above a hellmouth,

Alice fought to get her feet beneath her. Her legs shook but held, and she slowly crossed the space to join her grandma. Nana K looked both smaller than usual and larger than life at the same time. She offered Alice a tired smile.

"You okay, baby?" Nana K asked.

Alice nodded mutely, her brain having thrown out the meaning to every single word she'd ever known. What even were words?

"Good." Nana K lifted a hand to brush Alice's cheek. "I know you got questions, but you gotta make sure those things are gone for good. Then we'll talk."

Alice blinked, still very confused, before realization snapped her spine straight. She hurried past her grandma, stumbling to a halt just outside her bedroom door. Another Fiend was already trying to take shape amid the muck on the floor, snout bobbing up and out of the surface, claws grasping at the carpet.

"What the fuck is happening," she breathed. Her grip tightened on her sword. In truth, she was surprised she'd managed to hold on to it during all that. But now she wasn't sure what to do. Did she wait until the Fiend was fully formed to strike, or did she try and purge it as is?

As if sensing its impending doom, the Nightmare writhed and snapped, scrabbling at the edge of the pool of pitch.

"*Use it,*" something inside her whispered. And, to be honest? She wished it would shut up. She'd just fought off her second Nightmare attack today, in her house! Her mother could have been hurt, or worse, and her nana . . .

"*Use it.*"

She jerked in surprise when the sword grew hot in her hand, the hilt burning against her palm.

"Fine! I'll use the damn sword." She took a step toward the Nightmare.

"*Not the weapon.*"

Before Alice could even think to ask anything more, the warmth in her hand flowed up her arm and settled into her chest. It grew hot enough to hurt, then sharp enough to sting. Why did—

She clutched at her chest with her free hand, but instead of gripping her shirt her fingers curled around something small and hard beneath the fabric as well. Nana K's necklace. It glowed the same red, now streaked with gold radiance.

"*Use it.*"

A sudden pressure at her back made Alice turn to find her grandmother at her side.

Looking even more tired than before, Nana K smiled as one hand rubbed Alice's back while the other reached to take the sword from her.

"The dagger," Nana K said before Alice could protest. "If you don't stopper the flow, more will come."

The Figment Blade lay on the dresser spilling Slithe across the carpet. The newly formed Fiend at the center of the puddle had nearly pulled itself entirely free. And she'd just been standing here, this whole time! She started to ask what her grandmother meant by stopper the flow—and more importantly how Nana K knew any of this, was *doing* any of this—but instead of speaking, Alice acted. Or, rather, her body did.

Her hand reached out and closed around the dagger's hilt. Like with the sword, heat filled her palm, then pushed into the weapon, but instead of glowing white, the blade burned red. That crimson light spreading over the surface, sinking into it, enveloping the inky stain.

The dagger started to tremble in her fingers. Then it jerked and jumped, twisting as if to escape. She tightened her grip. It pulled in immediate protest, wrenching back and forth, desperate to get away.

Alice yelped in surprise and pain when a particularly hard lurch nearly took her off her feet. She latched on with the other hand and tried to anchor herself. This thing was going to pull her arm clean off!

"Hold on!" Nana K urged as she pressed to Alice's side once more. Her thin fingers curled around Alice's aching wrist.

The red glow intensified. A sound like nails dragging against glass filled the air. Alice's jaw clenched, her teeth set on edge. The dagger vibrated hard enough the bones in her hands rattled. The heat in her palm flared. *It hurt!*

Then, with a burst of red lightning that singed the air, the shadows vanished, vanquished. The dagger stilled. The Slithe was gone, the blade made whole again.

"Now!" Nana K called. "The purge!"

Without thinking, Alice lifted the newly purified dagger, then thrust it into the emerging Fiend's skull. The blade pierced inky flesh and drove into what she assumed was bone with a *crack*! The monster keened, jerked, then drooped. A familiar webwork of light crawled along its body as the purge took hold almost immediately. Instead of melting away beneath a pale glow, the Nightmare was consumed by the same red light that was now slowly fading from Alice's body.

The dead Fiend popped and hissed, buckling inward. The pool of Slithe began to shrink as well. Soon there was nothing left of the mess but the Figment Blade itself, sheathed in the carpet like the sword stuck in the stone.

Alice tightened her grip and pulled. The dagger came free easily, leaving the telltale scorch mark of a successful purge.

Then she stood there, staring. Silent. Weapon in hand. The dagger glowed faintly, a soft haze of red along the now perfect blade.

What . . . the fuck . . . just happened . . .

The trembling started somewhere in Alice's middle. It rippled outward, pouring through the rest of her. Her vision blurred. Her chest rose and fell with quickening breaths: there wasn't enough air in the room. She couldn't breathe, she—

Hands squeezed her shoulders. The returning panic had nearly overtaken her, but a sudden calm suffused her body.

"Breathe, baby," Nana K whispered. Her voice was a balm against Alice's frantic thoughts.

Alice inhaled slowly, automatically, then released it.

"That's my girl," Nana K coaxed, mirroring the slow inhale-exhale. "One mo'gain."

In, then out.

It took a few more deep breaths before the buzzing between Alice's ears faded completely.

Nana K murmured encouragements. "You done good, baby. So very, very good."

With her emotions mostly reined in, Alice turned to take in her grandmother, who smiled with both fatigue and pride shining in her eyes.

Something thumped behind Alice, and she turned to find her mother on her knees in the doorway, eyes wide, hands pressed over her mouth. She looked as frazzled as Alice felt.

"Well," Nana K breathed as she squeezed Alice one last time before stepping to the side and lowering herself onto the bed. "I suppose I got some explaining to do."

Mom made a choking sound that was part scoff part shout. "You think?!"

Nineteen
ALMOST

Humphrey withdrew to the far side of the room as everyone crowded around the injured Tweedlanov boy. Maddi worked over his injuries while Hatta coaxed the story of what happened out of him and this newcomer. Theo was the name he'd picked up on.

Chess and Courtney had emerged during the chaos and now occupied chairs to the side, watching, listening, both looking partially lost even as they appeared to be following the conversation well enough.

"At first, there was nothing," Dem said. "The ruins were empty. Regular day, all quiet. Then there was darkness everywhere." He flinched when Maddi started to lift his shirt.

"Nothing but doing," she chided.

"Madeline says she needs to get at your chest," Hatta explained.

Dem waved off Maddi's reaching hands, his head bowed slightly. "Don't worry about it. It's not as bad as it looks." He offered a faint smile.

Maddi frowned but turned her attention to his other injuries.

Hatta tilted his head just so, his hands clasped behind his back as he paced. "You were saying?"

"The Slithe." Dem swallowed. "It poured out of every door, every window. Nightmares started forming, far too many to fight. But we fought anyway."

Movement to Humphrey's left drew his attention. Theo settled into a nearby chair, offering a hand to Chess with a quiet introduction. Chess hesitated but then took it, clearly uncomfortable.

Then came Courtney's turn to shake, though she looked less bothered.

As he watched this seemingly innocent exchange, unease slithered down Humphrey's spine. Something was . . . wrong here. What that something was, he didn't know, but the sense of things being off rang in his mind like a warning bell. He tried to ignore it, looking back to the conversation as Dem dropped his face into his hands.

"I couldn't save him," Dem lamented. He shifted away from Maddi when she attempted to get his shirt up again, asking her quietly to please give him a moment.

She sighed, then yawned wide as she set her things aside. "Busy busy bumblebee." She moved to wash the gunk and blood from her hands in the sink behind where the bar once stood.

"She said don't go anywhere before she has a chance to look you over fully." Hatta paused and glanced toward Theo. "And how did you get mixed up in all this?"

"Anastasia told us she was sending the twins to the ruins and asked for assistance." Theo stroked his fingers along his salt-and-pepper beard.

A considering look crossed Hatta's face. His attention flickered back and forth between Theo and Dem every handful of seconds. "How did you get to Ahoon so quickly?"

Theo blinked as if not fully comprehending the question. "I'm sorry?"

Hatta shrugged, the picture of nonchalant curiosity. "It's just that Ahoon is nearly twice as far from your Gateway as it is Anastasia's. Even if she somehow managed to get you a message, it should have taken you twice as long to reach it."

There was a pause as nearly every pair of eyes swiveled simultaneously toward Theo.

"We made it a priority," Theo explained. "She said it was important, so we moved as fast as we could, even through the night."

Hatta nodded thoughtfully. "And it's fortunate you did, except . . . you weren't at your Gateway. It's Sunday. You and Theo are on patrol near Findest. Meaning it would take you at least two weeks to answer any distress calls for Ahoon; it'd be quicker to call me—so I ask again, how did you get there so quickly?"

Hatta had moved as he spoke. A seemingly leisurely stroll back and forth across the room. A ruse, one Humphrey saw through easily. Addison kept his elbows at his sides, no matter what he did with his hands. His steps landed him just outside of arm's reach from Dem but close enough to strike if necessary.

For some reason, Hatta was ready for a fight.

Humphrey straightened from where he'd tilted against the wall. His gaze bounced between Hatta and Theo as the two sized each other up.

"It sounds as if you doubt what I say," Theo said, smiling tightly. This was not an expression shared between old friends. "You know better than anyone how time passes differently between the realms. You can ask the boy if my word isn't good enough."

Hatta waved off the suggestion. "That won't be necessary."

"Good." Theo nodded. "Because we need to go after Mpho and the twin as quickly as possible. They will need our help."

"Of course," Hatta said, bowing his head. Then he lifted a finger. "One thing first." He pointed that finger at the Tweedlanov boy. "Demarcus?"

Dem blinked, looked to Theo, and then back to Hatta before nodding slowly. "Da?"

"Ahhh, see. Dem has a scar." Hatta tapped that same finger against his left cheek. "Right here."

Dem's hand went to his unmarred face. His eyes widened, then shot to Theo, who continued to smile. Then he started to laugh. Softly at first, the sound building as his shoulders shook with it.

"Ahh, well," said Theo, softly, almost apologetically. "About that." Then he lashed out, now inky arm and fingers stretching out lightning fast to catch a surprised Chess by the throat. "Kill the traitors," he growled, his voice gravelly and . . . inhuman.

The table with the medical supplies went flying as Dem—now half transformed into a Wraith—flew at Humphrey. Before he could react, Hatta stepped between them and, in one fluid motion, latched onto the creature, used its momentum to bring it around, then slammed it into the ground. His knee in the monster's back, he twisted a long arm, earning a sharp snap.

"Help Chess!" Hatta shouted over the Nightmare's pained yowl.

Across the room, "Theo" had curled blackened arms around the wriggling Chester, talons at his throat.

Humphrey let go of his hold on this realm and fell into the rush of the ether. He came out of it behind "Theo" and drove his foot into the side of the man's knee.

Crunch.

"Theo" loosed a keening howl. His head whipped around a full 180 degrees, and he bared jagged teeth in a snarl.

"Strewth," Humphrey hissed as he snatched at the nearest sturdy object—turned out to be one of the folding chairs—and slammed it into the beast. It lost its hold on Chester, who dropped to his hands and knees, coughing as he struggled to take in air.

"Theo" was already starting to recover. That is, until the business end of a pair of suture scissors was jammed into the side of his head.

Maddi scrambled back as "Theo" howled, her eyes wide and frightened, but also determined.

Impressed, Humphrey hauled Chester to his feet and shoved him toward the mousy bartender. "Get the girls to the back!" He didn't wait to see if his orders were followed, turning his attention to "Theo."

The Nightmare clawed at where the stainless steel protruded from its skull, unable to wrench it loose. Humphrey spun and drove the heel of his boot into the scissors's handle. With a sickening crunch of penetrated bone and flesh, the creature flopped over and fell still. Pitch oozed from the wounds on its head, pouring over its face.

Behind Humphrey there was a similar *snap*. He turned to find Hatta standing over the now mostly transformed "Dem," clutching a broken bit of construction lumber. The other end was lodged deep in the monster's chest. The creature lay sprawled on its back. A puddle of black seeped out from beneath it.

Panting, Hatta lifted his gaze to Humphrey, a silent question dancing in his eyes.

Humphrey nodded. He was fine. Relatively.

Hatta straightened and touched gingerly at a couple of cuts on the side of his neck as they bled freely. He stepped over his kill, eyeing "Theo." "Someone finished Madeline's work."

It took Humphrey a second to realize he was being spoken to, having been caught up in staring at the slowly melting face. That it had been recognizable at all made his skin crawl. "So it seems." He stepped to the side to avoid the growing puddle of pitch.

Hatta pinched the bridge of his nose, his expression stormy. "What happened to 'not possible without her'?"

Well, that was insulting. Humphrey leveled a look at the other former knight. "Oh, I'm sorry, shall we go back to the beginning where I said all of this was purely guesswork? Would you like to see my detailed notes on the matter?"

There was a pause, then a brief snort of laughter as Hatta shook his head. "You're right. You're right, and I'm sorry." For a moment it appeared as if he wanted to say more, but then thought better of it. "We'll look into this. Perhaps Madeline might be able to provide further insight given recent developments. For now, we need a purge, meaning you need to go and get Alice."

Humphrey agreed and moved to follow Hatta down the back hallway, already mapping out the path he would take to reach Alice's abode as quickly as possible. But as he stepped over the bodies, he paused, distracted. Something was off.

Kneeling, Humphrey studied the fallen creatures for a moment. Inky skin hung off bone like partially melted ice cream, the features identifiable as somewhat humanoid but no longer the faces that had been stolen. For all appearances, they were regular Nightmares. Except, Nightmares would have begun collapsing in on themselves by now. These remained slumped where they had died.

"We may need more than a purge," Humphrey muttered before finally stepping away.

Voices pitched high with quiet panic reached him before he reached the door to Hatta's office. This is where Chester had taken

Maddi and Courtney. The latter sat on the couch and curled over her knees while doing what appeared to be some sort of breathing exercises. Madeline paced on the other side of the desk, babbling at breakneck speed, gesturing to Hatta every other turn.

Hatta was trying to listen to her while speaking quick Russian into his phone. The words "Whitechapel" and "Ripper" stuck out.

With the already small office decidedly cramped, the former red knight elected to remain in the hall. This way he could keep an eye on the still-very-much-intact bodies.

"Do they have therapists in Wonderland?" Courtney asked, her voice slightly shaky. "Because I officially have no idea how to explain this to a human doctor."

Chester grinned a bit. "Fresh out of metaphors for watching your friends definitely but not really kill each other?"

Humphrey lowered his gaze. The remark was funny enough, but elicited something closer to guilt than amusement on his part. That's when he noticed the stains.

Three blotches of what looked like tar. Then a few more to the side, and even more. A clear trail led farther down the hall and around the corner. Humphrey followed.

The trail continued with the blotches reverting into what looked like footprints. They continued past the janitor's closet that housed the opening to the Western Gateway on to another closed door. There was only a moment's hesitation before he twisted the knob. Unlocked. He stepped inside.

It was a simple room, medium sized, filled with shelves that were stacked with items of various sizes and structures. He noticed a few things from Wonderland, baskets and tools, supplies and the like. What drew his attention when he flipped on the light was a small velvet pouch off to the side. He recognized it as the one filled with fragments of Alice's shattered dagger from earlier that day. He also recognized the thick black substance slowly oozing out of the bag like a faucet.

A pool of Slithe had formed, slowly spreading across the floor. It bubbled and roiled, seeming to realize it had been discovered. Hands erupted from the black, coated in pitch, scrambling for the edge of the pool.

Humphrey was out the door and down the hall in an instant, running as fast as he could while his mind tried to catch up with what he'd seen. In the few seconds it took to reach Hatta's office, he still had no clue.

"Slithe!" he shouted.

Four heads whipped around to stare.

"In the storage room!" he panted, frantic. "Coming from the dagger!"

For a split second, no one moved, confusion thick in the air. Then realization flickered in Addison's widening eyes just as Maddi loosed a scream, her finger aimed at Humphrey's feet.

Black ooze pooled across the floor. He made to step away, but a pair of those inky hands burst from the surface, grabbed his ankles, and pulled.

The world dropped out from under him, and Humphrey felt himself plummet.

Hatta shouted his name.

Fingers brushed his.

Then he was consumed by the frigid dark.

Twenty

LOST

Alice stared at her grandmother as her entire body buzzed. "How did you do that?" she asked. "How do you know about the dagger, the purge? Do you know about Wonderland?"

"One thing at a time," Nana K said with a small, tired smile. She was seated on Alice's bed, with Alice on one side and Mom, looking more than a little anxious, on the other.

After the initial shock had worn off, it was clear everyone was either uneasy about or exhausted by the entire ordeal. Probably both. Especially Alice's grandmother.

Nana K's hands trembled. She stumbled over words or repeated herself. She even dozed off a couple of times midsentence, just shut her eyes and started snoring until Alice or Mom called her name.

Alice did her best to swallow her impatience, and the accompanying irritation. She wanted, *needed* answers. So far, the only thing she got was apologies for messing up her room, which wasn't Nana K's fault.

"You don't have to worry about any of that," Mom had encouraged her every time. "Just . . . tell us what's going on, okay?" She was also eager for an explanation, and just as perturbed as Alice.

"One thing at a time," Nana K repeated, her voice somewhat breathy. She shook her head at nothing, humming softly as she started to sway side to side, just a little. "Sorry about the mess, Missy."

Mom sighed and patted Nana K's knee gently. "It's all right. I promise."

Nana K smiled. It was a bit strained. "My girls. Always looking after me. I'm just so sorry." A heaviness settled over as she spoke this time. Her shoulders sagged with it. It seemed to pull her very spirit down. "I'm okay. I'm okay. I'm okay," she repeated over and over and over.

Mom wrapped her arms around Nana K's shoulders. "Y-yeah. You're okay, Momma. But you shouldn't be tiring yourself out like this. You know that's . . . not good for you."

Alice's throat burned. It was clear Nana K was teetering on the edge of an episode. There was never a *good* time for those, but this was one of the worst for a number of reasons.

Alice *hated* this fucking disease. For what it stole from her grandmother. From them all.

And just like that, Nana K started snoring again, her head bowed, chin to her chest.

Mom sighed. "I need a drink."

Nana K jolted slightly, her eyes flying open. "You drinking, Missy? What about the baby?"

Mom blinked, then chuckled in that nervous way people do when they aren't sure if there's a joke they should be in on. "The . . . baby?"

"Yes!" Nana K raised her voice, her tone indignant as hell. "You and Syd said y'all was having a baby. You can't be drinking!"

Mom's shoulders slumped.

The fire in Alice's throat flooded her face and pressed in behind her eyes. She sniffed. Nana K turned toward the sound and gasped lightly when she saw Alice. "Oh, I didn't know we had company. Sorry I didn't see you, sweetheart."

Alice smiled so hard her face hurt. "I-it's fine."

"U-um. . . . mm-*nmm*." Mom cleared her throat. "Why don't we get you some tea, and you lay down in my bed."

"I'm gonna steal that bed from you someday. California king, fit for a queen." Nana K gave a sharp laugh, though she shook like a leaf as Mom helped her to her feet.

Alice knew she should help, knew she should support her grandma from the other side, but she couldn't move. She sat frozen, her entire body feeling like it might vibrate apart.

Once Mom got Nana K through the door, she threw a tearful look at Alice and mouthed, "I'm so sorry, baby."

Then they slipped out of sight.

"Oh, lord, what happened out here?" Nana K said.

"Redecorating, Momma."

Alice didn't hear the rest. She wished she had a door she could shut, but there wasn't one. So she sat there, her chest winding tighter and tighter, her breath coming quicker and quicker. A brutal buzzing filled her ears.

Her grandmother knew about Figment Blades. About Nightmares. Knew how to defeat them! Was . . . was Nana K a Dreamwalker? Had she known what Alice was doing all this time? No, that wasn't possible. Or was it? She didn't know what to think.

She didn't know what to say or do, so she sat there, her mind and her heart in turmoil.

"Alice?" Mom's voice reached her from the door. She braced herself against the frame, feet spread to avoid stepping on the purge site.

Alice quickly swiped at her cheeks, then wiped her hands on her sheets. "How is she?" Her voice sounded like a stranger's, haggard and frayed.

"She's resting." Mom crossed the room to join Alice on the bed again. She settled in close and took one of Alice's hands in both of hers. "Still stuck in the past, though. What about you, how you doing?"

A laugh slipped past Alice's lips before she realized it had even bubbled up. It was a hollow thing and left her just as empty. "I'm fine." She lifted her shoulders in a shrug. "In one piece, at least." Even though it felt like her heart had shattered and her mind was going in a million different directions. "What about you?" she asked, forcing that train of thought aside. "Sorry the house got tore up. Again."

Heaving a sigh, Mom lifted one arm to wrap around Alice, same as she had with Nana K. "Now you sounding like her. I'm not worried about that. I mean, I am, or I will be, but it's not a priority. Besides, I figure this might just be life, demons in my house, you fighting them, and now your grandmother." She shook her head, closed her eyes, and murmured a prayer Alice only half heard. Then she chuckled, soft, sad, but genuinely amused. "Your daddy would have had a field day with this."

Alice couldn't help her own slight smile. "Did he ever do anything like this?" she asked quietly. "Show that he maybe, might, kinda, sorta have . . . powers?"

"Oh lord no," Mom said a little too quick, and with a certain edge that made Alice feel kinda sorta like a freak. "What I mean is . . . I'm sure he'd be equally surprised. Thrilled, but surprised."

Mom patted Alice's hand. She hadn't let go yet and kept squeezing Alice's fingers. "I know you got questions, baby. I do, too. So many questions. But I'm afraid whatever it was she wanted to share will have to wait till she comes back to us."

Alice nodded. It was best to let her grandmother have some time to find her way. Until then, Alice knew someone else who might be able to tell her what was going on.

◊ ◊ ◊

Alice winced as she bit down a little too hard on her lower lip, which had spent the past ten minutes trapped between her teeth. "Come on, come on, pick up." For the third time in a row, her call went to voice mail. Weird. Courtney usually responded. Even if she didn't answer, she would at least send a text.

She's probably resting, too, Alice figured. Maddi had managed miracles, of course, but Court still looked pretty banged up after the crash. *Hell,* I *should be resting.*

But instead, she was tucked away in her mother's new bathroom, eager to tell Court about this latest family development.

Sure, she could talk to Mom about it, considering she'd witnessed it all, too, but Alice had spent the past almost two years bouncing Wonderland stuff off her best friend. It was habit.

Well, if she couldn't get ahold of Courtney, she should at least let Hatta and the others know what was up. Her thumb hovered over his name on the screen. She should call Hatta. She knew that, but her hand refused to push the button.

A million possibilities lay on the other side of that conversation.

One in particular had stuck out in her mind for the past half hour. What if he had known about her grandmother? And what if he had lied to her about it this entire time?

"No," she muttered, scrubbing her free hand over her face. "There has to be another reason. You can probably figure it out together, just make the call." She nodded and hit the pub's number.

The phone rang. And rang.

No one picked up.

Strange. Either Hatta or Maddi should've picked up, what with things being on possible-high-alert. Something was wrong.

"Or everyone's asleep because it's nearly midnight." She should probably get some sleep, too. But first, she had to wash off this Nightmare crud, and her mother's ridiculously large shower was the perfect place to do it.

She started gathering towels and things with one hand and picking through bottles with the other. Alice and her mother "shared" hair care products, which really meant they stole each other's when they ran out.

Turning on the water in the stall, she left it to warm up and planned to head back to her room to grab some clothes. She slipped out of the bathroom, then drew up short when she found her mother sitting on the edge of the bed, her head in her hands. Nana K was sound asleep behind her. "Mom?" Alice ventured softly.

Mom looked up in surprise, then quickly wiped at the wet trails on her face. "H-hey, baby. What is it?"

Alice fidgeted as her mother sniffed. "Nothing, I thought you were gonna make some tea."

"O-oh, I was—I . . . came up here for my owl mug." Mom glanced around for her favorite hot cup, then waved a hand when her search proved useless. "That doesn't matter, did you need something?"

"No! No, I was just gonna take a shower. Have you seen my co-wash?"

Even in the midst of trying to clean her face up, Mom managed to look playfully perturbed. "I told you, co-wash is something you do, not something you buy. Spending my money on a lie."

"If you don't believe in it, why do you use mine?" Alice asked, amused.

"Only when I'm out of conditioner. That's all that stuff is, anyway." Mom stood and shuffled past Alice and into the bathroom in order to check her reflection in the mirror. Then she pulled out a few more bottles and set them on the counter. "You in my shower again?"

"I like the water spray thingy." It was one of those that let water fall on your head directly like rain.

"It's pretty nice, isn't it? I was thinking, next time those demons show up, think you can fight them in the kitchen? I always wanted a breakfast nook. May as well get my money's worth if I'm gonna risk going to jail for magical insurance fraud."

Alice snorted a laugh. "I'll keep that in mind. Let me know if Nana wakes up?"

Mom's smile dimmed, but she nodded. "Of course, baby." She leaned in to kiss Alice's forehead on the way back into the bedroom. "I'm gonna make some food, what you want?"

Alice's stomach gave an eager burble. "Anything, really. I'm starving."

"How does shrimp and grits sound? I got—" Mom trailed off, her breath catching.

Frowning, Alice stuck her head out the door. The first thing she saw was her mother, standing frozen, staring across the room at the Slithe pouring in from the hall.

Her heart hammering, Alice hurried around her mother and

toward the door. She stopped just shy of where the liquid shadow oozed across the floor. It was worse in the hall. That disgusting shit covered the carpet, climbed the walls, sluiced between the banister posts to drip into the den below.

"The fuck," Alice breathed, her eyes searching the mess and pinging in on the source. A fountain of Slithe bubbled up and poured over itself same as it had in Ahoon or the football field, only this one was in her bedroom doorway.

Right where she'd killed one of the Nightmares. *Oh f—*

"What the hell is going on?" Mom gasped, clutching at Alice with a shaky hand.

They did not have time for an explanation. "We need to get out," Alice said, her head whipping around in search of a swift exit. There was the window on the far wall, but they'd never be able to get Nana K through there. And the Slithe was moving quicker.

"Get on the bed!" Alice shoved her mother in that direction. "Don't let it touch you."

Mom scrambled up onto the mattress, disturbing Nana K in the process.

The older woman flailed a bit as she shifted and rolled with Mom's movement. "Missy? If you wanted your bed back, you could've just said. You ain't gotta jump on me to—" Nana K went quiet when she caught sight of the mess sweeping toward them.

The Slithe filled the rest of the room. It bubbled and gurgled, writhing as if it were alive. It wasn't, but something lingering beneath was.

A shape rose from the mess. The inky ripple fell away, revealing a thin, curled hand. Pitch dripped from long nails that clawed at the carpet. Another hand sprouted nearby, then a third. They pulled themselves and the pitch toward Alice and her family. She scrambled back onto the bed, fear quivering in her middle.

More hands emerged, grasping at one another and at the edges of the blankets. A decidedly hard tug from one side sent her toppling over. She hurriedly pushed up and away from the reaching fingers.

"Momma!"

Alice spun to see her mother and Nana clinging to one another, struggling against where one of the hands had hold of Nana K's nightgown. A second latched onto Mom's ankle. The two were being pulled off opposite sides of the mattress.

Alice dove forward, arms spread. She managed to latch onto Nana K's hand, then scrambled to grab Mom's wrist. "I got you, I got you!" She pulled, but she couldn't anchor herself on the ever-shifting sheets. The hands grew more numerous, catching hold of Mom's free arm, crawling up Nana K's legs. Alice's hold on her mother's wrist nearly gave. She tightened it. Mom cried out as something shifted beneath Alice's fingers, bone grinding.

"I'm sorry!" Alice screamed, tears springing to her eyes. The muscles in her shoulders, arms, and back started to burn, but she held on. She wouldn't let go, she *refused* to let go. She couldn't lose anyone else, she couldn't . . .

"Let go, baby."

Alice blinked through the blur of tears. Nana K was smiling, actually smiling. She didn't fight the hands like Mom or try to pull away. She simply held Alice's gaze and set a hand over her shaky one.

"N-Nana," Alice whimpered.

"It's okay," Nana K whispered. "You don't have to fight this."

Alice could barely hear her above her mother's screaming.

Nana K's smile widened. "Let go."

Alice shook her head furiously. No. No! She flexed every muscle in her body trying to reel them. The resistance felt like she was being pulled apart.

"It's okay," Nana K repeated. The corners of her eyes crinkled. Tears gathered in her laugh lines. "Save your momma. Save them all. I love you."

Alice's chest tightened. "No!"

Nana K twisted her fingers.

Alice lost her grip. She stared, helpless, as her grandmother, still smiling, slid off the side of the bed and vanished into the liquid dark.

Agony howled in Alice's chest. It threatened to split her open from the inside, but she couldn't let it. Not yet. Alice wrenched onto her side and gripped at her mother with both hands. Then she tried to find some way to anchor herself to the bed.

Mom's wide, terrified eyes found Alice's. The darkness crawled over her body, clear up to her neck.

"No!" Alice tried to dig her heels into the mattress. "You can't have her!"

Mom started to say something, but inky fingers fell over her mouth, muffling her screams. She jerked away in reflex. The sudden movement yanked Alice forward. She braced herself against the edge of the bed! Which left her holding on to her mom with just one hand. That's all it took for the Slithe to snatch her mother out of her grasp and send Alice toppling over backward.

"NO!" Alice shrieked, her throat raw with it.

She flung herself at the edge of the bed, reaching it just in time to see her mother disappear into the black.

Twenty-One

A KNIGHT RISES

Humphrey was gone.

Beneath where he'd stood, the floor was covered in pitch.

Fear had spiked through Addison when a pair of inky hands emerged from the pool and latched onto the other knight. Dread quickly followed when Humphrey sank into that liquid darkness.

He hadn't spoken. He hadn't shouted. He hadn't even gasped. All he'd done was look at Addison, those blue eyes icy with terror.

Someone had shouted Humphrey's name.

Addison would later realize it had been him, crying out as he flung himself forward, pushing his body to move as quickly as it could, reaching for one of Humphrey's outstretched hands.

Their fingers brushed as he grasped at empty air.

And then it was done.

The dread filling Addison deflated into a sudden, sharp sense of despair as he stared at the slowly growing pool.

Not again.

Maybe he could reach him.

Not again!

If he was fast enough, he could get him out of there.

He took a shaky step forward, but fingers clamped down on his arm hard enough to bruise. Maddi pulled at him, telling him they couldn't touch the Slithe, it was dangerous, they had to find a way out of here.

Hatta gritted his teeth and pushed down the dark feeling welling up inside him. He had to keep his head, or they all might lose theirs. "On the desk," he urged those who remained.

Chess leaped up with little trouble, then reached to help Madeline and Courtney clamber up after him. The commotion sent papers fluttering. Addison maneuvered his way behind the desk, preparing to climb up as well, but a realization stopped him cold.

Get out, Madeline had said. But how? There were no windows, at least none large enough for them to squeeze through, and the only exit was blocked.

You know what you have to do. He did, but he'd sworn an oath. Never again. He wouldn't. He couldn't. Not after all this time, after he'd fought it for so long. *It's the only way to save any of them.* His eyes moved to Maddi, Courtney, and Chess, the two girls clinging to each other, the boy hovering protectively over them. *It's the only way.*

The only way. That was the lie he told himself last time. He wouldn't do so again.

Then they will all suffer her wrath. Your choice. Your freedom, for their lives.

Addison shut his eyes tight against the intrusive thoughts. But no matter how much he wanted to ignore them, no matter how much he wished it wasn't so, they were right.

A heaviness filled his limbs.

Pulling a small key hung on a chain around his neck, he shoved it into the lock on the cabinet. There was a *clank*, and the doors parted.

The Vorpal Blade hung before him, suspended in midair. The subtle shadows that had always shifted and curled around the hilt now waxed and waned ferociously, as if they knew what was coming. He had wielded the sword multiple times since his days as the Black Knight. That wasn't the true danger, though it was risky enough. But this? Allowing the sword, the knight's power, to take him again? Fully? He'd barely come back from it before. Would he manage it again?

In the back of his head, he registered that Madeline was screaming at him, telling him not to do it.

A sudden pressure at his ankle and the feel of ice shooting up his leg made him look down. The puddle had spread beneath the desk far enough that a hand managed to get hold of him, but it couldn't pull him under until it was beneath him as well. He had mere moments before it claimed him, but that was all he needed.

He took the blade down, grasped the hilt, and pulled it from the sheath. Instantly the light in the room dimmed, swallowed by the blade so black. It seemed to hum faintly in his grasp, almost eager. Madeline sounded beside herself, shouting and sobbing.

"I'm sorry," he murmured, the apology meant for her, for all of them. He drew a breath—"I am yours, so I swear"—then drew the blade along his palm. His skin split with a feeling like fire, and that flame spread through the rest of him.

It tore at his insides, gorging itself on muscle, sinew, and bone, eating away at him one instant, then filling him up the next. The pain was excruciating.

And an old friend.

Then it faded, drawn into him until a dull ache rested at his center. He opened his eyes, only then realizing he had closed them. The cut in his palm was gone. There was nothing but the burning.

The liquid black had finally covered every inch of the floor, save for a small spot beneath his feet. He shifted his stance. The Slithe shifted with him, clearing away before his boots touched the ground, and sweeping in to fill anywhere he was no longer standing.

A soft sound drew his attention to where Maddi stared at him, both hands pressed over her mouth. She shook her head, her small frame quaking with the force of her crying. Holding her up, Courtney stared as well with a haunted look that said she wasn't sure what was going on but she knew it was bad. Chess frowned, looking . . . apprehensive. His eyes were fixed on the sword.

Addison extended the blade forward. Like Moses parting the Red Sea, the Slithe split to reveal a clear path to the door. He moved slowly, carefully, stopping at the spot where he'd seen Humphrey vanish. A twinge of heartache wormed its way between his ribs. The other was truly gone.

There was no time to dwell. Shaking off the threatening despair, Addison aimed the sword down the hall to open the way, then extended the sheath toward the desk so the path behind him remained clear. "Come on," he said, once there was enough space for the others to follow. The three climbed down off the desk, clearly hesitant, but soon moved in behind him.

Addison "carved" their way out of the office, his mind working over the possibilities. They could go for the exit. Maddi's truck was at the front of the lot; if they reached it, they could get away. And possibly leave a trail of Slithe following them through the city. Bad idea.

The only other option was to go through the Veil, into Wonderland. There they could possibly find help, perhaps a way to undo whatever the hell was happening. There was the added benefit of Slithe being native to Wonderland. While it wasn't ideal, there would be fewer complications. Hopefully.

Decision made, he led the way along the hall, toward the closet that held the entry to the Gateway. The darkness followed them closely. Inky hands with thin, talon-tipped fingers emerged now and again to grasp at them, but a gesture from the sword made them withdraw each time.

"How the hell are you doing this?" Courtney asked.

"Th-the . . . darkness . . . obeys . . . the knight . . ." Madeline croaked.

Addison couldn't bring himself to look at her. This darkness was obeying, but barely. The effort to maintain a hold over it left a pounding behind his eyes so severe his vision nearly doubled at times. But he didn't have to keep this up for long, just long enough.

Finally, they reached the closet. Chess managed to get the door open, and they slipped inside. After making sure the Slithe had vacated the space entirely, Addison drew the sword across the door. It cut into the wood, leaving a clean slice singed at the edges. That should give them time.

"What . . . This is a closet," Courtney gasped. "Why are we—" She froze as understanding took hold. "We're going back to Wonderland?" Her voice trembled. So did she.

"There's no other way. Gather round, quickly." He sheathed the sword, and the light from the overhead bulb immediately seemed brighter.

Madeline shuffled in close, but not too close, he noticed.

Courtney and Chess pressed in behind her. Addison strapped the sword to his back, then took a deep breath as he prepared to drop them through the Veil. For the first time in centuries, the Vorpal Blade would enter Wonderland again.

And so would the Black Knight.

Twenty-Two
FOUND

Alice remembered the pain of losing her father sharply. She remembered the way it had hollowed out some part of her, way deep down, and no matter what she did, no matter how much time passed, it stayed empty. She remembered the ache of it spreading through her whole body as she sobbed for days, weeks, months. And whenever she thought she might finally be getting better, it would only get worse. Oftentimes there was no warning. The grief would rise up out of nowhere, slamming into her with the force of a freight train and knocking her back into the emptiness. Pain like that never dulled. It never went away. It was always there, around a corner, under a bed, through a door, waiting for her.

And now it had her again.

She sat on her mother's bed, an island of silks and cotton in a sea of writhing shadow. The darkness lapped at the edges of the mattress like waves along the hull of a boat. And though there were no choppy seas to toss her about, the sick feeling in her stomach would not abate. She wrapped her arms so tight around her knees her hands tingled with numbness, and sobbed into her sleeves. Her body buckled under the weight of her sorrow, her chest heaving so hard she felt it might cave in. Her throat burned. Her head ached.

Time ticked by. Seconds. Minutes. Maybe hours. She didn't know how long she'd been like this, didn't really care. All that mattered was that they were gone. Her family, snatched away. So she sat there, screaming until her throat was raw, crying until her tears dried up, waiting for when the hands decided to take her, too. But they didn't. They only tugged uselessly at the edges of the comforter. For some reason, they left her alone.

Alone.

She was alone.

"Whatchu gone do?"

Alice couldn't recall ever feeling irritation or anger at the memory of her father, but she felt it now. Hot and seething, the strength of the emotion took her by surprise. Apparently, she wasn't gonna do a mothafucking thing as two of the people she loved most were taken from her.

She snatched up the nearest thing, a pillow, and flung it across the room with a roar. She didn't see where it went. She didn't care. She just grabbed the next thing, another pillow, and threw it. Then the next, a lamp from the nightstand. An alarm clock, a book, and another pillow all went flying. Then she buried her fingers in her hair and bent forward, her knees tucked to her chest. Something cold and hard knocked against her chin.

Nana K's necklace.

The burn of tears threatened a new wave of sadness.

Sniffing, her chest spasming in hiccups like she was a child again, Alice clutched the necklace to her heart. She didn't know what to do.

She. Didn't. Know. What. To. DO!

Yes, you do, some part of her managed to whisper. *Say it.*

Alice shook her head.

Say it!

". . . I'm afraid," she croaked, tightening her hold on the necklace. It seemed to grow warmer in her hands.

Again.

"I-I'm . . . afraid."

AGAIN.

"I'm afraid."

Louder.

"I'm afraid!"

The heat in her palms spread through the rest of her. It filled her, almost to the point of painful, but there was no hurt that could touch her compared to what she was feeling now.

Good. Now, finish it.

"But fear . . . cannot . . . stop me."

The heat exploded, throwing Alice back against the headboard. Or it felt like an explosion, but instead of fire and destruction there was . . . ice? Alice blinked through the pain in her back, her vision white with it.

No, that wasn't it. Her vision was white because light hovered just in front of her face. Nana K's necklace blazed a brilliant mix of red and gold. It was like the necklace was forged from fire, jewel and all. It grew, chain and pendant morphing, folding, remolding itself until there was nothing of the original piece of jewelry left.

The necklace was gone, and in its place was a silver scepter. It hung in the air for a moment before plopping against the comforter.

Alice stared.

And stared.

And stared.

Her breath caught in realization. This was the same scepter Reflection-Alice had offered her in her dream some weeks ago, with hands cast in silver clutching what she now recognized as the jewel from the necklace. Only, in her dream, the jewel had been bigger and glowed bright purple.

Alice curled her fingers around the staff and lifted it. It was much lighter than she remembered. But how . . . how in the hell could she remember something she'd never held before?

"Because it remembers you," something whispered against her mind. *"And it will help you, guide you. You know what to do."*

Then the scepter vanished in a dusting of light, the particles re-forming into Nana K's necklace then dropping to the bed. Alice hesitated before picking it up. The chain and setting seemed to shine just a little bit brighter. She needed to put it back on. She didn't know how she knew, only that she did. That was happening more and more often. Damn, she was sick of this shit.

As she lowered the necklace over her head, Nana K's and Dad's voices warred in her mind.

"Whatchu gone do?"

"Save your momma."

"Whatchu gone do?"

"Save them all."

"I love you, Baby Moon."

"I love you."

"I love you," Alice murmured aloud. And though she was alone in this room, surrounded by darkness, she meant it. She meant it for her father, for her mother, for her grandma and her friends. She *meant* it.

And when you mean something, you act on it.

"Whatchu gone do?"

This. Alice pushed to stand. She wavered slightly, the mattress shifting under her feet. She didn't have her pack or her weapons. She didn't have any clothes but the ones on her back. She didn't have any idea what waited for her, but she had people counting on her. And she had no way out of this mess except through it.

So, with one hand wrapped tightly around Nana K's necklace, feeling the gem press into her palm, Alice shuffled up to the edge of the bed. Then she held her breath, and stepped off.

The darkness swallowed her. Ice coated her body, pressing down on her skin, scorching it. She fought against the primal panic that wanted to take hold, the burn in her lungs begging her to take a breath. She shut her eyes and allowed herself to sink.

Down.

Down.

Down.

Eventually, she blinked her eyes back open. There was nothing, only the darkness, only—

Something flickered across Alice's vision. A banner of light wavered in front of her, piercing the shadows, shining from somewhere above. If it could reach her, she could reach it.

Alice kicked her legs and pumped her arms, propelling herself upward. The burn in her lungs intensified. They felt like they were going to explode. Spots danced in her vision. Her throat tightened. She couldn't hold her breath any longer.

She broke the surface with a gasp, her lungs jackknifing as she coughed and flailed. Her arms splashed along the surface of the . . . water? The Slithe was gone, and Alice found herself treading bright green liquid. "I'm alive," she breathed, still gasping and a little light-headed. "I'm alive!" And if she was, did that mean Mom and Nana K were, too?

She had to find them. Her head whipped around, wet hair dangling into her eyes and clinging to her face. A shore lingered in the distance. She kicked off in that direction. There was no real way to tell how long she swam, but by the time she hauled herself onto the purple sand like some sort of drowned cat, her body was ready to give out.

She crawled the last few feet out of the shallows and collapsed. Her muscles ached. Her insides throbbed. She couldn't stop coughing, and with a familiar taste of copper on her tongue she threw up a short distance away. Scrubbing at her mouth with the back of her hand, Alice flopped onto her back. While her body fought to recover, her gaze roamed.

Overhead, the sky burned deep orange, but not the natural orange of sunrise or sunset. In fact, there was no sun. No clouds. Only endless color save for the familiar overcast of darkness in the distance, occasionally threaded by streaks of red lightning. The skyscrapers of downtown Atlanta twinkled beyond that.

The Nox and her world stood side by side, which meant she was in the In-Between. Again.

Only this time, instead of standing at the edge of a chasm, she lay along the shores of a beach. Purple sand clung to her wet clothes and skin, the texture oddly fine instead of coarse and gritty. It stretched on for miles in either direction, cradling an ocean of emerald waves that vanished into the horizon. The smell of seawater mixed with something faintly minty tickled her nose. This place was beautiful, there was no denying that.

Sniffling, and now shivering though she didn't really feel cold, Alice managed to get her feet beneath her. She folded her arms around herself, her gaze searching the green waters. There was no sign of her mother and grandmother, but that only meant they hadn't come ashore here. Alice believed they had made it. There was no other outcome she'd accept.

"Okay," she breathed as a spark of hope flickered to life inside her. Her family was out there, somewhere. And she was going to find them. "This is fine. We're gonna be fine."

Then she started walking.

And walking.

And walking.

For minutes. Hours. There was no way to tell, the day didn't appear to be shifting at all. This beach seemed to go on forever. She let her gaze roam as she went. Further back from the shoreline, yellow grass eventually spilled into a dense forest of what looked surprisingly like regular-ass trees. She debated heading that direction but every now and then thought she saw movement in the shadows. Without her weapons, and without shoes, the open space and soft sands of the beach were the safer bet.

So she kept going. Eventually her feet started to ache. So did her stomach. And she was no closer to . . . anything. It all looked the same. Same sand, same water, same boring beachfront. Her steadily building frustration finally spiked.

"UuuuuggghhhhAAAAHH!" she screamed at nothing and no one.

So she was hella surprised when someone answered.

"Ahh, there you are."

Alice whirled in the direction of the voice, her hands coming up. She might not have her daggers, but that didn't mean she was gonna go down easy.

Bushes rustled beneath the nearby trees before, once again, the last person she expected emerged. Actually, at this point? She should probably have expected him almost exclusively.

"You're a hard one to pin down." Sprigs ran a hand along the top of his balding head, disturbing the two tufts of white sticking straight up above his ears. He smiled. It stretched the lines in his deep brown face.

Alice relaxed. "You . . ."

He held his hands out to his sides as if presenting himself and chuckled in that gravelly voice of his. "Me. Well, hurry up, don't wanna be late." He beckoned her with a wave as he turned to back into the forest. They didn't get five steps before he paused, his head cocked to the side. "Or am I late? Or are you early?" He shrugged. "No matter, c'mon now!"

"Wait, where are we going?" She took a few hesitant steps after him. "Did Hatta send you?" The last time she saw Sprigs he'd said Addison asked him to help.

Sprigs angled his head around to peer at her as they walked, his expression giving him the look of an old dog that had perked up at the question. "Hatta? No, no. I live here."

Alice stared. People could live here? "And . . . you were looking for me?"

He nodded.

"Why?"

"Because you needed to be found," he said, as if this was obvious and she should absolutely understand.

Instead, she was all the more confused. "Found?"

"Yes," he sighed, and then he paused and faced her fully. That's when she noticed he was dressed kinda sorta like a Jedi. He had robes, boots, tunic, the whole thing. They were all various shades of gray, and impossibly clean considering he'd been rummaging through the woods looking for her, so he said. "All lost things are waiting to be found. Especially here." He gestured at their surroundings. "Which is everywhere, and nowhere, remember? Which is exactly where I knew you would be. I'm still a little fuzzy on the when, though. Sorry for the wait." A smile stretched his dark brown face, crinkling the lines around his eyes.

Alice couldn't help but return it. "Okay," she said. It wasn't like she was doing all that great out here on her own. "Guess I'm going with you, then."

He clapped his hands together. "Excellent. They'll be pleased." Then he was on his way, again.

"And who's they?" she asked, picking her way toward him. The sand gave way to soft grass, dirt, and scattered rocks. Hopefully, her bare feet would survive the trip.

"The other two. They were lost as well."

Alice's heart damn near leaped for joy. Other two? Her mom and grandma really were okay! Tears prickled at the corners of her eyes as she hurried to catch up with Sprigs just as he pushed into the brush.

Twenty-Three

FAMILIAR FACES

Humphrey twisted to try to free himself as he was pulled into the darkness. More hands emerged to grab at him, his wrists, his arms, attempting to pin him in place. But they were going to find it difficult to hold on to nothing.

Once more, he released his hold on himself. The ether opened before him. Then something strange happened. A prickling sensation filled his limbs. His senses wavered. And instead of feeling his body grow light as air itself, a heaviness soaked into him, followed by a sudden, sharp pain.

He wasn't . . . teleporting, he wasn't . . . Why wasn't . . .

That pain became a storm in his veins. Usually there was a rush of energy as he was transported from one place to another, unseen by most. Now there was this suffocating pressure that threatened to *crush* him.

He had to regain control, had to come out of the ether or it was going to shatter him. He took a shuddering breath, trying to focus past the hurt, focus on the fact that he *knew* he existed. A glimmer of self flickered, and he latched onto it. The ether loosed him with a sound like thunder.

The force of it slammed into the ground, sent him tumbling. He tucked himself into a roll, coming out of it on hands and knees, the world spinning. He gritted his teeth against the feeling of his bones vibrating.

The darkness was gone. As were the grasping hands. He was in agony, but he was free.

Carefully, gingerly, he pushed himself to stand. His legs held, despite the aches rolling through him. Once upright, he took in his surroundings, instantly recognizing the otherworldly quality of the In-Between. Night and day filled the sky both at once, a constant war of moonshine and daylight. In the distance, elements of Wonderland and the human world melded together in imperfect harmony.

He'd passed through this place a few times, though not *this* place specifically. The grooves from his tumble stuck out in hard relief along the otherwise undisturbed surface of purple sands. Emerald waves lapped at the shore, singing a gentle song.

The Eternity Shore, he realized. He'd never been here, but somehow, he knew where here was. Just like he knew where everywhere else was, and yet still didn't remember anything about himself, about his life before . . .

He shoved the thought aside. There were more pressing matters at hand, like getting out of here. "What was lost" wound up on the Eternity Shore. So it seemed he was going to have to wait to be found. Unless, of course, he found himself. Just where had those hands been trying to take him in order for him to wind up here?

"UuuuuggghhhhAAAAHH!"

Humphrey tensed as a shout echoed in the distance. *I know that voice*, he realized with a sudden jolt. What in the five circles was she doing here? No, that didn't matter; he needed to get to her. Running would be quick though traveling through the ether was always faster. Strewth, the ether had nearly *killed* him just moments ago. Or perhaps it was trying to vanish in that sludge that had hampered things. Regardless, there was only one way to be sure.

"Okay," he breathed, shaking his hands and arms out. "Slow going. Just a couple of yards to start." After a few steps, he loosed his hold on reality. The ether swallowed him whole, then spat him back out a tad further along the shore. Not far, but still forward.

The pain was instant, but not all-consuming. It radiated through him, causing him to sort of limp along. But as he moved, the hurt faded. Within the next handful of steps, it was gone completely.

He took a breath and jumped again. A little farther. More pain, but again it subsided.

After the third jump, he tried even further. And so he went, one, two, three, then further. That pattern, over and over. Eventually he was jumping a good distance, but never further than he could see. The ache was bearable and gradually lessening, like working out a cramped muscle.

Maybe half a kilometer along, he slowed to a stop when he noticed a disturbance in the sand. Footprints, a single pair that looked to have come from the opposite direction, for a good ways. They shifted back and forth a bit, then marched off toward the nearby woods.

That meant he wasn't just hearing things, which was somewhat reassuring. So was the fact that there weren't any signs of a struggle, despite what sounded like distress. Odds were she went that direction of her own volition. Or she was somehow coerced without force.

Without a second thought, Humphrey hurried after her, pushing into the forest. As he went, he listened carefully for any signs of life or movement. Well, life was an overstatement. Nothing "lived" in the In-Between. Things merely existed, creatures conjured by stray thoughts or incomplete ideals, battered and beaten into being as humanity attempted and failed to grasp certain concepts over time. Here, all was literally lost in thought.

That did not mean there was no danger, however, so he needed to keep his wits about him. Especially if his lady still visited in search of . . . whatever she was after.

And while he doubted Alice would be happy to see him, she wouldn't be actively looking to kill or capture him. Maybe. And it likely wouldn't go over well if he made his way out of here while knowingly leaving her behind, though he was curious as to how she wound up here to begin with.

But that wasn't the important bit. Right now, he needed to find her, but—to his annoyance—when he moved into the brush, he wasn't able to pick up her trail. Odd. She was having a physical effect on the land this time, he should be able to track her.

After an hour of searching, there was still no sign of Alice or whatever had drawn her away from the beach. He'd backtracked at least half a dozen times, followed what looked to be possible tracks, each chosen path ending with him right back where it started. It was infuriating, wandering around in endless circles, no idea how to navigate. There were few things Humphrey hated more than being lost.

"Trust yourself," Hatta had told him his first night staying at the pub. "Part of you probably remembers who you were, even if the rest of you doesn't. Listen to those instincts."

Very well.

Squaring his shoulders he closed his eyes. The sounds of the forest rushed in to envelop him. Birdsong. Insects. Faint whoops and trills, hollers and grunts, creatures and animals that had no true place in the human world or Wonderland. But in all that, he heard nothing that indicated there were people present.

And yet . . .

He felt a slight tug to the west. What or who could be pulling at him, he had no idea. Though he supposed if he was going to do this whole follow-your-instincts thing . . .

With a fortifying breath, he started in that direction.

The brush was easy enough to navigate, even without an actual path to wander. It was an odd mix of flora and fauna he recognized from Wonderland with bits of the same from the human world thrown in. Miraculously, the two habitats coexisted seamlessly, woven into and around each other, living as one, in peace.

Which was why he was surprised to hear the snarling and rustling of something in the brush.

"S-stay back! Stay!" someone cried.

Without a second thought, he bolted in the direction of the shouts. There was another scream, and the snarls grew louder. He let go of his physical form, allowing the ether to swallow him and spit him back out into a small clearing.

At the center, two scorch marks that had clearly been Fiends still bubbled and popped. A third still-very-much-alive Fiend snapped and snarled as it circled its prey: someone lying on the ground and, standing over them . . . Alice's mother.

He recognized the woman from the times he'd "visited" their home. She stood between the Fiend and the person slumped against the ground, brandishing a large branch.

His hand shot up, reaching for the hilt of his sword, and grabbed at air. He was unarmed, he realized with a sudden twist of anger.

Fine, then. He took a running start toward the beast, then let go once more. Pulling himself into being at the last second, he let the momentum carry him feet first into the monster's side. It howled and turned, but he was already dropping into the ether. He came out on the opposite side, landing another kick before dropping back again.

In and out, in and out, he appeared at various points around the monster, landing kicks and punches before vanishing again. The beast spun in futile frustration as it snapped and swiped at empty air. Meanwhile, fatigue started to pull at Humphrey's limbs. He had to end this.

And so he pushed to move faster. Faster. Each punch, each kick, spinning the beast around and around until he lashed out to drive the heel of his boot into the monster's jaw, connecting as it was coming around in search of him.

There was a sharp *snap* as the thing's neck twisted back. Then it slumped to the ground. He dropped similarly, catching himself on his hands and knees as his body ached and his lungs burned. His head hung forward, he closed his eyes against the dizziness threatening to overtake him. Everything seemed to tilt slightly as he struggled to inhale slow, deep breaths.

"Mom!" Alice's mother shouted.

Humphrey lifted his head in time to see her drop beside the other person, helping them to sit up. Another face he recognized, just barely.

What had Alice called the old woman? Nana K.

"Mom! Oh my god, are you—"

Nana K lifted a hand to wave her off. "I'm fine, Missy. Just tired," she croaked.

The sound of *that* voice sent a chill through Humphrey. He sat up, still kneeling on the ground, staring at the two of them as he fought to catch his breath.

Alice's mother helped Nana K into a seated position. As she did, he was able to get a closer look at the two. The former wore some sort of garment likely meant for sleep. Her feet were bare, her hair a mess of frizzy curls where it stuck out here and there. Her clothes and dark skin were covered in patches of black. She looked like she had been through hell.

So did Nana K, but she appeared to be dealing with it a bit better. Fear wasn't written over her expression, more a calm sort of resignation to the reality of the situation. He could see traces of Alice in both of their faces.

Right then, Alice's mom threw a look over her shoulder and straight at him. It made his spine straighten. This was definitely where Alice got her fire.

She eyed him as if she wasn't sure what to make of him but clearly had no intention of trusting him even if he had come to her rescue. "Thank you," she murmured as her gaze bounced between him and the slowly dissolving body nearby.

"You're"—he swallowed another breath as the tightness in his chest eased—"quite welcome."

"Humphrey?" Nana K called, louder this time. "What you doing here?"

The older woman stepped around Alice's mother so both could regard him curiously. There was something sharp in Nana K's eyes that cut him to the quick. He felt a sudden, powerful urge to take a knee. His head started to pound, his mind fighting to recall something he'd forgot forgetting. His brain warred against the recognition settling in his heart.

"How . . . how do you know my name?" he asked, his voice quiet, subdued. There was little possibility Alice had made mention of him to her family.

Alice's mom glanced back and forth between them, equally confused as to what was going on.

"You know him?"

"Yes," Nana K said, such surety in her voice. Surety that he didn't feel in the least. She narrowed her eyes, playing them over him. "And no . . . he doesn't look to be himself. Alice introduced us the other night. One of her lil friends."

Humphrey frowned. All right, perhaps Alice *had* mentioned him. Legitimately shocking.

As he stood trying to wrap his head around the puzzle before him, the pounding between his eyes intensified. He grunted, setting his hands to the sides of his aching head. What the hell was this?

"Do you remember me?" Nana K asked.

Humphrey started to nod, then thought better of it. "Yes," he hissed, blinking against the hurt. "N-no? I don't . . ."

Slowly, the older woman approached.

"Mom, wait," Alice's mother called, trying to stop her.

Nana K shook the other woman off and continued forward. "You remember me?" she repeated.

The pounding sharpened. His vision blurred. "N-No," he rasped. "No! I don't! Augh!" He doubled over now, the drumming in his head sending shards of agony down the muscles of his neck and shoulders, his entire body tensing. His breath came in quick, short bursts. His vision went white.

Fingers pressed to his shoulders. Nana K. He somehow knew it was her even without seeing. She grasped his chin and lifted his head. He blinked, trying to clear his vision, see past the pain.

Her silver hair seemed to shine, as did her eyes. He knew those eyes. All four of them. He still couldn't see straight and tried to pull away, but her hold was surprisingly strong. She gave him a slight shake, drawing his attention back to her.

"You know me," she said, though this time it was a command. There was power behind her words. Power that reverberated in the air between them, then reached down into him with a feeling like being filled with boiling water. It scoured away some of the muck clouding his mind. Enough that a memory, small but clear, surfaced.

He'd been kneeling then, same as he was now, though not from respect. The wound in his side had brought him low, but he refused to go down. His breaths rattled wetly. His strength had begun to wane. For the first time, he wondered if this might be his end.

This is it, he'd thought, struggling against gravity's grasp. *This is how I die . . .*

Then a hand had pressed to his shoulder. Another took his chin and forced his head up. His blurry vision, red with blood running into his eyes, focused on the face floating in front of him.

"You *will* survive this," a voice had said.

He had chuckled, a pained though amused sound. He made it now, the same faint smile pulling at his lips as it had then.

The memory vanished, leaving him on his knees once again, gazing up into a long-forgotten visage.

". . . I know you . . ."

Twenty-Four

WORN-OUT
PLACES

Alice marveled at the way the plants and brush from Wonderland mingled with the comparatively plain stuff from her world. And how Sprigs old-man-shuffled through all of it without any problems. Meanwhile, she was knees-to-chest in this bitch and still nearly tripping on exposed roots and vines. And her feet felt gross.

This is why God made Tims. Thankfully she hadn't hurt herself or stepped on anything. Sprigs had assured her there was nothing here to do her any harm.

"Besides," he had said, scratching at the top of his head, his white tufts shifting under his fingers. "Didn't your kind used to live in the wild?"

"That was thousands of years ago," she'd shot back while stepping over a particularly muddy-looking patch of ground. "We've evolved. And discovered Chucks."

"Who's Chuck?"

". . . Don't worry about it."

And so they'd gone back and forth a little whenever she grumbled or grunted.

"How much farther?" She swatted some hanging moss aside.

"Not too much. Just enough." He nodded without looking back.

"You said we going to your house?"

"Yes'm."

"So you live here?"

"That's what a house is for, ain't it?"

Her face heated in embarrassment. "I meant, I thought no one lived here. That's what Hatta says. S'what *you* said a little while ago."

"I'm nobody special. Not anymore, anyway." He rolled his shoulders.

"Who were you? If you don't mind my asking."

"I don't." There was amusement in his tone. "I wasn't nobody special then. Not really. But even queens gotta eat."

Alice's eyebrows shot up. "You were a chef?"

"No one stops being a chef. But yes." He glanced over his shoulder, the lines in his brown face stretching with his smile. "Best sweets this side of the Breaking."

"Huh." Alice blinked. She wouldn't have pegged Sprigs as a baker. Granted, she'd never really thought about what he did, but baking cookies wasn't it. "So you served the Queens?"

"For a time." He faced forward again.

"What happened?"

"The war." His tone dropped slightly.

She flinched. *Duh.* "I mean, do you still cook?"

"Sometimes. When the mood strikes. Here we are."

Alice tilted to the side to get a look around him. She nearly choked on a snort.

Sitting at the edge of a clearing, looking like something straight out of a Disney movie, was a quaint little cottage. Sunlight even poured across it in radiant beams.

Wait a second . . . Alice glanced up. Sure enough, there was the sun. "Where did that come from?" she marveled quietly.

"Wa's that?" Sprigs called.

"The sun. I didn't see it back at the beach."

Sprigs glanced skyward, then chuckled faintly. "Full of surprises, that one. Come on, now, don't wanna be late."

Alice followed him up a path marked with stepping stones, taking in the entire place. It was a squat thing, made of wood and stone, covered in vines and moss. There was even a little stack chimney with smoke coming out of the top. He pushed open the door and stepped through, holding it open for her.

As she entered, warmth and the smell of something sweet and spicy hit her. She glanced around the room. It was like one of those magazines where white people retire with millions of dollars then decide to go live in the woods for whatever reason. The stairs near the back took her by surprise. This place didn't look to have two stories. But this was Wonderland-ish shit, so that didn't matter.

"Make yourself at home," Sprigs said as he started removing his cloak.

Alice took a few steps, eyes roaming over the simple furniture, landing on the hearth where a small fire danced. Beyond that was the entry to the kitchen, she figured. And that's when she heard it, the faint yet familiar sound of bickering in Russian.

A smile broke over Alice's face, even as unease tugged at her heart. The twins and their fights were amusing, but if these were the two Sprigs meant, then . . . where were her mom and Nana?

The sudden sting of tears took her by surprise. She sniffed, hard, and took a breath. Breakdowns could come later, and the twins could help her look for her family.

This was good.

A hand patted her shoulder, and Alice turned to find Sprigs smiling at her, his expression—not exactly knowing. Maybe understanding?

"Don't worry," he said softly. "Your family is fine. They've already been found."

Alice's eyes widened. How did he—

"And they're already on the move. They'll no doubt meet up with you down the road, when the time is right."

Questions swirled in Alice's head, battering one another to the point that none of them came out complete. "How do you . . . ? When did you . . . ?"

Sprigs winked. "It's my job to know the comings and goings of this place, and to make sure that which needs to be found is. So, like I said, don't worry. Unless it's about yourself."

A grunt sounded from the other room, followed by a *bang!* as something wooden fell over. A brief moment of silence followed before the bickering picked right back up, louder this time.

Sprigs wrinkled her nose, chuckling in that way old Black men did that made their bellies jump. "Maybe worry a little about these two, too. Boys!" he called. "Come say hello."

The bickering quieted. After a few seconds, Dee and Dem appeared in the door and drew up short, wearing twin expressions of surprise.

The first thing Alice noticed was the bandages. Both boys were littered with them, and Dem even had his arm in a sling. But twin smiles broke over their faces before the two of them shouted at the same time, "Alice!"

She couldn't help smiling as well as they rushed toward her.

"H-hey! Whoa!" she said as Dee swept her into a hug and spun her around before setting her back on her feet.

"It's good to see you," Dem said, standing to the side.

"Good to see you guys, too." She squeezed Dee, gently, then moved to do the same with Dem, careful to mind his shoulder. Drawing back, she played her eyes over the two of them. "Though I'm starting to worry, you look like you got the shit kicked out of you. Again."

"Aaaah, it's not as bad as it looks. Some of this is still from your friend," Dem said. "But you are not wrong."

"What happened this time?" she asked.

"Ambush." Dee rubbed at the back of his head. "On the way to Ahoon."

Alice frowned. "How did you end up here?"

The twins glanced at each other, then back to her. "We don't know," they responded together.

"One minute we're fighting," Dee started. "The next, there is Slithe everywhere, and these hands . . ." He shudders, looking away.

Alice grimaced in understanding.

"We wake up on a beach, of all places." Dem rolled his shoulders. "Nathan found us, brought us here. Helped patch us up. Then told us to watch dinner while he went to find . . . you, I guess."

"How did _you_ get here?" Dee looked her up and down.

Her face warmed with embarrassment. "Jumped in the Slithe after my mom and grandma were taken. When he told me he found two people who would be happy to see me, I thought he meant them." Her insides started to twist again.

This meant her family was still out there, somewhere.

"They were taken," Alice continued. "But I don't know by who, or where. I was trying to follow them."

"And you still can," Sprigs said as he shuffled past and through the door the twins had emerged from. He called over a shoulder, "But we must be quick."

Alice glanced at the twins before the three of them followed him into the kitchen.

Well, not a kitchen exactly. At least, not the way she imagined a kitchen. There were no appliances, just a table, another fire pit in the center with a large pot boiling over it, and walls lined with bottles and books and plants and crystals. It was like a nursery and a hipster spirituality shop had a baby, and that baby threw up all over everything.

Sprigs moved over to the pot, reaching to stir the large spoon that stuck out of a purple liquid. "Thank you, boys, for keeping the fire hot."

The twins nodded and murmured responses she didn't exactly hear, thanks to the fact that she was distracted by something hanging on a nearby wall. A portrait of a white rabbit. The same portrait she'd spotted in Hatta's room at the pub the few times she'd gone. She wasn't exactly surprised to find it here, but at the same time, it shocked the hell out of her.

"Quickly now, here you go," Sprigs said.

Alice turned to find him offering a cup to Dem, then Dee. A third was offered to Alice. She eyed the steaming purple liquid, then gave it a sniff. Nothing. It smelled like nothing, which was a surprise. Nothing in Wonderland smelled like nothing.

Beside her, Dee and Dem examined their drinks similarly.

"What is?" Dee finally asked.

"A way for me to get you out of here safely, in case there are any eyes watching. There are always eyes." Sprigs turned away without further explanation and moved to a nearby cupboard. He pulled out what looked like a biscuit and placed it into a small black sack clutched in one hand. Then turned to look at them, blinking as if surprised to find they hadn't finished their drinks. "Well, go on." He waved.

"Are you a Poet?" Alice asked.

"I told you, I'm a cook. Though I know a thing or two. Down the hatch, quickly, before they arrive." He went back to fussing around the kitchen.

"They?" the twins chimed in perfect unison.

"You are being tracked. All of you, though I imagine you most of all." Sprigs's gaze found Alice's. "I can take you to the chasm, but not like this, or we'll attract the attention of those beasts." He spat the word, clearly not a fan. He pointed at the cups the three of them held. "This will help hide you."

Alice wrinkled her nose, not exactly sure, but beside her Dem slurped loudly on his drink. He pressed a fist to his mouth and burped before muttering what was likely *excuse me* in Russian.

Dee, eyeing his brother with some small amount of disgust, shook his head. "How is?"

Dem shrugged. "I've had worse."

Still glowering at his brother, Dee drank his as well. He smacked his lips and shook his head. Both of them looked to her.

Alice hesitated before finally taking a couple of swallows.

It tasted like nothing and was cold as it spilled down her throat, which was weird because it was still steaming. The chill settled into her stomach briefly before spreading outward, growing colder as it went.

"That's an odd feeling," Dem muttered, hand on his middle.

Alice started to agree but paused, blinking rapidly. Her eyes widened. "Am . . . am I tripping, or are you shorter than your brother?" she asked, her attention on Dem.

Dee turned and blinked as surprise played over his face. Sure enough, Dem looked a couple inches shorter. Then a few more.

Dropping his cup with a clatter, he splayed his hands over himself, shouting something in panicked Russian. Dee responded in kind, reaching out to his now much smaller twin.

"What's happening to him?" Alice demanded of Sprigs. "To them!"

Dem was about knee-high now, and shrinking. He shouted something in Russian, gesturing frantically at his brother, who was now also smaller. What the hell?

Alice shivered as the cold intensified.

"Don't worry," Sprigs said as he fiddled with a basket, though the sound of his voice was slightly muffled against the sudden rush of wind in her ears.

Her limbs tingling, her stomach twisting, Alice stared in horror as everything around her started to grow bigger and bigger, dwarfing her.

But that wasn't what was happening.

Just like the twins, she was shrinking.

Her thoughts raced, as did her heart. The world seemed to stretch and rise around her, furniture becoming skyscrapers. Soon, she was standing in the middle of the now city-block-sized room, with a pair of very tiny Russian boys at her side.

"What the hell is going on?" Dee demanded, his arm around his brother, who was bent over and throwing up some of the liquid.

Suddenly the ground shook with a sound like rhythmic thunder. Steps, Alice realized as she windmilled to keep her balance. Sprigs approached and knelt down near them.

"Mmm, looks like he doesn't take to it too well. No worries, though, it will pass." The old man's voice boomed. He set the basket he'd been fidgeting with on the ground.

"What will pass?" Alice shouted, doing her best not to let fear overtake her mind. "What did you do?"

"You can't be seen, not as you are. So I'll carry you to the chasm in this." Sprigs patted the basket. "But first, you have to fit. Which you didn't. Now you do."

Alice blinked, staring as the pieces started to click together in her mind. Her fear waned, only to be replaced with a sharp irritation. "You shrank us to carry us in a picnic basket?"

Sprigs blinked, then nodded. "That's what I said, young lady."

Freaking Wonderlandians . . . "You could have warned us!"

"And what would that have changed?" Sprigs opened the side of the basket like a little door. Apparently, this wasn't his first time providing tiny transport. "In you go. I've added some accomodations, for comfort."

The twins glanced at Alice before moving forward. She hesitated. That was a giant man, who was only giant because he shrank them without warning, asking them to step into his basket. Every warning bell in her brain should be going off, but it wasn't. She knew this man, after all. Hatta trusted him. *She* trusted him.

"Fine," she muttered before stepping inside.

Two things were nestled in the basket's interior. One was the little black bag that no doubt held the biscuit she'd seen earlier. The other was a bunched-up dish towel. The accommodations Sprig spoke of earlier.

It was . . . interesting navigating the bumpy surface of the bottom, but she picked her way past the bag and over to the towel. The twins were already seated amongst the folds. Sprigs peered inside at them with one giant eye blinking.

"Don't eat any of the cake, that's for later," he said. Then the side of the basket fell down, closing them off. "Hold on."

The basket jostled, then lifted. Alice threw her arms out to brace herself as her stomach dipped with the swift motion upward. She took slow breaths, tilting back against the side of the basket.

Of course today would end with her being shrunk to the size of a Barbie and carried around like a purse dog.

A groan pulled her attention toward the twins. Dem still looked a little green around the gills. Dee hovered over him, clearly concerned.

"So," she called over the steady thump of Sprigs's steps. "First time being carried in a basket?"

Both boys glanced at her with almost twin looks of confusion. One look was slightly more nauseated than the other.

"This is my second," she continued. "First time was with a dragon."

The boys blinked in unison, and Alice smirked.

Twenty-Five
DÉJÀ VU.
WAIT . . .

Addison stepped down from the platform that housed the now hastily closed Gateway. It was unlikely the Slithe would be able to follow, but he didn't want to take any chances.

Nearby, Chess checked over a reeling Courtney as Madeline paced in a small circle. She kept stealing glances at him, then looking away quickly instead of meeting his gaze. That, combined with the tension drawing her shoulders up, the way she worried at her lower lip with her teeth?

She was afraid. Of him. Rather, she was afraid of who he might become, again, and—since Madeline was one of the few who'd survived the Black Knight's tyranny—he couldn't blame her. Still, something inside of him twisted with that knowledge. But that was a worry for later.

Courtney sighed. "I gotta admit, beautiful as this place is, I'd sincerely hoped I'd never set foot here again. It's like a bad dream. Or . . . dark déjà vu?"

"I'm sorry to drag you here again," Hatta said. "And I promise I'll do everything in my power to return you home safely. Unfortunately, we can't go back the way we came. The nearest Gateway is to the north." He could imagine Anastasia's surprise when they popped up in her shop. "But without supplies, we'd never make it."

Chess folded his arms over his chest, brow furrowed. "Okay, so what do we do? Can't go back, can't go north, where *can* we go?"

Addison played his gaze over the glow, his mind working through the possibilities. There were some villages and towns within walking distance. Their group could make it to one of the more outlying settlements in a day or two, though he doubted showing up with the Black Knight in tow, reformed or not, would end well. And while Addison didn't care what happened to him, he wouldn't let his presence endanger his friends.

"There is a town maybe two days that direction." He pointed. "Possibly three, depending on your pace."

"Does cake come with picture?" Madeline demanded before he could continue.

Addison barely kept from grimacing. He supposed this should be expected. "Because I'm not going with you," he explained.

Three pairs of eyes widened, mouths dropping open in incredulity and likely protest.

He lifted his hands before anyone could voice the later. "I may be pardoned, but I doubt anyone else in Wonderland would be happy to have me show up on their doorstep. They might refuse to help because of me."

Maddi shook her head, all traces of her earlier fear gone, replaced with vexation. "Ice cream is for fish."

"That's not the point," Addison countered, feeling his own

irritation rise. "If I go, there's a chance we'll all be run off before we can ask for help!"

"Hold on," Courtney said, stepping forward. Chess kept a steadying hand at her back. She continued, "Are you trying to pull some 'it's better if you leave me behind' mess? Because, in case you forgot, you and I have already been through this."

The last time he had literally fallen into Wonderland, Courtney and Xelon had been with him. He'd been gravely injured and they'd been on the run. Then, like now, he'd told the others to go on without him. They'd refused.

"So you may as well pick another plan, because my answer hasn't changed," Courtney finished, folding her arms as well and sticking out her chin in defiance.

Chester didn't say anything, but it was obvious he agreed.

Madeline huffed in a silent "I told you so."

"Fine," Addison grumbled. "Fine!" He massaged the length of his nose, racking his brain for other options. "If we make for Legracia, there are a few places we can stop for clean water and forage a bit of food."

"Then that's the way we go," Courtney declared, then glanced around to see if the others were in agreement.

"Yeah, sounds good to me," Chess murmured.

Madeline remained silent, glowering at Addison.

"Very well, then." Addison turned in the general direction of the White Palace and started walking.

"Wait a second," Courtney called. "Before we go traipsing through the wilderness again, let's get everything out in the open. I don't want no creepy-crawlies or upset feelings sneaking up on us in the wilderness. That's what those monsters run on, right? So let's hear it. What's going on between you two?" She flapped a hand, indicating Addison and Madeline.

Addison sighed. "We really should get moving, I don't know if the Slithe will be able to follow us through."

"Fine," Courtney huffed. "Talk on the way. It'll be like listening to an audiobook." She strode forward and down the steps from the platform, tromping into the Glow.

Addison stared after her briefly before looking to Chester. "Is she always like this?"

Chess smirked. "This is actually pretty subdued. Count your lucky stars."

"Ahem!" Courtney's voice drifted back to them. "It's rude to leave a girl to get lost in a magic forest on her own without the entertainment she was promised!"

Blinking her maroon then lavender eyes, Madeline shot a look at Addison before hurriedly following after Courtney. Addison gestured for Chess to go ahead, and he brought up the rear.

The Glow was lovely as ever, undisturbed, for the moment, by the troubles of either world. The silvered branches and leaves glistened faintly in the daylight. All the flits and flowers were dormant, seeing as they were nocturnal, so the bell-like laughter that often hung on the wind was absent.

They walked in silence at first. Twenty minutes, maybe thirty. But eventually Courtney cleared her throat and declared, "I'm still waiting for my story. Don't think I forgot."

Addison barely bit back a groan. "Very well." He gestured to the sword over his shoulder. "This is the Vorpal Blade. The original, given to the original Black Knight, myself. After I was exiled, I was permitted to keep the sword for the sole purpose of putting down Nightmares when necessary. While it is not a Figment Blade and thus cannot *purge* a Nightmare, any it slays will take longer to re-form than if a regular sword were used. All of this can be done without invoking the sword's power, but . . ."

There was a brief moment of silence as everyone worked through what was said. Well, Chess and Courtney worked through it. He could practically see the process on their faces. Madeline, however, remained ahead of him and facing away, though her shoulders had hunched again.

"That's how you controlled the Slithe," Courtney mused. "How you were able to get us to the Gateway thingy."

"Yes," Addison admitted. "Though, technically, I couldn't control it. Not the way I was once able to. I could only hold it off long enough for us to make an escape." A stab of guilt moved through him. "Most of us, anyway."

"What do you think happened to Humphrey?" Chess asked quietly.

"There's no way to be sure. We can only hope for the best." And not just for Humphrey. There was no way to warn Alice, or anyone else, what awaited them at the pub. And even if there was, he had little idea what to do about it. Would a purge even work?

"Are you okay?" Chess's voice pulled Addison from his thoughts.

He glanced over to see the boy step in to help support a faintly panting Courtney.

"Just a little tired. I'll be all right," she said, waiving off concern as Madeline backtracked hurriedly to begin an examination.

Addison played his gaze over the injured girl, focusing in on how she favored her right leg slightly.

"There's a bit of lemon for the cake. Not to make a rabbit sing," Madeline admonished, her lips pursed.

Courtney and Chess simply blinked at her in that comically confused way Alice often did.

Addison smirked. "She said that you're healing well enough, but you shouldn't be on your feet right now. It might be exacerbating things."

"Well, we can fix that." Chess shifted around in order to kneel in front of Courtney, facing away from her. "All aboard," he called, grinning over his shoulder.

There was something . . . oddly familiar about his smile. It stuck in Addison's thoughts like a kernel of popcorn in one's teeth.

Courtney made a sound that was half laugh, half scoff. "You expect me to ride you all the way to Legra-place?"

"You expect to walk there?" Chess fired back at her. "I'm stronger than I look. Especially now. Climb on."

With obvious reluctance, and Madeline's aid, Courtney managed to clamber onto Chester's back. He got his arms beneath her knees and pushed to stand.

"You set back there?" he asked.

"I think I'm okay. This is weird, but okay," Courtney said.

"Let's keep moving, then," Hatta said. "Though please say something if you grow tired, Chester."

"I'm fine, for now." He started forward, with Madeline falling into step beside him. No doubt so she could keep a close eye on both of her patients.

Courtney, for her part, clung to Chess like a scared cat for the first few moments, but then eased her grip. At least enough to turn to face Addison.

"There's no chance you're gonna, like, go full Black Knight, is there?" Courtney asked. "I only ask because I don't think any of us can handle any more major betrayals right now. No offense," she said to Chess.

He grunted. "None taken. Though, technically, I was the only one who *wasn't* a Black Knight, thank you very much."

Addison smirked, though he couldn't maintain the expression. "I doubt it, but I can't outright ignore the possible effects that invoking the sword might have. The truth is, even before today, there has always been a chance I could revert. The Madness has been eating away at me since my time as the Black Knight, and while Madeline is able to successfully treat the malady, I can never be rid of it. Alone, there is little danger to anyone but myself. With the sword . . ." He considered his words carefully, not wanting to cause any undue stress or fear but not wanting to downplay the potential severity of the situation. "Let's say this. If Madeline feels the situation warrants being dealt with, defer to her."

Both Chester and Courtney turned to the poet at that. For her part, Madeline didn't appear outright troubled by the notion that she could at some point hold Addison's fate in her hand, but then again, why should she? That was true every day. Still, he could tell she was upset. At him more than the circumstances.

"No offense, again," Courtney started, "but I can barely understand her. You," she said directly to Madeline.

The poet simply chuckled, though there was no real mirth present. "There is to laugh but a not high on the winds of toast."

"She says none taken," Addison explained. "And while that's true, I doubt you'd have any trouble understanding her if things take that particular turn."

The story told and questions answered, the group lapsed into silence as they went, which was very different from what Addison was used to. Then again, his usual traveling companion was Alice. Something tugged at his heart at the thought of her, a mix of delight and worry. Lately, whenever trouble reared its head at the pub, it eventually made its way to her. Wherever she was, he hoped she was faring far better than him.

A few hours passed as they walked. There was little conversation, everyone left to their own thoughts and worries. Every now and again Courtney climbed down to walk on her own, or onto Addison's back in order to give Chester a rest.

Eventually, the group emerged from the trees onto a stretch of dirt. The beginnings of a road, Addison realized. Strange, he didn't remember any in this area. Then again, it looked relatively freshly formed. There were still patches of trodden grass scattered here and there, like small islands in a river.

"Recoup all the soup you can," Madeline murmured, surprise clear on her face.

"I don't know," Addison admitted. "There aren't any villages I know of out here. Looks like it heads north?" He glanced up and down the length of the road. "Or maybe south."

"Does either direction lead toward food?" Courtney half whined where she hung against Chester's back. "I'm not trying to be high maintenance here, but if I don't swallow some calories soon, I just may pass out."

"Wouldn't mind something myself," Chester murmured. He didn't look tired, but he certainly sounded it. Perhaps a brief break, then.

Addison hummed thoughtfully. "As a matter of fact . . ." He trailed off, then physically trailed off a short ways, gesturing for the others to remain where they were.

While the road was a new addition, the rest of the area was relatively unchanged. Which meant if he rooted around in this patch of bright blue bushes, careful to ignore the yellow thorns big as his fingers, he would find— "Aha," he said in triumph, plucking free a fleshy melancholy seed.

It was large as a grapefruit, colored blue with black spots on one side and completely white on the other. He plucked a few more, then made his way back over to the group to offer up his bounty.

"Dinner is served."

Chess lowered Courtney to stand as Madeline bit into a seed with a pleased sigh. Her eyes even rolled shut as she chewed.

Seeing this, Chester gave his a careful nibble. The taste of melancholy seeds was never the same twice, but they were always delicious. Chess clearly agreed judging by the way he went to town.

Courtney did not looked convinced. Despite both Chester and Madeline devouring their portions, she eyed hers like it might bite her instead. "What is this exactly?" she asked.

"Edible, which is what's important." Addison took a big bite, reveling at the tart and tangy taste. "Go on."

Her expression twisted, caught somewhere between intrigued and mildly disgusted.

"Alice makes that same face when she tries new foods from here," Addison remarked, with no small amount of joy at the thought.

"I can see why." Courtney finally bit into her helping. After a couple of seconds of chewing slowly, she lifted both brows. "Mmm! Tastes like a lime had a baby with a peach!"

"Knew you'd like it." Addison smirked and took another bite. "Take a moment to eat your fill, then we'll take a few for the road."

Courtney and Chess lowered themselves to sit, tilting into one another for support as they enjoyed their meal.

Madeline had moved off a short ways, already gathering fruit from nearby bushes.

Addison hesitated, debating whether to give her space or try to talk to her about, well, everything. After a minute or two of heated internal debate, he settled on something potentially in the middle: talk about anything else, and if she wished to discuss matters, he would let her bring it up.

"A shame melancholy seeds don't keep for more than a couple of days," he said as he drew near. "I'd like to think you'd come up with some fairly delicious concoctions if you could incorporate them into your recipes."

Madeline didn't look up from her harvesting but did respond. It was a start. "Rusted is a spoon. No stirring or writing since the quill has no ink."

"Vodka, I think. Maybe white rum."

"A blizzard roamed southward. Beneath the stars."

He blinked, tilting his head in thought. "I suppose you could try growing them. Don't know how they would take to earth soil. Perhaps putting them in the Glow would suffice."

She nodded in agreement, tucking a few more seeds into a makeshift pouch she'd fashioned from the light jacket she'd been wearing. She always said the pub was a little chilly.

"No weather warms winters," Madeline murmured, her hands falling still. She was finished, her "sack" full, but she didn't turn to him. Not yet.

"I know," he murmured, her words like stones in his heart. "And perhaps that makes me a coward. But seeing Humphrey vanish like that? I couldn't risk the rest of you . . ." His voice faltered, and he had to clear his throat to continue. "I couldn't lose anyone else."

Madeline turned to face him, finally. Her maroon, then silver eyes shone with unshed tears. "You could . . . lose . . . yourself . . ." she said, straining.

"Don't," he said quickly, concerned. "Don't force it. And you're right. I could. But that's about the only loss I'm willing to chance."

Madeline opened her mouth, clearly ready to protest, when a loud, shrill screech filled the air, taking the both of them by surprise.

"What the hell was that?" Courtney yelped as Chester shot to his feet.

The boy's hand went for a weapon at his left hip, then fell away slowly when he remembered he was unarmed.

"Nothing dangerous," Addison said, his gaze trained in the direction he thought he'd heard the sound. "At least, I don't think."

Another cry, this time closer, just as a cart rumbled into view at the far end of the road. A cloud of dust billowed in its wake. Pulling it was the source of the sound: a gryffthil, part bird, part horse. Lovely creatures, friendly as you please. It had been a while since he'd last laid eyes on one.

The cart approached them at a steady pace, and Addison gestured for everyone to clear the road. "Perhaps they can give us a ride," he thought aloud.

"What happened to people not liking you?" Courtney asked, sounding a little apprehensive.

"They might not, but I doubt there are more than two or three passengers, much safer than risking upsetting an entire town. If nothing else, they can take you three and—"

"No splitting the party," Chess interrupted.

"Fine," Addison sighed, waving a hand in greeting as the cart rumbled up to them.

A woman sat on the bench, guiding the beast with a steady hand on the reins. She pulled on it, drawing the gryffthil and thus the wagon to a halt.

Her bright face stuck out beneath the shadow of a wide-brimmed hat. Dark hair hung in a braid over her shoulder, and sharp green eyes played over Addison before moving past him to the others. Her attention lingered a bit longer on Courtney and Chess, before returning to him. "You good people lost?" she asked in English.

"On our way to Legracia," Addison offered. And that was all he offered, no need to go into detail.

"Same." The woman cracked a small smile.

Just over her shoulder, a slat in the wagon's front drew to the side, and another pair of eyes appeared to take in their little group.

"I'm Ramthe," the woman said, dipping her head.

"Greetings, Ramthe." Addison nodded. "This is Chester, Courtney, and Madeline. And you can call me A."

Ramthe arched an eyebrow. "A, huh? That short for something?"

Addison returned her small smile. "Always."

Ramthe snorted a laugh. "Cute."

Addison's smile widened. "I try. You say you're headed to Legracia?"

She nodded. "I imagine many are, given the state of things."

"And what state would that be?" he inquired, more than a little bit curious.

Ramthe didn't answer right away, instead lifting her brows as if surprised at the question. "You don't know about the attacks?"

Attacks? Addison's brow furrowed. He shook his head, truthfully surprised by the news.

"Nightmares." Ramthe lowered her voice, the words practically dripping with unfiltered hatred. "They seem to be all over, attacking the smaller villages and towns."

That was not a complete surprise. There had been increased

activity, but no outright attacks that he was aware of. "When?" he asked. "For how long?"

"Days now. Pinthiland was razed last night. The monsters struck without warning, tearing through houses, dragging people into the dark. Those they don't kill on the streets."

"Unfortunate, to say the least," Addison murmured, his frown deepening. Perhaps Humphrey's assumption was correct. Without the Bloody Lady to guide her mutated creatures, they were running rampant. And yet, something seemed off about this entire affair. So many random attacks, yet none close enough to the Gateway to betray the true numbers? And since when did Nightmares take prisoners?

"It's turning into a right mess," Ramthe said, drawing Addison from his thoughts. "Attacks on the main roads have people forging new ones." She gestured to the dirt beneath their feet. "The White Queen has opened the palace grounds and offered protection for any who seek it."

"I see," murmured Addison, tapping at his chin with the pad of one finger while he mulled all of this over.

If things were so dire, why hadn't he received word? Or any of the Gatekeepers? He shoved the line of thought aside for later. Right now, securing safe passage was the priority.

"I hate to ask," he began, setting a hand over his chest and bowing his head a touch. "But given the circumstances I must. Do you think we could ride with you as far as the castle gates?"

Ramthe's eyebrows lifted again, but she didn't say anything. It wasn't a yes, but it wasn't a no.

He continued, "Courtney is recovering from injury, and in no condition to travel so far on foot."

"Then why are you?" Ramthe asked. Her gaze pinged to his right shoulder, then back, no doubt noticing the hilt of his sword.

"Because we must. It's as simple as that." Addison held his arms out. "We can forage for our own meals, so you won't be out of any supplies. Chester and I can offer protection, in exchange."

There was a mumble from the slat, and Addison did his best not to glance that way. Ramthe leaned in, listening to whatever was said. After a moment, she nodded and glanced around. "It's gonna be nightfall soon. And I can't in good conscience just leave people stranded out here. Not with those monsters about."

Given the way the slat slammed shut, he imagined this wasn't the desired outcome.

"Thank you," Addison breathed, pouring as much relief into his tone as possible.

Ramthe nodded. "Three of you will have to climb into the back. One of you can ride with me."

Without a word, Madeline started toward the back of the cart. Chess glanced at Addison before moving to follow, taking Courtney with him.

"Guess that means I'm with you," Addison murmured.

"Guess so. Let's everyone get settled." She knocked against the front of the cart a few times.

At first nothing happened. Then she knocked again. Harder. "Cathsin! Don't be rude!"

With a bang, the back door swung open. "I'll show you *rude*," a woman called from inside. Definitely not the desired outcome.

Ramthe gave a bit of an embarrassed chuckle. "Don't mind her, she's just paranoid, what with . . . Well, you know."

"Indeed we do." Addison waited for the three of them to climb into the wagon. The door thudded shut, and the whole thing rocked slightly as everyone got settled inside.

When there were no shouts of surprise or pain, or calls for help, he moved to climb onto the bench beside Ramthe. "Thank you, again."

"You're welcome." Her gaze lingered at his shoulder briefly before she faced forward once more.

With a snap of the reins they were off, the cart lumbering down the road.

It didn't take long for the wagon to settle into a steady rhythm of creaking wheels and wood, though it did take longer than anticipated for the questions to begin.

"Sooooo." Ramthe drew the word out. "Would it be rude to ask what brings you three all the way out here with nothing between you but your wits and a single sword?"

Addison tilted back against the wagon proper, careful to keep one ear peeled for sounds of a struggle or anything from the cart. He wasn't normally so distrustful, but . . .

"We were attacked," he said. "Forced to run without time to bring anything with us. Took us by surprise."

She sniffed. "You and half the countryside."

"Things are truly that bad?" he asked.

"Worst they've been since the war. Don't know what's stirring them up, but I can't imagine it's good."

"Neither can I," Addison sighed.

Ramthe glanced his way briefly then back to the road. "We'll all be safe at Legracia, don't worry. The White Queen will know what to do. And maybe why the Gatekeepers aren't doing their damn jobs."

Addison did his best not to react to that, instead focusing on the road and keeping an eye out for possible trouble. "How long do you think it will take to reach Legracia?"

"Moonkin is one of the fastest critters around, aren't you, girl?"

The gryffthil cooed faintly, almost like a dove instead of the eagle the front half of her body resembled. "I figure she'll get us there in two, maybe three, days. Depends on how often and long we stop to rest. She's not used to carrying so many."

"Well then," Addison said, a smile dawning as his eyes moved to the creature. "I'll have to extend special thanks to our feathery friend here."

Ramthe smiled as well. "Her favorite snack is pop worms! That'll be plenty thanks."

"I'll be sure to procure at least a barrel once we reach the palace." With that promise, he settled in for the ride.

They made good time, thanks to Moonkin's remarkable stamina. By the time darkness fell, they'd already put plenty of miles behind them. Ramthe drew the wagon to a stop just long enough to light a couple of lanterns on either side of the driver's box. While she did so, Chess and Madeline climbed out to stretch their legs briefly, and Ramthe introduced Cathsin, her younger sister, who was most assuredly not happy with taking on additional riders but weathered it well enough. Courtney remained in the wagon, curled atop a pillow and sleeping off her hefty melancholy seed snack. Amusing how she'd been so apprehensive about them before.

Back on the road, they traveled for many hours more, until the gold lines of the Breaking started to crawl across the skies.

That's when Ramthe pulled on the reins. "Whoa, girl."

The gryffthil slowed to a trot and stopped off to the side of the road. Addison straightened in his seat, peering out into the night. So far, so good, no sign of Nightmares or any other troubles. But that could change in an instant.

"Cathsin, let's go." Ramthe knocked against the cart before dropping out of the box.

Addison climbed down as well. "Is there anything we can do to help?" He followed Ramthe around to where the door had swung open on the cart.

"Actually," she said as she reached to take a bag from Cathsin. "If you all prepare the fire while we prepare the food, it shouldn't take long at all!"

"Just tell us what to do." Addison offered an easy smile.

Between the lot of them, they were able to get a small camp fire set in a cleared-out spot and a meal cooking over it. Everyone gathered around as Ramthe passed out a bowl of something that smelled earthy.

Well, almost everyone. Madeline elected to remain in the cart, along with Cathsin. Chess sniffed at his bowl before trying a spoonful. Perking up, he ate eagerly.

Courtney eyed him while taking a few bites of her own. "Are you even tasting it?"

"Mm." Chess slurped rather enthusiastically. "It's pretty good. Better than anything you've ever cooked, so there's that."

"Ah!" she squeaked, affronted, though clearly for show. "I'll have you know my talents lie elsewhere! And you can't even manage Pop-Tarts without setting off a smoke alarm, so I wouldn't talk if I were you."

"It was one time," he countered, lifting a finger to indicate as much. "And your toaster has, like, eight hundred settings. Who needs that many options for heating up bread?"

Courtney sniffed indignantly as she took another bite. "Just because your palate is unrefined."

A light touch at Addison's elbow drew his attention away from the two friends. Ramthe held out a bowl for him. He took it with a quiet thanks.

"Those two argue like siblings," she remarked with a soft smile on her face while filling up a couple more bowls. "Are they?"

Addison shook his head while taking a bite. Chess was right; it was rather delicious. Hearty, though a little strong on the yarnl spices. "Just good friends. But who says friends can't be like family?"

Ramthe nodded in agreement as she gave the pot one last stir. "I'm going to take this to those two. Be right back." A bowl in each hand, she pushed to her feet and headed toward the cart. She clicked her tongue affectionately at Moonkin, who grazed nearby.

Madeline was seated on the wagon's foldout stairs, working a mortar and pestle she'd borrowed from the sisters. She'd agreed to make a few potions for them out of supplies they had in the cart. Nothing too fancy, something to bolster stamina and fight off aches and pains after days of riding in a wagon.

The poet glanced up when Ramthe approached and took the offered bowl with a smile. Ramthe then climbed into the cart to take a meal to her sister, who had elected to remain far away from the lot of them. Not fond of strangers, Ramthe had said in apology, been like that since they were little.

Madeline sniffed at the bowl curiously.

"How much longer till we get to wherever we're going?" Courtney asked around a yawn.

The question pulled Addison's attention toward her. "Another day, maybe two."

Chess tipped his bowl to drink the last of its contents, then smacked his lips lightly. "Wonderland food is pretty—" He paused to cover his own yawn. "Pretty good."

"Some of the best, depending who makes it," Addison said with a smirk while taking a few more bites.

Chess traced his finger along the inside of the bowl, then licked up whatever he'd gathered.

"There's more in the pot if you like," Ramthe called, amused as she retook her spot near the fire.

Chester's shoulders hunched sheepishly. "N-no, that's—" He yawned again. "That's okay."

"Stop! That's contagious!" Courtney complained while covering another yawn.

"I can't help it." Chess rubbed at his eyes.

"You two look tired as I feel." Ramthe kept stirring.

"It's been a long day," Addison murmured, surprised when his yawn set off another chain reaction. "Would have been even longer without your generosity."

Ramthe smiled, her face glowing in the blue light of the fire. "Think nothing of it . . ."

Something about her tone gave Addison pause. He lowered his bowl, studying her profile. She continued to stir the pot, the ladle scraping the sides slowly, almost rhythmically.

"Did anyone else want seconds?" she asked, her voice like a song.

Addison shook his head, then instantly regretted it when things went a bit fuzzy. "No, thank you, it . . . we . . ." There was supposed to be more to that sentence, he was sure of it. And he'd wanted to ask a question, but the words jumped right out of his brain. Why was it so hard to think?

Fwump.

Chester's bowl hit the ground with a muted thud just before he slumped over onto his side.

Courtney giggled and poked at Chester's head where it had

fallen across her lap. "Someone's got the iiiitiiiiiiis," she sang dreamily, then yawned wide.

Addison chuckled. Wait, no, this wasn't funny! He gave himself another shake, harder this time. That started a faint throbbing between his ears. "Wh-what . . ."

"No!" The shout came from near the cart.

He whirled that direction, nearly pitching himself over, to spy Madeline and Cathsin rolling in the dust, grappling with one another.

"Soup!" Madeline screeched. "Drugged!"

It took a second for the words to slot themselves into Addison's addled mind. The whole of him went cold, his eyes dropping to his bowl. Bowls? His vision doubled.

Oh no . . .

"Damn it all, Cat, you had one job!" Ramthe was on her feet and tromping toward the two wrestling girls.

Addison wanted to go after her, but his body refused to listen to his orders to stand up. "Ma . . . ddi . . ."

"Addison! Get up!" Madeline landed a blow that sent Cathsin rolling, then pushed to her feet. Her bright pink eyes widened, and she recoiled as Ramthe snatched at her.

"Get over here, you little—" Ramthe tried again, but Madeline was small and quick, ducking out of reach, her frightened gaze flickering between her assailant and Addison. She was outnumbered, and he was powerless to help.

Run, he wanted to say, but his mouth wasn't obeying him any longer, either. His eyelids grew heavier and heavier, his entire body tingling. ***Run!*** He urged silently.

With one last desperate glance, Madeline turned and darted into the night. Addison felt both relieved and frightened for her. While

Madeline had escaped whatever these two had planned, she now had to face whatever was out there alone.

Ramthe cursed before bending to help her sister. "Now, how'd you let her get the better of you?"

"Oh, shut it. This is your fault regardless." Cathsin held one hand over her left eye. "Stopping for vagrants."

Ramthe waved her off. "These aren't no vagrants. At least, that one isn't." She approached the fire, her eyes on Addison.

Shockingly, he managed to lift his chin just enough to meet her gaze as she stood over him, glowering at him with a look that sent a chill down his spine. "No, this one's not a vagrant at all. Pretty manners, prettier words. This one's been to court."

Cathsin's visible eyebrow shot up.

Addison's vision waned.

"Attendants?" Cathsin asked.

Everything started to go dark.

"No." Ramthe's voice still drifted in, crystal clear. "Look at his weapon. I'd wager we've got ourselves a knight. And I think I know which one . . ."

Twenty-Six

MY LADY

Humphrey repeated the words that had been drawn from him. "... I know you ..."

A slow smile broke across Nana K's face. "Yes. You do."

"Well, I don't!" Alice's mother stepped forward. Her wide brown eyes moved back and forth between them. "I don't know anything apparently! Where are we, what's happening, who is this? Am I dead? I can't be dead, Jesus help me—"

"You're not dead, Tina. You're lost. We all are."

Humphrey stared at the two of them, the buzzing in his ears intensifying once more. His thoughts kept drifting in and out of reach, unable to fully form, except for one. *I know you ...*

"But you're lost in more ways than one, aren't you?"

It took a second for him to realize the older woman was speaking to him. He nodded, slowly, certain that moving his head too quickly would worsen the pain. "You could say that."

Alice's mother—Tina, he'd heard—scoffed and started pacing. "That doesn't tell me where we are!"

"One thing at a time, Missy." Nana K took a slow breath and lowered herself to the ground.

Tina threw her arms into the air while shouting about . . . something; he couldn't make out her words.

No, he heard the words just fine, they just weren't coming out of her mouth. Or Nana K's.

Then who . . .

"One thing at a time, Emalia," this new voice said, wafting in from somewhere to the side. No, above. "Too risky. That's why you can't go through with it. Not when there's still Etton village, the cover, the northern fields, the Nox itself."

Humphrey glanced this way and that, trying to pinpoint where the words were coming from, but the moment he took his eyes away from the two women, they and the forest faded like an old photograph, until the trees were replaced by canvas walls lined with banners depicting scenes of battle and triumph.

He was standing in the middle of a tent, he realized. Furnished for one, but you could have fit at least a dozen people in there, maybe twice that. Torches burned with yellow flame, casting sunny shadows over the trappings here and there: a nearby table covered in picked-over food, a dressing screen to the side, a bed that looked very slept in, and beside it, a rack holding a set of bright red armor.

At the center of the space, a woman bent over a round table strewn with maps depicting various terrains and covered in battle figures. She frowned, her dark brown face pinched in concern. When she moved, to adjust a formation or reposition a marker, a thick band of bright red braids slid against her back where they were tied off. "I can feel you glaring, Emalia," she muttered without looking up.

Another woman, Emalia, stood on the opposite side of the table, tapping her gauntleted fingers against her folded arms. "If you looked up from your maps for more than two seconds, you'd see me glaring, too." She wore a suit of white armor, dented here and there, smudged and scuffed from recent battle. Snowy hair flowed down her back and framed her white face, which was presently flushed with anger.

Behind her stood a girl, her hair equally snowy with eyes to match. She wore acolyte robes instead of armor, though cradled Emalia's helmet in her hands.

Emalia, who began to pace on her side of the table, shook her head. "One thing at a time will have us losing more ground! We have to act soon, or she'll catch up with us; then all is lost."

The first woman chuckled faintly, the sound rich. "Patience never was your strongest suit, little sister."

Emalia snorted. "Patience doesn't win wars."

The other woman arched an eyebrow. "Doesn't it? Humphrey?"

Humphrey felt himself bow. "Yes, Princess."

"You have news from the south?"

He cleared his throat. "The situation in the meadows is dire. Our forces received a devastating blow to our numbers, which then bolstered the enemy's, to a slight degree. We were able to hold the line, but the Duchess said it will falter with another attack if they don't receive reinforcements."

The woman sighed as her eyes slipped shut. "Reinforcements we don't have . . ."

Emalia grunted in displeasure, bordering on disgust. "We're letting criminals lead battalions now? This isn't smart."

"Anastasia has proven herself on more than one occasion." The woman tucked a loose red braid behind her ear. "And we need all of the help we can get if we're going to—"

"Majesties!" interrupted a voice from outside the tent just before the flap was thrown aside to admit sunlight and yet another figure clad in white armor. A knight. She quickly strode up to the table, removing her helmet as she went. Dark hair fell free around her face and shoulders. She took a knee. "My ladies."

"Catch your breath, Romi," Emalia urged. "Then speak."

"Thank you," the knight, Romi, sighed before raising her head. Her face was rosy with exertion, and her eyes glinted with urgency. "Scouts say Nightmares approach Ahoon. They'll reach the village before sundown."

The woman near the map frowned. "How many?"

"An estimated thirty. Possibly more." Romi pushed to stand. "*He's* with them." Her tone dipped, jaw tight.

Humphrey felt his entire body tense. Metal creaked as his hold tightened on his own helmet tucked into the crook of his arm. *Addison* . . .

Emalia's eyes widened before she flung a look across the table at her sister. "What do we do, Kashaunte?"

A sound like rushing water filled Humphrey's ears. He knew that name.

Kashaunte . . .

Princess Kashaunte. *Queen* Kashaunte.

He frowned, blinking rapidly, trying to hear what was being said over the noise of his racing heart. Why did he feel so panicked all of the sudden?

"Ready your cavalry." Kashaunte tapped a finger against the map. "We'll set up defenses here and here. The archers can form ranks behind."

Emalia nodded before turning to sweep from the tent, her brilliant blue cape flowing behind her. The girl holding her helmet followed, then Romi. Only Kashaunte remained.

Humphrey chewed at his lower lip as anger, hurt, and no small amount of reluctance warred within him. "We've never won a battle when he was there."

"I know." Kashaunte stepped behind the dressing screen nearby, waving her hands as she went. The suit of red armor lifted from its place and drifted over to her. He could see her silhouetted form moving, limbs lifting and falling as it was fastened into place.

Humphrey cleared his throat and stood a little straighter before saying, "If Your Highness will permit me . . ."

"Speak."

"It's not a good idea for you or Princess Emalia to join the front. Romi and I are quite capable of—"

"I've no doubt you are." Kashaunte stepped from behind the screen, fully armored, redoing the tie that kept her braids back. "But my sister and I cannot hide from this, no matter how we may wish to." She plucked her helmet from the armor stand and came around the table to face him. "We will fight this darkness together." Her hand fell to his shoulder with a soft clank.

"Together," he repeated, nodding.

He shouldn't have moved his head so quickly; it started to pound again. The pain sent spots dancing across his vision. He blinked to try and focus, but everything swirled together. The princess, the tent, all of it a maelstrom of light and color that threatened to swallow him whole.

Then it all vanished, and he was left kneeling in a forest with two women standing over him; Alice's mother, Tina, and Nana K.

K.

"Kashaunte?" The name tumbled from his lips in a bewildered whisper. "Queen Kashaunte."

Whatever animated conversation the other two had been engaged in quieted. The world seemed to go still.

For weeks Humphrey had been haunted by a past he could not remember, a life he no longer lived. Surviving on puzzle pieces provided by forgotten friends desperate to regain what was lost. *Who* they'd lost.

All lost things are waiting to be found in the In-Between.

While he couldn't say he'd found himself just yet—there was still so much he didn't know, couldn't remember—one truth seemed to snap together in his mind. It wasn't a complete picture, but it was enough for him grasp the edges of his former self.

He was the Red Knight, and this woman, Nana K, was . . . "My Lady," he murmured, shifting once more to kneel, his head bowed low. "My Queen."

One of the women drew a sharp breath. Then silence stretched between them for several long seconds before Tina took a slow breath and declared, "The fuck you say?"

Twenty-Seven
GONE

Alice couldn't tell how long they'd been riding along in the basket, only that she'd nodded off once and her stomach was starting to get angry. She ignored its burbling protests, instead focusing on the current conversation.

She finished explaining the events that led to her arrival in the In-Between. From the Nightmares born of her dagger to her Nana K's secret magic! Then the Slithe that had dragged her family away . . .

The way her stomach twisted now had nothing to do with hunger. She brushed at some purple sand still clinging to her now dry clothes, trying not to think about the numerous ways her mother and grandmother could find themselves in trouble out here.

"Whoa," Dem murmured. "Magic grandmothers. Not the worst thing in the world."

Alice snorted. He had a point.

"Is it really so strange?" Dee asked. "You have powers."

"I'm a Dreamwalker, we all have powers."

"Not like you," Dem countered.

She arched an eyebrow in question.

"I saw you, the night we were attacked while escorting the princess and Xelon to the pub? I saw what you did with the sword. The light?"

Alice froze. She remembered that night.

Xelon had been hurt, was going to die! Alice had somehow used her sword to hurl blades of energy at the Fiends closing in on the injured knight, driving them off.

She snorted. "I didn't think you saw that," she said quietly, lifting her knees and wrapping her arms around them.

"Of course I saw it!" Dem said. "It was one of the coolest things I'd *ever* seen!"

"Why didn't you say anything?"

He shrugged. "You didn't look like you wanted to talk about it."

"Huh . . ." Sometimes Dem's insightfulness surprised her. Dee was usually the more aware of the two.

"Anyway," Dem continued. "I talked to Dee about it. He said we should wait to bring it up until you do."

"Maybe you get your magic from your grandmother," Dee offered helpfully.

"Maybe," Alice agreed, then groaned. If that was the case, where the hell did Nana K get hers?

Brrrglglglglgllg. Her stomach shared her sentiment.

"Ugh . . . I'm starving," she lamented. "And I can't think on an empty stomach."

"You're leaning against a literal biscuit." Dem didn't open his eyes as he spoke.

"That we're not supposed to eat yet. For whatever reason." Though it was tempting as hell. Pushing to her feet, Alice shifted as she adjusted her balance for Sprigs's gait, then wandered over to sit in front of the twins, away from the biscuit and thus temptation.

She was lowering herself when the basket gave a sudden shudder and she toppled over backward. The twins shifted as well, throwing their arms out to hold their balance.

"Here we go," Sprigs's voice called.

There was a shift and then sunlight poured in around them. Alice shielded her eyes, blinking to clear her vision, before Sprigs's massive brown face appeared above them. "We're here. The chasm. The only way out of the In-Between."

"Where up is down," Alice murmured, recalling the old man's words from her last visit.

Sprigs smiled. "Exactly. When you land, split the biscuit between the three of you. Start with small bites, don't wanna have too much."

"Wait." Dee sat forward, alarm slowly spreading across his expression.

"Land?" Dem frowned.

"You two should brace yourselves," Alice said, moving to press against the wall.

Sprigs's smile widened. "Good luck."

The lid closed, blocking out the sun once again. Alice took a deep breath.

Then her stomach dropped as the basket and everything in it plummeted into the breach.

◊ ◊ ◊

"One, two, three, push!" Alice counted down, then threw her weight against the lid of the basket. The twins did the same, the three of them grunting with combined effort.

Of course the basket had landed against something that blocked their exit, so they had no choice but to try and pry open the top.

"One more time," Alice panted, adjusting her stance. "One, two, three, *push!*"

The three of them roared with their efforts, giving it everything they had, until, finally, the lip popped open and sent them spilling into the night.

"Oh thank god," Dem grumbled as he rolled onto his back on the ground. "Freedom."

Alice pushed to her feet, brushing off her butt as she took in their surroundings.

Starlight and moonlight filtered through the canopy above. So did the brilliant gold of the Breaking. They were definitely in Wonderland proper, though she couldn't begin to guess where exactly. Last time she fell from the In-Between she'd landed near the Eastern Gateway, clear across the world.

"Well." Dem clapped his hands together, glancing around. "We'll have to thank him for dropping us in the middle of nowhere, at night, all while we're perfectly bite-sized."

"Quit your crying." Dee clambered his way back into the basket. "This isn't the first time we've been here at night. And the old man said this would help with the being-small part."

Alice followed, though not before wedging a small rock into the opening to keep it propped up.

It was dark inside, but she could just make out Dee's lithe form as he chopped at the biscuit with his sword. Three fairly equal chunks about the size of Bundt cakes soon rested at his feet. Alice bent to snag one while he hefted the other two, offering one to his brother when they rejoined him outside.

"What did he say?" Alice asked as she turned the pastry over in her hands. It was light and fluffy, a few pieces crumbling between her fingers. Perfect, really. Her stomach gave an eager grumble.

"Start with small bites," Dee said. "Like a mouse."

"He did not say 'like a mouse,'" Dem countered.

"It was an example!"

"Guys!" Alice cut in before another argument could start. "Eat, then fight."

Glowering at one another, the twins took simultaneous bites of their biscuit chunks. Alice did as well, delightfully surprised to find it tasted like brownies. She was so delighted, she took another bite before she could help herself.

"How long until it works?" Dem asked around a mouthful.

Alice started to say that she didn't know, but a sudden twist in her stomach knocked the wind and the words right out of her. Heat flashed through her limbs, followed by an uncomfortable tingling. Then her insides quivered right before she shot upward into the sky, the branches overhead rushing toward her. Only her feet never left the ground.

She was growing, she realized. The sudden rise left her light-headed.

An elbow caught her in her side. She grunted in pain, stumbling off a short distance in a flail of limbs. Behind her the twins windmilled similarly, battering one another on accident. Maybe they should have spaced themselves out.

Alice patted herself down. All body parts accounted for, and the correct size.

"Bozhe moi . . ." Dem murmured. Or maybe Dee. She couldn't tell when they were quiet like that.

She glanced up to find the two of them staring at her, eyebrows raised. "What?" she asked.

Dem aimed a finger at her. "Were you always that tall?"

It was then that she realized she was looking down at him. At both of them. Her hand went to her mouth, eyes wide. She'd taken two bites, she realized. Damned sweet tooth. *Good job, Kingston. How the hell you gonna explain this?*

She had no idea, nor the time to come up with one, because a sudden rush of sound and movement exploded from the nearby underbrush and a figure came careening toward them in the dark.

Whoever it was didn't get more than a few steps before Dem had a blade to their neck. They screamed, blinking wide blue, then purple eyes. Dem yanked his weapon away, recoiling as a shocked "Maddi!?" left his lips.

The mousy girl was clearly frantic about something, face streaked with tears, the whole of her shaking like a leaf.

Alice hurried forward, arms out to wrap her friend. "What are you doing here? What's wrong? What happened?!"

Maddi shrugged off the hug, practically shoving Alice away. "Echoes! Echoes and not!" she cried, instead latching on to Alice's wrist and hauling her forward.

Alice let herself be tugged along. "Whoa, calm down, I don't—"

"No! Not a how, please!" Maddi pulled harder, dragging Alice now.

"I think she wants us to follow," Alice called over her shoulder as she broke into a jog, trailing after the bartender.

The four of them practically plowed through the undergrowth, though Alice was slowed now and again by having to pick her way over roots and around boulders with her bare feet. Twice Maddi pulled ahead and Alice nearly lost her in the night, calling for her to slow down.

Maddi shouted nonsense and gestured impatiently each time.

Finally, they broke free of the trees onto an empty dirt road. Maddi stopped in the middle of it. Her fingers curled into her fists as she panted, her chest heaving, her head whipping back and forth.

"No," Maddi gasped. She jogged over to a small clearing on the side of the path, up to what looked like a fire pit. A few embers still glowed blue between rocks.

"What is this place?" Alice asked, following her.

"No, no no!" Maddi pressed her hands to the sides of her head. "A rumor. A whisper. Gone. Not at all. Not at all!"

Dee and Dem joined them, both boys scanning their surroundings, alert.

Watching the other girl, Alice felt her stomach clench anxiously. "Maddi, I know it hurts to talk like us, without your potion? But none of us can understand what you're trying to say."

Maddi whimpered, scrubbing at her face before swatting her cheeks with her hands. "You must . . . *you* must."

"Slowly," Alice coaxed. She set a hand on the mousy girl's shoulder. "Take your time."

The twins gathered in close to listen.

Maddi took a careful breath. Her face twisted in pain, her lips quivering as they worked to form words.

"Addison. Courtney. Chester. Captured . . . Gone."

Twenty-Eight
SIR ADDISON HATTA

Addison rocked with the swaying of the cart. With his hands tied behind him, he had no way to brace himself when they hit a bump or hole. To his left, Chess lay similarly bound, still unconscious thanks to whatever had been slipped into their food. Courtney was knocked out as well and tucked against Addison's other side, her head resting on his shoulder, her hands in front of her.

Across from him, Cathsin sat with her bright yellow gaze trained on them. Her jaw set, her lips pursed. She held the sheathed Vorpal Blade against her lap.

Addison shifted slightly and immediately regretted it when pain shot through his torso. His ribs were definitely bruised, if not broken. It could have been worse. Much worse.

After Madeline disappeared into the dark, Cathsin and Ramthe had gathered around their trio of drugged captives.

For a moment, neither of them had said a word. They simply

stood in shared silence, watching. Waiting. What for, he couldn't fathom.

Then Ramthe lashed out, delivering a sharp kick to his side that sent him sprawling. Any attempt to pick himself up was met with a similar blow. Then another. And another. Even when he lay still, she kicked, and kicked, until the whole of him throbbed with it.

Finished, she stumbled backward, her chest heaving, her pale face slick from her efforts. Addison could only stare up at her, helpless as pain radiated through his body.

"Is . . . is that really necessary?" Cathsin had asked as she bent to retrieve the Vorpal Blade where it had fallen a short distance away.

"You have no idea," Ramthe muttered darkly.

Cathsin turned the sword over in her hands. "It *is* a fine bit of craftsmanship. You can tell by the hilt alone."

Addison coughed as his lungs fought to take in air. "You're . . . bandits?"

"You take that back!" Cathsin hissed. Then she bit into her lower lip. "What I mean is . . . n-no, we're not. We just . . . I don't . . . It was Ramthe's idea."

"Cathsin," Ramthe said in a warning tone.

"Well, it was! All because you saw this." Cathsin held up the blade, then looked to Addison. Her face twisted a little as she took in his state. "Sorry about my sister, I don't know why sh—"

"Don't apologize!" Ramthe roared. "Not to him!"

Cathsin, her shoulders rounded, took a couple steps back. "Heavens, fine! You don't have to shout." Her attention returned to the sword. She'd started to unsheathe it before Ramthe clamped a hand down over the one wrapped around the hilt.

"Don't!" Ramthe had hissed, her eyes wide in the light of the fire. "Don't release that thing."

Cathsin frowned. "What . . . what's wrong with it?"

"It belongs to a monster." Ramthe knifed a glare at Addison.

Cathsin, clearly confused, glanced between her sister and their captives. "Now's not the time to talk in riddles."

"You *dare* show your face here again? Now?" Ramthe's voice was low and laced with barely contained hatred. Her gaze remained locked on Addison. "When our homes, our families, are being ripped apart by those beasts! *Your* beasts."

Cathsin, her irritation waning, reached to set a hand on her sister's arm. "Ramthe?"

Ramthe's fingers curled into fists at her sides. "Da said it was foolish to leave you alive," she bit out at Addison, ignoring her sister's attempts to offer comfort. "That it would only end badly. But Mother said we should trust the judgment of the new queens." She scoffed. "And here we are."

Addison had tried to focus on what was being said, to form a response, but the drug in his system dulled more than his senses.

"What, no words?" Ramthe asked. "No excuses?"

Cathsin once again glanced between Addison and her sister. "What's going on? Who is this?"

"This, dear sister, is the venerable Sir Addison Hatta of the high realm," Ramthe spat the words.

Cathsin actually gasped, one hand going to her mouth. She stared, wide-eyed, in horror.

"Deserter. Traitor. Murderer," Ramthe continued. "Monster. The Black Knight. I thought I recognized you, but I wasn't sure. Until I saw your sword." She aimed a finger at the weapon now clutched to her sister's chest. "After watching, helpless, as it cut down my brother, I'd know that vile thing anywhere."

Cathsin flung the sword away. It hit the ground with a heavy thunk and a faint whisper only Addison could hear. If he could get his hands on it . . .

"Pack up," Ramthe barked, interrupting his already shaky train of thought. "We're leaving."

Cathsin blinked out of her terrified stupor, her fingers tugging at the ends of sleeves frayed from years of anxious fidgeting. "What about the girl that ran away? Madeline?"

Ramthe busied herself with putting out the fire. "It doesn't matter. If she's with him, the woods can have her."

"And these two?" Cathsin gestured at Chess and Courtney.

Ramthe eyed them for barely a second. "Slit their throats."

"What?!" Cathsin squeaked.

"Don't!" Addison shouted, pushing himself onto one arm. The effort left him dizzy.

"Give me one good reason why we shouldn't," Ramthe demanded.

Cathsin stared at her sister, mouth agape. Clearly this wasn't part of their impromptu plan. "Rammy . . ."

Ramthe kept her eyes on Addison. "Why shouldn't I?" There was a dangerous edge to her voice.

"Because," Addison panted around the pain eating at his insides. "They're my protégés. Dreamwalkers."

The girls exchanged a glance.

"The Dreamwalker from the West is said to be a girl," Cathsin said. "But that doesn't explain him."

"With Nightmare activity picking up, it seemed prudent to train a second." Addison continued to fight the drug. He'd only ingested a few spoonfuls, so it likely wasn't a full dose, but whatever they'd used was slowly winning. Darkness pressed at the edges of his vision, unconsciousness likely beyond.

Ramthe straightened. "And this is reason enough to spare them because?"

Good. They believed him. "Your grievance is with me, and I gladly bear that weight, but they are innocent. And I don't imagine killing humans would go over well with the Queens, especially since that's what started this whole mess to begin with."

Cathsin bit into her lower lip. "He's right," she started quietly.

"I don't care," Ramthe said.

Cathsin frowned. "We can't kill Dreamwalkers."

"Can't we?" Ramthe demanded. "Who will know? Who will care?"

"I will!" Cathsin raised her voice, surprising both her sister and herself. She cleared her throat, averting her gaze briefly. "They're not part of this. It wouldn't be right."

For a moment, it seemed as if Ramthe would simply ignore her sister's plea and put an end to the three of them right then and there. But then, thankfully, the lines in her face eased. She released a breath. "Fine," she muttered.

Cathsin seemed to deflate as well, this time with relief. "What do we do with them?" she asked.

"Take them back to the Gateway," Addison offered. "Let them go home."

Ramthe snorted. "And put you in a better position to get away or for someone on your side to mount a rescue? No. You escaped justice once." She stepped over Addison in order to approach Chess and Courtney, kneeling to shake their shoulders. When neither roused the barest bit, she nodded. "Sound asleep. Good. We'll take them with us."

Surprise flickered over Cathsin's face. "And do what with them? Do what with *any* of them?"

"We sell the sword." Ramthe started packing up their gear. "We drop the Dreamwalkers in a town and keep going. And him." She looked to Addison again. "Him we make suffer, like he made Jalsin suffer. Either way, we need to get a move on, in case his little friend doubles back and tries to attack us in our sleep."

And so they were loaded into the back of the wagon, Addison moving on shaky legs, and Chess and Courtney all but hauled in like sacks of potatoes. He hoped this didn't aggravate her injuries.

The sisters spoke in hushed tones, almost too low for him to hear, but he picked up on a few words and phrases. They were trying to decide on where to dump the Dreamwalkers. It sounded like Legracia was the closest option, but maybe not the smartest. A decision was made, but he didn't hear it. Cathsin joined them in the cart while Ramthe took the reins once again, and they set off.

Now here they were, with the three of them still trussed up and Cathsin settled in, the Vorpal Blade across her lap. She clutched her own weapon, a short sword that could do with a bit of sharpening, her eyes trained on them.

Addison glanced at Chess, who'd started to snore. Courtney remained silent. And Madeline . . . Strewth, he hoped Madeline was able to get away safely, find shelter before anything that went bump in the night caught up with her.

At least she was free. Now he had to work on that for the others.

"Will your sister keep her word?" he asked quietly. "Will she let them go?"

Cathsin bristled slightly. "Ramthe is not a liar."

"But she *is* angry," Addison said softly. "And rightfully so."

"It's you she's angry at. *We're* angry at."

"Mmm." Addison tilted back against the side of the cart. "Anger makes people do things. Things they normally wouldn't. Especially anger fueled by pain." He shut his eyes, and an image of Portentia curled atop a small crystal coffin played against the backs of his lids. His chest tightened with a sudden swell of emotion that accompanied it.

"She's not a liar," Cathsin repeated.

And the Queen wasn't a murderer, he wanted to say. *Not at first. Neither was I.* But he swallowed those words. "I'm glad. Thank you for agreeing to spare them."

"Keep your thanks," Cathsin snapped, but she didn't sound nearly as menacing as her sister.

"If it's any consolation, I have nothing to do with the Nightmares on the loose right now."

"No?" She gave a faint laugh. "You just happen to be wandering around with this while they're out here roaming the wilds?"

He cracked his eyes open to find her clutching his sword in a death grip.

"We were actually running from them," he said. "The four of us." Worry ate at him even more now, for Madeline. She was a capable Poet, and would likely be able to survive off the land for a bit, but she wasn't a fighter. And if Nightmares were indeed running loose in Wonderland . . .

But he couldn't think about that now. He had to focus on getting them out of here, especially if he wanted to go back for her.

"Running from them? I thought the Black Knight controlled them," Cathsin said.

"He did. Or I did. But that was a long time ago." He rolled his shoulders and winced in regret. His ribs, while healing, were still sore. "As part of my exile, I gave that power up. Hell, I would've given it up anyway. I didn't want to be part of that anymore . . ." He released a slow sigh.

"Then why do you have the sword?" she asked.

"It was the only way to escape with our lives."

And he recounted what had happened, how Nightmares had taken the shape of their friends, ambushed them. How these new creatures, these Wraiths, were rising in number. How that sludge had swallowed Humphrey whole—though he didn't mention his name—and nearly got the rest of them, but he'd made the decision to use the sword and what little influence he could muster to hold the darkness back while they fled.

"We were on our way to Legracia, to warn Her Majesty, when our paths crossed with yours."

Cathsin looked disbelieving, but only barely. "If you didn't summon the Nightmares that've been rising, then . . . who did?"

"That's what we're trying to find out. Or were, before we were attacked." He shifted, trying to get comfortable. His shoulders were starting to ache, and his arms were starting to tingle. "We have an idea, but we can't be sure. We were hoping Her Majesty could help with that, as well. If you're going to kill me, and I very much believe that's the end goal, please carry this message of warning to the Queen in my stead. Something is stirring up Nightmares, and new evils. You've already seen the results, and I fear this is only the beginning."

Heavy silence filled the space between them, save for the faint creak of wood as the cart swayed, the roll of the wheels, and the clomping of the gryffthil's hooves and feet.

Cathsin opened her mouth to speak, but it was Ramthe's voice that spilled in through the little slat in the front wall.

"You expect us to believe what comes out of your mouth." She huffed a laugh. "Like you won't say whatever you need to, to save your skin."

Addison gingerly rolled his shoulders. "I have no reason to lie, especially about something that would implicate me as culprit. And especially when there's no chance you'd believe it. But something *is* happening, and Legracia needs to be warned. All of Wonderland does."

Ramthe shot a glare through the slat. "Just . . . shut up. I don't want to hear another word out of your mouth, or I'll stop this wagon, come back there, and cut your tongue out to give to Moonkin for breakfast."

The gryffthil gave a short call at the sound of her name.

"And I'll cut out the humans' for lunch," Ramthe continued.

Cathsin frowned. "You said they could live."

"And they can. Tongues are optional for survival." The slat slammed shut.

Addison fell silent, his eyes trailing from the now closed slat to Cathsin. She looked uncertain as she settled back into her spot, lowering her weapon.

"Please," he said, quieter this time. "No one else should pay for my mistakes."

Cathsin lowered her gaze to her lap. "My mother used to say that time was the only one who could know a person fully. It would reveal who they truly were in the end. Seemingly good people would be shown to be villains. And seemingly evil ones heroes." Her eyes lifted, rimmed with tears. "I miss her. And my brother."

Addison remained silent. He doubted his condolences would mean much more than hollow niceties.

"Neither of them would approve of anyone innocent being punished," she went on. "Ramthe has her heart set on vengeance. I don't think I can change her mind about you, but I'll do what I can about your friends."

"That's all I ask." Addison looked to the sleeping boy as well.

"Whatever was in that stew looks to have really done a number on them." His attention moved back to Cathsin. "Are either of you Poets?"

A bit of color touched Cathsin's cheeks. "I dabble, from time to time. Father didn't approve. Still doesn't."

"If it's any consolation, I work with one of the best Poets in all Wonderland. She'd be impressed, I think." If she hadn't been chased into the night, but he kept that part to himself for the moment.

"I doubt it. It's just a sleeping draft, and it didn't even put you under for very long."

"It's not your fault. I have fairly potent potions and poisons moving through my veins; nothing else has much of an effect unless mixed for compensation."

Cathsin hummed thoughtfully, no doubt mentally adjusting her mixtures for possible future droughts. Not that it mattered, he wasn't going to be eating or drinking anything else they offered.

"They should come around in another hour or two," Cathsin said quietly.

Addison nodded. Hopefully, that would be all the time he needed to come up with a proper plan to get out of here, and not die trying.

◊ ◊ ◊

The cart finally rolled to a stop, rocking a bit more forcefully. Addison blinked away the vestiges of fatigue as Chess finally stirred beside him. Courtney, however, remained unmoving. It was only thanks to the slow rising and falling of her chest that Addison could tell she was still with them.

Chess grunted and groaned, tugging weakly where his arms were bound behind his back. "W-what?" he rasped.

"Shhh," Addison cautioned.

Across from them, Cathsin shifted slightly where she'd drifted off. She still clutched his sword and her own weapon, though her hold had slackened.

Chess jerked upright as his mind finally caught up with what was happening. He glanced around, his eyes pinging immediately to the sleeping girl on Addison's other side.

"Courtney," he whispered urgently. "Courtney!"

"She's fine. Relatively. Now, shhh." Addison kept his own voice low.

Chess turned wide eyes toward him, still understandably panicked about waking up like this. That's when Addison noticed their violet coloring. Strange, for a human.

"We're *all* fine," he continued. "At least for now."

Chess panted, twisting his wrists. "What . . . what happened? Where are we?" He glanced around the cart. "Where's Maddi? I . . . everything's all fuzzy."

"We've been taken captive. She escaped." Hopefully she would avoid harm and find her way to safety.

"Captive? What . . . why is . . . ." Chess winced and sagged back against the wall.

"You all right?"

"Pins and needles in my arm. Think I slept on it wrong. Dizzy."

"Work your wrist, gently. Don't burn yourself on the rope. And go slow, the drug is still in your system."

The door yanked open, pouring daylight into the space.

Cathsin jerked upright, glancing around in surprise. The weapons tumbled from her lap and she snatched them up, blinking against the brightness.

"Good morning." Ramthe stood silhouetted against the light. "Cathsin, a word."

Cathsin spared Addison a glance before moving to step out of the cart. There was a brief pause where he was certain Ramthe was glaring at him, then she slammed the door.

The girls' voices picked up, their words muffled but their tones clear. Ramthe was upset about something. He could guess what.

The voices quieted as they moved away from the back of the cart.

"All right, we don't have much time," Addison said. "How's your arm?"

"Still tingly, but fine. Why did they do this?"

"Pain makes people do many things." The memory of Portentia tried to press in, but he pushed it back. "They have their reasons. This is my fault, and I'm sorry you two were caught in the middle of it all," he murmured as he peered around the inside of the cart. He'd been studying the space, hoping to find a means of escape. The only spot he hadn't been able to search was where Cathsin had been sitting. He stretched out his leg and kicked over the crate she had been sitting on.

"Their plan is likely to kill me, or worse." Addison toed the spilled contents. Mostly cooking utensils, but no knives. "They said they would take you and Courtney to a village or town to let you go, but I doubt that. Not sure what else they would do with you, and I don't want to find out. We have to find something to cut these ropes."

Chess grunted as he pressed himself flush against the wall. Then he scooted forward, wriggling his arms behind his back. He did it again, back against the wall, then sliding his hips forward. When he repeated the action a third time, Addison paused.

"What are you—"

Chess winced as his arms slid forward beneath his backside. He wriggled and brought his hands up to the back of his knees.

Addison watched on, impressed, as Chess then pulled his arms up under his legs and free.

"Well. That'll do it." Addison grinned.

With his hands in front of him, he shook Courtney gently, calling her name. At first, she didn't respond, and then she groaned, asking her mother to leave her alone.

"Courtney, you gotta get up!" Chess urged.

Finally, she blinked into wakefulness, her eyes fluttering open partially as she glanced around, then between the two of them.

"Y'all let me fall asleep with make—" Courtney froze where she'd lifted one hand to rub at her face, then noticed the other was bound to it. She stared, blinking, her eyes widening when she started to realize just what was happening.

"Don't panic," Addison cautioned when it looked like she might scream. "Long story short, those women blame me for some bad things that happened to their family, which they plan to kill me for, and I'm not sure what they're going to do to the two of you. We have to get out of here."

Courtney stared at him like he'd told her to shave her head and dance naked in the wylds.

Chess pushed to stand, though he had to bend over slightly to keep from banging his head against the pots and bottles dangling from the roof. He started rummaging through what looked like the cookware. Wooden plates and utensils clapped together.

Addison stole a glance at the door. "Quiet," he urged. "And hurry."

Chess grunted as he continued looking. "I *am* hurrying." His brow pinched, his hands worked back and forth until he drew them free with a small "aha!" of triumph.

He held a ladle.

He cursed and tossed it aside.

Courtney was still fixated on the rope around her wrists.

"It's a lot. I know," Addison said, his attention boomeranged between her, Chess's search, and the door. "How do you feel?"

She blinked, swallowing thickly as she finally tore her gaze away from her bound hands. "Well rested, weirdly enough, for having been kidnapped."

Addison nodded. She didn't panic. Good. Not entirely surprising considering she'd been ready to face a Fiend armed with nothing but a Gucci pump a few weeks ago. He shifted to face away from her. "Do you think you can work on my bonds?"

"Y-yeah. I can try." Her fingers fell to the ropes, and he felt her pulling at them, digging and tugging to try to work at the knots, cursing faintly as she did.

The door yanked open.

Everyone froze. Once again, Ramthe filled the space, sword in hand.

The Vorpal Blade, Addison realized with a start. "What're you—"

"Silence," she snapped, then aimed the weapon at Chess, who lifted his bound hands in front of him. "Outside. All of you."

Chess hesitated before glancing back at Addison, who nodded. He went first, stepping around Addison and Courtney, then climbed out of the cart, following Ramthe's instructions to move a short distance away. Addison followed, though he waited as long as he dared for Courtney to make her way forward and down the small set of stairs.

His eyes went to Ramthe, to the sword. "You really shouldn't have that out," he started.

Faster than he expected, the back of Ramthe's hand connected with the side of his face. His head whipped around and pain exploded along his cheek, followed by a rush of heat.

"Hey!" Courtney shouted.

"I said silence," she hissed. "Or I'll kill them, then you, too."

Copper filled Addison's mouth. He spat a bit of red at the ground, but didn't speak again.

Courtney glared at Ramthe before stepping over to Addison and curling her fingers around his arm. He led the way to where Chess stood a short distance off.

As they walked, he noticed her limp was more pronounced, likely from having slept with her legs folded under her like that, but she didn't let whatever pain she had to be feeling show on her face.

Not too far off, Cathsin was busy setting up a pit for a fire. She stole glances at them, her expression cowed.

"On your knees," Ramthe ordered.

Addison lowered himself gradually.

Chess was slower to obey.

Courtney remained on her feet.

Ramthe's eyes narrowed. "I said on your knees."

"I heard you," Courtney shot back at her.

For a moment the two girls simply glared at each other. When Ramthe lifted the sword to aim the tip of the blade at Courtney's throat, Addison shifted as if to rise. He heard and felt Chess do the same beside him.

"Don't move, or I kill her," Ramthe said.

Courtney continued to glare. "Look, I don't know what your issue is, and I don't really care. I have been attacked by Wraiths, run off the road by Nightmares, nearly drowned by Slithe, dropped through a hole in the world, my car was totaled, my whole body hurts, and now I've been kidnapped by . . . Wonderland's version of *Little Women*." She glanced back and forth between the sisters. "That was just this weekend. This past month alone has been a disaster." She narrowed her eyes. "You do not scare me."

Ramthe's lips curled back in a silent snarl. Her fingers tightened on the hilt.

"Ramthe," Cathsin called, moving forward a few steps. "Please. We don't harm the innocent."

The older sister shot a glare at the younger, her body all but trembling with her barely controlled fury. "Very well," she finally relented, lowering the sword.

Cathsin sighed, her relief draped over her entire body.

Ramthe stepped away from Courtney and stopped in front of Addison. She glowered down at him, her eyes wide and furious, her hands shaking as she gripped the sword. "Do you remember him? My brother? Do you remember any of them?" She started to circle him then.

He remained still, his gaze flickering over their surroundings. They were along a more prominent road now that they'd reached the edge of the forest. The Glays plains stretched on to one side, the rolling hills to the north. They were much closer to Legracia now.

"I remember. I was there." She came back around to face him. "It was a beautiful day, like this one."

Addison kept his gaze on Ramthe but remained silent. Something told him any attempts to reason with her would likely end with his throat slit.

"He was on his knees, just like you are now." The flat of the Vorpal Blade tapped his shoulder. The daylight around it seemed to fizzle and lessen, drawn in by the sword.

"You need to sheathe that." He lifted his gaze from the sword to her. "Nightmares are attracted to it."

Ramthe seethed. "I told you to sh—"

"The sheath binds its power. If you leave it out too long, you'll draw them here."

"Nightmares don't attack during the day," she muttered.

"No, not usually, but something's changed," he urged. "These attacks clearly aren't normal, even you can see that."

"They attacked us during the day," Chess said. "Twice."

Ramthe scoffed. "So, what, I put it away and forestall your proper judgment?" She continued to stare at Addison.

"I was thinking more along the lines of forestalling our collective slaughter. Please, Ramthe, I know how you feel."

"You can *never* know how I feel," she hissed.

"I can at least know what you want. But you won't get it if you're dead."

She narrowed her eyes. "Are you threatening me?"

"Never. I am trying to save your life, all your lives. Put the sword away."

She glared at him, seeming to consider something. "All right." She came back around the opposite side. "I'll put it away."

Addison watched her movements carefully. There was a dangerous glint in her eye. One he knew all too well.

"After I take your head."

Metal bit at his skin where she pressed the blade to the back of his neck.

"No!" Courtney screamed. She started to come toward them, but something made her stop.

"Careful," Ramthe said. "Don't want me to slip."

The sting of the blade bit deeper, and he felt blood run warm against his skin. Now, finally, panic sliced through him. "I already told you, you can have my life. Just . . . not like this. Use something else."

"Why? So you don't end up a monster?" She snorted. "Oh yes, the stories of the Vorpal Blade, the blade so black, are widespread. Those slain by it rise again as part of the Nightmare army, controlled by the Black Knight. It's how my brother met his end—why should your fate be any different?"

Ramthe pulled the blade away, but only to raise it overhead, gripping the hilt with both hands. "My brother begged for his life. You will beg for yours."

Addison drew a slow breath. He'd imagined his end many times, usually in the jaws of a Nightmare, at the ends of its claws, or perhaps via assassin when his goodwill with the Queens ran out. He'd even pictured someone hunting him down in some back alley to exact their vengeance in the dead of night.

But he never imagined he would find himself back in Wonderland, no longer burdened by the pain of the exile curse. And he never imagined it would be bright out, daylight warm on his face, the smell of flowers on the breeze.

"Beg!" Ramthe shouted.

"No," Addison murmured.

Someone screamed.

Cathsin, he realized. His eyes flew open to see her scrambling backward on all fours as a Fiend stalked her from the tree line.

"Cathsin!" Ramthe cried. Vorpal Blade in hand, she darted around Addison and toward her sister.

Chess sprang to his feet, his gaze fixed in front of him.

"Hatta!" Courtney hurried over to him. "You're bleeding!"

"Just a scratch." Addison whipped around just in time to spot another Fiend, lips pulled back in a snarl, claws digging grooves into the dirt as it raced along the ground, coming at them.

"Get back!" He shifted, trying to get his weight under him to stand.

The Fiend leaped.

Twenty-Nine
MEMORIES

Humphrey had never been one for butting into anyone else's business. At least, he felt he wasn't that type of person. He didn't actually know for sure, but the way his stomach squirmed uncomfortably while he stood in the midst of a verbal tug-of-war between Tina and Queen Kashaunte more than convinced him he did not like getting caught up in other people's personal . . . stuff.

Everything had been fine until maybe five minutes ago when Kashaunte suddenly felt weak and looked as if she might faint. Humphrey had moved to steady her, but Tina got to her first, bracing her up with a surety and swiftness born from practice.

Once they were settled on a nearby rock, the Queen glanced around and asked why they were in their nightgowns at the park. Then she'd looked at Humphrey and loudly inquired, "Who's the white boy? One of Alice's friends?"

Tina had pressed her hands to her face and shook her head. "Not now." She'd uttered more prayers and pleas between declarations of needing a drink. Then they'd starting arguing about alcohol consumption while pregnant.

Throughout it all, Humphrey got the distinct feeling this was something of a regular occurrence, and that he should very much stay out of it.

That was until his Queen looked directly at him once more and pulled him into it. "What's your name?"

He blinked rapidly, caught off guard by the question. "I—I . . ." Then he dropped to one knee. "Humphrey, Your Majesty."

"Majesty?" Kashaunte snorted a delighted laugh. "You hear that, Missy? Your Ma-je-sty."

Normally he would wait to be bidden to stand, but something told him that likely wouldn't happen. At the risk of impropriety he rose. "I—I . . . I'm sorry, I don't understand." His attention flickered between the two women. "You knew me not five minutes ago, you . . . knew me before I knew myself—is this a jest?"

"She's not joking," Tina sighed. "Er, jesting. She has a condition where she forgets things. Whole parts of her life, just . . . gone."

Humphrey could sympathize. Nay, empathize. "Is it permanent?" Perhaps what had happened to him had happened to her.

"Yes and no. Usually, she comes back to the present, but there's no telling when that'll happen." Tina sniffed, wiping at her face. "It's been getting worse. Jesus, I can't do this. Dragged down by monsters, my mother-in-law doing magic, now folk showing up calling her *Queen*." She started pacing. "Lord, gimme strength. Gimme strength, Je—" She paused. "Actually, never mind. No more strength. No more trials. This is too much."

Humphrey stole a glance at the Queen, who'd gone oddly quiet. She sat with a vacant though saddened expression pulling at her face, at least what part of it he could see. She'd pulled the collar of her garb up to the lower half of her face, the fabric bunched in her fingers.

"I'm sorry, Missy," Kashaunte murmured. "My mind, it's . . . not so good anymore."

Tina sighed. Her shoulders sagged. But then she took a breath and squared them. Making her way back over to the Queen, she sat beside her and wrapped her in her arms. "You ain't got nothing to be sorry for, Momma. None of this is your fault, and your mind is just fine." She dropped a kiss to the Queen's forehead.

In that moment, she looked so much like her daughter, resigned to the moment while simultaneously determined to make it right.

Humphrey averted his gaze, turning to face the forest and keep watch, and to afford the two a moment of privacy.

After a bit, Tina cleared her throat. "So, Humphrey."

He turned to face them once more. The Queen sat with her eyes closed, her head on Tina's shoulder.

Tina held her head high, chin lifted. He could feel her eyes taking him apart.

"Now that we got a moment, I have a few questions. Are you part of this monster-slaying business? Do you know my daughter?"

He felt a flush crawl up his neck. "Ahh . . . yes. You can say that."

"Then you know where we are, what's going on?"

"Yes, and no." He moved to lower himself to kneel in front of them. "This place is called the In-Between. It's what you might call a pocket dimension cradled between your world and mine."

Tina arched an eyebrow, recoiling slightly. "My world and your world? We aren't from the same place?"

"No," he said, somewhat amused. "I'm from Wonderland. That's where the monsters come from."

"Monsters?" the Queen barked, straightening and looking around.

"Yes, Momma, monsters. You fought some off earlier."

"I did?"

"You did."

"Hmm." Kashaunte looked quite pleased with herself, and Humphrey couldn't help the faint smile that pulled at his face.

"So, Humphrey," Tina continued. "We between places."

"Yes. For all intents and purposes."

"Okay. Well, how do we get home? My home, not your home. I mean, *you* can go to your home, but we gotta get back to mine."

Humphrey sighed. "I'm . . . not sure."

"What you mean you're not sure?"

"I mean I may know a way, but it might not be available to us at the moment." The four Gateways were the main means of traveling between Wonderland and the human world. They provided a natural bridge that could be crossed expediently, but there were instances where weaknesses in other parts of the Veil could be exploited.

Being what he was, he was often able to use the ether to shore up those weak spots for his own travel. He'd never made an attempt to enter or exit the In-Between with anyone else, and he didn't want to try now, when he wasn't sure he'd make the journey in one piece himself. Something was . . . wrong with his abilities.

But he didn't say that. Instead he offered, "It's also very dangerous. And I've never taken anyone before."

"Are there less dangerous options?"

"Perhaps . . . I need time to think."

"Time, I don't have time! I've got to get back to Alice!"

Humphrey blinked, slightly taken aback by the volume of her voice. "Is she in some sort of danger?"

"My house was covered in that black shit, of course she's in danger!"

He lifted his hands in what he hoped was a calming gesture. "Let's not lose our heads."

The glare leveled at him said he was incredibly close to losing more than that.

"Sorry," he added quickly, reminded that this was indeed Alice's mother. "It's just . . . I've only known your daughter for a short period, but she's quite the capable warrior. I'm sure she'll be able to handle whatever was happening when you left." He stroked at his chin lightly. "I actually thought I heard her here, but I suppose it's you I heard. How did you end up here, anyway?"

Tina launched into a somewhat frazzled explanation of a Nightmare attack at her house, Kashaunte and Alice fighting them off, and some black sludge coming to life and dragging them under. The Queen seemed confused and distracted during the tale. Tina kept hold of her when she tried to get up and wander off a couple of times.

"Your experience sounds eerily similar to mine," Humphrey remarked. "In any case, I'm glad the two of you are unharmed, and I assure you I will do everything in my power to keep it that way."

Tina, for her part, managed to look slightly relieved.

The Queen looked like she wasn't paying attention, her eyes fixed on some point off to their right.

"What is it, Your Highness?" he asked, peering in that direction. He didn't see anything but more forest, perhaps a couple of creatures scurrying away as they caught sight or sound of the three of them.

"Your who?" She didn't look away from whatever had her attention.

"Why do you call her that?" Tina asked.

Before he could answer, Kashaunte lifted a hand to point. "Something's out there." She frowned. "I don't like the look of it."

Humphrey peered in that direction once more. There was still no sign of danger, but if something bothered the Queen enough for her to draw attention to it regardless of her condition, it was best to heed her warning. He did not remember much, but he somehow knew Kashaunte's intuition was not to be trifled with. "I'm certain there are many somethings out there. We should get going."

"To where?" Tina asked even as she climbed to her feet and helped Kashaunte to hers.

"For now? Anywhere but here," he murmured. "Follow me." He decided to head back to the Eternity Shore. No one had ever truly mapped the In-Between. There were rumors that it went on forever, unlike the worlds on either side of the veil. The prospect of endlessly wandering was not an appealing one, and things lost near the waters usually tended to wind up coming ashore wherever they were supposed to be. Not much to go on, but Wonderland simply worked things out at times. It was best not to question it. That way lies madness.

Eventually the woods thinned out. The ground grew harder, rockier. The sky darker. Night was falling early? He didn't understand at first, until they finally broke out of the woods and into the open.

His body froze up. His insides went cold.

"What . . . is that place?" Tina asked. There was an edge of fear in her words.

Humphrey bit into the inside of his cheek. The pain shook him out of his stupor.

"This . . ." The Queen stepped forward. The look on her face was a mix of confusion and regret. "This is home."

She swallowed, her eyes wide and glossy as she looked over the broken, barren, and blackened land before them. The ground was fissured, pierced through by rock and what looked like jagged black crystal. Solidified Slithe.

Overhead, the sky roiled as black clouds boiled over, bloated and blotting out the day. Arcs of red danced through the billows.

The Nox. And a short distance away, the darkened towers of what was left of Emes stood like sentinals in the artificial night.

The palace, like its queen, had earned a new moniker among the people of Wonderland. They called it the Hollows, named so for the emptiness that would forever sit at the center of Wonderland, and at the hearts of its people.

"Emes," the queen whispered, almost reverently. "It's been so long."

Humphrey felt a swell of sadness as he watched the recognition flicker briefly in Kashaunte's eyes.

"Not quite, Your Majesty," he murmured, turning to face the landscape once more. "This is still the In-Between."

"Momma?" Tina called when Kashaunte stepped forward, her stride steady and sure. "Momma, what are you doing?"

"Your Majesty, we should turn back," Humphrey called after them.

The Queen ignored both of them.

Tina glanced at Humphrey before hurriedly picking her way after the older woman. He sighed and brought up the rear. Just like old times, in a way. Maybe. He felt like it was, even if he didn't recall exactly.

Thunder boomed overhead. Each time, Tina started slightly or hunched her shoulders. She kept calling out that they needed to stop, that they shouldn't be here. The Queen maintained her pace, undeterred.

Humphrey followed along, offering reassurances that this place looked dangerous but was nothing compared to the real thing. They were safe here.

He hoped.

Eventually, they wound up at the base of the grand staircase that led up into the palace. In the shadow of Castle Emes, Queen Kashaunte paused only for a moment before taking off at a run.

"Momma!" Tina hurried after her.

Humphrey followed easily enough, up the long stairs, through the huge doors, down darkened halls and corridors. Tina's calls for her mother to stop echoed through the space, the high ceilings catching the sound of her voice and pitching it around them.

But the Queen did not stop. She kept running, almost frantic, as she made her way toward the center of the palace.

With each step, Humphrey's chest tightened. He didn't like this. He didn't like being here. He . . . couldn't remember, but something deep inside told him nothing good would come of this.

And yet, duty bound, he followed.

Finally, bursting through one last set of doors, the Queen came to a stop. Her chest heaved, her breath coming in harsh pants. The dulled light from outside poured through the high ceiling, casting the room in shadow and silver. There was just enough brightness to take in the intricate carvings and trappings, many of them marred by the emergence of more crystallized Slithe.

"What the hell is this place?" Tina murmured.

"This is where it all began," Kashaunte said, her tone low and even. "And where it ended."

Humphrey watched her closely as she started forward, her steps measured. Her bare feet carried her across the room to where two crystal structures stood in the center. One was a throne, similar to the one the Bloody Lady had often sat in. Humphrey immediately tore his gaze away. The other was a long container of some sort, much smaller than the throne. The pink color was brighter, but the luster had dulled. Once-translucent crystal was now cloudy and dim, covered in the evidence of years gone by.

A *coffin*, something inside him whispered.

A subtle throbbing picked up between his ears. He pressed the fingers of one hand to his temple.

"What do you mean?" Tina asked.

The Queen released a shuddering breath as she set her hand against the coffin's lid. She played her fingers through the dust and sniffed. It was then Humphrey noticed her face was streaked with tears, her expression contorted in quiet sobs.

"Momma, what's wrong?" Tina took a step forward, but didn't move any closer. Something seemed to hold her back, an understanding of the situation Humphrey did not possess.

"This is . . . where we left them." Queen Kashaunte's voice trembled with the weight of her emotions. "This is where we said good-bye."

"Good-bye? To who?" Tina asked.

"My sister." Kashaunte patted the coffin gingerly with trembling fingers, like she was afraid it might shatter under her touch. Then she reached out with the other hand and set it against the throne. "My mother." She bowed her head as sobs shook her body.

Tina moved forward then, gripping her nightgown and taking the steps two at a time until she was able to wrap her arms around the Queen, murmuring reassurances and other words of comfort.

Humphrey looked away. He let his eyes trail over the somewhat familiar room. Flashes of a brighter, warmer space full of laughter played through his mind. Images of a queen and her three daughters, together and happy, followed.

He closed his eyes, letting his mind wander, trying to follow along with whatever it wanted to show him. He'd walked these halls. As a knight, as . . .

"Oh god." The Queen's panicked voice cut through his thoughts.

He was instantly on the alert, glancing around for signs of danger. Once again his hand went for a sword that wasn't there, and he cursed quietly. He was going to have to find a way to keep some sort weapon on his person at all times. When he didn't see any threats, he looked to the women. Kashaunte was on her knees between the structures, only they were different now. The lid on the coffin had been shoved aside, and the throne was gone, torn away, leaving behind jagged crystal in its place. Slithe burbled lazily where it stretched between them.

Humphrey hurried forward, eyes moving over the scene, intending to pull them both away, but there was no danger here. This . . . wasn't real. Still, what he saw made his stomach twist.

The coffin was empty. At least, there was no body, only the stain of what looked like the remains of a fallen Nightmare before a purge. It stretched over the lip of the coffin proper, then poured down its side. Something had crawled out and landed on the floor, then made its way to the throne, leaving a long-dried and crusted trail behind it.

Without warning, the entire scene flickered and shivered as if shaking itself off before changing before their eyes. The coffin lid slid closed. The throne was once again whole.

No one spoke. They barely breathed. Then, just when it seemed like things had settled, the scene shifted again, dancing back and forth between everything being broken and made whole.

"The hell is going on here?" Tina asked, looking more than a little frazzled.

Humphrey was having a hard time wrapping his head around it as well. "I . . . don't know."

"It's because of where we are," the Queen explained. "The In-Between isn't real, though it's not *not* real. It's a reflection of reality and remembrance." She reached to set her trembling fingers against the edge of the coffin once more. "This . . . my fault," she murmured.

"I don't understand," Humphrey said, his eyes playing over the scene once more. "Why did it change?"

"Because it's caught between my last memory of this place and the reality of what it is now." Kashaunte withdrew her touch and the room fluctuated again.

Broken, unbroken, broken, unbroken.

"You were here?" Humphrey asked quietly. "After everything?"

"Yes. And I believe I've made a terrible mistake. We . . . we have to leave." She sniffed and pushed to stand, with some help from Tina. "We have to go. We have to find Alice, we have to warn Emalia."

"Who?" Tina asked. "Why? What's going on?"

"The White Queen," Humphrey offered in explanation, his eyes on Kashaunte. "You remember who she is?"

Kashaunte turned to him. Her chin lifted, her shoulders drew back. There was regality in her bearing, grace in her being. The transformation was instantaneous and all consuming, and somehow equally minimal. Because this was who she had always been, regardless of what happened to her body or mind.

The clarity in her gaze shook him to his core while simultaneously bolstering him. He dropped to one knee, one fist planted on the ground, the other over his heart.

Queen Kashaunte took a slow, careful breath.

"I remember everything."

Thirty

BIG PROBLEMS CALL FOR BIG SOLUTIONS

Alice paced as she stared down the dirt road in the direction Maddi had indicated, which had been confirmed by Dem when he examined the tracks.

"They're in a cart," he said, brushing the dirt from his hands. "We'll never catch up with them, not on foot."

"We have to try." She didn't stop moving or draw her gaze away. Anxiety rolled through her, twisting up every inch in her body until she felt like her skin was on too tight. Her friends were in trouble.

"My brother is injured," Dem said. "And you have no shoes. We wouldn't make it more than a mile."

She whirled on him. "We can't just *sit* here!"

Dem lifted his hands. "I'm not saying we should! Only that they're moving faster than we ever could. We'd need a miracle to catch them. Or for them to stop long enough."

"Okay, so help me think of how to fix problems, don't just point them out!" She started pacing again, staring down the road.

Tears burned her eyes and the back of her throat. Her chest rose and fell with hard breaths that rattled something inside her.

Silence settled over the group, thick and uncomfortable. Her fault. She needed to calm down. No one here was to blame for what happened.

"I'm sorry," she finally offered.

"No apologies needed," he said quietly. "You are angry. I understand."

"You're right." She shook her head, rubbing at her face. "We won't catch them on foot. We need a plan. Or a dragon."

"Klassno," both boys responded simultaneously, sounding quite impressed.

Alice smirked, then went back to pacing. They had to think of something, some way to get after her friends before anything happened to them.

A hand fell on her shoulder.

Dem offered her a faint smile. "We will fix this. We always fix it, da?"

"Da," she returned, setting her fingers over his.

"Good. And stop pacing. Save your energy. We don't have much food. Magic cookies don't count."

"It's a biscuit."

"Whatever." He turned to move back over to where Dee stood with a frazzled Maddi, the two of them somehow discussing . . . whatever they were discussing.

"Magic cookies. Right." Alice shook her head with a faint laugh. Then she froze, eyes flying wide. "Magic." Her eyes went to the basket at Dee's feet. He'd snatched it up when they took off after Maddi.

She hurried over, bending to scoop the basket up and rip the lid off.

"Something wrong?" Dee asked as he took a step back.

A wide smile broke over her face. "No! It's perfect!" The black bag rested at the bottom, along with a few largish crumbs left over from when Dem had hacked it into thirds. Or had that been Dee? It didn't matter! She tipped the basket to pour the crumbs into her hand. There was enough for her to squeeze together into a decent sized chunk. "I've got an idea!"

"What kind of idea?" Dem started to say at the same time Maddi's eyes went wide.

"The baker is not a fisherman!" Maddi snatched at Alice's arm but wasn't fast enough.

Alice tipped her head back and shoved the entire thing into her mouth. She chewed, and chewed, and chewed, then swallowed, coughing afterward. "Why's it so dry?"

Maddi stared at her, shock painted over her features. "Ooooooooooh, mooses and mice," she murmured.

The twins stared as well.

Alice released a quick breath and braced herself.

Nothing happened.

She blinked and lifted her hands to glance at them, turning them over. "Um . . ."

"Bozhe moi," Dee murmured. Or was it Dem? Shit, she was losing track.

She glanced up to find them and Maddi backing away. "What?"

"Mooses and mice," Maddi said. "Mooses and mice!" She pointed at Alice.

"Your eyes," Dee said.

Alice touched her face, then immediately felt foolish. She couldn't see or feel anything different. "What about them?"

"They're glowing," Dem said, equally awed.

She blinked, then glanced around for something to maybe see her reflection in. That was when warmth suffused her body. Only this wasn't the gentle roll like last time; this was a searing heat that bit at her nerves.

She doubled over with the pain, choking on it. It intensified, dragging a scream from her and pulling her to her knees.

Someone shouted her name, one of the twins. They said something else, but she couldn't hear over the sudden pounding in her temples. She pressed her face to her arms where they folded in the dirt and tried to concentrate on breathing.

It didn't help.

So stupid! Eating something like that all at once, without knowing what would happen, without trying it first.

"Only take a nibble, though." Sprigs's voice echoed in her ears, along with more screams, her screams.

She felt like she was going to burst into flame and burn into nothing.

Then, as suddenly as the agony had overtaken her, it subsided. She panted as her body attempted to adjust to the sudden freedom in her nerves, everything buzzing and tingling. Her muscles ached. Her head throbbed. Each breath she took was like sandpaper against her raw throat.

"Mother bitch," she panted, dropping to the ground to lie against the cool earth, hoping to temper the heat that remained. She didn't care what happened to her clothes. They were probably dripping in sweat; she felt herself covered in it. "That was . . . that—" She tried to roll onto her back, but something stuck her in the side. Several somethings, actually.

She hissed and pulled away, opening her eyes to see what she'd nearly rolled onto. "What in—" She froze. Trees. Those . . . those were trees. At least, she thought they were trees. They looked like trees, only small.

"U-um," one of the twins called in a soft, squeaky voice.

Both boys and Maddi had moved to the edge of the road. They looked so far away, for some reason, but . . . not? No, they weren't far; she was just up high. Which was kind of the same thing when she thought about it. How did she get up here? Her jittery thoughts swirled, eventually landing on the truth of the moment.

"It . . . it worked," she breathed, staring at her now massive hands. Massive compared to everything else, they were normal to her. "Holy shit, it worked!" Wonderland spread out before her like a miniature set piece. Patches of light near the horizon were likely villages. A body of water a short ways off shone brightly with the light of the moon. Grinning wide, Alice peered down at her friends. Her very little friends. There was a *Scarface* joke in there somewhere.

Dem looked her up and down, which took some doing.

"This . . . was your plan?" Dee asked.

"Yes!" she shouted, then placed a hand over her mouth when they all slapped hands over their ears. "Sorry! Yes. I didn't think I'd be this big, but this is great! Now I can cover more ground faster. We can go after them!"

"And just how are we supposed to go with you?" Dem asked.

Alice blinked. Thaaaat was a very good question. Another quick glance around didn't reveal anything helpful. What did she expect, a giant fanny pack to fall out of the sky? "Um, two of you can go in my pockets. Or I can carry you. I . . . didn't think that far ahead."

The three of them exchanged glances before seeming to come to a reluctant agreement.

"All right. Just, please don't crush us," Dee said.

"A right way is wrong for someone else," Maddi murmured, looking less than thrilled.

"Come on, we need to hurry." Alice shifted, a little hesitant about the possibility of maybe crushing her friends, before reaching to gently curl fingers around Dee and pluck him up.

He made a sound that was half yelp, half grunt. Any other time it would've been funny, but now it just made her anxiety spike. "Are you all right?"

"I'm . . . I'm fine," he called. "This is weird, but I'm fine."

Nodding, Alice carefully slipped him into one pocket, then Dee into the other. Once they were settled, she held a hand out for Maddi.

The mousy girl crawled across her fingers and settled into her palm. It tickled slightly, like holding a squirmy critter. Only this was a whole person.

So . . . freaking weird, but she would have to be freaked out later.

"Okay," Alice said, pushing to her feet. "Hold on."

"To what?" Dem shouted.

She started walking first. So far, so good. It was a little disorienting being this tall but no major complications.

Little faster now. A jog.

Her balance shifted, and she nearly tripped over her own feet as they propelled her forward faster than she anticipated. It was like her first night in Wonderland when she had to get used to her new-found strength and speed, only this time she knew how to compensate. She adjusted and leaned into the run.

"Everyone okay?" she shouted.

Three thumbs-ups eased some of the worry in her gut, but not all of it.

Her feet bounded against the earth, the left one kicking up the dirt in the road. She was damn near flying along the path. The trails from the wagon wheels were faint, but she could just make them out.

This is going to work, she realized, with a sudden thrill. They were fast enough to catch up now. She pushed herself to go faster. *Hold on. I'm coming.*

I'm coming . . .

Thirty-One

THE RED QUEEN

Humphrey played his gaze over the blackened wasteland around them. It seemed to go on forever, which made no sense considering they'd made their way here via a forest, one that seemed to have vanished the instant they emerged from the trees.

"This is why no one comes here," he muttered to himself before turning to make his way down from the outcropping of rock he'd climbed for a better vantage point.

Kashaunte and Tina waited below, the latter peering around like a frightened rabbit, as if she expected the very shadows to snatch her up. Which . . . had happened, so he could not blame her.

"Did you see anything?" Kashaunte asked.

"No, Your Majesty. Just more of the Nox. It seems to go on forever."

Tina made a frustrated sound, mumbling to herself about nonsense.

"I . . . do not wish to question you, my Queen," he started, turning to face Kas. "But this place can be difficult for the most capable of navigators. You're certain the chasm is this direction?"

"I told you to stop with the 'Your Majesty' and 'my queen' stuff. That was a lifetime ago. You can, call me Kas." She smiled. "That's a literal question, by the way, and I'm more than sure. You of all people should know that." She stepped past him and once more took the lead, traversing the uneven terrain with uncanny ease, her footing having grown more and more sure.

"Apologies," he murmured. "There's . . . much I remain ignorant of."

"Because of your memory, I know."

He could hear the frown in her voice.

"I promise, when this is over, I'm gonna see what can be done about that," she offered.

"Thank you, Your Maj—Kas." He fell silent, even as everything inside him urged him to ask the question that had been knocking around in his head since they left the reflection of Emes.

"*Speaking* of memory," Tina said as she picked her way along. "Let me see if I got this straight. You're telling me you're from this outrageous, upside-down world, too."

"Mmhm," Kas said.

"And you and Humphrey came to our . . . my . . . damn it all, you came to Earth!" Tina swatted at something that dared swoop too close to her face."

"Mmhm."

"Then you both lost your memories and, what, just went on living your lives not knowing nothing?"

"I don't know what happened to his memory." Kas pitched a sympathetic glance over her shoulder, then faced forward again. "And I feel responsible for that, to a degree. Far as mine, well, I got old."

Tina stared at Kas like she was a total stranger. And Humphrey supposed she was. At least, this information made her seem like one.

"But you remember now?" he asked.

"I remember *more*," Kas said. "Not everything."

"But you said—" Tina started.

"I know what I said." Kas's brow furrowed. "And I do. Sort of. It's the same as before. Right now, I know everything. I remember losing my sister. My mother falling to grief. I remember the war. And I remember becoming Queen."

"Queen." Tina nodded sharply as she heaved a breath. "I'd almost forgotten about that part."

"Don't act too surprised." Kas waved a hand at Tina, smiling. "I always been queenly."

"So," Humphrey dared interject. "You remember everything *except* what happened to me."

Kas's smile dimmed. "Unfortunately."

"I see." He couldn't keep the note of disappointment from his voice. It surprised him, honestly. The issue hadn't bothered him before.

"But I remember who you were before," Kas said, throwing him a lifeline. "You were quick to smile, even quicker to laugh. Great sense of humor, constantly pranking Addison and the others. But when it came down to it, you took your duty so seriously, you always had, so when I told you my plan to bring the Heart to the human world to keep it from the Loyalists, you were determined to come with me. I should've known you would be, even if it meant leaving everything and everyone else behind.

"Maybe you wouldn't be like this if I had gone on my own, like I planned. But I was glad to have you along. You're good peoples." She smiled at him, and he couldn't help but return it. "Emalia agreed that it was best I not be alone with my grief. She knew what I wanted to do. But neither of us knew what would happen."

"And what did happen?" Humphrey urged.

"The only thing capable of throwing a wrench in it all. Love. I fell in love, with a human, of all possibilities." Kas snorted a laugh. "All that time ignoring courtiers and potential wooers, and it's a boy who gives me free oranges from his shop that wins. Go figure. Henry was one of a kind, though."

"I was . . . present for all of this?" Humphrey asked.

"In your own way. You remained close, but you busied yourself with odds and ends here and there. I *urged* you to return to Wonderland on several occasions, but you refused. You said there was nothing for you there. It bothered me to see you so upset and not be able to do anything."

Humphrey frowned. It was so strange to hear these details about his life and not be able to remember a thing. Like hearing a fairy tale.

"But you perked right up when Sydney was born," Kas said, her tone wistful but sad.

Beside her, Tina's entire being tensed, almost painfully from the look of it.

"Sydney?" Humphrey asked.

"My son. And the then heir to the throne, even though neither he nor his father knew anything about that."

"They weren't the only ones," Tina muttered.

Kas squeezed her hand, but kept going. "You were . . . not exactly a nanny, but not exactly an uncle. Somewhere in between. You were good at it. Which is why I was surprised when one day you just up and vanished. No good-bye, no nothing. I'll admit, I was salty for a bit, as the kids say. But then that's hypocritical as hell, considering I did the same thing. I thought you'd just gone back home. I didn't know what was happening, I didn't know you were in trouble, I didn't . . . I'm so sorry, Humphrey."

"It's not your fault, my lady," he murmured. And while part of him was glad to have these bits of his life laid out so he could try to piece things together, he still didn't know what had robbed him of himself. "It sounds as if I vanished long before you lost your memory. Do you know what happened to cause that?"

"The natural order of things," she said. "When we cross into the human world, we start to fade. The farther we are from the Veil, the longer we're away from Wonderland, the faster it happens. Soon the human world starts to affect us. We grow older, losing more and more of who we were as we become who we are. I don't think that happened to you, though. I actually have no idea what might have done this, outside of some powerful Verse."

"I can't believe this." Tina shook her head as she stomped along. "You really lived some secret double life and never told any of us. Are you why Alice ended up mixed up in this mess?"

"Now, Alice is part of Wonderland, and Wonderland is part of her, but her dad went all his life without anything happening." Kas frowned. "I had no idea Alice was a Dreamwalker. And I don't appreciate your tone. But believe you me, I'm gonna have words with Addison Hatta 'bout this. Lots of four-letter ones."

"If it's any consolation, I don't think he's aware of who she is," Humphrey said. "Neither is she, for that matter."

"No, she has no idea. And she has no idea just what she's capable of, as a child of both worlds. Which is why we need to find her, before my sister does." Kas's tone dipped dangerously.

"The White Queen?" Humphrey asked.

"'Fraid not."

Thirty-Two
BURNED OUT

Addison could see little more than the claws splayed as a Fiend went for the kill. His body reacted, not waiting for his brain to fully process as instinct took hold. He rolled onto his back, feet up to catch the creature and use its momentum to pitch it overhead.

Only the monster adjusted for the throw and pressed into the lunge. Instead of flying, it damn near fell on top of him. He barely managed to tuck his knees in time to provide a barrier, just enough to keep those jaws from clamping down on his throat. Pain burned along his nerves when claws caught his shoulders. He wasn't going to be able to hold this thing off, not with his arms pinned behind him like that.

Chess slammed into the Fiend from the side. It went tumbling, howling in rage. Addison grunted as Courtney helped haul him to his feet.

"Thank you," he panted.

Courtney nodded, fear bright on her face. Addison shifted around, placing himself between her and the Nightmare as it regained its feet.

Chess did the same.

Not far off, Ramthe swung the Vorpal Blade wildly, fending off one of the monsters. Cathsin cowered behind her.

"Cut us loose!" Addison shouted. "Free us so we can fight!"

"I'd . . . rather die than join you!" Ramthe grunted, then roared as she swung the sword again, clipping the beast. It withdrew, circling them.

"You will! And so will your sister if you don't—"

Before he could finish the statement, Cathsin snatched a knife from her boot and came racing over. She sawed through the ropes around Addison's wrists, then Chess's, and finally Courtney's.

"What're you doing?" Ramthe screeched, indignant, though she didn't take her eyes off the Fiends.

"You want your vengeance, you have to live to take it!" Cathsin offered her dagger to Chess, along with the short sword once she unbuckled the belt from her waist.

Addison shook out his arms, eyes playing over the Fiends as they circled, searching for an opening. Beyond them, more Nightmares emerged, pouring from the forest. Natural ones, Fiends, far more than he and Chess could handle alone. At least, not as he was.

"Ramthe," he said quietly, ushering Cathsin behind him to join Courtney. "Give me the sword."

"No!" she hissed.

"Don't be foolish!" Cathsin called to her sister. "We can't fight them. He can. Please, Ramthe!"

A number of emotions played over the older girl's face: anger, pain, fury, and finally resignation. She thrust the sword toward

Addison, her jaw clenched, her eyes blazing. This was not a deci-sion she made for him, but he didn't need it to be.

He wrapped his fingers around the hilt just as one of the Fiends lunged. Pushing himself in front of her, he drove the sword into the thing's chest. It howled in pain before he kicked it away, sending the body tumbling across the ground. Yellow and black stained the blade, glistening in the daylight.

To his right, Chess dodged a swipe of claws, slicing at the monster as he danced around it. Seeing him move like this was still a shock, especially since Addison swore he knew that fighting style . . . but he couldn't dwell on that now.

Like before, a feeling of icy flame spread through his body. The Vorpal Blade vibrated in his hold, its power flowing into him. Behind him, one of the girls gasped. He focused on the burn licking at his skin, spreading in his bones, growing hotter and hotter until it felt as if the flames might consume him. Then he held out a hand.

Cease . . .

All at once, the Nightmares froze. Wherever they were, what-ever they were doing, they went still as stone. Then their heads turned, angling around to regard the one who wielded power over them, even after all this time.

"What . . . what's happening?" Cathsin whimpered.

"He is," Ramthe bit out, disgust stinging her words and clear in her gaze.

Courtney shoved the girl, though not hard. Just enough to get her attention. "And he's going to save your ungrateful life."

Addison focused on the Nightmares. He could feel them, each and every one within his sight, as well as the ones that had not yet broken the tree line. At least a dozen more.

"Traaaaaaaaaaaiiiiiiitooooooooor," a voice rasped. The Fiend nearest to him jerked and twitched, fighting his influence to try and close in. "Traaaaaaaaaaaiiiiiiiitoooooooooor."

Soon other voices joined it. "Traaaaaaaaaaaiiiiiiiitoooooooooor," the Fiends called in unison, over and over as they slowly forced their way forward.

"I can't . . . I can't maintain this for very long," Addison panted. It was like trying to hold back a hurricane with his bare hands. It had been too long, his powers were weakened, even with the sword. This wasn't right, this wasn't . . .

He didn't have *time*.

"Then let's thin the herd," Chess said, moving forward to strike the nearest beast. The dagger drove into its skull with a crack. It jerked, then pitched over. He moved on to the next one. Then the next. Black blood and ichor stained the grass at his feet.

He'd killed four of the creatures in a matter of seconds, but there were still too many for them to handle, and their movements were gaining speed and fluidity as Addison's control weakened.

"P-pull back," he grunted. "Make for the cart." They could barricade themselves inside, maybe strike at the monsters from relative safety. Or perhaps they were only delaying the inevitable. Either way, there was nothing else for it.

Chess immediately altered course, stabbing at Nightmares on the way. Courtney raced after him. The sisters hesitated, sharing anxious glances as they shifted on their feet. The cart wasn't too far off, but it might as well have been miles with the Nightmares between them and it. The gryffthil kicked and shrieked, pulling at the rope that kept it from bolting.

"Our only chance is to run," Addison gritted out. "Go!"

Cathsin took off first. Ramthe shouted something after her sister. Addison couldn't make it out over the rush of blood in his ears.

She spared him one last mistrusting glance, then quickly followed. Addison hurried after them. As he raced past Nightmares, they swung their heads around, not quite able to follow with their bodies. Their snarls of "traitor" rose around them.

Chess was nearly to the cart when, without warning, the ground heaved beneath their feet. Chess and Courtney kept running, but Cathsin stumbled to a stop, her head whipping around in search of the source.

"Keep going," Addison urged, the burn against his nerves weakening, which meant his control was as well.

A nearby Nightmare snapped at him in passing.

He jerked to the side in what should've been a simple maneuver, but the ground quaking beneath his feet threw him off. He toppled over, catching himself in a roll. The fall didn't injure him, but it broke his concentration. He felt it snap like brittle bone. Felt the Nightmares shake free of his will.

He pushed to his feet, still moving, still racing forward, his long strides catching him up to the group. The Nightmares closed in easily.

Cathsin screamed as the nearest one pounced.

And a massive foot came down on top of it.

He . . . he stared, not really sure what he was seeing, his eyes traveling upward and nearly popping from his head in surprise.

"Alice?"

Stepping over the nearby tree line, she lifted her foot with a sound of disgust and wiped it against the ground nearby.

"Gross," she muttered, before kicking out at another Nightmare, sending it flying.

Then she squashed another. The rest of them scattered, snapping and snarling, scrambling forward to scratch and bite at her ankles.

She winced before bending over and swiping them away with the back of her hand. "Addison? Chess? Courtney!" Her voice echoed in the empty air.

"Here!" Courtney hollered, waving her arms in the air as she jumped up and down.

Alice caught sight of them and smiled. It broke across her face like sunshine. "You're all okay! Hold on a second!"

She bent forward to set a windswept-looking Madeline on the ground. The Poet appeared unharmed, if a bit shaken. The twins were placed beside her, looking equally ruffled, one a little worse for wear.

Her passengers safely out of the way, Alice threw out a hand, sending more Nightmares tumbling. They yowled and cursed, calling to one another to bring the big one down, their previous prey all but forgotten.

"Woooooooo!" Courtney cheered. "That's my big best friend!"

Chess stood silently beside her but was no doubt just as thrilled.

Cathsin and Ramthe clung to each other, their eyes wide as saucers.

While Alice went about kicking and stomping Nightmares left and right, Madeline and the twins joined the rest of them at the cart. Dem drew his sword, cutting down a Nightmare that had broken away from the frenzy.

"What happened?" Addison asked, eyes moving to the gigantic Dreamwalker as she battled her enemies like a titan of legend.

"She ate this cake thing Nathan gave her," Dee said.

"Biiiiiig piece of it," Dem finished, lifting his fingers to offer an approximation of size.

"She *what*?" Addison glanced up when the ground suddenly shook under their feet. "Alice!"

She'd been brought to her knees, slices along her legs bleeding. Still, she swung and kicked. The ground was littered with dark stains where the Nightmares had fallen. She'd taken out more than half of them single-handedly, but she was starting to tire. And ingesting that much Emtae was eventually going to drain her.

"She needs help," Addison said, tightening his grip on his sword and darting forward. Chess and Dem moved with him.

Together, they cleared the field of the remaining Nightmares. The few they didn't kill fled into the shadows of the nearby forest.

"Everyone all right?" Addison called.

"Relatively," Alice said as she dropped to sit. The ground shook slightly.

Courtney hurried over, gazing up at her friend, smiling wide. "I always knew you'd make it big!"

Alice snorted. "Really? Puns?" She stretched her legs out and hissed faintly as she fingered the cuts and claw marks along her ankles and feet. "Damn. Even when they tiny, this shit still hurts."

"That's not the worst of it." Addison fetched his sheath from where Ramthe had literally been about to execute him. That was going to have to be addressed. But first: "I'm told you ate a rather large piece of Emtae."

"Em-what now? Ow!" Alice flinched and glanced to where Madeline examined her large, though not severe, injuries.

"The worm is a bird at heart," the Poet called.

Alice made a face. "What?"

"She said stop squirming. And Emtae, the thing that made you so large." His attention shifted to the cart where Cathsin came racing out with a few healing vials clutched in her arms. She handed them over to Madeline, then made her way back to the cart. The twins and Chess sat on the ground near the stairs, talking quietly among themselves.

Ramthe stood apart, patting the gryffthil's head, glowering at the lot of them.

"I had to," Alice explained. "Maddi told us y'all had been taken, and we had no way to catch up to you. Well, no other way."

"And what in either world gave you the idea to grow fifty feet tall and come running after us?" he asked.

"*Attack on Titan.*" She tilted back against her hands, her chest working in harsh pants.

That was decidedly not good. "Hard time catching your breath?" he asked, trying to keep the worry from his voice.

"Well, I did run however many miles, then fought a bunch of Nightmares, so a little."

"And I imagine the Emtae isn't helping. We need to reach Legracia."

Alice blinked. "Not . . . go home?"

"Afraid not. We were attacked at the pub, driven through the Veil. Going back the way we came is nigh impossible."

"That's becoming something of a thing," Courtney said while she rubbed at Alice's wrist soothingly.

"And even if it weren't," Addison continued, "we need to warn Her Majesty about what's happening both in your world and this one. Again."

"Something's *always* happening." Alice flung her hands into the air. When they came down against her thighs, the ground trembled almost hard enough to topple the rest of them over.

"Sorry," she said with a wince. "For that and the fact that I can't go with you. My mom and grandma are here, somewhere."

That bit of information gave Addison more pause than anything else she said. "Your family is in Wonderland?" How was that possible?

"Not on purpose! More Nightmares showed up at my house. I got rid of them, but the purge sites started bleeding Slithe! That shit ended up everywhere. We tried to run, but these hands popped out of it and drug us down."

Several details in Alice's story were unsettlingly similar to what had transpired at the pub. Too many to be simple coincidence. Troubling, to be sure.

"Then I ended up on some beach in the In-Between," Alice continued. "That's where Sprigs found me, took me to the twins. Then he shrunk us, put us in a basket, dropped us off a cliff. It was a lot! We're okay, though. The three of us ran into Maddi and, well, here we are."

"Here we are indeed," Addison said, massaging a temple as his mind worked to make some sense of it all. This couldn't be random happenstance or wild Nightmares acting on the final orders of a fallen master. There was something far more sinister at work here.

Addison released a heavy breath as he strode over to join Courtney, placing his hand on one of Alice's massive fingers. He gazed up at her, marveling just briefly at how incredible she truly was.

"You won't want to hear this," he began. "But the best thing all of us can do is go to Legracia. I know." He lifted a hand to cut off her retort. "You are concerned for your family. Humphrey was taken similarly. And if whoever is responsible for their disappearances wanted them harmed or worse, efforts toward capture would not have been made."

A muscle in Alice's jaw flexed. It was large enough and he was small enough that he could see it.

"Rushing in to save others is what you do. It's what we all do." He swept his gaze over Madeline, the twins, even Courtney and Chess. "But doing so without fully understanding the circumstances has only ever made bad situations worse."

Alice averted her gaze. She huffed an annoyed breath through her nose, nostrils flaring. No, she didn't like what he had to say, but she was accepting it. Thus the face.

He rubbed at her hand gratefully, a tad worried. "Then there's the matter of the Emtae in your system. You've eaten far too much. If left to run its course, it could burn through you, which is dangerous. We need to get some Emknird in you before it's too late. You can't save anyone if you've gone up like a Roman candle."

She huffed and drew her legs in to fold them under herself. The resulting shock waves were like a small earthquake.

"Don't want you burning out," Courtney called. "And as hot as big girls are, this is a little much. You'll never fit into any more of your clothes or shoes or, hell, your house!"

Alice rubbed at her face with one hand. "I can't believe this is happening," she mumbled. "How far is Legracia?"

"On foot?" Addison asked. "Another two, three days depending on whether we make good time."

"Well, we don't have three days. *I* don't have three days. I'll carry you. Everyone." She started to push to her feet, earning a shout of surprise from Madeline.

"You'll *carry* us?" He arched an eyebrow.

"Yes. Two of you in each pocket, one of you by hand. Or you can all pile in that thing." She pointed at the cart.

"I . . . doubt that would go over well," Addison murmured.

"You let me do the talking, then." Courtney glared in the direction of the sisters.

Leaving Alice to recover, Addison and Courtney rejoined the rest of their oddly growing band near the cart.

Cathsin glanced up from where she sat on the stairs. "Is she all right?"

"She's fine, for now, but that Emtae is going to cause problems. We still need to get to Legracia, and she's offered to give us a ride. All of us." He looked pointedly to Cathsin, then Ramthe.

The latter snorted and looked away.

Cathsin stammered lightly. "It . . . what? You want us to come? Even after . . ."

Addison sighed. "I don't begrudge your sister her pain, or anger. And, in the end, we fought together. Sort of. Besides, the easiest way is for all of us to pile into the cart and have Alice carry it. She'll reach the palace before sundown—otherwise, it'll take us days."

"You really think we're going to travel with you," Ramthe muttered, her expression a quiet thunderstorm. "Like everything is fine? Like none of this happened?"

"Look here," Courtney started, moving to place herself between Addison and Ramthe, aiming a finger at the woman. "Since you've been too busy shoving your head up your ass to notice, Nightmares are all over the damn place, and you two are useless in a fight."

"The same could be said for you," Ramthe bit back at her.

"I know my strengths. Hardened battle ain't it. But that's not the point. Ain't nowhere safe right now, it's best we stick together. Especially with them." She gestured at the twins. "And Giganta back there. They're the only reason you're alive to bitch about all that. So you can shut up and come with us, live to fight Hatta another day or whatever, or we can leave you here and you can deal with whatever comes out of those woods by you damn self. You let me know if immediate satisfaction is worth your life."

Addison, impressed, looked from Courtney to the sisters.

Ramthe opened her mouth to speak, but Cathsin beat her to it.

"It's not." Cathsin pushed to her feet and moved over to her sister. "Just like it's not worth dying over this. I'm angry and hurt, too. I want justice, too. But it's clear that's not an option, at least not right this moment. We're outnumbered, for one." She gestured to the twins and Chess. "And I don't want to lose my sister over it."

Ramthe pursed her lips, glaring as tears gathered in her eyes. She scowled at her sister, then to the side, patting at the cooing gryffthil's head.

Cathsin wrapped her arms around her sister before turning to face Addison. "We'll go. But I don't think we can *all* fit in there."

"I'll gladly ride in a pocket," Addison offered. Besides, he didn't want to make things harder for the girls by invading their space for longer than necessary. "Either way, we need to prepare to leave. These Nightmares don't purge, and we don't want to be here when they re-form."

"They don't . . . purge?" Cathsin's eyes widened.

"I told you, we had an important message to get to the Queen."

"Question." Dem raised his hand. "What are we going to do about scary Big Bird here?"

"I can ride her." Cathsin reached to pet Moonkin's white feathers.

"All right, we have a plan. Let's get to it, we don't have much time."

◊ ◊ ◊

With help from Cathsin, Madeline was able to provide basic treatment for Alice's wounds. It wasn't up to par with her usual work, but it was better than nothing. Dee and Chess helped Ramthe unhook the gryffthil and get her saddled. Soon enough, everyone climbed into the cart. Everyone but Addison, who elected to ride in Alice's pocket.

She placed him inside gently enough, but it was still like being squeezed by the world's softest wrestler.

When she lifted the cart, a few surprised shouts sounded from inside.

"Everybody ready?" Alice asked.

Someone stuck their hand out the slat to give a thumbs-up.

On the ground, Cathsin climbed into Moonkin's saddle. With a snap of the reins she was in the air, circling overhead.

Alice took off, setting in a jog. By the Breaking, the ground she managed to cover in just a few steps. She truly was incredible.

And she continued to be so, falling into a steady pace and continuing on. They only had to stop a few times, mostly for her to take a moment to catch her breath, get a drink—it took some convincing for her to sip from a few of the natural rivers and springs here and there—before, eventually, the sparkling towers of Legracia came into view on the horizon.

"We're nearly there," Addison hollered up at her. Then he noticed the the subtle shifts in her body.

Sweat glistened bright and shining on her face. Her eyes looked somewhat glossy, her lids fluttering. What he'd thought was the wind was actually her labored breathing. The Emtae, it had run its course sooner than he thought!

"Alice!" he shouted.

She didn't respond.

"Alice!" he tried again, waving his hand.

It was no use; she was in a daze. And she was going down.

First, she stumbled, then went to her knees. Then the whole of her pitched forward. The ground rushed toward them as a groan left Alice's lips.

Addison ducked into the cocoon of cloth and braced for impact. It rattled his bones, pain jolting through him. There was the sound of wood splintering, then silence.

"Alice," Addison breathed, fighting against the ache in his body and the fabric holding him tight. He needed to get out of here to check on her. There wasn't a single thought in his brain beyond making sure she was okay.

Damn it all but he couldn't get loose of her clothing! He snatched the Vorpal Blade from his sheath and sliced his way to freedom, stumbling a bit before immediately putting away the weapon. If Nightmares attacked while Alice was down . . .

A short distance away, the others were pulling themselves from the remains of a busted cart.

"Is everyone all right?" Addison called, his eyes on Alice as he circumvented her shoulder, trying to find her face.

"What happened?" Courtney demanded as she emerged.

Cathsin came swooping in on the gryffthil. "She's fainted!"

"What can we do?" Dem asked. They'd all followed him around.

Addison racked his brain for a solution. He fought to ignore the throng of voices as everyone started to panic. Someone shouted to check the cart for supplies; maybe Maddi could mix a potion.

It wouldn't be enough. Alice needed Emknird. They would have some at the palace; there was always a supply. But there was no way to get her there.

So they would have to bring it to her.

Addison whirled to face the group, searching out the sisters who still stood slightly apart. "Which of you is the fastest flier?"

Both women looked surprised that he was talking to them, but then Cathsin hurriedly stammered, "A-ah, Ramthe is."

Addison turned to her. "Whatever ill will you feel toward me, you need to put it aside. Fly to Legracia, find Odabeth or Xelon, tell them what's happened. We need Emknird, as much as they have, and we need it fast. Please," he pressed when Ramthe looked to Alice. "Please, or she'll die. After saving you, after saving your sister. After saving all of us on more than one occasion."

Ramthe pursed her lips, her glare still firmly in place, but nodded. Without a word she rushed over to the gryffthil and climbed into the saddle. With a "Hyah!" she took to the sky, flying in the direction of the palace.

Addison watched her go, willing the winds to push her faster somehow. She had to make it. So Alice could make it. The thought of anything to the contrary squeezed the air from his lungs.

Closing his eyes, Addison willed his racing heart to slow. He couldn't panic, not now. Not when Alice needed him. It took a few seconds, before he felt the jittering in his body lessen. Then he opened his eyes and turned to find Madeline and Cathsin kneeling in front of Alice's sweat-slicked face. Her eyes rolled beneath fluttering lids. Her breath still came in quick pants, washing over the blue grass like wind.

Madeline said something and pointed at the cart, which sent Cathsin running.

"What else can we do?" Chess sounded as worried as Addison felt.

He chanced one last look in the direction Ramthe had taken off, then rolled up his sleeves. "Whatever those two tell us."

Thirty-Three

SO ORDERED

Addison paced a short distance away from where Madeline and Cathsin worked frantically at Alice's side. They'd plastered purple leaves from muden trees coated in something silverish against the exposed skin of her arms and neck, hoping to provide some relief from the Emtae burning away inside her. There was nothing else to be done. Without a dose of Emknird, there was no way to undo this.

Addison tensed every time she groaned, the sound of her in pain shooting straight to his heart. *Please, hurry,* he silently urged, his gaze drifting toward the direction Ramthe had vanished.

"You should sit down," Courtney murmured from nearby. "You're going to work yourself into a fit." She was planted on the ground, tilted into Chester. Her eyes were red, her face slicked with tears.

Chess curled his arm around her shoulders, holding her close.

The twins stood behind them, silent sentinels, though they were similarly tilted against one another. Dem supported his injured brother's weight. The two of them watched the scene across the way with dual looks of concern.

"I'm fine standing," Addison insisted. He looked to the gradually pinkening sky for signs of Ramthe or anyone who might be coming to their aid. It had already been two hours.

"She didn't say you weren't," Chester murmured.

Addison frowned, his mouth opening in order to . . . argue, agree, he wasn't sure. But before he could offer up either response, Cathsin approached the group.

He spun to face her. "Any change?"

"She okay?" Courtney asked at the same time.

Cathsin swiped at her own brow, her pale face flushed. "She's . . . I wouldn't say stable. But the leaves are working. Her temperature isn't decreasing, but it isn't rising, either." She and Madeline had worked hard and fast to apply the cooling layer as quickly as possible.

"I sense a 'but' in there somewhere," Dem murmured.

Cathsin's face scrunched slightly. "But," she continued. "If she doesn't get any Emknird in her system to counter the Emtae, it will kill her."

Courtney made a pitiful sound that was part gasp, part sob. She pressed her hands over her mouth. Chester tightened his hold on her.

The pressure in Addison's chest tightened as well. He swallowed thickly, taking a slow breath to still his racing thoughts. "How . . . how much time does she have?"

"That's hard to say. Madeline estimates another three, maybe four hours. Could be more, could be . . ."

"Alice is stronger than even she knows," Addison cut in, his eyes moving to the giant girl. "She's faced worse. Recovered from worse. She'll get through this."

Cathsin shuffled away to return to her patient, leaving the lot of them to process this news. It wasn't the best, but it could be worse. That's what Addison would hold on to. She could pull through. He couldn't comprehend the alternative.

Addison lowered himself to Courtney's other side. He was surprised, but at the same time not, when her hand found his, and she squeezed.

"Did you really mean that?" she asked, her voice thick with emotion. "You weren't just saying some bullshit in order to make us feel better?"

Addison returned the squeeze. "Yes, I really meant it. No, I wasn't just saying it." He glanced back across the field. "Alice is perhaps the strongest, most capable Dreamwalker I've ever trained. She likely wouldn't believe me if I said so, but . . . she's accomplished more than she ever should have to. Especially now."

"Da," Dem murmured. "She will get through this."

"She always gets through it," Dee said.

"Always," Addison agreed, confident in the truth of this.

Though that confidence started to fade as yet another hour crept by. Then another.

The fourth was starting to sneak up on them, and Alice's once quick but steady breathing was now labored, rattling even. Her body was drenched with sweat, and heat washed off her in waves they could feel, even at a distance.

Addison had set to pacing again.

The twins remained close to Chester and Courtney, who was crying outright now, though silently. She jolted every time Alice couldn't catch her breath, gasping, groaning.

Come on, luv, he urged quietly, watching her struggle. *Hold on for us.*

He'd wanted to go to her, be by her side. Had tried at least thrice, but Madeline shooed him away. No excess body heat, no matter how faint. She and Cathsin had covered themselves in a cooling layer by then in order to stay close to Alice and work, swapping out swatches of the leaves as they dried. But there was too much to do, not enough leaves, and not enough hands.

Even when all of them had offered to help, Madeline said it would do more harm than good. None of them were Poets. None of them knew how to make the mixture. And covering them in a layer of the salve so they could work would just waste what few resources they had.

And yet, with all that, the last of the layer was applied and now dried up. They were out of time.

Alice took another gasping breath.

Addison shut his eyes, biting into the inside of his cheek. It already stung where he'd done that numerous times before.

Hold on . . .

"Cathsin!" Rathe's voice called out.

Addison jolted to his feet, his eyes immediately going to the sky.

There. A slash of movement across the deep orange sky. Moonkin.

The relief, the outright joy that poured through Addison made him weak in the knees.

The gryffthil soared toward them, her wings beating the air. She grew larger and larger, and so did her rider. No, riders, plural. Ramthe sat at the front of the saddle and, behind her, Xelon held tight.

Gripping the reins, Ramthe guided the beast to land. The instant they hit the ground and Moonkin came to a stop, she all but leaped out of the saddle and raced toward her sister and Madeline.

Xelon climbed down as well, her armor gleaming. Her cape swept in around her, the blue material shining almost as bright.

She played her whitened gaze over the lot of them, smiling wide as she was all but rushed. Courtney reached her first, throwing arms around her in a tight hug, thanking her repeatedly for coming.

The twins each clasped her arm in turn in a warrior's greeting. They spoke to one another quickly, though Addison didn't really hear what they were saying.

His attention was focused across the field where Ramthe had joined Cathsin and Madeline, the latter holding a massive glass jug containing a bright blue liquid.

The Emknird.

The cart had been hauled over to Alice's head, and the girls worked together to get on top of it, handing the jug off as they climbed. As they went about what seemed like the arduous task of getting the mixture into Alice's mouth, Xelon finally made her way to Addison's side. He nodded at her, then looked back to what was going on.

"I think we made it in time," Xelon murmured.

Addison didn't respond. He couldn't. All he could do was stare as the blue liquid finally disappeared between Alice's lips.

For a precious stretch of seconds, nothing happened.

Then even more time passed.

And even more.

Xelon rested a hand on Addison's shoulders. "Hatta . . . I . . ."

Everyone jumped when Alice's body jolted. The ground shook as her limbs flopped against it. She twitched and writhed, her head jerking around. It was like riding a bucking bull, only the ground was the animal in question. Everyone toppled over like dominos.

Madeline, Cathsin, and Ramthe quickly climbed down off the cart, screaming when Alice's arm swept it over onto its side, nearly catching them.

Ramthe pulled her sister to her feet, and the three of them ran toward the group. All the while, Alice's body pitched and thrashed, sending tremors through the earth.

"What's happening?" Courtney shouted, her voice panicked. "Is it working?"

"See for yourself!" Ramthe pointed.

Alice continued to shake, but her body had begun to shrink. Smaller and smaller, fading away into itself until she looked . . . Alice-sized again. At least, she did from a distance.

Addison was at her side in an instant. He threw himself down beside her, ignoring the ache in his knees. He gathered her body into his arms, gasping faintly at the heat that still wafted off her. Had the Emknird not worked?

"Alice," he whispered, his voice cracking on her name.

"Mind the snowdrop!" Madeline was suddenly beside him, pulling Alice from his grip.

His hold tightened briefly, reflexively, a primal part of him not wanting to let her go, but reason won out. He handed her over gingerly as Cathsin joined them. The two bent over their patient, coaxing her mouth open, pouring a multicolored liquid between her lips, slowly, carefully, getting her to swallow.

Addison drew back, nearly tumbling over Courtney, who'd pressed in beside him, her shoulders shaking, an equally distraught Chester at her side.

"Hear me, Alison," Madeline murmured as she touched her hand to Alice's face.

With another jerk, Alice started coughing. Hard, harsh convulsions that shook her entire frame and likely rubbed her throat raw. But she was breathing, steady, even. It was the most beautiful thing he'd ever heard.

"Oh thank god," Courtney whimpered before practically melting into Chester, crying into his shoulder as his arms went around her. He buried his face in her hair in turn.

Addison pressed his hands over his face and . . . just sat there, his body shaking outside of his control. The twins celebrated somewhere behind him.

"She's okay," Xelon murmured as she came up to his side. "She'll live."

"That she will," Addison croaked, sniffing and swiping at the blur in his eyes.

"Mmm." Xelon watched him for a moment before quietly asking, "Where's the sword?"

At first, he didn't know what she meant. "In the cart." It had been a compromise of sorts after Ramthe left.

Cathsin, while she seemed to trust him more than her sister, had said she would feel better and likely work faster if she knew he didn't have direct access to it. So he put it in the cart for safekeeping.

Xelon nodded. Despite the happy turn of events, there was still a sorrowful twist to her expression. No, not sorrow. Regret. But not from anything she had done. It's what she was about to do. "I'm sorry," she murmured.

"I know," he whispered.

Then she stepped back, drew her sword, and aimed the tip of the blade at his chest.

Cries of shock and alarm went up around him, but Addison did not react for his part. What could he say or do in this instance but accept his fate?

"Addison Hatta," Xelon said, raising her voice. Her gaze bored into his. "Having abandoned your assigned post as keeper of the Western Gateway and ventured into Wonderland beyond the allotted territory deemed necessary for the fulfillment of your duties, your previous sentence is hereby revoked, and you are to be placed under immediate arrest and brought forth to answer for your crimes. So ordered by Emalia of Legracia, the White Queen."

Thirty-Four

REUNITED

Alice's entire body felt like one giant bruise. The very thought of moving sent ripples of agony radiating through her. Every inch of her skin was on fire, the heat eating her alive.

"I've got you!" a familiar voice said from somewhere overhead.

She tried to open her eyes, but they refused to obey. It was the same with the rest of her mutinous body, arms, legs; nothing worked.

Something cool pressed to her lips. Her head was tilted up, and sweet, soothing cold flowed down her throat. The flames eating away at her insides flickered in defiance, then faded.

Sweet relief. And she could tell the instant her body was back under her control, it was like someone had lifted a boulder off her chest.

Finally, she opened her eyes.

The world floated around her in amorphous blobs of color that gradually came into focus, along with a familiar face staring down at her.

Two familiar faces, actually.

"Oh thank god," Courtney breathed.

"Hey!" Haruka smiled brightly, her dark eyes twinkling. "You're okay!"

"Relatively," Alice muttered. God, her head was *pounding*. She groaned, closing her eyes again, lifting a hand to press over them. Her arm felt like it weighed a hundred pounds. "What happened?"

"A lot. Apparently you OD'd on some magic biscuit." Courtney retook her seat on one side of the bed, Haruka on the other.

Alice couldn't help the exhausted chuckle that escaped her. "I *what?*"

"That stuff that made you go all big, your *Attack on Titan* plan?" Courtney snorted. "It burned you out like a bad transmission. Almost. Luckily, help arrived, got you shrunk, and we brought you here."

"Here being Legracia," Alice assumed. She hadn't gotten a good look around, but fancy white walls covered in portraits and an even fancier ceiling made it easy to guess.

"Yup," said Courtney. "This place is ridiculous, no wonder Odabeth's spoiled."

"How are you feeling?" Haruka asked, concern clear in her voice.

"Like somebody put my head in a blender and the rest of me in a pizza oven." Alice opened her eyes again.

Courtney smiled and squeezed Alice's other hand.

"Here," Haruka said, holding out a glass. "Drink."

Alice didn't need to be told twice. She tipped to her lips and swallowed the contents easily, surprised it was just plain water. The best plain water she'd ever tasted.

After downing two more glasses, and feeling less like she was going to vibrate apart if she moved too quickly, Alice pushed herself up to hang her legs over the side of the bed.

"Go slow," Haruka cautioned. "Maddi said you might be a little weak."

Alice nodded mutely, her attention fixed on where Haruka had gently clasped her arms in order to help steady her. Warmth blossomed where skin met skin, so different from the oppressive heat that had tried to devour her earlier.

"What are you doing here?" Alice asked, trying to ignore the fluttering in her middle.

Haruka shrugged. The muscles in her bare arms rippled with it.

Alice tried and failed to ignore that, too.

"Same as everyone, I imagine," Haruka said. "Increased Nightmare activity, kill sites that won't purge. Romi came for answers, and I came with."

"Oh . . . well . . . it's good to see you," Alice said, smiling gently.

Haruka returned it, and the butterflies in Alice's stomach went ham.

A distinct "ahem" sounded behind Alice, and she suddenly remembered her best friend was in the room, too. She glanced over her shoulder and right into Courtney's smug smirk.

"We're supposed to let Maddi know when you wake up, but I can give you a minute if you want."

"That, um, that won't be necessary," Alice said, feeling the temperature in her face rise a hundred degrees.

Was it a trick of the light or did Courtney's smirk widen?

Alice gently tugged her arms out of Haruka's careful hold, murmuring a quiet "Thank you."

The other Dreamwalker merely nodded before turning to pour another glass of water. This gave Alice the few seconds she needed to take a deep breath and get herself together. *Come on, Kingston!*

"I'll go deliver the news." Courtney rose from her chair and sashayed across the room, humming jauntily. When she reached the door, she pitched Alice one last knowing look.

Alice scowled back at her, then at the door when it closed behind her.

"Your friend is very funny." Haruka offered her the refilled glass.

"She *thinks* she is," Alice muttered. She finally tore her gaze away from the door and looked at Haruka.

"I don't know," said Haruka, sitting back fully in her chair. "She told me a few stories that were pretty good. Nothing about you," she added when Alice choked a little on her water. "Mostly about her family and her many sisters."

Family. That word made Alice sit up straight. Her family, her mother and grandmother, she still didn't know where they were!

"What's wrong?" Haruka asked, a frown creasing her brow.

"Nothing," Alice said softly, shaking her head. "At least, I hope it's nothing."

Sprigs had promised Mom and Nana K would be all right, and would find her when it was time, whatever that meant. And as much as Alice wanted to race out of this room, out of the palace itself, and go off to find them, she knew it didn't work like that.

She took a deep breath to calm her jumping nerves, then looked to Haruka again. Damn, she looked good, the tank top, those arms, whyyyyyy.

Clearing her throat she shifted to try and get to her feet. She waved away Haruka when the other girl reached out as if to help.

"I'm okay, just need a second." Her knees knocked, and her ankles felt like they had the bearing strength of toothpicks, but she stayed on her feet. She even managed a few testing steps. So far, so good.

"When I OD'd on that biscuit or whatever," Alice began as she walked in a small circle before lowering herself back to the bed. "I was carrying a wagon full of people. I must have dropped it or . . . or something. Is everyone okay?" She imagined Courtney would have said something if anyone was hurt, but she wanted to be sure.

"Everyone is all right," Haruka said. Then, after a moment, added, "Physically."

Alice did *not* like that. "What do you mean?"

Haruka chewed at her lower lip, reluctantly. "No one has been harmed, but . . ." She finally lifted her gaze to meet Alice's. "Addison Hatta has been detained, charged with violating the terms of his exile."

All the air fled the room. Haruka kept talking, but Alice didn't hear a word she said. She couldn't. Everything around her had faded to the background, swept beneath the sudden storm rising in her veins.

She was up and striding toward the door in an instant, her aches and pains forgotten, brushed aside by worry and adrenaline.

"Alice!" Haruka called after her.

She didn't exactly ignore her; she just didn't stop. Snatching the door open, she drew up short so as not to barrel right into the body waiting on the other side.

Anastasia Petrova, the Duchess, peered down at Alice. A single red brow hiked toward the woman's crimson hairline. Her usual single braid hung partially over shoulder. She'd been waiting. "Going somewhere?"

Alice felt the storm inside her intensify. She scowled. "To see the White Queen. Please move."

The Duchess did not budge. "That's not a good idea."

"And why not?"

"Because nothing you say will help him."

Alice felt a muscle in her jaw twitch. "You don't know that."

The Duchess folded her arms over her chest. "I know a great many things, such as how you feel right now. But you ca—"

"*Oh* really?"

"*Da*, really. Addison has been my friend longer than he's been yours, so I am very aware of how upsetting this is. But the White Queen already overlooked one infraction, she will not forgive another."

Alice scoffed, mostly to keep from laughing in the Duchess's face. "Infraction? You mean running for his life? He didn't have a choice, none of them did!"

"I know," Anastasia said calmly, which only served to irritate Alice more. "But the law is the law, regardless of how we feel about it."

Alice scowled. Her fingers curled into fists at her sides. "This isn't about my fucking feelings."

"No?" The Duchess's already hiked brow lifted even higher. "You're certainly acting like it is."

Alice's vision doubled she was so angry. She started to tremble with it. "Odabeth pardoned him," she said, fighting to keep the words from shaking with the rest of her.

"True," the Duchess admitted. "To save his life, in exchange for having helped save all of ours. The exile verse would have killed him otherwise. But that doesn't mean the conditions of his sentence had changed."

Alice's father had once told her that anger can make a person foolish. You get someone mad enough about the right thing at the wrong time, there was no telling what they might say. Or, worse, what they might do. Anger made people reckless.

Right now? There was nothing Alice wanted to be more than reckless.

As if sensing this, the Duchess tilted forward slowly, a dangerous glint in her eye. "Poslushay menya. Listen to me and listen well," she began, her voice low, edged like a razor blade. "Now is not the time to be ruled by emotion. This matter is far more complex than you know, and there is not enough time in this world or yours for me to explain it to you, so I will simply say this: Addison is alive. He is alive and unharmed, and the palace grounds are presently full of people who would very much like to change that. People who were hurt by events that transpired during the war, who believe he deserved execution instead of exile, and some of them would do almost anything to see him lose his head. Addison is a prisoner, but this also means he is protected."

She was right. Alice *hated* to admit it, loathed the very idea with her entire being. But that wouldn't change the fact that Anastasia was right.

Alice's anger deflated like a balloon, popped and left to flail about uselessly until there was nothing more to keep it afloat. She felt empty without it. Then she felt the sting of tears, sharper, more pronounced in the wake of her dwindling fury.

A hand fell to her shoulder. Haruka's.

Blinking through the blur, Alice wiped at the few drops that had managed to fall. She wouldn't allow more than that. Then she took a breath and met the Duchess's gaze.

"Can I see him?" Surprisingly, her voice was far steadier than she expected.

The Duchess straightened, then sighed. Her expression softened with understanding. After a few moments of contemplation, she nodded. "I will take you to him."

Alice followed the Duchess through the grand halls of Legracia. Haruka had given Alice a lingering but comforting hug, promising to find her later after checking in with Romi, so it was just the two of them. The palace was every bit as beautiful as before, though much, much busier.

As they walked, they ducked around dozens of people carrying medical supplies, armaments, even baskets of food. Or stuff that looked like food. There were also a lot more guards than she remembered, a pair stationed at every door, every corner, or on patrol. All of them armed and armored. Shit was getting real.

Questions bubbled along the surface of Alice's mind. One question in particular. She wasn't sure if asking it would start trouble or not, but it itched at her all the same. She stole glances at the Duchess, debating whether or not to voice them.

"Something on your mind?" the Duchess asked without turning. "Besides the obvious."

"What makes you think there is?"

The Duchess spared once glance over her shoulder, then faced forward almost immediately. "You look like something is on your mind."

Okay, fair. "I had a question."

"Just one?"

Alice grunted. "For now. It's . . . I don't want to be rude . . ."

The Duchess gave a thoughtful "mmmm." "You want to know why Addison is imprisoned and I am not."

"It . . . No, I . . . Well, yeah . . . kinda . . . I mean, you were both exiled, right?"

"Da, though the terms of my sentence were not as severe. I can return to Wonderland for brief periods under very specific and extenuating circumstances, all having to do with my charge as a Guardian and my duty to protect Wonderland."

Alice frowned. "Okay, second question."

"Knew it."

She ignored that. "*Why* was your sentence less severe?"

The Duchess paused. Just stopped in the middle of the hall. Alice nearly ran into her but managed to pump the breaks as well.

For an instant, the warrior's mask fell from Anastasia's face, and Alice caught a glimpse of the sorrow beneath. It was brief. Blink and you'd have missed it. But it was there. And it reminded Alice of the look on her mother's face every time someone mentioned her father.

"Because I never threatened Wonderland itself," the Duchess murmured. And then she kept going, and that was that.

Alice followed, her mind turning over those words.

"Do not worry too much," the Duchess said, derailing Alice's train of thought. "Addison's 'prison' is nicer than several homes I've been in. Lucky for him the actual dungeon is being used for extra storage."

They rounded the corner and came to a stop in front of a large door flanked by guards, two on each side. Four pairs of eyes moved between Alice and the Duchess.

"I am here to see the prisoner," the Duchess declared.

Each pair of guards exchanged sideways glances before one of them reached out to press a patch of metal on the door where a handle should have been but wasn't. After a few seconds, the tumblers clicked and the door swung inward.

That quick, huh?

The Duchess nodded and stepped through. Alice quickly followed, the door swinging shut behind her.

Well, the Duchess was right. Again. This place was more parlor than prison. At least, Alice thought this was a parlor. It looked like it would be called a parlor, full of fancy-looking tables, chairs, and a couple chaises. Addison sat on one of them, book in hand. The title was indiscernible from this distance. He did not look up as they entered.

"Anastasia," he said evenly while flipping a page. "To what do I owe the pleasure?"

In lieu of a verbal response, the Duchess simply stepped to one side.

Addison glanced up. The moment his eyes met Alice's, the widest smile broke over his face, sending every butterfly in her stomach into overdrive.

"Alice." He sighed her name like a prayer, and then her arms were around him.

She didn't know if he came to her or vice versa, or maybe they met in the middle, but she buried her face in his chest and breathed him in. He smelled like he always did, faintly of alcohol and something sweet she couldn't place.

"You gave us quite a scare, luv," he murmured into her hair, pressing a kiss there. "How are you feeling?"

"Better now," she said, her voice muffled against his shirt. "Considering I almost OD'd on a biscuit."

He chuckled, and the sound moved through her.

"What about you?" she asked as she finally withdrew.

"Well, things could be worse. Much worse. Her Highness is far more forgiving than I expected her to be with my return."

"I suspect that has more to do with the Nightmares threatening to overrun the land and less to do with your charm," the Duchess said, a smile pulling at her face.

The White Queen wasn't being *that* forgiving, in Alice's opinion, but it was clear that things could be worse, and might very well soon be.

"I guess that explains why this place is so busy." Between the new flavors of Nightmares, from face-stealers to unpurgables, then ones that apparently can hide in Figment Blades and create living Slithe that swallows you whole, it made more than a little sense that everyone was on edge.

Addison nodded. "The Queen has been preparing defenses and sending forces out to protect the people for weeks now, apparently. As least here in Wonderland. Though I am curious as to why none of the Gatekeepers were alerted."

The Duchess made a noise that was part contemplative, part concerned, all annoyed. Then she murmured something in Russian, her tone dipping.

Addison answered in kind, the two of them going back and forth, growing more and more animated each time. Something was clearly up.

"So, uuhhhhhhmm, y'all wanna share with the class?" Alice asked.

The conversation petered out, with Addison massaging a temple and the Duchess pursing her lips as she glowered at the floor.

"It could be nothing," he said.

"Or it could be everything," the Duchess immediately countered, knifing a look at him that could have slit his throat.

Alice set her hands to her hips, in no way shape or form in the mood. "I thought we were done with all the secrets and cryptic bullshit."

"It's not a secret, luv. Just an old concern possibly rearing its head. A theory, really."

Alice gestured for him to continue. He hesitated, but when she cocked her head to the side and narrowed her eyes in warning, he relented.

"Very well," he sighed. "There was an . . . incident in your world during the late 1800s. A series of unsolved murders in England. Human authorities believed it to be the work of a madman, but Anastasia and her Dreamwalker discovered a Nightmare was responsible. And not just any Nightmare, but a sort of mutation we had never seen before and haven't since. At least until recently, when I attended the costumed event with you and Courtney."

"The Wraiths," Alice murmured, picturing the "people" who had chased them through the convention center, their arms and faces contorting into claws and fangs. She shuddered.

Addison nodded. "Yes. Granted there are differences. These Wraiths merely mimic human appearance instead of cobbling a disguise out of dead bodies."

Alice recoiled both mentally and physically. "Waitwaitwait. Dead bodies?"

"Mmm." Anastasia picked up the story. "The mutation had taken over the corpse of a young man. We're still not sure if it killed him first or found him after he was already dead, but it inhabited the cadaver, taking control in order to murder others and use their flesh to mend its broken form. To what end remains a mystery."

The back of Alice's throat started to tingle with the need to throw up. "That . . . that's all kinds of fucked."

"You don't know the half of it," Addison growled, his disgust clear on his face. Something about this seemed personal, but she didn't press.

"The mutation was slain and purged," he continued. "But we never did discover its origins. Had it developed the same way all Nightmares do, or was it created by someone harnessing the power of the Nox? The same way Portentia used her power to make Fiends."

He shrugged. "It remained a mystery, until Chester was slain, then resurrected by Slithe."

Chess? What did . . . ? Oh no . . . Panic started set in. Alice's entire body started to vibrate with it. It wasn't hard to guess what Addison was getting at. "No." She shook her head. "He's not. He can't be!" She didn't want to believe it, but part of her knew. Had always known. From the day he came to her outside Nana K's building. The moment he lifted his shirt and she saw the wound in his chest. It had been lethal. She'd seen him die, she—

A gentle touch to Alice's cheek brought her out of the spiral. She blinked rapidly as Addison's face came into focus. He brushed a thumb against her cheek, slow and steady. A grounding sensation.

He smiled softly. Sadly. His gray eyes full of understanding. "Do not worry, milady. Chester *is* stable. Madeline made sure of this when she was being held prisoner by the Blood Lady. But . . . in doing so, she inadvertently refined the process for creating the Wraiths. And while she was able to sabotage many of the Bloody Lady's other experiments, she could not bring herself to do the same to him."

Alice's thoughts spun in fifty different directions. Did this mean Chess was a Wraith? Or was he a mutation like that thing they killed way back when? Did being stable mean he wouldn't need body parts to stay alive? She shuddered, revulsion rolling through her.

When she could manage words without risking puking, she asked, "Does he know?"

Anastasia nodded. "I imagine this is one source of the strife between you all. Addison has kept me appraised of his behavior, for obvious reasons."

Alice shut her eyes and breathed deep. So, one of her best friends might be a literal monster. One she maybe might have to kill one day. Fucking fan-tastic.

"There is good news, of sorts," the Duchess said. "The sample of Slithe you gathered at Ahoon? I have been studying its properties. It is incredibly potent, unnaturally so. Most likely a result of the initial failed attempts to create the Wraiths. This strain, and any Nightmares born from it, are more resilient and thus more difficult to purge, but all degenerative properties have been greatly reduced. In plain terms, it is keeping Chester alive, sparing him the gruesome fate of the boy in England."

Good, Alice thought, still breathing deep to keep from having a full mental meltdown about her friend being turned into a monster and it being partially her fucking fault. Keeping him alive is good. No need to start harvesting body parts. But something didn't sit right in all this. Hell, none of it did, but something in particular the Duchess said stuck out.

"If we found this super Slithe in Ahoon, that means it's part of Wonderland now," Alice said. It was coming out of the ground.

"And that's the rub," muttered Addison. "We hope the naturally occurring Slithe will eventually dilute it, but only time will tell. Meanwhile, stronger Nightmares and pools of creeping dark may be a thing for a bit."

Alice nodded slowly. Okay. Okay. Stronger Nightmares she could deal with. Had been dealing with. And it was nice to finally know what the hell was going on, but . . .

Her thoughts were interrupted when the parlor door swung open again. One of the guards filled the frame. She nodded, bright gray eyes flickering over everyone present. "Alice Kingston.

Her Majesty Queen Emalia of Legracia requests your presence at once."

◊ ◊ ◊

The Duchess had offered to accompany Alice, but the guard had insisted the White Queen wanted to see her and her alone. Which was fine. Perfect, really. That whole conversation about Chess and the Wraiths had sent Alice's head spinning, and a silent march through the palace gave her a chance to get her shit together.

The throne room doors were large and wide, ridiculously ornate things with silver hinges and jeweled handles the size of her forearms. Of course there were even more guards stationed on either side. Alice recognized this pair from her last visit. Malal and Kapi, the siblings that were part of the princess's personal guard. Guess they were the Queen's now.

Kapi nodded to Alice in silent greeting as he and his sister both gripped a massive handle and pulled. The doors swung open slowly.

Inside was absolutely stunning, all clear crystal and bright daylight glistening overhead, reflected off the dazzling marble floor beneath her feet. A luxurious silver rug split the cavernous chamber in half, providing a clear path right up to a rise of circular stairs set against the far wall.

At the center of the landing, poised like the topper on on a wedding cake, stood a throne of glass cradling a single occupant. A woman. Even at this distance, which had to be at least a hundred feet if not more, Alice could tell it was the same woman from the portrait she'd seen of Odabeth and her mother.

As Alice approached, she was able to study the woman, comparing her with the memory of the painting, and it was easy to tell something was wrong. The Queen was thinner, her complexion more gray, her features not exactly gaunt but narrowed just so. Symptoms of being poisoned, most likely. Still, she was one of the most beautiful women Alice had ever laid eyes on.

The Queen was dwarfed by her throne, sunken into it more than sitting on it. To her right, in a smaller and slightly less impressive chair, was Odabeth. Save for the gorgeous glow of her amber skin and round features, she was the spitting image of her mother. She held her head high, chin out, looking bougie as ever. It made Alice smile, if only a little.

"Alice!" The princess bounced up from her seat, gripped her skirts, and practically floated down the stairs and across the room like an enthusiastic cloud.

Alice opened her arms for the hug she knew was coming.

"It's so good to see you." Odabeth squeezed Alice tight enough it actually hurt a little before drawing back.

"You too! You look . . . queenly!" She shot a look at the throne, then back to the princess and lowered her voice. "How's your mom?"

Odabeth's smile waned a little but remained bright and hopeful. "I know it may not appear so, but she's doing much, much better. The treatments are helping, and the search for a cure continues. But the Eye's vision has been, how do I put this. It's as if the Eye is confused."

Alice frowned. "What you mean?"

Odabeth huffed in frustration. "When I try to see the Heart, I'm shown a room covered in shadow and crystal. But before I can pick out many details, the vision changes! Into a bedroom. I think. There is a bed, a short armoire covered in small figurines with large heads and oversized eyes, like big black buttons."

Alice blinked. Had Odabeth just decribed . . . Funkos?

"No one knows what to make of it," the princess continued, her brow furrowed.

"Odabeth, darling, please," a gentle though tired voice echoed softly through the air.

Odabeth straightened, and her frown vanished. "Yes, of course. Apologies, Mother." She gave Alice one last squeeze before hurrying back to her seat. Then she reached to take her mother's hand, smiling faintly.

The Queen returned the smile before looking to Alice and drawing herself up, just slightly. "Alice Kingston. Approach."

Alice swallowed thickly before making her way down the carpet, her steps muted by the lush fibers. She stopped a few feet in front of the stairs and curtsied, pulling at the hem of her shirt, which had definitely seen better days. "Your Majesty."

The Queen's white eyes followed Alice's every step. "It is my understanding that I have you to thank for saving my daughter's life, on multiple occasions, as well as my own."

Alice fidgeted under the power in that gaze, despite the Queen's somewhat frail appearance. "I was glad to. And I'm glad to see you're recovering."

Odabeth made a faint sound and bit into her lower lip. The Queen sighed softly.

Alice frowned. "You . . . are recovering, aren't you?"

"Not as quickly as I'd like. But, thanks to Naette, I am stable."

There was a silent "for now" at the end of that sentence if Alice ever heard one.

The Queen cleared her throat. "That's not why I asked you here. I wish to reward you for your great deeds. I offer one boon of your choosing, within reason and my power."

"Boon?" Alice asked.

"My daughter's life is worth more than I can every repay, but if you have a price, name it. And I will see it done."

Alice didn't know what to say. When she'd come to Legracia, it was to save Addison. That's all she'd wanted. And to fix the mess she'd unintentionally made, but that's neither here nor there. Everything that happened after was her doing her job, fighting to protect the people, the world she cared about. She was a Dreamwalker. Saving people was part of the deal, right?

Though, now that she thought about it, there was one thing she could ask for. One thing only the White Queen might be able to give her. Well, not *her*.

Before she could voice this, the doors boomed open and Malal fell into the room. "Your Majesty!"

Alice swallowed an annoyed sound. That's twice now someone came bursting in and interrupted her. She was starting to feel a way, for real.

Malal's chest heaved as she trotted forward, quick, powerful strides carrying her swiftly to Alice's side where she immediately took a knee. "Y-Your Majesty!"

The Queen frowned, her eyes fixed on the kneeling guard. "What is it? Are we under attack?"

Malal gestured frantically at the door, stumbling over her attempts to speak. "Y-you . . . your—I—I don't . . . It's . . . !" Girl was shook.

The Queen heaved a put-upon sigh. "Malal, this is hardly appropriate. I insisted I not be disturbed."

"Then it's a good thing I don't give a damn about what you insist."

Alice spun toward the door so fast she nearly flung herself over sideways.

320

"Nana!" she gasped, eyes fixed on her grandmother as the older woman came shuffling down the silver carpet.

And beside her . . . "Mom!" Alice broke into a run.

The chamber hurtled by in a blur of light and crystal. Then Alice was in her mother's arms, face buried in her shoulder.

"I'm sorry, I'm so sorry!" she sobbed, choking on the words as they poured out of her. She couldn't stop them, or the tears.

"Shh, shh, it's okay, baby," came the whispered reply, trembly with relief.

More arms wrapped around her, squeezing tight. Nana K. Alice reached for her as well, fingers clutching weakly at the fabric of her gown. Relief had stolen her strength.

"Thank you, Jesus," Mom sighed, dropping kisses all over Alice's face. Then wiped the tears from her cheeks. "My baby."

"I tried to hold on," Alice stammered, swallowing hard around the lump in her throat.

"We know," Nana K assured. "It wasn't your fault."

It took a second, and a few deep breaths, for Alice to rein in her runaway emotions. She'd believed Sprigs when he said her family was safe and they would be reunited, but seeing her mother and grandmother here was like a balm on a wound she didn't know was there.

Alice drew back, laughing through more tears. It sounded a little manic, but she didn't care. Because nothing and no one else mattered.

For about two seconds.

Then someone shoved her from behind. She turned, *immediately* ready to throw hands, until she saw the White Queen hanging off her grandma.

"It's okay, Em," Nana K murmured as she consoled the weeping monarch. "I'm here."

Alice blinked several times, wiping the last of the tears from her eyes. Briefly, she wondered if she was hallucinating. Maybe the biscuit was still messing with her system, but no. The White Queen was still clinging to Nana K, who had wrapped her into a bear hug. This didn't make any sense. What the hell was happening right now?

"Mother?" Odabeth approached slowly, her brow wrinkled, her fingers twisted in her skirts. "Mother, what . . . what's going on?"

Good fucking question.

"I can't believe it," the White Queen said, the whole of her trembling. "After all this time. Sister, I feared the worst."

Sister? At that moment, every thought bouncing between Alice's ears ground to a halt as her brain short-circuited.

Thirty-Five
WAR COUNCIL

A lice stared.

Sister?

And stared.

Sister . . .

And stared.

Sister!

Then she felt her mouth move, but couldn't remember making the decision to speak. "The hell do you mean, *sister?*"

Mom wrapped her arms around Alice's shoulders, patting and rubbing as if trying to calm a skittish animal. "Language, baby."

Language?! Alice gawked at her mother, who was entirely too calm about this situation.

"It's . . . a lot," Mom started. "I know."

She was interrupted by the White Queen, who spoke slowly, as if having realized this was a somewhat precarious situation. "I meant exactly what I said. This is my sister, Queen Kashunte of Castle Findest, finally returned to us."

Nana K made a sort of strangled noise at the back of her throat as her eyes fell shut. "I haven't heard that full title in decades."

Alice's entire body went ice cold. Her heart hammered wildly in her chest. This wasn't possible. It had to be a dream. She was still in bed, high on magic biscuits or something. That had to be it, because if she wasn't, if this was really happening, that meant . . .

"You're the Red Queen." It was supposed to be a question. Instead, it came out more as an affirmation. Maybe even a little bit of an accusation.

Nana K nodded. Her silver afro bounced slightly with it. "I am."

Those two words landed like a gut punch. Alice felt the world tilt, and had to fight to keep from tilting with it.

"You're the Red Queen," she repeated. "*How* are you the Red Queen?"

It didn't make sense; this was her grandma! A constant in her life for as long as she could remember. Nana K had gone to her recitals and concerts, plays and school programs. She baked cookies for the church block party and made her famous banana pudding for the family reunion every year, where she would exchange stories and memories with distant relatives from bygone times. There was just no way she could be the Red Queen.

But then Alice remembered the other night, how Nana K had defeated those Fiends at the house. Then she showed Alice how to dispel the Slithe corrupting her dagger like it was nothing and . . .

"Holy shit."

"Language!" Mom snapped.

Nana K reached to take Alice's hand without letting go of the

White Queen's. "I will explain everything, to everyone, but right now we got bigger problems."

Alice briefly wondered what could possibly be bigger than revealing yourself to be the long-lost monarch of a magical kingdom, but her attention was diverted when Nana K turned toward the throne room doors.

"Tell them," she called to a figure lingering just inside the chamber.

It was Humphrey. Had he been there this entire time? She hadn't even noticed. Then again, she was pretty distracted.

"By the breaking," the White Queen gasped. "Is that—"

"Yes," Nana K cut in. "But we don't have time to get into it. Listen to what he has to say."

Humphrey pushed away from the wall, looking all kinds of uncomfortable with being here. His shoulders hunched, his eyes darted about the room as he crossed to kneel in front of Nana K and the White Queen.

At least, he stared to kneel, but Nana K flapped a hand at him to remain on his feet.

"An army of Nightmares marches on Legracia," he said. "I saw them gathered in the Middler Forest when I scouted for provisions after we emerged from the In-Between. If they travel through the night, they will be here by morning."

Silence descended, thick and crushing. Alice could see this news crash over the White Queen like a tidal wave. She actually swayed on her feet and might had fallen over if not for Nana K's hold on her. The two exchanged a wordless look, but Alice could tell more was said in that brief glance than some people manage with whole speeches.

Finally, the White Queen turned to Malal. "Assemble the war council," she ordered, then hesitated a beat before adding, "and bring me the Gatekeepers and their charges. All of them."

◊ ◊ ◊

Alice hadn't known what she'd expected from a war council assembly, but when several runners scurried from the throne room to carry the command to all corners of the palace, rumor that the Red Queen had returned went with it. What followed was pure chaos.

Almost instantly, a crowd gathered at the throne room entrance. People whispered and pointed, some staring wide-eyed and open-mouthed. Malal and Kapi did what they could to keep onlookers back, but more and more showed up with each passing minute. Those who couldn't squeeze in at the door pushed onto their toes to peer over shoulders and heads, trying to catch a glimpse of the once missing monarch. Even some of the surrounding guards had stepped away from their posts to see what all the fuss was about.

This had led to even *more* guards being called from the surroundings halls to corral the swelling throng as it threatened to spill into the throne room. Chants of "Long live the Queens!" in various languages shook the palace walls and echoed through the corridors. These people were ready to throw a party in the antechamber.

Through all of that, Alice had teetered between bouncing off the walls and having an anxiety attack. One second, she would be ready to burst, smiling so big her face hurt. The next she couldn't breathe, it felt like an elephant was sitting on her chest, and she wanted to sink into the floor. A pretty normal reaction to finding out you're related to a queen. Maybe. She had no freaking idea.

On the one hand, who wouldn't want to discover they were secretly royalty? This was some real Sailor Moon meets Princess Diaries type stuff. On the other, guards were already calling her "Your Majesty" and shit and she just . . . couldn't. She didn't want to think about it. About how people would start treating her different. How her life would probably change, in both good and not-so-great ways. No. She had enough to worry about, since there was apparently a Nightmare army on the way, ready to storm the castle gates all Helms Deep like.

It took a while to clear the throne room completely. Partially because Alice's mother refused to go, at first. But when the White Queen explained that only military personnel—which included Dreamwalkers—were permitted to attend the council, Mom relented.

She'd hugged Alice tight enough to hurt, but it was a good ache; then she was escorted out by a pair of guards who would take her to have a bath, change her clothes, and get some food.

The Duchess and Romi arrived shortly after that, with Haruka and the twins in tow. Dee looked much better, no doubt thanks to Maddi. The three Dreamwalkers joined Alice where she stood off to the side while Romi and Anastasia were reunited with Nana K.

It was weird seeing people bow to her grandmother. Even weirder to see her wave them to their feet all regal like with the declaration that she ain't been bowed to in decades, she wasn't having it now. Instead, hands were clasped and quiet words of reverence exchanged. The whole time, Alice tried not to squirm while she waited for either of the twins to catch on.

Dem put it together first. Then both boys exploded in an excited mix of Russian and English, earning sharp glances from the Duchess. Apparently finding out your friend is a princess is no excuse to wild out in the presence of royalty.

Haruka's reaction was more reserved in comparison. She said something about how a kiss from a princess was supposed to be good luck. Ignoring knowing looks from the twins, and how the temperature in her immediate area had risen several degrees, Alice kept stealing glances at the throne room doors.

A handful more people she didn't recognize came in. More shock, more bowing, some of it to her. Alice tried not to squirm. She decided she didn't like this part. Not that there was anything *wrong* with it, just . . . it made her feel weird. No thanks.

Addison was the last to arrive. Well, second to last. He came in ahead of Xelon, who had escorted Odabeth to her chambers and on the way back retrieved him from his "cell."

His gaze found Alice's and he smiled, his chin dipping ever so slightly. She returned it, or tried to. It felt more like a grimace. Probably looked like one too, given how his brow furrowed slightly in concern.

"I'm fine," she mouthed. Which was true. Mostly. She was nervous as all hell. Felt like her skin was going was made of Pop Rocks and someone had poured soda over her head.

He nodded and faced forward again. The entire exchange took mere seconds, and he didn't even stop. He couldn't, not with the White Knight guiding him steadily forward, until he came to stand in front of both Queens of Wonderland, together again.

To Alice's astonishment, Addison barely reacted to her grandmother's presence. He didn't look shocked, didn't gasp or swoon like everyone else had. He simply strode forward and dropped to a knee.

"Majesties," he murmured.

Nana K peered down at him. "Addison Hatta."

"It is good to have you with us again, Queen Kashaunte."

"You don't seem very surprised to see me," she said, arching an eyebrow.

Alice felt a nervous sweat break out on the back of her neck. Here she'd been worried about the day Addison might cross paths with her mom, and it was her grandma who might break him in half. Or have someone else do it.

"Word of your return spread quickly," he said, still kneeling. Nana K hadn't waved him up yet.

"Mmm." Nana K's gaze flicked upward, catching Alice's briefly. She winked before looking back to Addison.

Uh-oh. Alice felt her stomach tighten. Her grandmother was up to something.

"You not gonna bow to the princess?" Nana K asked.

Ahh hell.

Addison lifted his head but didn't rise. His gaze moved to Odabeth's empty throne, then back again. "The princess is not here, Majesty."

Nana K's smile stretched the full width of her face. "I mean my grandbaby."

Kill me now.

Addison blinked rapidly. His mouth worked for a second before he tilted his head in question, clearly confused. "Your grandbaby, Majesty?"

Please. End it. I won't fight.

Nana K extended a hand Alice's direction. "Alison Kingston. My granddaughter."

All eyes shifted to her. While most of the room was already aware of the familial connection, one person in particular was not.

Addison's jaw nearly hit the floor. His head whipped back and forth so fast Alice was afraid he'd give himself whiplash. "Y-you," she said, staring at her, then at her grandma. "She's your . . ." Alice didn't think she'd ever heard him sound so flustered before.

It would have been cute if it wasn't mortifying.

"Yeah, it's news to me too," she blurted, trying to sound nonchalant. "Not the being-her-grandbaby thing, the whole Queen . . . development." She let the tiniest bit of annoyance coat her words.

Nana K chuckled, though her eyes narrowed. "I hear you made her a Dreamwalker."

Addison continued to flounder for a second before dropping his head and bending even deeper into the bow. "Apologies, Your Majesty. I was not aware." Was that regret in his voice?

"I know," Nana K chirped. "Which is the only reason I ain't had Anastasia tie you in a bow. Now get up. We got monsters on the way."

Thirty-Six

LIES WE TELL OURSELVES

Humphrey didn't remember ever setting foot in this place. He didn't remember walking these halls, but something was familiar in the path he took.

Maybe it was because of the time he spent with the Bloody Lady at the Red Palace. Findest, they called it.

Around him, people raced up and down the hall, calling to one another as preparations for battle were made.

They needed to bring as many supplies for those inside the palace walls as possible. They needed to arm every able-bodied fighter they could. More guards. More soldiers. Armies that hadn't been called to serve since the days of the war.

A war he fought in but still didn't remember.

The hallway leading to the armory, or what he assumed was the armory, bustled busier than the others. Murmurs about the missing Queen floated just beneath the wave of orders being shouted.

The one known as Xelon stood at a round table placed at the

center of the room, people flowing around her as weapons were handed off. The one named Anastasia, the Duchess, stood beside her, the both of them bent over what looked like some sort of map stretched along the table's surface.

"You should join us," a voice said near Humphrey's ear, and he turned to find himself staring into the familiar face of Addison Hatta.

Something . . . strange happened in Humphrey's chest, an almost painful fluttering of what he refused to call excitement that left him feeling uncomfortable, and irritated. "What for?" He looked away from his fellow former Black Knight, letting his gaze roam over the room.

"You may not remember who you are, but you clearly haven't lost your knack for strategy." Hatta stepped back as someone swung a lance around to exit.

"My strategies were limited to outsmarting a handful of warriors, not an entire army." Humphrey rolled his shoulders. "And I'm not certain if the plan originated in my head or if it was put there."

"Still fuzzy on a lot of the details?" Hatta asked.

"More than I like." He grunted and shifted to tilt against the wall. "I'm not sure where . . . he ends and I begin, right now."

"I see. Unfortunately, what happened while you were the Black Knight is a part of you, for better or worse."

"Speaking from experience?" Humphrey asked.

"Somewhat. What you went through wasn't your fault. That's where our experiences differ." Hatta set a hand on Humphrey's shoulder. He stiffened but didn't pull away. "You're still one of us. And you're still a warrior. One who knows *this* enemy better than any of us. We could use your help on this. And I mean *your* help. The you standing here now, not who we remember you as." Hatta stepped past him and into the room.

He greeted the two women, who welcomed him to the table. The Duchess caught Humphrey's eye as she shifted to the side, and he nodded in greeting. For a moment she paused, as if to say something more—perhaps to extend an invitation similar to Hatta's—but she seemed to think better of it and looked back to the map.

Humphrey finally stepped into the room, though he didn't move for the table. Instead he looked over the weapons hung on the wall nearest him. Long swords, short swords, broadswords, great swords. He could wield any of them if he so chose, of that he was certain.

"The river near the rear of the castle will provide cover if Madeline's Verse holds," the Duchess said, her voice able to carry now that there were fewer people in the room.

"That leaves the meadow to the east," Hatta said.

"Reports say the army approaches from that direction." Xelon ran her finger along the map. "If we can meet them here, it's possible we'll—"

"Ahem."

Distracted from eavesdropping as he perused the weapons, Humphrey turned to find a guard watching him, almost . . . nervously? She shifted slightly, as if uncertain she had permission to speak with him. "The knights have asked that all those who have come to fight take their weapons and report to the front gate."

He opened his mouth to respond as Hatta's voice leaped across the room.

"He's fine, Pehrta, being the Red Knight and all."

The guard bowed and slipped out of the room, positioning herself outside the door.

Humphrey grunted and glanced toward the table where the three of them watched.

He fought the urge to fidget under their gazes. "I'm not a knight."

"Maybe not," Hatta said. "But neither am I."

"Nor I," the Duchess offered.

"We trust you, all the same," Hatta said.

"Your mistake." Humphrey looked back to the weapons.

"You're talking about fighting an army of creatures that can only be killed by humans. The best bet is for the Dreamwalkers to face it here, with the help of trained allies, instead of later, after we're all dead or scattered," a woman said, pulling on what looked like a long, crooked pipe before blowing a plume of white smoke into the air. It curled in and around itself, seeming to take on the shape of dancers before fading. Romi, she'd said her name was when she introduced herself. Another person from his past he couldn't remember. Another name and face to add to the growing list.

Silence fell over the gathering as glances were exchanged.

Humphrey rolled his eyes, exhaling softly before saying, "She's right." He didn't let the sudden influx of attention bother him, meeting those gazes with his own. "If we fight and fail, the rest of Wonderland is doomed. As is the human world. Our best chance, our only chance, is together."

A smile pulled at Hatta's lips. "Together?"

Humphrey lifted a hand. "Don't make this into some sort of grand gesture, I'm simply agreeing with the most rational option."

Romi tapped the map, running her fingers along the topography. "Battalions positioned here and here should slow them. Haruka and the twins can hold this position with Anastasia. You two with me here." She gestured to Humphrey and Hatta, then pointed. "The rest of the army can move into position behind us and provide reinforcements when necessary."

There were nods all around before Romi knocked her knuckles against the table. "Arm yourselves."

Everyone turned to securing their weapons and grabbing whatever else they thought they might need.

Humphrey moved to do the same, but was drawn up short by a hand on his shoulder.

Hatta, he thought to himself before turning and confirming his suspicion.

"Can I speak to you for a moment?" Hatta asked. "Alone. Won't take long."

Humphrey hesitated. There was something about the look in Hatta's eyes that gave him pause, but he found himself nodding anyway, then silently following him.

They wound up in a small room off a relatively quiet hallway. Shelves lined the walls stacked with books and scrolls, ledgers and journals. A miniature library perhaps? Or storage for records of some kind.

Hatta closed the door behind them, his hand lingering on the knob. "Thank you for agreeing to this."

Humphrey shrugged while eyeing a nearby stack of books. No titles. Definitely records. "Seemed rude to refuse considering we might all die in the morning."

That earned a chuckle. "Indeed we may." Hatta joined him near the shelf. "Which is what I wanted to talk to you about. Not the almost dying, but . . ."

When there was no follow-up statement, Humphrey turned, half expecting to find Hatta lost in thought, his eyes unfocused, his lips moving in silent mumbles. He did that more and more recently.

Instead, Humphrey found Hatta focused on him. Those gray eyes were crystal clear, shining with a vulnerability that made something inside the former Red Knight squirm.

Hatta drew a steadying breath. "When you went missing, I couldn't forgive myself for how things were left between us."

"Don't let it trouble you too much." Humphrey plucked one of the books from the nearest shelf at random, flipping through it. "I don't remember how things were at any point, so no need to lose any sleep over it." He read maybe two sentences about crop rotations before putting it back.

Hatta sniffed a faint laugh but shook his head. "That isn't what I meant."

When Humphrey reached for another book, Hatta caught his hand, drawing it and his attention around.

"You were my heart," Hatta continued, his voice soft, quiet. "And I lost you."

Humphrey's heart sounded like a thunderstorm in his own ears in comparison.

"I wasn't there when you were taken. I should've been, but I was in exile. My own fault." He seemed to struggle for a moment, his brow furrowed. His thumb played over over Humphrey's knuckles. "I swore to be at your side, always. And when you needed me most . . ."

Addison's brow creased, his expression pained. The urge to smooth away the lines in his brow nearly overtook Humphrey, but he locked his arms in place. What the devil was wrong with him?

"I'll never forgive myself. And I know things are different now, in more ways than one. What's done is done. There's no changing the past. And, truth be told, there are many things I wouldn't change. But I can't . . ." He winced but shook it off. "I can't do this again. I can't go into battle knowing either of us might fall, and I could have felt your lips against mine one last time."

The uncomfortably eager feeling from before kicked itself into overdrive. The clothes on his body suddenly felt too small. There wasn't enough air in the room, he was suffocating. He needed . . .

more. Of what, he didn't know. How much, he wasn't sure. But that didn't stop him from wanting it.

"I'm going to kiss you," Hatta purred, unaware of the hurricane currently raging inside Humphrey. "If you'll let me."

There were no words that he could manage. No response he could give that would adequately express what he was feeling. All of it fizzled out, like a flame without enough oxygen. Apt, because he was having a somewhat hard time breathing in that moment.

Hatta stared, equal parts hope and fear clear on his face, but he didn't move. He waited for an answer that Humphrey couldn't give him. Not with words, anyway.

Humphrey felt himself nod. The first dip of his chin was faint, but the next much more assured.

By the third, Hatta had closed the distance between them.

Fingers slid against Humphrey's cheek before lips found his, soft and hot. A tingle shot down his spine, and he felt himself tense. But the warm, runny feeling that followed loosened the tension in his body.

He couldn't remember ever being kissed, but part of him knew this, knew the way he tilted his head to open up to it. Knew the way Hatta's fingers slid up into his hair, anticipated the faint tug that resulted in another tremor.

That part of him told him to press closer, and he listened. The faintest edge of hunger slipped into the kiss, and a sudden, furious rush filled his ears. His chest heaved, his breath stolen as it left him.

More, that same part of him whispered, ever so faintly. But just then, it was over.

Hatta drew away, those brightly colored eyes of his flickering over Humphrey's face.

The fingers in Humphrey's hair loosened and slid away as Hatta put more space between them.

Neither of them spoke. What was there to say? Words seemed so inadequate when so much could be conveyed in a single glance. And the way Addison looked at him just now . . .

Hatta cleared his throat. "Thank you," he murmured.

Again, Humphrey nodded.

"I . . . We can't . . ." Hatta struggled for words again.

Humphrey picked them up easily. "We won't."

Hatta nodded, understanding washing over his expression. "See you out there."

"See you after," Humphrey returned, the words leaping from his tongue of their own accord. He hadn't even thought to say them; they just fell from his lips.

Hatta paused at the door. He didn't glance back, simply stood there, looking like he wanted to say more. Instead, he twisted the knob and slipped from the room.

Humphrey listened to his retreating steps until the sound was swallowed by the surrounding quiet. He waited a minute or two more, just to be certain no one would see them both leave before making his own escape. As he slipped down the hall, his mind kept replaying the last few minutes over and over, to the point where he could almost feel Hatta's lips against his again.

"We can't," Hatta had said.

"We won't," had been Humphrey's reply.

Liar, that part of him that had wanted the kiss seethed from somewhere deep inside him.

And he knew it was right.

Thirty-Seven
ROYALLY
SCREWED

Walking away from Humphrey had been one of the hardest things Addison could remember doing in some time, but he knew he had to. For himself, for Humphrey, and for what was blossoming between him and Alice.

Nearly every bone in his body bade him turn around, go back, but thoughts of her kept him moving forward.

One kiss, he had told himself. To assuage the rather insistent memories he'd tried to unsuccessfully bottle these past weeks. For what they once shared and how it had never received a proper burial. One kiss, so the want to do so whenever the former knight was near would finally fade.

By the breaking, he'd thought he'd finally put all of the emotions surrounding the other knight to bed. He'd thought, after so many years without feeling like a broken thing pieced together without glue at the slightest reminder of him, he was over it all. He'd even opened himself up to the possibility of feeling for someone like that again. He *did* feel for someone like that again, and now . . .

Well, now it seemed whatever fate or destiny guided his path saw fit to present him with yet another trial.

And he'd thought, he'd truly believed, this would put an end to the entire affair. He'd finally get some sense of true closure.

How wrong he'd been.

If the memory of Humphrey had been under his skin, now it was in his blood. He'd have to find some way to be rid of it, though the threat of battle would provide ample distraction.

He hoped.

He turned his mind to the preparations that still needed to be made. Voices called out around him, Anastasia and Xelon and even Romi barking orders. The battalions were soon armed and ready to ride out to meet the Nightmare horde. Hatta looked over the shield he'd been given, along with the original Vorpal Blade.

"If we're lucky, you might be able to control them," Xelon had said in response to what Hatta had assumed was quite the surprised expression when she returned the weapon to him. "Even if only for a moment."

"I assume Madeline explained what happened at the pub," Hatta had asked, without yet taking the blade.

"She did. And if you can manage that here, it'll give us a much-needed edge over the enemy."

"I'll try," Hatta had said, wrapping his fingers around the sword's hilt. He'd felt the faint thrum of power, the undercurrent that was always there, always pushing in at the farthest edge of his mind. "For as long as I can."

Humphrey similarly would wield his weapon. The more former

Black Knights able to potentially influence the enemy army, the better, it seemed.

Along with a shield, Hatta clutched a belt to which a pair of sheathed daggers were strapped. Figment Blades very similar to the kind Alice was used to, provided courtesy of Anastasia and Romi. Now he simply had to find Alice and hand them over.

Alice . . .

No, Princess Alice of . . . he wasn't sure. Findest was her grandmother's palace. And while the Red Queen might be all right with moving back to Wonderland and inhabiting the old place once more, he doubted the Red Princess would feel the same. She was human, at least in part. One of the many things Addison loved about her.

She was likely in the throne room with her newly discovered family. He headed that direction, very aware of the looks cast his way. These people didn't trust him. Might never trust him again. He'd made his peace with that long ago. Or so he'd thought. It had been an easier task when he faced exile.

It didn't take long for him to spot Alice. She stood at the base of the stairs along the front of Legracia. She looked good in a new set of deep red battle armor. A pair of Figment Blades were strapped to her back; he could see the hilts crossed over her shoulders. A chain was coiled at her hip, similar to the one from the convention but glittering with the same glassy silver finish as her daggers. She shifted her weight from side to side anxiously while keeping her head bowed in conversation with her grandmother.

The sight of the Red Queen made Addison draw up short, both from the shock of seeing her after all this time, and the double stunner of just who she was in more ways than one. Alice's grandmother. Skies above.

As he watched the pair, standing still while everyone and

everything moved around, he once again noticed the now plainly obvious family resemblance and wondered how he truly did not see it all the time. The adorable way Alice's brow furrowed in concern and made her nose scrunch was somehow identical to the way the Red Queen's expression crinkled in scathing disappointment.

Out of respect, and a little fear, he waited until the Red Queen hugged Alice, then stepped away to join the White Queen on the dais.

"Behold Alison Kingston of Earth, Red Princess of Findest," Addison said as he approached.

Alice spun, her expression already pinched. She aimed a finger at his face. "Don't you start with me. And 'of Earth' sounds boring as hell."

He scrunched his nose briefly before smirking as he took hold of that pointing finger. "What would you like to be 'of,' in that case?"

Her expression went thoughtful for a moment before she snapped fingers on her other hand. "Of the moon."

"Of the moon?" he asked, recalling her mild obsession with that particular celestial body.

"Yup," she said, now looking expectant.

"Very well." He cleared his throat before bending into a formal bow. "Behold Alison Kingston of the Moon, Red Princess of Findest." He straightened to find her clapping.

"Very well done." She laughed now, her face lighting up with it.

Addison reached to play his fingers against one of those cheeks. It was reflex by now. She tilted into his touch, her hand coming up to fall over his. That's when he noticed her fingers were shaking. It was subtle but there. So was the tremble that moved through the rest of her. She was scared. Of course she was, and he wanted nothing more than to pull her into his arms and hold her, squeeze her, keep her from this. He knew he couldn't, and—despite her fear—she wouldn't want him to.

So instead, he drew a slow breath, pulled her tight against himself, and spoke. "I'll protect you. You have my word, Your Highness."

He felt her nod as much as he saw it. Felt her shaking as well, though that gradually subsided. So did the noise of orders and organization. Everything drifted away, and for a brief moment there was nothing else, only here, only now.

"Alice," a voice called from behind them.

He withdrew, and the both of them turned to find her mother entering the throne room.

"Wooo," Alice called over the low roar of voices. "Don't we look fancy."

"Hush." Her mother waved a hand, one of her sleeves billowing slightly. But Alice was correct—she did look stunning in what was likely one of the White Queen's dresses.

"This is going to take some getting used to," Queen Mother Tina said in a low tone. "Never in my wildest dreams would I imagine any of this were possible. But . . . something tells me your daddy might. That he, even not knowing all of the details either, would've seen something like this coming from a mile away. You're both like that, bright eyes and deep minds."

Alice fell silent at the mention of her father. Addison had seen this silence, had come to know it well, when she disappeared into some part of herself that took all of her. She probably wondered what he would make of all this.

"I think he'd be surprised." Alice stole a glance at her mother. "And worried. This . . . isn't your fault."

Queen Mother Tina looked at her daughter, blinking in surprise.

"There isn't anything you could've done or should've done to 'protect' me and keep me from this."

"I don't want to—"

"Of course you do," Alice laughed. "I wanted to keep myself from it, at first. But . . . with things with Nana, it's clear that would've never worked. And I think I'm okay with that."

Queen Mother Tina shook her head. "Well. I'm not. But I'll work on it. Especially since I'm gonna have to watch you go off and save the world a few more times, it seems." Then she turned to Addison, and her eyes narrowed.

They were the same brown as Alice's, he noticed, though they glistened with the promise of harm. "I'm told I have you to thank for that."

Addison . . . didn't have anything to say to that. It was the truth, after all. He had pulled Alice into this world, something he'd blamed himself for many times over the past few days.

"Later, Mom," Alice said, giving her mother's arm a shake and saving Addison from losing his head before the battle even started.

Queen Mother Tina hmphed just as the White Queen rose to her feet. That simple movement sent a ripple through the rest of the room. Everyone started moving at once. The Red Queen joined her sister and gestured for Queen Mother Tina and Alice to do the same. They climbed the stairs, wearing identical forced smiles to mask their anxiety.

Similarly, Odabeth joined her mother. The room quieted as everyone drew near. Anastasia, Romi, Xelon, and Humphrey huddled to the side, with the former Red Knight hanging back just a bit. The twins and Haruka weren't far, sporting their own gear and weapons. Courtney had looped her arm through Chess's, holding tight. She wasn't dressed for battle, but he was, with a longsword strapped to his back.

Courtney smiled and flapped her free hand in the air. "That's my best friend! Go, best friend!"

A wave of uncertain but polite chuckles filtered through the crowd and Alice, smiling, waved back.

The White Queen stood with her hands folded in front of her, waiting until as many people filled the room as wanted to be there, most dressed in silver armor bearing the white and blue standard of Legracia.

Addison joined his fellow former knights. Xelon and Anastasia smiled and nodded in greeting. Humphrey met his gaze a split second before taking interest in the enchanted ceiling. Romi seemed content to ignore him altogether, which was fine. It was a mercy, all things considered.

The White Queen cleared her throat. "I know many of you are thinking about the mass of Nightmares on its way, and it's easy to give in to the fear of what may come, but I charge each of you to—"

The large doors into the throne room banged open. Addison spun, his hand going to the sword at his hip.

"She has to know!" someone shouted among demands for silence.

"You're not well! You need medical attention, please!"

"No! Not until I tell the Queen!"

The one causing the commotion was a Legracian guard. At least, he looked to wear most of the armor of one. His helm was gone, as were his spaulders and greaves. Blood smeared the side of his pale face, dry and flaky in some spots. His left arm hung at his side and he shoved at his fellow guards with the right.

"Please, she must be told!"

"What is this?" Queen Emalia asked.

One of three guards trying to wrangle him back turned and bowed. "Apologies, Your Highness. He just arrived, injured, raving about a conspiracy."

Alice frowned and shifted forward, presumably to get a closer look.

"What sort of conspiracy?" the Queen asked.

"To steal the throne!" the injured guard hollered. "To steal it from its rightful ruler! An assassin has been sent!"

Gasps went up around the room.

Humphrey groaned faintly, setting a hand to the side of his head.

Addison leaned toward him. "You all right?"

The former knight nodded, his eyes shut tight. "Yes. Sudden headache. I'll be fine."

Addison nodded and looked back toward the commotion.

Xelon moved forward from her place behind the throne, glided down the stairs and over to the guards in just a few strides. Her face was carefully blank. She waved a hand, and the guards adjusted their efforts from trying to remove the man to simply restraining him.

The White Knight narrowed her eyes. "What's this of an assassin?"

The guard swallowed as he looked from her to the Queens, then back. "Someone is trying to steal the throne. So she sent an assassin to stop them." He smiled. It stretched his face impossibly wide.

"Nng!" Humphrey doubled over then, shaking his head. "She's . . ."

Chess straightened from where he had bent as well, his expression twisted in pain, but his eyes wide. "Here!"

The Legracian guard flung out his arms, which grew to be much longer than they had any right to be. The guards holding him went flying into the others gathered. As Xelon went for her sword, a massive fist caught her across the face, flinging her away at a spin.

"Defend the throne!" someone shouted.

Swords were drawn.

The guard, now with blackened skin stretching to elongate limbs and claws, raced toward the stairs, impossibly fast. But Addison had a bead on it. He darted forward, drawing his sword and swinging it out in a single motion. The black blade arced through the air. He felt the give of inky flesh, but there was no resistance. He whirled with the momentum of a missed swing, thrown off balance.

As he shifted his weight to correct for the swing, he realized he was far too slow for this creature. It reached the top of the stairs, where Alice had taken up a defensive position in front of her grandmother.

"No!" Addison flung himself forward.

The creature dissolved, melting away to ooze that bubbled over and spread along the marble floor. Odabeth lifted her feet as he swept beneath her throne, and then the others in the next instant. It coated the entire level in a blink.

Get away! he wanted to scream, but the thought had barely formed before inky hands darted out of the black. They latched onto a shocked Odabeth, who screamed as she was hauled toward the darkness.

Similar hands snatched at the White Queen, who struggled against their hold. The Red Queen was also caught, the hands wrapping around her arms and face, pulling.

"Let GO!" Alice screamed, just as a clammy hand clapped over her mouth. She stumbled forward, unable to dig her heels in.

"Alice!" Addison rushed forward to slice into the tendrils of black, but for each one he cut down, three more seemed to spring forth. There was shouting and screaming as the other guards charged.

Fury and fear warring within him, Addison twisted and yanked at the hands that had hold of him, but he couldn't shake them loose. Someone shouted his name.

Humphrey, he realized.

In a flurry of steel, the Red Knight was at his side, cutting into the tendrils, trying to get him free. Behind him, Chester hacked and sliced, trying to clear a path to Alice, but the darkness just kept coming, growing, oozing out of the portal.

Addison twisted, pushing against the pull, but it wasn't enough. His feet were yanked out from under him, and he was hauled across the marble floor. His stomach pitched. His senses wavered.

"Addison!" Humphrey's voice reached him before fingers clamped around his. "I've got you!"

The strength, the warmth, was a familiar balm against the aching cold climbing through his entire body and the last sensation to register before the two of them were pulled into the waiting dark.

Thirty-Eight

BLOOD IS THICKER

Alice's body felt heavy, her limbs slow to respond to her commands. Her thoughts were equally stubborn, refusing to crystallize into any useful information. Where was she? What was going on? What happened? All questions she could answer if she could just get her eyes to cooperate and *open*.

She focused all of her energy to the front of her face. *Open. Open, damn it!*

Her lashes fluttered, and her lids finally lifted. Stone. The first thing she saw was stone. The first thing she felt was stone. Stone rose around her. Stone pressed against her face, against her body. An ache started to register in her limbs, delayed, along with the rest of the feeling in her body. She was cold, she realized, a chill sliding through her.

She groaned, the sound distant even to her own ears. Her arms shifted, slow at first, like they were filled with sand. It was a struggle, but she managed to push herself up into a seated position, glancing around.

More stone rose toward a ceiling hidden in shadow. In fact, shadows hugged every wall, every corner, every crevice. Except for the ceiling. It was made of the purest glass, allowing black clouds, thick and ominous, to be seen as they tumbled over one another.

Someone groaned. Alice spun, her heart in her throat. She spotted Odabeth fighting to push herself upward same as she had just a moment ago.

"Ahh, I see the prodigal princess awakens," a voice hissed, the sound slithering across the open space.

Alice twisted around, trying to see more, but there was nothing else. She and Odabeth had landed at the base of a set of stairs that led up to a broken throne, and beside it, something that looked like one of those things they put pharaohs in on the Discovery Channel. A sarcophagus?

"So rude, this one," the voice spoke again.

Where was it coming from? Her gaze flickered back and forth, searching the shadows.

There. The outline of a person was slumped against the chair, covered in Slithe, wearing it like a second skin. That's why she didn't notice them at first.

She tried to push herself upward, her hands going for her daggers, but her body was still so slow to respond.

"Easy, now. Traversing the Veil within can be taxing. Are you all right?"

"Where are we?" Alice asked.

Beside her, Odabeth finally managed to push herself upright, for the most part, glancing around groggily. "M-Mother?"

Alice didn't dare take her eyes off the figure, who seemed content to sit and watch them in the dark. For now. Another groan from behind, this voice familiar.

Alice dropped to her knees, reaching to help her grandmother sit up. She kept stealing glances at the now silent figure that continued to watch from the darkness. Nana K pushed upward, taking slow breaths.

"I'm okay," she said through clenched teeth as Alice fretted.

"What happened?" the White Queen asked, a hand going to the side of her head.

"I don't know," Odabeth said.

"Why don't we ask her?" Alice muttered, her eyes still on the figure.

The figure laughed, the sound filling the odd room, washing over Alice and everyone else present.

Alice shuddered, shifting to help her grandmother to her feet, then moving to place herself in front of her. "You sent that guard, didn't you? The Wraith?" Nightmares that could pretend to be human. The thought sent another shiver through her.

"Who are you!" Odabeth demanded, her words sharp and loud. "Where are we?"

"H-home." The word was barely a whisper, breathed in shock. The White Queen glanced around from where she rested on her knees, her wide gaze moving around them. She pressed a hand over her mouth, whispering what sounded like a prayer, though Alice couldn't make out the words.

"My lord," Nana K echoed as she took in their surroundings, though she looked less surprised and more resigned to what was happening.

The figure finally moved, lifting its arms slowly, carefully, the joints popping wetly, before it flung its hands outward. Dark sludge sloshed against the ground and stairs. "Welcome to Emes."

"This . . . this isn't possible," the White Queen murmured.

"It very much is, Emalia." Nana K didn't take her gaze off the figure. "I believe my granddaughter asked a question of our gracious host."

All eyes went to the figure, who continued to chuckle, the sound sloppy and thick.

"Why, do I need a reason to want to see family?" that raspy voice scratched. "My sisters. My nieces."

Surprise straightened Alice's spine, and Odabeth's and her mother's given their shocked reactions.

But Nana . . . she simply shut her eyes, heaving a slow, tired breath.

"Odette." She said the name like she was whispering a prayer for some great wrong already wrought.

The White Queen's head whipped around so fast Alice swore she heard her neck crack.

"Odette?" The White Queen looked to the figure. "But that's—"

"Impossible?" the figure finished. It waved a hand, and some of the shadows pressing in around them lessened. They drew back, allowing more of the already too dim light to filter into the space. The clouds above prevented daylight, but there was still a sickly cast over everything, sharpened by a flash of red here and there. Crimson lightning.

This was all familiar to Alice for some reason, but she couldn't think on it. She was distracted by the dark parting and revealing this . . . Odette.

When the shadows settled, the Bloody Lady stood at the top of a nearby staircase similar to the one she'd stood atop back at Castle Findest.

Behind her, a shattered throne cut a profile against the black. Something large and crystalline stood beside it, covered in Slithe. Behind everything, a wall of sharp shadow stabbing jagged into the air loomed over them all.

"Odette," the White Queen repeated, her voice strangled by the sudden rise in grief that flushed her face red and filled her eyes with tears. "How . . . how are you alive?"

The figure, the Bloody Lady, chuckled. She smoothed a hand over red strands stained with Slithe. It nearly covered her entire body, the darkness crawling along her limbs, turning her fingers to talon-tipped claws. At the center of her chest, the shattered remnants of the Heart glowed the faintest rest.

"Alive?" the Bloody Lady scoffed. "This isn't living. This is having purpose. Driven by pain. By hatred." She chewed the words, forcing the last of them through her clenched teeth. Her eyes, wide and wild, flickered between all of them, almost as if unable to focus.

"She's alive because of me," Nana K murmured, her voice soft, reserved. "Because of my weakness."

"I don't understand," the White Queen said.

That makes two of us. But Alice kept her mouth shut. Something was going on here that she had no part of.

"I saw this. In the In-Between," Nana K continued. "A vision of this place. Of Odette's casket beside Mother's stasis crystal. Of the former broken open . . ." Nana K took a slow, careful breath. "The darkness having shattered it."

"Mother set me free." Odette smiled, twisting her body around. She reached to play fingers against the jagged shadows just behind her.

That's when, through the faint haze of dim light, Alice was able to make out the silhouette of something inside the crystal.

"She set me free, and her power showed me what happened." The smile on the Bloody Lady, on Odette's face, melted into a snarl. "How her own daughters betrayed her."

"You think we wanted to fight her?" The White Queen finally found her feet. "That we wanted any of what happened after you passed? She went insane with grief, Odette. She called on the darkness, forged herself with it, to try to bring you back. And when that didn't work, she was determined to avenge your death, only . . . we had no idea what had killed you."

"She blamed the humans," Nana K said. "Said she would wipe them out. She meant to wipe them out. But . . . if she did that, she would wipe us out. Wonderland cannot exist without the world of man, or vice versa."

Odette chuckled, shaking her head. "Mother only wanted to protect her family, her children. And then her children betrayed her."

"She betrayed us. And Wonderland. Please, sister," the White Queen said, her tone pleading. "We don't know how this happened, but . . . we have a chance to be a family again."

"No." Nana K shook her head. "That looks like Odette, sounds like her, but . . . Odette died. And after we locked Mother away, I . . ." Nana K's voice broke. Alice reached for her but she waved her off. "Instead of doing my duty and hiding the Heart, I brought it here. I broke it in two, then I left one half inside Odette's coffin, laying it over her heart."

Alice's eyes shot to the jagged mess at the center of Odette's chest.

"The other half I took with me to the mortal world, intent on leaving it there. But . . . as the kids say, shit happens."

"Both of you . . . went on with your lives. Fell in love. Had children." Odette snorted as she approached them. Her body continued to jerk and twist, her feet barely able to get beneath her in order to catch her weight. "You created new families, while leaving your real family in the grave."

A bit of motion just to the side caught Alice's attention. The shadows were shifting again, moving in response to Odette's steps. Limbs pulled themselves free from the black, dragging bodies to follow. Nightmares hissed and snarled softly, their whispers filling the air.

Odabeth noticed as well, gasping softly and drawing back a step.

Odette chuckled. "Now you will be powerless, as I was, to protect those closest to you."

The shadows continued to ripple, and as Odette lifted her arms, they rose, taking form.

"Get behind me," Alice said, reaching to pull her grandmother back, her hands going to the weapons at her hips.

"Please, Odette," the White Queen called. "If we'd known there was any chance you were alive, we would've—"

"That's not Odette," Nana K snapped. "It's the corruption of the Nox. Of this place. Over time, the Heart allowed the dark power here to infect Odette's body, but that wasn't all, was it? The Slithe crawling from throne to the coffin. Mother's influence. You're right about one thing, we failed you. I . . . failed you. By placing that shard there, I opened you to her power. I didn't know that would happen, but that doesn't matter. You're not Odette. Not really. You're Mother's will."

Odette chuckled darkly. "More lies. Your silver tongue will not save you this time, Kashaunte." Her fingers twitched, and the Nightmares solidified.

As they slithered forward, Alice readied herself, dropping into a fighting stance. She . . . she didn't know how they were going to get out of here, but they would find a way. They had to find a way.

"Join me, sisters. Nieces. Join me in the dark." Her fingers twitched.

The Nightmares lunged.

Thirty-Nine

BEWARE

Humphrey was not unaccustomed to pain. It was familiar. An old friend. A long-lost lover. One he was quite ready to be rid of. He lay against a hard, rough surface. Stone, he realized, as his fingers brushed it. He opened his eyes to a world of shadows and silence. He struggled into a sitting position, his hands going to his face. His entire body throbbed with the effort.

"Strewth," he hissed.

A moan answered, and he turned to find Addison recovering similarly, movements slow as he pushed himself up. "W-where . . . where are we?"

"Not sure," Humphrey said. "Wherever those things brought us."

He glanced around. The stone beneath them was cracked and uneven. Dust covered everything in layers, so much so that their slight movements had stirred enough of it to leave them wreathed in a fog of sorts. There was little light, save for the faintest haze that managed to reach them through dirtied and shattered windows lining the high walls. There was something . . . familiar about all of this.

They were in an antechamber of some sort, a large door at their backs, a hall across the way. He couldn't see any farther than that, not without any light.

As if summoned by the thought, an arc of red lightning appeared above them, glimpsed through the fractured high ceiling. It illuminated the world for the briefest instant, but that was all Humphrey needed. He knew where they were.

"Dammit." So did Addison, it seemed. "The queens. The princesses. We have to find—"

Another groan echoed in the dark. Humphrey snatched the sword at his hips free, spinning up onto his knees despite his body's protests. Addison drew down as well, the two of them facing off against . . .

"Chester?" Addison called, his voice high with confusion.

Chess lay on the ground and rolled onto his side to face them, his armor clinking against the floor. "That sucked."

Humphrey sheathed his weapon and moved to help the boy to sit up. "Are you all right?"

"Define all right."

"Sounds fine to me," Addison said, lowering his sword but not sheathing it. "Sorry to see those things got you, too."

Chess shook his head. "They didn't."

Humphrey arched an eyebrow. "Then how did you get here?"

"I don't know, I . . . I saw everyone vanish. I wanted, no, *needed* to follow." He frowned as if confused. His gaze danced around a second before he blinked at Hatta, as if suddenly realizing he was there. "So, I did. I think. This wing came out of nowhere. I felt it pick me up, then pull me apart into a million pieces. It didn't hurt, just felt weird. Then I woke up here."

Humphrey mirrored Chess's frown. What the boy described sounded awfully close to what it felt like to teleport. But that couldn't be it, could it?

The look on Addison's face said he was just as confused, but whatever he was thinking beyond that he kept to himself.

"Have you ever done anything like that before?" Humphrey asked.

Chess set a hand to the side of his head and grunted. "Like what?"

"Wanting to be somewhere, then just appearing there," Humphrey said.

"N-no, what . . ."

"Teleporting," Addison explained. "Like Humphrey when he pops up seemingly out of nowhere. It's an ability only some of our people possess. Very, very few of them."

Chess's frown deepened. "I'm not from Wonderland."

"Maybe it's a side effect from the Slithe?" Humphrey offered, not liking the strange itch at the center of his chest he hadn't noticed until now, nor the way Addison was looking at him.

"Slithe can't just make someone a Tirip." Addison slid his gaze to Chester. There was something unreadable in those gray eyes. "You have to be Wonderland-born."

Humphrey looked to Chess as well now.

The boy, his head swiveling back and forth, his mouth working, looked positively lost. "I'm not . . . That's not . . ."

Addison drew himself up, sword still in hand.

"What are you doing?" Humphrey asked.

Chess's gaze pinged to the blade, then back and forth between it and Addison's face.

"I don't know how I didn't see it," Addison muttered, his voice low, his words edged. Dangerous. "No. I saw it. But I thought I was imagining things at first. Then I reasoned them away. Tch, you're just that good."

"G-good?" Chess asked.

Humphrey felt a twisting in his stomach at the noise and hurried forward to set his hand against Addison's arm. "Don't do this."

"He's lying," Addison said without taking his eyes off Chester, but he lowered his weapon at Humphrey's insistence.

"But is it a lie if you don't know what's true?" a new voice cooed from the darkness, the words spoken in singsong, a faint rasp of breath, like there wasn't enough to fully form them.

Addison glanced to Humphrey, then the two of them turned to search the shadows briefly.

"That wasn't your . . ." Addison started, throwing a glance at Humphrey. "Was it?"

He shook his head. No, that wasn't the Bloody Lady. "And I'm guessing it wasn't yours?"

Addison shook his head as well.

So, not the Bloody Lady or the Black Queen. Then who the hell was it?

Behind them Chester scrambled to his feet.

Addison whirled, sword lifted. "Don't. Move."

Chester's hands went up, his back once again pressed to the wall. "Wasn't me! Wasn't . . ."

"Careful," the voice called again, seeming to come from everywhere and nowhere at once. "We wouldn't want to act rashly, would we? Do something we can't undo."

"What do you want?" Humphrey asked.

"Oh, a great many things," the voice answered. "But I'll settle for being entertained by your current predicament."

"Who are you?" Addison asked. In a flurry of motion, he had

his arm braced against a terrified Chester, the Vorpal Blade at his neck. "And answer truthfully, or I'll slit your spy's throat."

"Addison!" Humphrey pressed.

"You think he's with me?" the voice called, clearly amused.

Addison was decidedly not. "I'm to believe he's not? That it's a coincidence you show up right when he's cornered?"

"What you believe is your business, but beliefs and truths are very seldom one and the same." The words seemed to slither through the air. Humphrey could imagine whoever spoke them crawling across the ceiling overhead. But even in the low light, brightened by the occasional flash of lightning, it was easy to see there was nothing. "You wish to know the truth. Ask the right questions."

"You didn't answer the one I already asked," Addison said, his blade still at Chester's throat. "Who are you?"

"Mmmmmm, very well," cooed the voice. The pressure in the room seemed to shift, and the words smoothed over Humphrey's skin, the contact nearly physical. "'Twas brillig, and the slithy toves did gyre and gimble in the wabe. All mimsy were the borogoves and the mome raths outgrabe."

Humphrey froze as shock stabbed through his body. He knew these words. And the way Addison stiffened similarly at his side meant he did as well. He stepped back, leaving Chester to clutch at his thankfully unslit throat.

"I have no name, though I am known," Humphrey began.

Addison immediately added, "No future and no past."

"With eyes of flame, and heart of stone," Humphrey continued.

"My first will be your last . . ." Chester finished, and both Addison and Humphrey spun toward him. "H-how . . . how do I know this?" the boy whispered, eyes wide, desperation clear on his ashen face.

"Because all know me," the voice said, practically giddy this time. "And none know me, though I know all. Most. I know most. For I was at the beginning of this world, and I will be its end. Mm, excuse me, *at* its end. It's important to be exact with your words, you see."

"I have no name, though I am known," Addison repeated. "Only you do have a name. Most have simply forgotten it."

"But not youuuuu," the voice crooned now. "You know my name because she knew it, your heartbroken queen, who came to me and spoke in the old ways. Mmmmm, how I miss the old ways." The pressure shifted again, and the darkness seemed to thicken, ripen, closing in around them. "She spoke my name then. That's the reason I answered her, you know. Well, part of the reason. And I gave her what she wanted. What she thought she wanted. I can give you what you want as well. Answers to your questions. Truths to balance out your beliefs."

"No," Addison bit out through clenched teeth. "To speak your name is to give you power. I will not."

"Oh. Pity." The voice sighed. "Guess we have to do this the hard way."

Humphrey never saw it coming, but he heard. The thick, raspy press of something like scales against stone. It came at them, lightning fast. He barely had time to get his sword up, hoping to fend off whatever was moving out there, in the dark. But then it had him.

It wrapped around his legs, and pulled. He went down.

Chester must have as well, given the shout and the thud of a body hitting the ground.

Humphrey tried to catch himself, but whatever was around his legs kept him from twisting far enough to brace himself. Pain exploded against the backs of his eyes when he slammed into the stone. Pain that rolled through his body when he was dragged across stone and lifted, Addison shouting his name.

He hung in the air, unable to see, but he could feel the shift of gravity, feel it pull at him, feel its grip where he hung from his ankles in the air. He tried to orient himself, blinking rapidly to clear his vision, but he could only hear as Addison begged.

"Don't! Don't hurt him, I—I . . . please, just . . ."

Somewhere to his right, Chester groaned.

"Hurt him? Oh, well, that's up to you, now, isn't it?" the voice trilled. The pressure from before was much more intense now, digging into every inch of Humphrey's body. He bit back on the pained sound that tried to claw its way free. "I'll give him back to you, both pieces, if you do as I ask."

Addison fell silent now, somewhere below Humphrey. He could hear him breathing, the rough pant, could imagine his chest rising and falling with them. And then he heard the sigh. The resignation.

Forty

HEARTBROKEN

Alice snatched her daggers free and readied herself as the first Nightmare came at her. She dove around the swipe of claws and lashed out, driving one blade into its head and the other into its spine. The beast yowled and thrashed, but couldn't get at her. With a twist of both pommels there was a sharp *crack* before the monster went limp. She kicked it away and turned to face the next.

There are too many! She wouldn't be able to protect the others.

Lucky for her, she wouldn't have to. The White Queen threw out a hand and a bubble of light rose around her, Odabeth, and Nana K. Nightmares slammed into it, clawing and scratching but unable to get through.

"Alice!" Nana K shouted upon seeing her outside of the protective field.

"I'm all right!" Alice called as she yanked her dagger from another Nightmare's gut. It wailed and dropped with a wet thump, dead before it hit the ground.

She turned on the next one, cutting through it, and then the next, making her way toward the throne and the woman standing near it.

"Enough!" Odette shouted, her hands lifting, red lightning striking her raised hand before she flung it forward. The electricity arced through the air and slammed into the bubble with an audible crash, but it held fast. Again and again, it was struck.

"Fine," Odette hissed. "If that is how you wish to play it." She gestured and, to Alice's shock, the floor beneath the dome melted away.

"Look out!"

Her voice echoed around them, but it was too late. The shadows swept up and over her grandmother and the others. Their shouts were immediately muffled.

Fear bolted through Alice, sharp and hot. "No!" She raked her gaze over the swell, but they . . . they were gone.

Laughter erupted from the throne; the Bloody Lady was doubled over with it.

"How fitting!" she howled with delight. "That you should be as helpless to save your family as I was to save mine." Her smile stretched her face unnaturally, looking like it cut across instead of opening, and she appeared to have more teeth than any human or humanlike being should.

"Portentia," Alice muttered, watching as the transformation continued, Odette's skin going pale white, her red hair darkening along with the bloody tears in the flesh where the piece of the Heart still protruded from her chest.

"Not quite," the monstrous woman hissed. "But close." She lashed out, her arm stretching black and talons as long as Alice's arm slicing at her. Alice dove to the side, twisting around and rushing forward. She had to make this fast; Nana and the others likely didn't have long in that stuff.

She leaped, driving down at the woman with the daggers.

Odette lifted her arm, blocking the blow at least in part. Alice felt the give of flesh as the daggers found purchase, but Odette only laughed.

"You'll have to do better than that, little girl." The words were a hiss against pointed teeth snapping in Alice's face.

Alice twisted, trying to pull her daggers loose, but they were stuck in the white flesh that now started to melt around them, consuming them.

"No!" She managed to snatch one weapon free, but the other remained stuck.

"There will be no more running, Alice. You've nowhere to go . . ."

The jagged crystal at the center of Odette's chest began to glow. So did the amulet in the necklace hanging against Alice's chest.

"I can think of one place," Alice said before reaching to grab hold of the Heart.

The glow exploded, consuming the both of them.

"No!" Odette's shout echoed around them, fading. Everything faded, until there was nothing but darkness.

Alice could . . . could feel herself, feel her fingers flex, thankfully free from whatever had been consuming her, but she couldn't see them. At least, not at first.

As quickly as the darkness had risen, it fell, and the throne room came back into sharp clarity. At least . . . she thought it was the throne room. It looked like the throne room, but was decidedly . . . more cheerful.

Realization moved through her as she recognized the trappings of Emes from before it fell to the Nox.

It was empty. Well, mostly empty. Someone sat on the throne.

The little girl with pink pigtails from every vision she'd been shown of the royal family. Odette.

The child had her hands pressed to her face as she sobbed.

Alice stared for a second, unable to tell exactly what was going on or . . . why.

"Hello?" she said finally.

The girl lifted her head, eyes wide as she gasped. "You . . . you're not supposed to be here . . ."

"I don't even know where here is," Alice said, glancing around. Well, she kinda did.

"You have to leave!" the girl cried. "Before she returns!"

Alice wanted to ask who, but she was interrupted when a shadow fell over her from behind. She spun and found herself standing face-to-face with Portentia of Harts, the darkness draped over her like living fabric.

"Thank you for returning my heart to me," she murmured, her eyes falling from Alice's face to her chest. "It will be that much easier to reclaim from your corpse . . ."

Alice glanced down and found the pendant pulsing faintly, the red light brightening and dimming in a steady rhythm. A rhythm that matched the one pulsing in the Queen's chest.

"Nnnnn!" The pained sound made Alice glance over her shoulder to where the girl clutched at her chest. Between her fingers, red shards slick with blood erupted from her sternum, just as they had the Bloody Lady's. She doubled over, her body heaving as her limbs elongated with the sound of tearing flesh. The little girl grew, gradually looking more like the woman Alice remembered fighting at Findest, and again just moments ago.

"Be a good daughter, unlike your ungrateful sisters," Portentia cooed, her voice saccharine. "Kill her for Mother."

Odette jerked and whirled, her wide, wild eyes fixating on Alice.

She drew a step back in reflex, fear seizing her throat and squeezing. But she swallowed and forced the words past the feeling like fingers gripping her neck. "You can fight this, Odette. That . . . that's not your mother. A mother wouldn't do this to you, make you hurt like this."

Portentia chuckled. "You hear how she seeks to turn you against me? When all I've done, I've done for you. End her. Then end the others, but it must begin with her."

Odette whimpered as lengthened nails dug into her scalp, tearing it red. "I . . . I can't help it! I—I'm sorry!"

Alice turned to try and go to her, but her feet caught, and she tripped forward. At least, she wanted to, but the ground had turned to liquid darkness, as it had with Nana K and the others.

The panic started to set in. Alice glanced around for something, anything that could help. When she glanced down, she caught sight of herself and froze. Her reflection, she could see it against the surface of the Slithe.

As always, Reflection-Alice stood in a dress, holding the silver scepter. Their eyes met, and she extended her hand.

Alice took a breath as a realization settled against her mind. She braced herself and dove. Her arms locked around Odette's waist, and she pulled. The girl didn't fight her as she lifted.

Portentia watched on, confused at first, but then fury crossed her face as Alice tipped her weight backward.

"No!"

Alice shut her eyes, held her breath, and braced for impact. She hit the floor and the entire thing gave, like breaking the surface of water. She and Odette sank into the black. Away from Portentia. Away from everything. Just away. Where, she hoped . . .

Hello? she called, glancing around as her legs kicked, her arms locked around Odette, who'd gone limp.

You're here, I know you're here!

More nothing. Just darkness, in all directions. Alice felt her chest jerk. She let go of Odette, her hands going to her own throat. Her lips parted involuntarily as her body tried to take in air. But there was none. Only the shadows that swept over her head, and she found herself drowning in them.

Her lungs spasmed.

Her insides twisted as liquid black poured into her.

I saw you! Please, help us! I know you can help us!

Her arms and legs kicked and swung, the weight of the waves pulling her under.

Fire erupted in her chest and poured up through her throat.

"What you gone do . . ."

She screamed. The sound filled her ears. The pounding behind her eyes swallowed her entire body. Her throat tightened, constricting uselessly around water. The burn from before intensified. Then, in a rushing cough that shook her to her core and scorched her insides, she rolled onto her side and the shadow poured from beneath her lips. Her stomach roiled. Her body trembled. Every inch of her throbbed white-hot. But she could breathe. She was alive.

"That's it," a voice coaxed, shockingly gentle. "Breathe."

Alice lay there against something hard and wet while gasping sobs racked her body. She sniffed and gagged, struggling to get her arms beneath her, to push up.

Her vision was blurred and didn't clear for several blinks, but eventually the world stopped pitching in circles and steadied. She sat in a cave, the dark, jagged stone jutting up around her and dangling from above, glittering with water droplets. The space was illuminated with the faint light of thousands of blue orbs clinging to the rocks above like stars. The taste of salt on her tongue and in her nose gave the place the scent of the sea. She gasped, her lungs jackknifing, still suffering from being filled with water. She'd drowned. She should have drowned. But she was alive.

"W-what . . ." she gasped, but no more words would come.

"You almost lost sight of me," the voice called, echoing all around her, sounding from nowhere in particular and everywhere at once.

As if summoned by Alice's confusion, her reflection appeared before her, dressed as always in that flowing white gown.

"I can't win this alone," Alice said.

Her reflection shook her head. "But you're not alone."

"No, I mean . . . you're not enough!" Her shout echoed around her. "I'm . . . not enough."

A hand fell to Alice's shoulder and squeezed. "But you don't have to be." She set a hand to Alice's chest, and the red pulse began again.

"Draw on your true strength. Your heart," her reflection murmured.

A twin point of light emerged from the dark, followed by the shape of the young Odette, the shards of the Heart pulsing in her chest.

Odette gazed at Alice and her reflection, the fear and pain that had been written on her face no longer there, now replaced by confusion. "What . . ."

"I brought you here, to be safe with us. But it won't last long," Reflection-Alice said.

Alice herself knew the truth of that statement when she heard the roar of darkness at the edges of her hearing, like a distant Nightmare waiting to slide back into her mind.

"You know what you have to do," Reflection-Alice said.

And Alice did. She moved toward Odette, drifting over to her in the open dark. "Don't be afraid," she said when the girl flinched away from her. "I'm here to help."

"How?" Odette asked, her voice small.

"That." Alice pointed at the girl's chest. "It looks like it hurts. Let me help you with that . . ."

The girl hesitated but nodded, and Alice reached to set her hands over it.

The sudden burning that flew up Alice's arm made her recoil with a shout. Odette shouted as well, hands on her chest. "It hurts!"

"I—I know," Alice said, shaking out her hand. "But you have to be brave. We have to be brave together. A little bit of hurt now, to spare you all the hurt later."

The girl nodded again, and again Alice reached. The burn returned, shooting up Alice's arms, flowing through her. She wanted to pull away, but instead she held tight.

The pulsing quickened, the red light blinking furiously until it solidified into a solid glow. It grew brighter, hotter. Alice felt the skin on her hands curl away as the burn intensified, but she held on.

CRACK!

A sound like thunder filled the void. Alice's hands came away, the fire dying instantly. The lack of heat felt like ice. She glanced down and expected to see mangled fingers, but instead she simply held the fissured bit of the Heart.

Her eyes flew to Odette, who hung in the air like a rag doll, panting raggedly, though she no longer looked to be in pain. As a matter of fact, she smiled.

"I-it's gone . . ." she said, her voice barely above a whisper. "It's gone!"

Alice couldn't help returning her smile.

"Thank you," Odette murmured before her eyes fell shut and her body went limp.

"Hey . . . hey!" Alice reached for the girl, but her fingers passed through her. Then, before her eyes, Odette faded.

Leaving Alice standing there holding the Heart. At least, part of it. Then she reached beneath her shirt and pulled out the pendant her grandmother had given her. The other half of the Heart. She held them together and, like before, the light intensified. The burn returned, but this time, *this* time, instead of pain, a thrill swept through Alice.

The red light faded, and instead of holding two halves of the Heart, Alice held what looked like a handle in one hand and a sickle in the other. A long silvery chain connected the two. The blade glinted faintly, silvered glass swimming with a soft, dark mist in constant motion. But that wasn't what drew Alice's attention.

What caught her eye was the bit of heart embedded on the end of the handle. She saw its match at the end of the other. The . . . Heart was the weapon?

"What is . . ." she started to say, but then the light from before returned, growing so bright that Alice had to shield her eyes.

She felt herself yanked out of the air, pulled down in a rushing current of some kind. Wind howled in her ears. Gravity let her go, sent her flying. Then there was a loud pop, and gravity took hold again, dropping her to the ground.

She hit it with an oomph, twisting onto her knees, glancing around. She was back in the throne room, the real one, with Portentia wearing Odette's body standing at the throne. Mom, Nana K, and Odabeth were back, too!

". . . Impossible . . ." Portentia whispered, staring at Alice. Then she clutched at her chest, clawing at it when she realized the shard was no longer there. Instead, torn flesh bled black. "No, no! Kill them!" She thrust a bony finger toward the other three.

Nightmares of all sizes, including Fiends and Wraiths, raced forward, eager for the kill.

Alice darted over to where her grandmother, the White Queen, and Odabeth were recovering, picking themselves up. Odabeth threw up her hands, the bubble forming around them once more, just in time to keep the nearby Nightmares from ripping into them.

Nana K coughed and sputtered before taking a few deep breaths. "What . . . what happ—" Her eyes fell to the weapon in Alice's hand, and she went silent. "It . . . transformed?"

Alice looked to it as well. "I guess . . ."

But there was no time for that.

A scream drew all of their attention to where the Bloody Lady thrashed and shrieked, screaming for the darkness to destroy them.

"Oh, Odette . . ." the White Queen whispered.

Fingers curled around Alice's wrist, and she glanced down to find her grandmother clutching at her.

"Free her," Nana K whispered. Her eyes were wide, glossed with unshed tears.

A heaviness fell over Alice, and she nodded.

She pushed to her feet. The silver chain clinked as it unfurled. She darted forward, feeling the cold wash of magic as she exited the bubble.

The Nightmares were on her immediately.

She roared.

So did the creatures.

They collided.

Forty-One

MANXOME

Addison couldn't remember the last time he had been so afraid.

No, that was a lie. He remembered when Odette had gone missing. He'd been afraid then.

When Portentia swore herself to the darkness. He saw it chipping away at who she was, saw the burden it placed on her. And so he offered to help her carry it, hoping to one day bring her back. He'd been afraid then.

And when Alice had faced down that monster at Ahoon only to return nearly torn to pieces? Madeline had worked through the night to put her back together. He'd been so very afraid.

Now, with Humphrey hanging there, the darkness threatening to swallow him unless Addison spoke a single word, he was yet again afraid.

"You can end it," the voice coaxed, sugary, pleasant almost. "Just say one word. *The* word. And I'll make it stop. Make it all go away. That's fair, isn't it?"

". . . Manxome."

It was as if the room, the very darkness, drew in a breath, then released it.

"The first Nightmare," Addison continued. "The . . . the source of the Nox."

A throaty chuckle filled the air. "Thank you. That's all I wanted, a little recognition." As if waved away, the darkness withdrew, leaving Humphrey and Chester curled against the floor. The two of them shivered audibly.

Addison threw himself down beside the other knight, helping him to sit up. He reached to help Chester with the same, but the boy recoiled at his touch.

"W-what . . . what's going on?" Chester panted, the whole of him shuddering.

"Oh, that's right," the voice said, almost sympathetic. "You still don't remember. I suppose recalling things can be difficult when one has been split so completely."

"Split?"

"Right down the middle, so much so that you don't even recognize yourself. Literally." The voice sighed. "I'm afraid Addison was correct, Chester. You're not human. You're not anything, really. Except lost. It seems your heartbroken Queen didn't know the strength of your devotion when she asked you to kill your charge."

"M-my charge?" Chester swallowed. "I'm . . . I'm not a knight."

"No, you're part of a knight who was captured and tortured, his mind taken so he would obey. But the mind is easy. The heart is not so easily swayed."

Chester shook his head. "I—I don't . . . that's not . . ."

"Isn't it, though? Just a little over a year ago, you met Alice Kingston. To be precise, it was just a few days after her father died.

A task the knight was charged with. That is when you freed yourself of him. And when he lost enough of himself to forget himself. So while his mind bent to the will of the . . . Black Queen, you call her? His heart tore free and developed a mind of its own. A will. Don't know where you got the name. Chester Dumpsky."

As the voice spoke, Addison saw the shock he felt in his very being play out over Chester's face, then Humphrey's, as realization dawned over the three of them.

Chester turned to Humphrey, his chest heaving, his mouth working uselessly. Humphrey had gone stone still, staring not so much at Chester as through him.

"The dream," he murmured, his voice somehow hoarse. "It's a memory. Our memory. My . . . memory . . ."

"Nooowww you get it," the voice called. "Now it's clicking. But, unfortunately, we are running out of time. Your princess needs saving, and I need her alive. I also need the knight who stole her heart and a knight without one, so count yourselves fortunate."

Addison started to ask questions, to demand answers, but when he tried to open his mouth, his body would not move. Nor when he tried to lift his hands. He was stuck, frozen. Panic fluttered to life in his chest like a frightened bird, and it only beat its wings faster when it saw Humphrey's eyes widen, but he didn't move otherwise. He was stuck, too. So was Chester.

"Now, now, don't struggle," the voice said. "It wouldn't do much, and I can't have you hurting yourselves."

The panic in Addison's chest tightened. He . . . he couldn't breathe. It felt like his lungs were filling with water. They burned. He tried to cry out, tried to scream, tried to reach for Humphrey!

All he could do was stand there.

Forty-Two
ENOUGH

Alice yanked her sickle from the body of a felled Wraith and whirled to face any other attackers.

There were none. Because every other Nightmare had turned to attack the shield. Odabeth withstood the onslaught, radiating power, her body illuminated from within with the Eye beaming at the center of her forehead. The White Queen and Nana K huddled behind her, shielded by the princess's glow as it littered the ground with massive, inky bodies and a number of humanoid ones. The sounds of snarls and the smell of black blood filled the air.

"Down!" Odabeth shrieked.

Alice dropped reflexively, rolling to the side as a Nightmare lunged, swiping at the empty air. It hit the ground and lumbered around to face her again, its lips curled back from a drenched maw to snarl. It started forward.

Alice paced around to face the monster as it came between her and her intended target: the warped body of Odette, twisted and bleeding Slithe, still controlled by Portentia. She clutched her chest.

"You . . . you are nothing . . ." Portentia hissed. "Human . . . filth. I will never . . . allow you . . . to take her place . . ."

"Sorry," Alice murmured, adjusting her hold on her weapon. "You don't get a say." She drew a slow breath, focusing on the balance in her step, the strength of her stance. She could do this.

As that thought filled her head, she felt heat sweep along her arms, to her palms. The sickle began to glow red. She let it drop, the chain sliding through her fingers. Her wrist flicked, bringing the weapon up and around her head in a wave of crimson light.

She drew back and, with everything she had, hurled her arms forward. An arc of red energy exploded from the blade, careening toward Portentia in Odette's bloody body.

Portentia flung out her hands, and Nightmares threw themselves in front of her. The light slammed into them. Their bodies erupted, ichor spraying the ground.

"Hauh!" Alice twirled the chain overhead, flinging it out again and again, sending more light arcing toward her target.

Again and again, Nightmares leaped to their mistress's defense.

A river of black snaked around the stone. Chunks of shadowy flesh clung to the walls, the floor. Alice wiped the splatter from her face, her chest heaving. She couldn't keep this up forever.

"There is nothing here for you," Portentia crowed, her hands cupped near her chest. A swirling mass of black energy crackled with red lightning, pulsing between her fingers like the beating of a heart. "You are in my domain. I command an unending army of Nightmares here."

With a wave of her hand, the shadows rose. Claws tapped at stone as six more monstrous beasts stalked forward from the edges of the room. Panting, her limbs burning, her hands on fire, wet and warm where her palms had split from gripping her sickle and chain so hard, Alice tried not to give in to the terror worming its way into her heart. If she lost faith in herself, she was doomed. But she couldn't see a way out of this.

With snarls and hisses, the Nightmares swept toward her.

Alice lifted her weapon. The pieces of the Heart pulsed faintly.

A blur of motion above snatched at her attention as, from seemingly nothing and nowhere, Humphrey, Chess, and Addison faded into sight.

Blades drawn, the latter two came down on top of the attacking Nightmares, driving their weapons into their spines with the sickening snap of bone. The other Nightmares scattered. Agonized howls rose and were abruptly cut off.

Alice felt the widest smile break over her face. "Guys!"

Chess straightened, glancing around, then at her. He grinned. "Hey."

Behind him Humphrey lowered himself to the ground, shifting around behind Addison, who crossed the space between them in a few quick steps, pulling her in against him, burying his face in the side of her neck.

"My lady," he murmured, the sound of his voice vibrating through her.

"You came," she whispered, her fingers digging into the fabric of his shirt.

"I told you I would."

"This is sweet and all, but, um . . ." Humphrey said.

Addison drew back and turned to face the still-growing line of Nightmares, and standing behind them . . .

Alice heard his breath catch.

"Is . . . is that . . ." he whispered.

"It's Odette," she murmured. "But Portentia is controlling her body."

The haggard thing that had once been a girl laughed, the sound wet and choppy. "More traitors. Thank you for saving me the trouble of hunting you down."

The ball of energy in her hands was bigger, twice the size of her head as she held it out in front of herself. Inky shadow rippled across it like the surface of water disturbed, still pulsing and charged with red lightning.

"Once more," Portentia snarled. "Once more grant me your power. Callooh . . . Callay . . ."

She flung the orb forward, with some difficulty. It hit the ground and expanded, carving a hole into the air. It reminded Alice of a Gateway, only the edges were ripped and jagged. It looked more like a wound torn open than a door. Two massive hands emerged, gripping the "frame" and hauling a mass of shadow, skin, and fur forward.

A wolfish thing that looked like perhaps it had once been a man emerged. It sniffed the air, lips curling away from massive fangs. The beast prowled back and forth, great claws tearing grooves in the wet mud. One hand snatched up a smaller Nightmare, the thing squealing as it was lifted and then bitten in half, the wolf devouring it within seconds and tossing what remained aside. The other Nightmares sniffed at the corpse but then their attention returned to potential live prey, all of them circling in once more.

Portentia aimed a bony finger Alice's direction. "Time to die, usurper."

Spines that resembled black bone protruded from the wolf's back as it hunched forward onto all fours and fixed its gaze on Alice.

Her mind went to the new breed of Nightmares, and something sour twisted in her stomach.

"Nnnng!" Odabeth's groan echoed through the chamber. She kept her hands up, but her arms shook and her knees buckled. She looked like she was struggling to hold up some great weight despite her hands risen empty in the air. "I—I can't . . . hold it!" Both Emalia and Nana K were at her sides, their arms around her, trying to keep her up.

"We have to end this," Alice said. "Before the shield comes down."

"You heard her," Addison said, moving around to her side. "We hold the line." He lifted his blade.

Chess did the same, as did Humphrey.

The monsters came at them with a swipe of their massive mitts, reaching to tear throats free. Chess and Addison drove forward, heading two of the creatures off as Humphrey dropped in from where he'd hovered above. The wolf came straight at Alice. She threw herself to the side, narrowly escaping being slashed to ribbons. The Nightmare landed after its miss and whirled around to lunge again. There was a flash of black as Alice dove forward, her sickle slicing into inky fur and flesh.

The creature howled in pain. Alice grunted similarly as the two of them went tumbling. Pain blossomed along her entire body as she hit the ground and it landed on top of her, forcing the air from her lungs with its weight.

"Alice!" Addison's panicked shout filled the air before he dove in, driving his sword at the monster's side.

The Nightmare roared. Despite its injuries and Hatta's attack, it pinned Alice to the ground with crushing force, teeth gnashing above the narrow barrier of the sickles now caught between its jaws. She managed to hold it off with the brace of her arms, its mass pressing in from above. Its breath was hot and foul in her face, bloodstained teeth just inches shy of chewing into her. She fought to keep it at bay as it scrambled to bite into her, its claws digging into her arms. She screamed. It snarled and snapped, growing more furious and frantic as it sliced itself open again and again on her weapons. The smell of its own blood was driving it mad, and it fought hard for the meal it was denied.

The beast was so focused on its current prey that it did not see Addison coming around again. He drove his foot into its side, the force of the kick hurling it from atop Alice. It yelped as it was sent rolling.

Hands gripped Alice and yanked her to her feet. "Are you all right?"

She didn't have time to answer. The monster was on its feet and racing at them again, a furry blur in the darkness.

Chess yanked his sword free from where he'd driven it into something that resembled a hog. He spun into a crouch, sweeping the blade along the backs of the wolf's legs. It yowled as it crashed to the floor, its limbs flailing as it tried to stay upright.

Addison raced forward, twisting around with another kick aimed at the beast's head this time. The speed from the spin drove the heel of his boot into the side of the monster's face, and when the kick connected, the beast's jaw caved in with the sickening crunch of bone. It yowled, stumbling away to crash against the ground.

It lay still, its ragged breaths wet and raspy as blood filled its maw. It struggled briefly to regain its feet before succumbing to the exhaustion from its efforts and its wounds, whimpering and whining piteously now.

Humphrey came down on top of it, seemingly out of nowhere. There was a wet crunch as he drove the blade into the beast's skull and it ceased to writhe, the glow fading from its great red eyes.

Alice dropped her arms to her sides, the slashes along them screaming, her nerves alight. But she gritted her teeth and held on. The boys shifted in beside her again, readying themselves.

"Your efforts are futile," Portentia crooned. "My army is endless." Another wave of her hand summoned a wall of undulating dark. Hands, claws, talons twisted into the air, ripping free bodies big and small, slim and thick. Nightmares sloshed forward, freshly born. But they didn't peel away to attack. No, instead the largest ones lay down so the smaller creatures could skitter over them, tearing at quivering flesh with claw and fang until a mass of heaving shadowy flesh and bone stretched to lurch across the battlefield.

"We . . . we might be in over our heads," Chess murmured.

"Eyes forward," Humphrey said.

Addison's fingers found Alice's and squeezed.

"Tear them apart," Portentia whispered.

The Nightmares roared as they swelled, a massive mass of tentacles, talons, and fangs. Inky skin, slathered in fur, scales, torn tissue, and blood rippled like water. Massive, lidless yellow eyes rolled in hundreds of sockets spread across its body, some too large or too small for the glowing eyes within. Mouths split across the creature's singular body, teeth gnashing at its own flesh, rending it free with a tearing sound that sent shivers down her spine. It was the largest Nightmare Alice had ever seen.

Behind it, Portentia crowed with laughter, her head thrown back, her cracked mouth wide and frothing. "Manxome! I envoke thee, callooh callay." The words crackled like thunder. The sky darkened.

The clouds thickened, spitting crimson lightning. "By the might of the first, I will have my vengeance."

Vengeance . . .

That word. Alice's body trembled. Her hands shook. Her knees knocked. But it wasn't fear that had hold of her. It was rage.

If Portentia's horror got past them, her family would be slaughtered. Torn to pieces.

Then everyone in Wonderland, in the world, would suffer Portentia's wrath.

"No . . ." Alice whispered. Then she turned and ran.

One of the boys called her name. Addison, she thought. She didn't look back. She raced the distance to the shield, pounding against it with her fist. A feeling like lightning shot up her arm.

"Odabeth!" she shouted at the princess, now kneeling on the ground. "The Eye!"

Odabeth lifted her head.

"Give it to me!" Alice screamed, trying not to focus on the sounds of battle behind her, the shouts of effort and pain, the scrape of claws against metal, the thud of bodies or limbs. She blocked it all out.

Odabeth groaned, her fingers going to her forehead. The shield faded, and with it her light. She dropped her hand, the Eye clutched between her fingers.

Nana K snatched it up, hurrying forward to press it into Alice's hand, her eyes wide as their gazes locked.

"I love you, Baby Moon," Nana K breathed.

Love. She would do this for love.

And if she failed . . . she would do that for love as well.

Alice didn't take the time to answer, though she hoped her grandmother could see the truth in her eyes, before she lifted the Eye and brought it down against the blade of her sickle.

There was a resounding *crack!* And then the world went white.

A storm erupted in Alice's chest. It raced down her limbs and up into her skull, filling it to bursting. Every inch of her burned. It felt like her skin was being peeled from her body, but she did not scream. She could not. She floated in a sea of agony, blazing as it burned through her.

But then, as quickly and as hotly as it had consumed her, it was washed away by an icy embrace. Something soft brushed against her arms, her legs, encased her torso. She opened her eyes.

A dark glow wreathed her body like fabric, dazzling against her brown skin.

This power . . . she knew it. Had seen it before.

And like before, it painted her curves like a luminous corset, the hints of silver and gold vine-like detail bursting with red blossoms along the bend of her body. Red swirled with black, and the two fell in folds along her legs.

The fabric of the dress swirled around her, billowing in a breeze that came from nowhere. A breeze that held her weapon aloft in front of her.

Alice reached for it. As her fingers brushed the metal, the chain broke free, snapping out like a whip to wrap around her legs. It embedded itself in her dress, the links soaking into the fabric like silver ink.

She curled her fingers around the sickle, and the handle lengthened in a blurry blink, the metal morphing like liquid silver until it no longer formed a sickle but a scepter, crowned with a stone glowing deep purple. A hand fell over hers where she gripped the scepter, and in the blinding haze, Alice saw the reflection of herself.

Reflection-Alice smiled, gripping the scepter as well.

When she did, a tingle raced up her arms, pinpricks that

were just the right side of painful. The numbness spread from her palms, the staff shimmered, and with a sound like glass shattering, the purple stone split outward. The metal formed two hands cast in silver, the purple gem cupped by their fingers.

It was exactly like what she had seen before, only now . . . now she saw that it wasn't purple but instead a deep, gorgeous black swirled with the twinkling of bloodied stars. The Eye, and the Heart, were one.

"*Finally . . .*" Reflection-Alice whispered, her voice echoing in Alice's ears. "*The Soul of Wonderland has awakened.*" She breathed a sigh before fading, leaving Alice to grip the staff with both hands.

Alice felt the ground push up beneath her feet. She blinked open her eyes, not realizing she'd closed them. Around her, the darkness had receded. Light poured from her body, from the scepter, forming a dome similar to what Odabeth and her mother had conjured before, but this one was different. The Nightmares could not even draw near it to beat against it. When they did, their skin sizzled as if dropped in a pan of hot oil. They howled and recoiled.

But Addison, Nana K, and everyone else were unharmed. They gazed up at her, their faces a mix of shock, awe, and something she couldn't recognize. Humphrey, Addison, and Chester all went to their knees, their weapons dropping to the ground with a clang. The Vorpal Blades shone black and brilliant, the light spilling into them until the darkness began to peel away, flaking off to be carried into the air like ash, torched in the fire of her radiance.

Radiance, Alice thought. And it was true. She was radiant.

"No," Portentia gasped.

Alice finally looked to the fallen Queen, whose face was slicked with Slithe, her pale skin turning ashen gray now that more of her was poking through her dead daughter.

"You," Alice hissed. Her words shot forth, the air trembling with the power in her voice.

"No!" Portentia shouted now. "You can't do this! I can't . . . my baby . . . they need to pay! All of them must pay! She . . . must be avenged! Manxome! You promised!"

"Odette deserves more than vengeance. She deserves peace." Alice lifted the scepter overhead. "And so does the rest of this realm."

A pulse of power flowed from the crystal down the staff, into Alice's arm and through the rest of her. She winced under the strain, suddenly feeling like she was a balloon with too much air. But she knew she would not burst. Because . . .

"I am Alice Kingston."

"Stop her . . ." Portentia gasped.

The massive Nightmare hesitated, trembling.

"And I am afraid," Alice cried. Heat gathered in her palms. It felt like her skin might melt right off her fingers, but she tightened her grip and gritted her teeth. It was only pain, and she was no longer scared of being hurt.

"STOP HER!"

The beast bellowed and beat at the shield, its tentacles burning away to nothing as it screeched.

"But fear cannot stop me." Energy filled Alice from the soles of her feet to the crown of her head. She could see the folds of her dress fluttering wildly in the breeze, billowing around her as if to shield her. But it wouldn't last long. She needed to finish this!

Portentia wailed and flung out her arms. A wave of living shadow rushed forward.

Alice reached for that power, but she didn't seek to pull it from the same source as Portentia. No. Instead of digging into the raw essence of Wonderland, Alice dug into herself. The words were there. She tore them free.

"I . . . am Alice Kingston. Daughter of Tina. Heir of Kashaunte. Pride of Sydney!"

Her voice cracked, but this time she did not.

"Dreamwalker of the Western Gateway. Guardian of Prima Terra. Soul of Wonderland."

Her knees buckled, but this time she did not bend.

"And I am afraid! I have *always* been afraid! But fear cannot stop me! *You* cannot stop me!

"Nothing can stop me!"

A gentle pressure fell onto Alice's shoulders. Warmth flowed through her, wrapped around her, held her close.

"Nothing can stop you, huh? That's what I like to hear. Let's do this, Baby Moon."

Tears streamed down Alice's face. Her hands shook. Her stance wavered. But she would not, could not, falter. Not when something stronger held her up.

Alice brought the scepter down. The crystal hit the floor. The force of the blow erupted outward.

The Nightmare howled.

Portentia screamed. She held her arms out, trying to shield herself against the flare of black and red energy. But it was useless, as bits and pieces of her were torn away as if by razor on the wind.

Then the whole of her shattered.

Forty-Three

LONG LIVE THE QUEEN

Legracia was under siege. The Nightmares had torn through the front lines. The cavalry was in shambles. Anastasia's soldiers were bloodied and broken, but still on their feet somehow. And yet she couldn't help the sinking feeling that it wouldn't matter. Their numbers were thinning out.

But she would not give in.

Beside her, Romi lowered her black-streaked sword and glanced around, chest heaving as her gaze played over the battlefield. She came to the same conclusion as Anastasia, it seemed, because a smile started to pull at her face.

"I think . . . this may be the end, Duchess."

Anastasia felt her own smile begin to stretch. "If it is, then it has been an honor fighting at your side again . . ."

"Behind!"

Anastasia whirled toward the shout.

Romi spun as well and cursed.

A wave of black crested the far hill and washed toward them. A second horde, more numerous than the last.

A sort of peace came over Anastasia. *We're going to die out here.*

"Re-form the line!" Romi shouted.

It was echoed along the field as everyone still on their feet hurried into some semblance of a formation.

All the while, the rising tide of shadow raced for them steadily.

Soon the ranks were re-formed. The guard held their weapons aloft. Some of them with fear in their eyes. Others with resignation. And still others with determination.

Anastasia looked back to the wave of black. She could make out individual monsters now, see their limbs, their mouths, their tails and horns. Some of them Fiends, some of them great beasts, and some once again humanlike.

"Steady," Romi called aloud.

The horde was close enough that Anastasia could pick up the sounds of their roars and snarls, their gnashing teeth. She could feel the ground rumble.

Closer they drew. Now she could make out the inky ripple of their skin. An army of terror and pain on a collision course that would surely wipe them out.

One hundred meters . . .

Fifty meters . . .

Twenty-five . . .

"For Wonderland!" someone shouted.

Echoing cries rose around them, voices rising as well, Anastasia's among them.

She braced herself.

Light erupted from seemingly nowhere, spilling into the air in a flash. It rose like a wall between the line of warriors and the beasts, the Nightmares slamming into it from the other side.

People shuffled around her, equally confused before someone called out, "The Queen!"

"No, the princess!"

Anastasia spun around so fast she nearly fell over.

Romi turned as well, to see Alice gripping some sort of staff, her entire body engulfed in light. The shield was coming from her.

"Alice," Anastasia breathed, her name like a relieved prayer on her lips. She smiled, though it melted into confusion when she saw Alice lift her hands, a strange staff held in her grasp.

A flare of red and white energy swelled, enveloping the gnashing horde. The light grew bright, blinding, the sound like thunder and bells filling the air.

Anastasia turned away.

When it faded, the battlefield was empty. There was a burn along the ground, a groove dug into the earth where the shield had been, but that was it. The Nightmares were gone.

The victory shout was instantaneous and deafening, soldiers clapping one another on the shoulder or lifting their weapons as they screamed.

Romi turned to push her way toward Alice and the others. Anastasia followed.

"One side!" the Duchess cried, pressing her way through the throng. "One side! Move!"

They broke through the edge of the crowd, coming upon the scene of Addison holding on to Alice, cloaked in some ridiculously puffy dress and looking half ready to pass out. She clutched a sickle in her hand, one that snatched at Anastasia's attention, but that would have to come later.

Xelon was helping Princess Odabeth climb out of what looked like a hole in the ground. The Queens stood nearby, aided by Chester and Humphrey.

"Is that it?" Anastasia asked, her chest heaving, her lungs hot with the strain of battle. "Is the day won?"

"That . . . and so much more," Addison said before he looked down at Alice. "Thanks to her."

Alice, visibly weak but still standing, glanced up and around as all eyes turned to her.

Queen Kashaunte, on Humphrey's arm, made her way over to her granddaughter. She reached to set a hand against the staff. "Been a long time since the Eye and Heart were one."

Murmurs surfed the crowd.

Alice stared at the staff a moment before holding it out to her grandmother, who waved her away.

"This is your doing, your path. I'm here to support you while you walk it, though."

With a sniff, Alice wrapped her arms around her grandmother. At least until the staff started to shudder. She drew back to grip it with both hands, and as she did, it snapped in half. The look on her face said she hadn't meant to do it.

She opened her mouth, likely to apologize, only for the words to evaporate as the halves of the staff, one white, one red, molded themselves into chained sickles, blades sleek and edged in silvered glass.

Anastasia felt her breath catch. "Is that . . ."

"Figment Blades," Addison answered as he inspected one of the weapons. "The Eye and the Heart have taken the form of Figment Blades." He sounded as shocked, and as impressed, as she felt.

"Not surprising," the Red Queen said. "A princess of Wonderland, and also a Dreamwalker."

Anastasia gazed at Alice Kingston in a new light. The girl that had dragged her deeper into Wonderland than she had been for the first time in over a century.

Alice Kingston, who'd bested a Mort Nightmare single-handedly, then the embodiment of Portentia's rage, twice.

Alice Kingston, human, Dreamwalker, princess.

Alice Kingston . . . one day Queen of Wonderland.

Epilogue
FORWARD

Alice stared at her hands where they were bunched in the red of her skirts. There was so much fabric! It flowed down her arms, swallowed the lower half of her body, and continued on in a lengthy train that would've been as long as she was tall, if she wasn't sitting on it.

Her heart hammered like a trapped hummingbird in her chest.

"You can do this," she whispered to herself. She closed her eyes, took a slow breath, and repeated the affirmation. "You can do this."

"You ready to do this?" Court called from across the room.

Alice blinked her eyes open and glanced to the door as her friend strolled through, wearing her own bright pink gown. It wasn't as long, or wide, or fancy, and Alice was a little envious.

"Can I say no?" Alice asked.

Court waved a hand with a snort. Her face was flawless, as always. "To being a queen?"

"I'm not a queen. Not yet."

"But you *will* be, yeah? Everyone is talking about it. What with you wielding the Soul of Wonderland or whatever."

Alice glanced toward the wardrobe where she'd shoved her sickle and chain after it had reverted from the scepter. She'd already tried, and failed, to get it to transform again. Nana K said not to worry about it right now, the point was that it had revealed itself.

A gurgle sounded in Alice's middle, and she pressed her hands over her stomach. "Can princesses retire?"

"Um . . . maybe?" Courtney arched an eyebrow. "But not before they become princesses, I don't think, so you at least have to go through with that part. Besides, you'll be great at it!"

Alice wasn't so sure about that, and she'd only agreed to this whole coronation thing to make her grandmother happy.

"Doubts already?"

Alice glanced up to find Chess standing in the doorway, dressed in some fancy duds that made him look like he was right out of a storybook.

"There never weren't any," Alice said, pressing her hands to her twisting middle. She felt like she was going to be sick, had since she went to bed last night.

"Hey." Chess came to kneel in front of her, setting a hand on her knee. "I've seen you slay a shit ton of monsters in one fell swoop." He grinned. "You can do this."

Alice couldn't help the smile that pulled at her face, or the warmth that spread through her as Court took one of her hands and squeezed it. She squeezed back. "Having you guys here helps." Then she paused, her back straightening as her gaze wandered over him, kneeling there.

This time she leaned forward. She could see Chess's eyes widen in confusion and something close to fear, but then her lip brushed his forehead.

"Having *you* here helps. You're going to be okay." She took both of his hands this time. "I'll make sure of it."

For a moment, neither of them said anything, simply holding each other. It didn't mean anything more than what it was, and that was okay.

A door to the left opened and Alice's mother stepped out, dressed in an equally fancy red dress. While Alice was to be crowned princess, her mother would be crowned Queen Mother, on account of having married her dad, who was a prince.

He . . . died without knowing.

The sting of tears was sudden and caught Alice off guard.

Mom turned, her smile fading when she saw her. "Baby, what . . . ? Give us a minute, you two, we'll be along."

Chess and Court took turns hugging Alice, whispering encouragements before slipping from the room. Alice's mom came to sit beside her on the lounge, wrapping arms around her and pulling her in.

"I know, baby . . ." she said without having to be told.

"I—I just . . . I just wish he was here," Alice whispered, sniffing.

"I know." Mom pulled back and brushed fingers along Alice's cheeks, catching the few tears that managed to slip free. "He would be proud. *I'm* proud enough for the both of us. And he wouldn't want you to ruin your makeup." Mom smiled, earning a chuckle from Alice, then she sighed. "After everything you've told me, there's no doubt in my mind he's here with us. Or that he's been watching over you this entire time. And he'll keep watching over you. We both will."

"Thanks, Mom." Alice leaned in for another hug.

There was a knock on the other side of the door before it swung open. Haruka stood there wrapped in a swath of crimson fabric dotted with pink and white blossoms that gathered at the waist in solid color then dappled along the length of the outfit the further the eye trailed from the belt. She'd called it a chu-furisode, and it was gorgeous. Behind her, Alice could make out the twins arguing with each other, looking pretty damn sharp in all black, three-piece suits.

"They're ready for you," Haruka said, her eyes wandering over Alice in a way that made her flush just faintly. "You look stunning."

"Thank you," Alice said as she stood, Mom rising beside her.

"This way, Your Highnesses." Haruka left the door open and stepped back out, gesturing to the small crowd that likely included Chess and Courtney on down the hall.

Alice drew a deep breath.

I am Alice Kingston.

She moved to follow her mother out of the room and down the hall. The sound of the voices filled the air, people speaking to one another further on in the throne room. A great MANY people from the sound of it.

And . . . I am afraid . . .

She paused, letting everyone else continue for a moment. Beyond them, she could glimpse the throne room of Legracia, sparkling and bright. She could see Nana K seated beside her sister, the two of them chatting. She could see Odabeth in her own chair, and the empty one beside her.

"But fear cannot stop me," Alice said to the empty hall.

"I actually don't think anything can stop you," a voice called from behind her.

Alice smiled, turning to find Hatta standing there in gold

armor, a dark black cape speckled with red starlight draped over his shoulders.

"Wow, you clean up nice," she said.

He chuckled. "And you look incredible."

Alice felt her face heat, and she ducked her head. "Everyone keeps saying that . . ."

"And everyone is right." He stepped forward, reaching to take her hand. "Are you ready for this?"

She couldn't help but groan. "Maybe . . . though I kinda wish people would stop asking me that."

"Ahh, apologies, my lady."

"I didn't think you'd be back in time," she murmured.

"Come now, a little cleanup wouldn't keep me from your coronation, even if it is important to prepare Findest for the Red Queen's return." A smirk pulled at his lips. "Besides, Queen Nana—"

"Ohmigawd, does she *really* have y'all calling her that?"

"I rather like it. Anyway, she told me personally that if I missed it, she'd string me up by my toes. So, here I am."

"Oh, so you're here under threat of bodily harm and not to support me." She struggled to keep her straight face.

"You've met your grandmother, right? She might not look it now, but once there was no one in the land who could best her with a blade."

"Somehow I'm not surprised." Alice squirmed slightly, her eyes moving to the throne room again. Anastasia stood at the mouth of the hall, her hands folded in front of her skirts, patiently awaiting a signal from the Queens. She was dressed in her formal best as well, bright blue skirts and frills that were a far departure from the combat clothes Alice had seen her in.

Silence descended, broken only by the faint sound of voices in the hall beyond. She and Addison just stood there, not talking, not really looking at each other. He adjusted some strap near his elbow, and she fluffed at the front of her dress. It really was huge.

Unable to take the quiet, she cleared her throat and pointed. "How's your head? Anything come back?"

"There's little pain. The Madness has quieted, though I still don't remember what happened after we went through the portal."

Chess and Humphrey were suffering from similar memory loss, unable to recall what happened after they were snatched from the throne room. Apparently, they had simply found themselves waking in the antechamber of Emes and, hearing the sounds of battle, Humphrey phased them in quick as he could.

A once-over from Madeline, and a nice lady named Naette—she came highly recommended by both Addison and the White Queen—cleared all three of them.

"A side effect of not being the intended target of the Verse," Naette had suggested.

Alice was still concerned, but . . . Portentia was gone. *Gone* gone. Alice's . . . cosmic moon powers—that's what she was calling them, no one could convince her otherwise—had evaporated her essence and that of the Nightmares, leaving Emes, and Odette's body, purged. While the shadows of the Nox would eventually retake the palace, they had managed to carry the lost princess out and lay her to a proper rest.

The Black Queen was dead.

Wonderland, and the world, were safe.

Alice blinked out of her thoughts and chanced another glance up at Addison, only to find him still smiling gently at her. "What?"

"Nothing, just . . . thinking about how I was right."

That made her arch an eyebrow. "About?"

"You being special."

The jumping in her stomach intensified, but not unpleasantly. "Huh. Last I heard I had been stripped of that title, after not letting you get through your serious complimenting."

"Okay, wait."

"Unspecial, I was called."

"Alice . . ." He tried to sound chiding, but it only came across as amused.

She lifted her chin. "Stripped of my serious compliment!" she lamented.

"Now who's fragile," he muttered before pressing a kiss to her laughing mouth.

She sputtered briefly. To his credit, he held the kiss, drawing her into it. His lips were soft, his arms firm around her. She drank him in, the feel of his hair as she threaded her fingers through it, the spicy sweet scent that always lingered in the air after him. And when he made this little sound at the back of his throat she did everything she could to draw it and others free so she could swallow them. He was hers. Her knight.

Her hands moved against the warmth of his armor and she wished briefly she could feel the muscles of his chest instead, but she let herself get swept up in every other sensation.

When they finally broke away, her head was fuzzy and her lips tingled lightly.

"You have always been special, my lady." Addison released her, stepped back, and bowed. "My Queen."

She started to correct him, but the Duchess cleared her throat. When Alice glanced toward her, she waved them forward, smiling.

"Well, here we go." Addison offered his arm.

Alice took it, her pulse racing, her stomach fluttering, her nerves jumping.

"Breathe, Baby Moon."

So she did.

And then she stepped forward.

ACKNOWLEDGMENTS

First of all, giving all glory and honor to my heavenly Father, without whom none of this would be possible. I thank the Lord each and every day I'm allowed to do what I love for a living. His grace, mercy, and blessings sustain me. Thank you, Jesus.

To my agent, Victoria, it's finally finished! This trilogy is complete. Here's to many more. To my editor, Holly, thank you for being a fan of my work and fighting to get this book to where it is.

My family, my loved ones, my friends. There are far too many of you who were there for me during the exhaustive process that has been this third book. I'm not going to name anyone, because I don't think I'll remember to name everyone, and I don't want to forget folk. Mom, Dad, my sisters, baby brother, y'all are my heart. Thank you for holding me down through everything.

And finally, to my readers. My road dogs. My ride or dies. *Alice's* ride or dies. Thank you for taking this journey with me. Thank you for falling in love with Wonderland and each of its colorful characters. I hope one day we get to return to this world, because there is so much more to explore. Don't forget to mind your Muchness, and keep moving forward.

Thank you for reading this Feiwel & Friends book. The friends who made *A Crown So Cursed* possible are:

Jean Feiwel, Publisher
Liz Szabla, VP, Associate Publisher
Rich Deas, Senior Creative Director
Holly West, Senior Editor
Anna Roberto, Senior Editor
Kat Brzozowski, Senior Editor
Dawn Ryan, Executive Managing Editor
Jie Yang, Production Manager
Emily Settle, Editor
Foyinsi Adegbonmire, Associate Editor
Rachel Diebel, Associate Editor
Brittany Groves, Assistant Editor
Meg Sayre, Junior Designer
Ilana Worrell, Senior Production Editor

Follow us on Facebook or visit us online at mackids.com.
Our books are friends for life.